THE

ORDEAL BY TOUCH.

A ROMANCE.

———

"Hush—stand aside! Behold the crimson stream!
The life-blood flows—woe on the guilty head
Heaven has given its verdict!"

———

LONDON:

PUBLISHED BY E. LLOYD, SALISBURY SQUARE, FLEET STREET.

George Webster Taylor

Kings Langley

Hertfordshire

June 21st 1847

PREFACE.

In presenting the Romance of the 'Ordeal by Touch' to the Public in a distinct and separate form from what it originally wore, an opportunity is afforded both to the Author and the Publisher to say a few words with regard to the Work itself—its public reception, and the manner of its production.

For himself, the Author is well pleased at the circumstance of being able to make some written acknowledgment to the public, the real patrons of literature, for the very great degree of commendation which it has pleased such kind friends and critics to bestow upon the work. He is most especially well pleased to find that the work has given satisfaction, because the circumstances under which it was written were entirely peculiar.

He knew that he would have to compete with gentlemen of great talent, and of great knowledge and learning ; so that when, after much anxious consideration, he put pen to paper, in the production of the Romance of the 'Ordeal by Touch,' he did so with an amount of shrinking diffidence, for which he hopes the public will give him some degree of credit.

It is a gratification, likewise, to find that there has been so unanimous an opinion on the part of the Press as regards his choice of a subject, and the stirring period of England's history at which the Tale is laid.

At no time in the history of this country were there so many strange and romantic adventures as when that great change was taking place in the habits, feelings, and manners of society consequent upon the abandonment of the superstition and the priestcraft of papal rule for the, at all events, much more tolerable and milder dominion of a Reformed Church. The falling party brought into the field every means they could devise to procure for themselves a victory over the Protestant party ; and upon the old principle of Papacy, as well as of some sects of philosophy, that 'the end sanctifies the means,' every description of crime, including murder, was freely had recourse too, to crush the opponents of the Church of Rome !

Under such circumstances it may be well imagined how many personal collisions and conflicts must have arisen, even among persons not connected with affairs of State.

It is then most pleasing to the Author of 'Ordeal by Touch' to find that the great interest he himself has taken in the events of that period of history has been so fully responded to by his readers.

To the publisher, likewise, Mr. Lloyd, it is a source of much gratification to find that the experiment of offering a large sum for a work which was open to fair competition, has so fully succeeded in the production of a gratifying result, and he does not feel that the time of the literary gentlemen, who were most careful in their examination of the works sent in for perusal, has been otherwise than well employed.

There were certainly many works of great merit read by those gentlemen, and it was pleasing to them and to the publisher to find that so much talent was evoked by the offer he had made.

With the sanguine hope, then, that any other works—one of which he is now producing under the title of the 'Iron Mask,' and which is in course of publication in 'Lloyd's Entertaining Journal,'—may meet with a like amount of favourable consideration from the public that has been awarded to the 'Ordeal by Touch,' the Author of that Romance most respectfully submits this volume to the World of Letters.

LONDON,
December, 1846.

THE
ORDEAL BY TOUCH.

𝔄 𝔓𝔯𝔦𝔷𝔢 ℜ𝔬𝔪𝔞𝔫𝔠𝔢,

FOR WHICH ONE HUNDRED GUINEAS WERE AWARDED.

INTRODUCTION.

THE casual observer who glances at the picture in the Exhibition of the present year, at the rooms of the Royal Academy, may ponder over the figures there represented, and create in the chambers of his own brain some history of moving accidents, of dark passion, dire revenge, and frightful murder, which shall, in the progress of its harrowing details, embody the figures and the countenances of the persons there represented. He may fancy, that still figure lying in the repose of death—so calm—so cold—so passionless, to have played its part in some domestic drama—the last scene of which, to him, has become so awfully tragic.

He may imagine too, how that female form, now so bowed down with agony, was once erect with all the pride and consciousness of beauty; and, even as he gazes upon the pictured scene which represents the outlines of a frightful story, he may fill up for himself details full of the wild and the wonderful.

But let the spectator of that picture task his imagination to the utmost—let him dive deep into the very penetralia of thought—let him pluck up from the very bottom of the human heart the wildest slumbering passions, and by a human touch awaken them to life and energy—let him picture to himself woman's love in all the exquisite purity of the heart's devotion—let him look upon the lurid eye of hate and jealousy, and then placing together such antagonistic principles as rage and gentleness, love and despair, hate and most heavenly goodness, yet shall he not succeed in depicting a series of circumstances so absorbingly terrific as the truth

The picture tells something of a frightful tale, but it tells it not all: one incident is graphically depicted, but only one; we see there the murderer and the murdered, the destroyer of God's image, and the casket without the glorious gem which made it what it was— we see those who are heart-stricken by the consciousness that such a crime has been committed, but we know not why it was so done—we know not how it was that suspicion has fallen upon that bold, yet shrinking ruffian who advances his rigid hand to touch the lifeless form of him who, but for that hand, urged only by a demoniac spirit, would not have lain there so cold and motionless.

No. 1.

We see that the warm blood gushes from the congealed wound—we see that there is a witness against man, r even ... the dead—a witness, mute, but oh! how eloquent! a witness harmless, yet oh! how terrible!

He who painted that scene of desolation, of death, of terror, and of surprise, knew the circumstances which will be here recorded, else had he not succeeded in imparting such a touch of nature to that all but living group.

And with a painter's license some costume may be changed; what occurred in one age may be transferred to another; but human feelings and human passions, love, hatred and revenge know no change—they are eternal, commencing with creation, existing in all climes, and under all circumstances, exhibiting under different colours the same real aspect, and so will they continue until time shall be no more.

Let our readers judge for themselves—let them look at the picture, and then bearing faithfully in the mind's eye the magic of the painter's art, let them look for the causes and the details to the following pages.

CHAPTER I.

The Body on the Bier—The Challenge—The Hidden Man—The Ordeal—The Wound, and the Condemnation.

THE doors of an ancient church had yielded to the pressure of a countless multitude—God's temple shall not be a sanctuary for murder: shrieking, shouting, calling aloud for vengeance, and hurrying on with them many an unwary and unconscious spectator, a furious mob in a few short moments filled the whole area, and press distractedly even unto the very altar steps; but there they pause, and as if some charmed potent spell kept them from too great a profanation of that holy temple, the foremost of the throng prostrate themselves, and make a living barrier of their bodies against the pressure of those behind.

And all eyes are fixed upon one object—an object lying upon the topmost step, within some slender rails, that scarce would afford a momentary check to the dense pressure of the multitude that throng the place, but still which serve to mark beyond where they are not to intrude into that holy of holies—that sanctuary of priesthood.

But hark, all is hushed!—there is the low tinkle of a silver bell—a massive drapery is moved aside, noiselessly and gently, as if done by some invisible hand—the multitude is hushed—the cries of discord have ceased—those who have suffered cease to clamour—even pain (for many were hurt in the dense pressure) forgets for a moment its agony, as an aged priest, bent low with the weight of years, and in whose deep furrowed cheeks might be traced the march of more than a hundred years, came slowly forward, carrying in his hand the honest symbol of Catholicism—the consecrated host, before which all bow down in trembling adoration.

How wonderful is the power of such a feeling over the mind of the most turbulent—the war of words is hushed—there seems no angry passion in that vast multitude, and the soft musical tinkle of a silver bell reaches the ears of the most distant listeners in the profound, devotional stillness that reigns around.

The vast amphitheatre of faces—for such, viewing the church from the altar, was the aspect of the place—all bent slowly forward in lowly worship, and then from out the entrance whence the aged priest had stepped, came two young boys, swinging with a slow and graceful movement vases of incense, hung by golden chains.

And then another, and then another priest, in richest costume, blazing with gems, until the whole of the sacerdotal host belonging to that sacred edifice are assembled at the altar-foot.

Hark! there is a strain of melody, rich, full, and glorious as it floats up the vaulted roof, as if carrying up to Heaven on its dulcet wings the lowly uttered words of prayer from the aged priest, who is now himself kneeling at the altar-foot.

And now, amid that universal stillness, ere yet again an angry passion mar the unruffled surface of the multitude, we have space of time to look upon the object that occupies the topmost step of those white marble approaches to the altar-foot.

It is a bier rudely constructed, partially of wood and partially of wicker—a bier for the dead, and not unoccupied—for in it lies what in health and in life must have been a form of rarest workmanship.

A sheet, of pure and spotless whiteness, covers the whole of the body up to the throat, but the face is exposed—that face, so pale and wan, and yet wearing upon it the impress of high intellect—the impress of nobleness of soul, and of many a godly deed, and now also bereaved for ever. A silver coin is placed on each of the eyes, and at a distance they look like eyes themselves, giving to the face a strange and unearthly aspect.

On the breast is placed a small silver salver, in which is some fine-ground salt, and at the feet and head burn tapers.

The aged priest still prays, and all is still as the calmest summer ocean, until his last words of orisons to heaven are over; then he rises, trembling, from his knees, and stretching forth his hands as if invoking a blessing upon that vast multitude, while his hoary locks shiver with the tremulous movement that pervades his whole system, he speaks to the people:

'My children, why is this? Come ye here to pray or to condemn—come ye here to seek man or to seek Heaven? Vengeance is God's; he hath said it and he will have it.'

'Justice, justice, justice!' shrieked a female voice. 'Blood for blood! that is God's mandate, too. Justice on the murderer. Shriek, ay, children shriek for justice on your father's murderer.'

Then, as if the loud wailing voice had broken a spell which had been cast over the entire multitude, there arose a shout that made the old roof ring again; but then even almost on the instant it is as if each shrank from the profanation of which he was guilty, the strange preternatural silence came back again, and all was still as the very grave.

The old priest folded his arms across his breast, and seemed lost in thought. He then clasped his hands and held them up to Heaven, as if mutely seeking council of that supreme Power whose minister he was; and then he sunk upon his knees and smote his breast, prostrating his white hairs to the dust, and appearing in sore trouble and vexation of spirit.

And the people watched him with anxious fears, and some, with lips apart and staring eyes, drew their breath short and thick, and swayed to and fro in deep sympathy with the movements of that aged man who was so sorely troubled.

But suddenly he arose and spake again.

'Let them who seek justice,' he said, 'come forward to the altar-foot and ask it there. Who speaks?—as there is a heaven above us, justice shall they have.'

There was a movement among the mass of people—the throng divided, and through a living lane there came a female form, pale, and with the marks of agony upon her countenance—her hair dishevelled, her lips closed and bloodless and by either hand she led a child, while a third clung to the skirts of her garment, and all were terrified, for they knew not what it meant, and only recognised the common accents of grief and despair incidental to human nature.

'Come forth,' said the old priest, 'come forth and be not afraid. There are earthly judges to hear complaint of earthly wrong; but yet, Heaven forbid that we, the spiritual teachers of the people, should shrink from any appeal that the unfortunate or the afflicted can make to us. Speak, woman! what is it you require?'

'Kneel, my children, kneel,' cried the woman, in frantic accents, as she flung herself upon her knees on the altar steps, with the trembling, shrieking children clinging to her—'kneel my children, and bless Heaven's minister that promises so much!—Justice, justice, justice on the murderer!'

'Be patient,' said the priest, 'you shall have justice, but none the more for clamour—none the less for gentleness.'

'Thou shalt commit no murder!' shrieked the woman, 'that is God's command. Have we not all heard it a thousand times from the lips of good and holy men—have we not been told that the blood of the murdered will cry out aloud for vengeance on the guilty? Justice, justice! Holy sir, I ask it of thee. I ask it of you all—I ask it of Heaven, and I shall have it!'

'Peace, peace,' said the priest; but he said it kindly. 'Come nearer, and bring with you the little ones. Has not our great Master said, of such is the kingdom of heaven? What complaint hast thou to make? Speak freely in this temple, there are none so lowly but may speak—none so high but may listen.'

'Your tones sink into my heart, and I am pacified. I know now that I shall have justice—the spirit of my murdered husband stands by his bier, and listens to us all.'

'Woman,' said one of the other priests, 'look not o
that which is ba........................'

'Hush, hush,' said the aged man. 'Who shall say it is
not so? let her proceed.'

'Look upon his face,' she cried—'did you not know him?
was he not devout and good, and full of holiness—was not
he all that even you, holy father, would wish him to be? Did
he not love God and the Church of God, and the ministers of
the Church? Aye, well we all know he did—he was a peni-
tent of yours.'

'Heaven's will be done,' said the aged priest. 'The corpse
was brought hither at the early dawn. My eyes are aged and
I have not looked upon the face. Heaven has granted me the
weight of years, but has not absolved me from human infir-
mities—methinks, too, that I have lived too long, for I have
heard in this temple sounds of uproar and of strife, such as
have stricken me to the very soul.'

'And such,' said the other priest, stepping forward, 'such
sounds could never have profaned this holy temple, but
that an arch-heretic, the Eighth Henry, sits upon the
English throne.'

'Hush, hush! my holy brother; your tongue is rash.'

'Nay, if you fear——'

'Fear—fear!' cried the old man, and he drew himself up
to a height, which in youth must have been gigantic; 'I fear
an earthly crowned monarch? Arm me but with the thunders
of the Vatican, and I will seek the tyrant, even at the festive
board, and hurl them in his teeth. Talk of fear to me—fear?
I—I—but no matter, no matter! Peace, peace, woman!
what is your complaint? Let us not travel from this matter
now in hand.'

'My husband has been foully murdered!'

'His name—condition?'

'His name is Randulph Hensman. I am his wife, these his
children, and there is all that remains of my husband, and
their father and protector. Bear with me, holy father, I
must weep; and it seems to me that when tears are denied to
us, we must rave and talk loudly in the agony of our despair.
Bear with me, holy sir; you know the sight that is before me.
Look at that mute face, from which I cannot turn my eyes—
those pallid cheeks, upon which I have seen the manly glow of
health—those lips, which never parted but to utter noble sen-
timents—those eyes, now hidden for ever, which flashed with
all the fire of life's true devotion. Look at him, my children—your father's corpse! Oh, holy sir, can you wonder
that I am nearly maddened?'

'It is a sore trial. Say on; and Heaven grant that your
affliction may be chastened down to the calmness of resignation—to the decrees of that Providence, which giveth and
taketh, as best it pleaseth infinite wisdom to direct.'

'Yes, I will be calm, because I shall have justice.'

'I have a remembrance of your husband's name.'

'He was secretary to the Lord Warden of the castle.'

'The castle here of Winchester?'

'The same. A worthy gentleman—one who held my husband highly; and who, were he now here, would bear him
witness to the spotless fame, high reputation, and unbounded
honour of the mute form that lies before us.'

'Heaven grant him rest eternal! Who has done the
deed?'

'A man upon whose very visage shall be seen the reflection of his crime—a man so steeped in guilt, chicanery,
and deceit, that surely none but he could arm a weapon
against such a precious life as that which he has let out,
through the gaping orifice of a wound, which has reached the
noblest heart that ever beat.'

At this moment, the excited feelings of the bereaved wife
again burst through all bounds of reason and reflection. She
turned from the priest, and, with wild gesticulations, again
appealed to the people.

'Justice on the murderer!' she said; 'Justice on Sir
Rupert Brent! Blood for blood! Shall he who has committed such a deed as this live? Justice! justice!'

The multitude, ever prone to excitement, took up again the
shout. These were ticklish times for the priesthood and the
sanctity of their temples. From a thousand throats rung
out the words,—

'Justice! justice!' and then a single voice that was heard
above all the rest of the clamour, shouted,—

'No sanctuary!'

The priests glanced at each other, as these ominous words
rung in their ears; and then a suspicion came across them,

which before had not been uttered, of the reason why the
body had been brought to that church in particular, and why
so great a popular tumult had been excited upon the occasion.

'You named some one,' said the aged priest. 'Is that the
man you charge with the commission of this crime?'

'Yes, Sir Rupert Brent; that is the man. It is his sword
that has drunk my husband's blood. The weapon broke; one
half of it is here, let him produce the other. He did the deed
that calls aloud for vengeance. Sir Rupert Brent, I accuse
him of my husband's murder!'

'What motive had he for the deed?'

'Holy sir, it is not for the accuser to supply a motive to the
criminal for the evil that he has done.'

'Well reasoned,' said the priest; 'and yet there is a motive:
not that I should compel you to avow it, if it please you not.

One of the priests now stepped up, and took the aged man
aside; he whispered to him energetically for several moments,
and what he said appeared to produce a considerable effect,
for an expression of deep anxiety ran over the old man's
face, and he said, mournfully—

'Is it indeed so?'

'It is,' was the brief reply.

Three times to the woman the old priest spoke with a
greater smoothness of aspect than he had hitherto assumed.

'Rest assured,' he said, 'that you have accomplished all
that you desire—rest assured that you shall have ample
justice against the oppressor—retire in peace, and take with
you your friends, if those persons present are entitled to that
appellation. Be fully assured, upon the word of a minister of
Heaven, that all that can be done shall be done.'

The woman looked in his face, and seemed about to speak,
when again the same voice that had rung so loud and clear
above all other sounds, shouted out, in a tone that sounded
like the blast of a trumpet,—

'No sanctuary!'

This time the words had a greater effect than before, for
they were taken up by the whole multitude; and strange,
indeed, was it to hear a Catholic church echoing with
such a sound.

'No sanctuary! no sanctuary!' was the cry, until at last
the bereaved wife herself shrieked it in the ears of the priest,
and dashing aside the long raven tresses of her hair, she with
hysterical vehemence clasped her hands like one possessed,
shrieking, 'No sanctuary! no sanctuary!' until the whole
church echoed to the sound, and the priests shrank back
aghast towards the door at which they had entered; while the
affrighted boys who bore the incense by the golden chains,
cowered down and trembled at the uproar that was around
them.

'Yes, yes,' she cried, 'that is what I came to say, no
sanctuary! no sanctuary! for the murderer—drag him forth
to the light of day—let the eye of Heaven beam upon him—
No sanctuary! no sanctuary! I heard the voice—it is
John Elkington's—I know him well, my husband's friend,
a good man and true—no sanctuary! no sanctuary!'

And now the mob opened again like parted waves of the
ocean, or like some rock riven asunder by the vivid power of
lightning, and there came forward to where the widow raved
and screamed, a young and stalwart man.

His dress was plain; a sad-coloured close-fitting doublet
comprised the whole of its upper portion, and long buff
leather horseman's boots defended his feet, and came half way
up the thigh.

He was fair, but there was a bold sparkling freedom about
the blue eyes, which were a remarkable feature of his face. The
mouth was small and well chiselled, and there was about his
bearing a lofty and a noble air, which, but for the plainness
of his appellation, and the meagre state of his attire—for that
was a time when dress made the man, and the distinction of
such was well kept up—might have proclaimed him one accustomed to command.

The old priest, as he saw this man advancing, fixed a keen
glance on him from beneath his shaggy brows, but the other
did not quail—he was not to be abashed by any priestly scowl,
and advancing to the side of the bereaved wife, he stooped
and spoke to her, saying:—

'Dame Hensman, the popular voice is with you, and this
priest, I am sure, will do you justice—so aged a man must
know the value of that commodity.'

'My son,' said the priest, 'be calm—this is not a moment
for such counsels to the ear of the distressed—there is bitter-

ness in your speech, more then your recorded words would convey—be calm! be calm! come to me to-morrow, and we will weigh this matter well.'

'Holy sir,' said John Elkington, 'I much regret that long habit induces me rather to do to-day what might possibly be as well to-morrow; had we the power to strip the interval of time of all its accidents and chances.'

'What is it that you require?'

'I have spoken twice—the popular voice has echoed with a roar that which I expressed—you have heard it from the lips of the bereaved wife—the demand made is comprised in those two words—no sanctuary!'

'Audacious caitiff!—durst thou thus at the altar's foot make war against the Church's ordinances? Can you hope for consolation here, or mercy hereafter, by thus coming in as a brawler to that temple which surely you have been taught to revere? I know not who you are, your dress would say you are one of lowly condition; but that there is a certain air and manner about you, which tempts me to believe you are not what you really seem.'

'Holy sir,' said the stranger, 'I am humbly of opinion, that all that is beside the question. I know not how and why my dress and appearance should in the least affect the question at issue. This woman asserts her husband to be foully murdered. If it be so, what imports it that I am what I seem, or not?'

'And the Church has promised to do all that may be done. Whoever yet heard the ministers of religion called upon to act in the capacity of prosecutors on account of crime committed? These questions are for the civil power, and not the ecclesiastical. Begone, all of you, or dread the anathemas of the Church!'

It was evident, during this brief colloquy, the people who were present listened with the greatest interest and attention. There was something about the manner of John Elkington, their spokesman, although he was a stranger to all but the bereaved wife, that gave them great confidence in what he could achieve.

And at the same time they listened with eager curiosity to the remarks of the aged priest, whose opinions had been considered for years past little less than oracular by the ignorant multitude.

But the supremacy of the Catholic Church at that period had received several severe shocks: the contentions between the king and the priesthood had already taken the form of open hostility; and it would seem as if Henry the Eighth had began to shadow forth in his own mind the gigantic scheme of confiscation respecting Church property, which he afterwards carried out so relentlessly.

Several things had occurred to do away with much of the respect the people had been in the habit of entertaining for the clergy; and but a few years before those who now filled the cathedral of Winchester, and gave utterance so unrestrainedly to their opinions, would have considered they were rushing upon certain perdition to have done so.

As the bold stranger thus confronted the priest, murmurs of applause came from the multitude; while, occasionally, some bolder and more reckless spirit would utter some loud expression of approval, or otherwise, according as one or other of the parties were speaking.

'Urge him again, urge him again, John Elkington,' cried the widowed mother. 'You knew my husband well—call aloud for justice upon his murderer.'

'I will do so to my utmost power,' said he, who was thus addressed.

'You have done so,' said the priest; 'depart now in peace, and leave us to say masses for the departed soul, whose mortal remains lay before us.'

'Far be it from me,' said John Elkington, 'to detract in the slightest degree from the efficacy of those masses, but still it does appear to me, that while we accord to them their full amount of importance, we should not forget that there is an earthly justice to be asked for as between man and man.'

'Go, then, to the ministers of that earthly justice.'

'Most assuredly we shall; but when we are asked by those ministers where is the accused man, and we find we are compelled to say that he has taken sanctuary from the arm of justice, it will be paralysed, and nothing can be done.'

These words were ostensibly addressed to the priest; but, before he had finished the bold speech, John Elkington had turned to the people, and when he had ceased, there arose

again such a shout of 'No sanctuary! no sanctuary!' that even the bold-hearted spirit of the aged ecclesiastic shrunk before it.

Turning from the altar, he snatched from it an ebony cross, on which was a sculptured figure in ivory, of the suffering Saviour, and holding it forward to the full extent of his arm, in the faces of the people, he cried aloud:—

'You may trample this sacred emblem under foot you; may take the lives of those who are its guardians; you may desecrate by riot, bloodshed, and confusion, this holy building, but dreadful should be the retribution, as well in this world as in that which is to come, for those who take part in such a fearful work.'

'He denies me justice! He denies me justice!' cried Mistress Hensman. 'You hear, all of you, he denies me justice. He knows well that the murderer of my husband is within these walls.'

'Woman, I know nothing.'

'Justice! justice!' she continued, 'and no sanctuary. Look here, at the bloody witness of a crime, denounced alike by man and by divinity. Does not the sight of that still face move you? It was but yesterday he walked among you, and had any one of this assemblage met with such a death as he has, who but Ranulph Hensman would have come forward to demand justice and no sanctuary?'

'We will have it, we will have it!' shouted the people 'Where is the murderer?'

'You hear, holy sir,' said John Elkington to the priest, 'you hear what the people say.'

'And how long,' said the priest, bitterly, 'how long is it since the people have governed?'

'They have not yet governed in England, but like an infant Hercules, a people is beginning to feel that it has strength and power. When the popular voice does rise as it has this day risen, let me tell you it is wiser to swim a little with the torrent than attempt to stem its dangerous waves.'

The old man shook as he looked in the face of the speaker.

'Never!' he said, 'never! This may be, and probably is the last day of my mortal career. It is likely, in the unavailing opposition I shall offer to brute force, that I may be killed. I care not—I am prepared to offer that opposition at the hazard of my life.'

'Even now you said you knew nothing; will you say that you are not aware of the fact that Ranulph Hensman's murderer has sought sanctuary in this place?'

'I am not aware of that fact. I have been made aware within these few moments past of two circumstances that occurred close upon each other. In the small hours of night, the doors of this temple have never been closed but once, and that once was to-day, when you and your companions, evidently intent upon far other than holy thoughts, approached its sacred precincts.'

'Go on, holy sir, what occurred?'

'Some hours before day-break then, as I am told, the priest whose duty it was to watch the altar during the night, saw a man prostrate himself upon the steps; he claimed that which we dare not deny him; we inquired not his name, his crime, if crime it was, nor his condition. Were he the most abject beggar that ever crawled, or the heartiest prince that ever wore a jewelled diadem, his reception with us must have been the same; he asked for that which we dared not refuse him.'

'And that was——'

'Sanctuary,' said the priest.

'You hear,' cried Mistress Hensman; 'you hear they have given protection, under the name of sanctuary, to my husband's murderer, it is not even sought to be denied, and therefore is it that I cry, No sanctuary.'

Again the mob took up the cry, but John Elkington by gestures implored their silence; and when all was still again, so still that the slightest whisper might have been heard, he turned again to the priest, saying—

'You spoke, holy father, of two circumstances occurring last night, you have told us but of one.'

'The other was the arrival of this body some half hour after sanctuary had been claimed by him who was unknown to us. This murdered man, as it appears, was brought within the church and placed upon the altar steps, the body was found in the public streets, no indication was found upon it of who or what he had been in life, and so, for recognition, remained. I have no more to say.'

'It is enough,' cried the widow; 'it is enough, by your own admission, the murderer has found a refuge within the walls of a building reared to the service of Him who has said most emphatically, "Thou shalt commit no murder."'

The people at this grew more violent than before; the admission of the priest, for it really amounted to as much, that the murderer had found a refuge within the walls of the sacred building, inflamed their passions to the utmost.

From some evidence which she must have gathered from foregone circumstances, Dame Hensman, when she heard of her husband's death, at once accused Sir Rupert Brent of the deed, and a more unpopular name with the multitude could not have been found.

This circumstance, combined with the wild and vehement eloquence that came to her aid as she flew from house to house proclaiming the deed of blood, had in an incredibly short space of time got together the vast assemblage that had accompanied her to the church.

Now a most dangerous crisis seemed to have arrived, and it evidently depended upon the man called John Elkington, whether the multitude should proceed to the utmost violence or not. It was a strange and significant sign of the times that a perfect stranger should thus have it in his power, in such a place as that, to exercise a much more powerful control over men's passions than the priesthood to whom they had been habitually deferring on all matters whatever.

But so it was: the impolitic and most unjust exercise of this power of sanctuary did more, in the minds of the common people, to excite hatred against Catholicism, than any other single circumstance whatsoever.

Probably, too late, the ecclesiastical authorities became aware of this fact, but yet to have given way upon such a point would have been such an acknowledgment of their want of supremacy that it could not for a moment be thought of, and they were forced to abide the full consequences of the act.

John Elkington, as before, succeeded in completely silencing the people, such was the power he had obtained over them in consequence of the bold manner in which he had maintained their rights, that almost at a glance, or with a waive of his hand, he could accomplish anything he pleased.

Then, turning to the priest, he gave him, probably, the soundest advice that could be given under the circumstances.

'You perceive,' he said, 'that this is a matter that must and will be settled by the people. Give way while yet there is time; what object can it be to you to shield a murderer from the just reward of his crimes?'

'Regain some of your vast power over the minds of the people by an act of justice—give up the murderer.'

'We know of no murderer; we know of no criminal; a man has sought sanctuary, and he has found it; we know no more; we seek to know no more.'

'You hear, Dame Hensman, what the holy father says; are you satisfied?'

'Satisfied!' shrieked the widow; 'satisfied while my husband's blood calls for vengeance! satisfied when I see these little one's clinging to me for a sustenance they can no longer receive, since their natural protector is no more; can you, dare you ask me if I am satisfied?'

'It is enough!' said John Elkington in a loud voice; 'the appeal to those who call themselves the ministers of One, with whom justice is indefeasible and eternal, has failed; this bereaved mother accuses Sir Rupert Brent of being the murderer of her husband; she further declares him to be within these walls.'

'He is, he is!' cried a hundred voices.

'Shall we then calmly depart and leave this monstrous act unavenged?'

'No, no, no!' almost shouted every throat then present.

'I may be,' said Elkington, 'doing myself great peril, but being always willing to answer for my acts, I declare my name is John Elkington; I am a sincere and humble follower of the Earl of Surrey, my most honoured master.'

'Beware,' said the aged priest; 'beware, I say, unless your name become a bye-word and reproach. I will warn you three times, and then your sin be upon your own head.'

'Most certainly,' said Elkington, 'I seek to share the consequences of my acts with no man; and, first of all, I advise that the doors of this cathedral be guarded by some of those persons who have an antipathy to murder.'

There was a rush of persons to the massive doors; they were closed in a moment, that the escape of any one by that mode of egress was a matter of impossibility, and then John

Elkington waived his hand again, and all was peaceable as before.

'For the second time,' cried the aged priest, 'I warn you, and bid you beware. Do you not fear some sudden judgment from Heaven for this impiety?'

'In truth do I not; were I clear upon the subject of its impiety, I might so fear; but, in the name of eternal justice, I protest for myself, and for all human nature, against what is called sanctuary—against that worst designation of Heaven's temple, which converts it not into a place of refuge for the great and the good and the pious, but into a mansion, where can be screened those who have committed the worst of vices, that I protest against.'

'Go on, go on!' cried Dame Hensman, clasping her hands, 'we shall have justice now, justice and no sanctuary for the murderer: look, my children, look, kneel by that bier, on it lays all that was once your father!'

Up to this point of indignation the most violent excitement of feeling had carried the widow on; she had shed no tears, but when she saw the children, in obedience to her commands, creep gently forward, and kneel by the bleeding corpse, the well-spring of her heart gushed up, and the frantic burst of tears came to her relief.

CHAPTER II.

The Search for the Murderer—The Cathedral Vaults—The Discovery—The Proposition, and the Death of the Aged Priest.

THERE was something so sacred about the grief of the bereaved one, who thus upon the altar steps gave way to such a frantic burst of grief, that all around became so still and hushed, one might have imagined she was the only person present within the ample verge of the sacred building.

The people waited until a greater calmness should come over the mourner's heart, ere they proceeded to the perpetration of acts, entailing perchance, in their execution, some bloodshed and certainly much violence.

It was a mercy that she was thus permitted to shed tears so abundantly, for by that natural outlet much of the fevered agony that had almost turned her brain to fire, left her, and she became comparatively calm.

The gush of tears ceased, and was succeeded by low hysterical sobs, these then passed away into gentle sighs, and then, clasping her hands, she knelt down with the children by the side of that melancholy spectacle which was before her, and seemed absorbed in her own reflections.

John Elkington had not taken his eyes off her during the few minutes that this wild excess of passionate grief had lasted, and when he saw that it had passed away, and she was calmer than before, he drew a long breath as if he too felt much relieved.

'Those tears were a mercy,' he said, in a low tone, as if rather making the remark to himself than to others—'those tears were a great mercy; I have been most anxiously looking for them, and, thank Heaven, they have come at last.'

Then he drew himself up again to his full height, for he had stooped low to look upon the mourning face, and once more he addressed himself to the people.

'It is now our duty' he said, 'a duty which we owe to immutable and sacred justice, to leave no spot unsearched in this building for the criminal, who shall find that Heaven's temple will not shield him from his deep iniquity.'

'Rash man,' said another of the priests, stepping forward, 'rash man, you neither know that he who sought sanctuary within these walls last night be Sir Rupert Brent, or if he be you know not that he is the murderer of the man called Ranulph Hensman?'

'The production,' said John Elkington, 'of the individual who sought sanctuary, will at once answer your first questions, the second can be then entered into; no injustice shall be done, it would ill become us to come here with the words "justice and no sanctuary" on our lips, and then convict any man on insufficient evidence.'

'The search, the search!' cried several voices, 'search for the murderer, drag him forth, kill him, slay him, the priests have hidden him.'

Some of the more daring of the crowd began to break open some of the small confessionals, fancying it possible that in one of those moments that they thought he might be induced, but they were ... ... that he had ... ... and to ... ... make his way over the gilt ... that marked ... the progress.

This ... ... the latent fire that was in the old priest's disposition; he snatched from the altar a heavy silver crucifix, which would have required a man of no ordinary strength to wield, and with one frightful blow he sent the intruder headlong down the steps.

There wanted but one such incautious act to inflame all the worst passions of the people.

The yell of rage that arose from among them was positively terrific, and there cannot be a doubt but that the life of the aged man would at once have been sacrificed, had not John Elkington flung himself before him, and cried aloud—

'Forbear, forbear, I implore you to forbear; as you value the cause you come here to espouse, harm not a hair of this aged man's head; let us, even while we are opposed to him, remember who and what he is.'

The heavy silver cross dropped from the hands, that only for a few brief moments had gathered strength from intense excitement to wield; and then the aged ecclesiastic tottered backward until he came to one of the costly chairs which were reserved within the sacred precinct of the altar for high Church dignitaries.

Into this he sunk with a deep groan, his head reclined upon his breast, and his arms hung powerless by his sides.

John Elkington turned, and pointed to him as he continued his address to the people.

'There you see.' he said, 'the unavailing opposition is over, and you must bear in mind that this old man has but done his duty to the order to which he belongs; forgive him, therefore, and let us pass on to the purpose which we have resolved upon.'

'Long live John Elkington!' cried a voice; 'let old father Wynell it alone, he was a soldier in his youth.'

'Yes,' said another; 'but he never struck a better blow than this, and he has proved, what we all doubted before, that Drunken Hugh of the Old Crickens had some brains.'

'Come on, search well, but search quickly,' pursued John Elkington; 'injure no one, destroy nothing, but leave not a hole or corner unlooked at. By dragging forth this criminal to justice we strike the first great blow against the privilege of sanctuary.'

Elkington stood himself by the altar, while the mob dispersed itself about the sacred edifice, and when the whole area of the church, with all its nooks and corners, and richly sculptured niches, had been searched in vain, he selected twelve men, from whose appearance he thought he could depend upon; and then, addressing the others, he said—

'Let me implore you all to remain here, with the exception of these twelve, who shall accompany me. We shall be able much more effectually to search for the man whom we believe to be hidden than a larger number of persons. We are enough to overpower all opposition, and if the criminal be here we shall produce him. One of these lads, too, will accompany us.'

As he spoke he took by the arm one of the terrified incense boys, and conducted him at once through the opening which had been disclosed by the massive curtain drawn aside for the entrance of the priesthood.

After traversing a narrow passage, the little band that was led by John Elkington came into a profusely and richly decorated apartment. The most superb hangings depended from the walls, and on a table in the centre of the room were refreshments in plates and dishes of burnished gold.

Goblets of the same costly material were likewise there, and a single glance was sufficient to show that they contained something much stronger, and more exciting to the palate than water.

In fact, take this room for all in all, it was a tolerable specimen of the height of luxury to which the priesthood had attained at that period when their downfall was so very near at hand.

A glance was quite sufficient, likewise, to convince them that nowhere was the person hidden whom they sought, and John Elkington, without making any remark as to what he saw, passed onward through another doorway which led to a staircase, part of which ascended and part descended.

He paused for a moment, as if in doubt, which of these routes he should take, and then turning to the boy, who from fear had crept tremblingly by his side, he seated him so high upon the staircase, that their faces were upon a level; and then, as he fixed his eyes upon the embarrassed and frightened countenance of the lad, he said,—

'Now you will tell me, and tell me truly, where the man who sought sanctuary last night is hidden?'

The boy looked doubtful and terrified for a moment or two, but the stern and steady glance of Elkington completely cowed him. He did not speak, but he pointed with his finger down the staircase.

'Good!' said Elkington; 'I understand; in the vaults?'

'The vaults!' said the boy. 'Don't take me, for there are evil spirits.'

'There is one, at all events, which we will rid the vaults of. Let two of you remain above here as sentinels, in case we should pass him in our search, and he should make an attempt to escape this way.'

This was done, and John Elkington, accompanied by the ten remaining men, proceeded down the staircase, which each moment grew darker and darker as it dived beneath the level of the earth.

They had paused, and were debating the propriety of one of their body returning to procure a light, when Elkington, who was first, perceived that a little in advance there was a niche in the wall, from which proceeded the dim rays of a burning lamp. It was most probably a shrine, at which a light was continually kept burning.

'This will answer our purpose,' said Elkington; 'that lamp which is most likely shining upon some image of the Virgin, cannot be used for a better purpose than that for which we require it, therefore shall I take it without scruple.'

The lamp was burning very dimly, but by trimming it a little with a small poniard which hung by his girdle, which was then an allowable, as well as a fashionable weapon, he made it burn brightly, so that it shed quite sufficient light around it, to enable him to see what he was about, and in this way they all descended to the vaults of the ancient cathedral in search of one who no doubt thought himself extremely safe in such a place.

When they reached the bottom of the staircase they found themselves in a vaulted apartment paved with stone, from which branched two passages, establishing again a necessity for placing sentinels, so that John Elkington got rid of two more of his number in this way, and then proceeded down the passage, which was to the right hand, not from any particular preference for that, so much as he felt it absolutely necessary to lose no time in the prosecution of his project, lest the priests should adopt some plan of foiling him.

After they had traversed this passage for some distance they came to an iron door of apparently great strength. It yielded, however, to a touch, and it conducted the adventurers into a place, the details of which for a few moments completely fixed their attention.

It was an exceedingly capacious vault, and contained a number of tombs, on each of which reposed some sculptured figure, made to represent the individual who slept the long sleep of death beneath.

The roof of this subterranean place was supported by numerous stunted pillars of Gothic mould; and a damp unwholesome atmosphere seemed to them to pervade the entire space.

A single glance round the walls was amply sufficient to show that there were no places for concealment; but John Elkington, who himself carried the light, seemed dissatisfied, and lingered near its entrance.

He appeared lost in deep thought for a few moments, and then one of his companions said to him—

'There are no places of concealment here; this is the house of the dead, not the living; let us leave it, the atmosphere is noisome, and full of unwholesome exhalations—let us leave it.'

'In a moment,' said Elkington, 'in a moment; I wish to make a little experiment first.'

As he spoke, he took the poniard, which we have previously mentioned, from its sheath, and carrying the light in the other hand, he walked among the tombs, making a thrust with the sharp-pointed weapon he carried against the sculptured images of saints and warriors that lay around.

The persons who had come with him to the vaults, looked with surprise at this excess of suspicion, which could not even leave statuary untouched, but they soon had occasion to perceive that, if John Elkington had his suspicions, they were extremely well founded, for upon approaching one of the statues, and gently trying it about the region of the ribs, to the amazement of all, it sprung to its feet, revealing a living man, and without doubt, from his anxiety to conceal himself, the one whom they sought.

He was plainly attired and a sword hung by his side, which, however, he made no effort to draw, although he placed his hand upon its hilt.

With eyes flashing fire, and a countenance altogether expressive of the greatest anger and ferocity, he confronted him who had been the means of discovering the well-laid plan he had conceived for eluding capture.

'Sir Rupert Brent,' said Elkington, 'I am glad to see you; it is true we have had some trouble to find you, but you are well met at last.'

'Well met for what?' cried the captured man as he glanced upon the faces of those who now thronged around him; 'well met for what ? can a man not get into a street brawl, and choose then, of his own accord, to seek sanctuary, without being hunted out by all of you ?'

'You are accused,' said Elkington, 'of the murder of Ranulph Hensman.'

'Who accuses me ?'

'His widow and myself.'

''Tis false; I did not do the deed!'

'Wherefore, then, did you think it necessary to hide yourself from its consequences?'

'I was not hiding; an innocent man may repose himself upon a tomb, surely, without that being construed into a presumption of his guilt.'

'Bring him along,' said John Elkington, 'we will talk no more; bring him to the church, and let us then see how his boldness will avail him.'

Several of the men laid hold of him, to urge him on, and as he marked their resolute countenances, the colour wholly forsook his own, and for a few moments he exhibited every symptom of the most abject fear.

'I am in sanctuary,' he said ; 'then cursed shall be the hand that tears me from it—the malediction of the Church will fail upon you all. Beware of what you do !'

'We have had this warning before,' said John Elkington, 'we have had it from worthier lips than yours, and it has not moved us. Bring him along, my friends—bring him along.'

'I shall appeal to higher powers,' muttered Sir Rupert Brent, as he was hurried from the vault, 'I am quite safe, you dare not harm me, you know you dare not ! I am in sanctuary, and therefore safe.'

It took but a few brief moments to convey him into the upper air. When John Elkington and his companions entered the cathedral, conveying with them their prisoner, the shout of exultation that burst from every one present was more than sufficient to terrify a far bolder heart than his.

He shrunk back perfectly appalled; and, doubtless, would have fled again to the fancied security of the vaults, but that he was effectually prevented by his capturers.

A look of intense mortification was evident upon the countenances of the younger priests, as they saw the prisoner thus brought forth. As for the aged man, who sat upon the chair at the altar, he spoke not, and moved not, but preserving the same attitude he had assumed when he had there seated himself, he seemed to have given up all interest in what was passing around him.

And the widowed wife still knelt on the same spot where she was left, ere the search begun for him whom she accused of being her husband's murderer. The children were huddled close to her, still lost in wonder and full of terror at the strange proceedings they were called upon to witness ; she did not look up, though the shout of execration, which announced the arrival of Sir Rupert Brent, wrung up on her ears.

It was not until John Elkington advanced, and stooping, whispered to her, 'He is here!' that she awoke from the sort of stupor and grief that had come over her after the burst of energetic agony had subsided.

These words, however, seemed to act as a most potent spell to rouse her; she looked up on the moment, and clearing from before her eyes the tangled masses of hair, she glared around her in search of the countenance of him whom she accused of inflicting upon her so great an amount of evil.

Then she sprang to her feet, and pointed at him with outstretched arms.

'It is he, it is he!' she said; 'look upon his face—do you not see there a thousand of bloody guilt-less marks ? How he quails before me—he dare not look upon me—he shrinks. Murderer, look upon your victim !'

He followed the direction of her eyes, and for the first time then seemed to be aware of the presence of the murdered body. It was with something of a cry between a shriek and a groan that he stepped back from too close a proximity to those ghastly remains. Mistress Hensman then shrieked out her charge against him in accents that made every one tremble, so fearfully condemnatory did they sound at times, and then again so full of solemnity and the very majesty of pathos.

'Yes,' she said, 'he is here ! I see him now ! I look upon the face of the man who has made me a widow, and these children fatherless. He may deny it with his tongue, but the tell-tale countenance will still confess the deed. I denounce him ! My husband was the secretary of the Lord Warden. He was detained late on business of great import. In vain I waited for him ; this man slew him, ere he reached his own threshold.'

''Tis false!' said Sir Rupert; 'I have not seen him for many an hour.'

'You hear him,' said the widow; 'your hear him, friends all. He says that it is false, and therefore demands proofs. He shall have them. Look at this ; here is part of a sword drawn from my husband's breast. Where is the remainder of the blade?'

As she spoke she unfolded from a cloth which she had with her a piece of a sword blade of about six inches in length, which she placed upon the altar steps.

'You have a weapon by your side, Sir Rupert Brent,' said John Elkington; 'draw, and let us see if it be perfect.'

'No, no, no,' cried the conscience-stricken ruffian; 'not in a church, and, besides, this is not my sword. I picked it up in the streets, and girded it on, as being the easiest mode of carrying it. I have not examined the blade, and cannot know if it be perfect or otherwise.'

'Then,' said Elkington, 'to save your scruples, we will ourselves satisfy the doubt.'

As he spoke he advanced, and seizing the handle of Sir Rupert's sword, he drew it from its scabbard, and then not a soul in the church could do otherwise than perceive that it had lost some portion of its length.

'The proof, the proof!' cried Mistress Hensman ; 'look to his broken sword. Who shall now doubt his guilt? Look again, my children, into his face, and should you live until old age bend you nearly to the earth, ever dread such a countenance as that. It is the likeness of your father's murderer.'

The children gazed at him with awe and wonder; and then, by a desperate effort, Sir Rupert yet attempted to turn the tide of feeling in his favour.

'I can disprove this charge,' he said, 'most easily; and at the same time I can well forgive its being made, because I know that appearances are against me. I was going home last night from the castle, when, on suddenly turning the corner of a street, I heard the clash of swords, and I perceived that one man was contending with several. The man who thus fought single-handed was Ranulph Hensman; his assailant I know not. I drew my sword and joined the affray to rescue him, but my weapon was beaten from my grasp, and what became of it I know not.'

Dame Hensman seemed about to speak, but John Elkington motioned her to be still, and she was so.

Then Sir Rupert Brent, who had paused while this little interruption took place, continued his narrative—

'At that moment I saw Ranulph Hensman fall, and, stooping as I thought to pick up my own sword, which had fallen from my grasp, I instead snatched up this, which now you see, and followed the fast-retreating ruffians who had slain Hensman. One of these turned upon me—we fought for a few moments, and I think I slew him; he fell into his companion's arms, and I, on the impulse of the moment, sought for sanctuary in this the nearest church.'

'The tale is well told,' said John Elkington, 'and well contrived; but it is no marvel us to me how you could another person's sword fits your scabbard. You cannot that away; and see, the garnishments upon the sheath are of a pattern with those upon the sword-hilt.'

8

ORDEAL BY TOUCH.

'That is accident—a man should not be condemned upon such mere coincidences. I claimed sanctuary, because I feared that in my wish to defend Ranulph Hensman I had slain some man of rank.'

'Heed not this specious tale,' cried the widowed mother, 'oh! heed it not, you who are friends to the fatherless. He is guilty; he knows full well that he is guilty.'

'Nay,' said Sir Rupert, 'I know full well otherwise; and could Ranulph Hensman now give evidence as to the cause of his death, he would, in a few words, clear me of the crime.'

Elkington was about to speak, but Dame Hensman stretched forth her hands, crying,—

'Let me speak—let me speak—this suggestion surely comes from Heaven; let me speak, and weigh well the words I utter.'

She stood upon the altar steps like one inspired. A flush of exultation sat upon her brow, and when all was hushed and still, she spoke, saying,—

'This man denies his crime; there lies the mute witness of a deed committed by some human arm. We are here beneath the roof of a building reared to the service of Heaven—the ministers of religion are present—we have abundant witnesses—and Sir Rupert Brent has called upon the dead to testify to his innocence. I likewise call upon the dead to bear witness to his guilt.'

'The dead!' said John Elkington.

'Yes,' she cried, elevating her voice; 'yes, I claim the *Ordeal by Touch!*'

These words produced an immense sensation among the multitude. It was one of the most current superstitions of the day, that if a murderer touched the corpse of his victim, the blood, although apparently congealed and motionless, would flow again in a fresh and ruddy stream from the wound which had produced death.

In thus claiming the ordeal by touch, Alice Hensman by no means uttered anything which her auditors considered to be absurd or outrageous. Perhaps, there were scarcely a dozen persons in the whole assembly who doubted for one moment the efficacy of the trial; and among that dozen, probably, we ought to include the priests, who were far above in education all other classes of society.

When the first feeling of surprise was over—for no one had expected such a termination to Alice Hensman's speech—the eagerness of the multitude to give effect to the proposition knew no bounds; scarcely one was silent; and if before, the cathedral had echoed with the words 'No sanctuary!' the groined roof seemed now to shake again, as, with one voice, the dense crowd shouted—

'*The Ordeal by Touch! The Ordeal by Touch!*'

And now Sir Rupert Brent shrunk back, presenting a picture of the most abject terror. This proposition had taken him most completely by storm; he knew not what to do or what to say, but stood trembling in every limb, as if waiting his instant condemnation.

'This may not be,' said one of the priests, stepping forward, 'except with the express permission of your superior, who you perceive is in deep and holy meditation.'

'How can he object?' said Elkington.

'Were I in his position I should not object; because in my own opinion I hold Sir Rupert Brent to be guiltless, and to have fairly explained the proceedings of last night.'

'Then we will disturb his reverence's holy meditation, and procure his permission.'

John Elkington stepped up to the aged priest, and touched him lightly upon the arm.

'Holy father,' he said, 'the widow of the murdered man claims that he whom she accuses shall go through the *Ordeal by Touch.*'

There was no answer, and John Elkington then looked more nearly and anxiously into the face of the old priest. Then he drew back, and in a voice of some emotion, he said:

'He is dead—peace be to him! he is no more!'

The other priest stepped up to the chair, and a moment's examination satisfied them of the fact. There could be no doubt but that the agitation consequent upon the whole affair had been too much for the aged, worn-out frame of that venerable man.

All the energies of an existence which might, with no disturbing cause, have lasted for a considerable period, had been completely exhausted in that one stupendous effort he had made to resist aggression upon the inviolability of the altar. Probably the moment he sat down upon that chair he had breathed his last.

CHAPTER III.

The Ordeal, and its Results—The Challenge—The Champion of the Oppressed.

This incident seemed to have a subduing effect upon everybody. Those who were before most clamorous spoke in whispers, and even Alice Hensman, when she saw that death had laid low another as well as her husband, felt, for the moment, better able to sustain her great affliction.

'This is the will of Heaven,' said John Elkington. 'I much rejoice that not a soul of all here assembled laid a finger on the aged man.'

'And I—and I!' said Alice Hensman.

'You, however,' continued Elkington, turning to the other priest, 'you who have already said that, were you in authority, you would grant permission for this ordeal to take place, can now do so.'

'I can, truly; and since I have said so, I may not refuse.'

John Elkington then turned to Sir Rupert Brent, and said,—

'Now, mark me, you shall understand your real position; sanctuary shall not avail you. You shall be taken from here, and upon such evidence as can be brought against you, you shall be arraigned for the murder of Ranulph Hensman.'

'I am innocent!'

'As you assert; but now, as regards this ordeal by touch, you shall not be compelled to undergo it, and for one reason shall you not be compelled: I cannot myself believe that such a result, as is by many confidently expected, would ensue. When human means are sufficient to prove guilt there needs no special act of Providence to fix it in the proper quarter.'

This was unpalatable to the crowd, who again shouted, 'The ordeal! the ordeal!'

'I care not,' said Elkington; 'be it as you please.'

'I should not,' said Sir Rupert Brent, 'shrink from this, being guiltless of this man's death;' and then, he added to himself in an under tone, ''tis but an idle superstition. If I shrink from it, I am lost, and it will be evidence in my favour to have passed through it unscathed.'

'The ordeal!' cried Alice Hensman; 'let him touch the corpse, and, if the blood flow not, I will forgive him. I call upon Heaven to confound the guilty, and to do this great act of justice.'

'Be it so,' said Sir Rupert, boldly, 'I will prove to you that the tale I have told is a true one; you shall admit that you have wronged me. I am content to go through the ordeal which you propose.'

This was said boldly, and was almost enough to stagger any one as to a presumption of his guilt. The priest looked on with cold calmness; John Elkington folded his arms, and rather with an air of indifference than interest, awaited the result, while the spectators crowded nearer, and but a small space was left in which the strange, superstitious rite could be performed.

And in that space was Alice Hensman, and likewise her children; there were John Elkington and Sir Rupert Brent, and lastly, although not least in interest, there was the dead form of Ranulph Hensman, which presented so solemn and afflicting a spectacle to all beholders, and more especially those who had known what he was in life.

No one spoke, so Alice Hensman herself appointed the proceedings, and amid such a breathless stillness that the faintest whispers could have been heard, she spoke:—

'Sir Rupert Brent, you know you were my husband's enemy, you know that he had cause of quarrel with you, and that for that cause you wished him dead. He is no more, and although I accuse you, you declare yourself guiltless of the deed; place your hand now upon that cold, still breast, once full of noble and generous feelings, and call upon Heaven to open again the gaping wound which let out his life blood, if you be guilty, and let that blood flow forcibly.'

There was a death-like stillness. The cold perspiration stood upon the brow of Sir Rupert Brent in heavy drops, his lips were colourless, and he shook in every limb.

'Will you do it, or do you now shrink from the ordeal you affected to dare?'

'I—I dare it still,' he said; 'I do not shrink. Who says I shrink? I am calm and cool and steady; for I am innocent.'

Another step brought him close to the corpse, so that by stretching out his hand he could, if he so pleased, have placed it over the region of the heart. Once, twice, thrice, he raised his hand, and as often drew it down again with a shudder.

'Guilty, guilty!' cried Alice Hensman. 'He shrinks—he dares not essay the ordeal.'

'Guilty, guilty!' echoed the crowd; and the word rung fearfully in the affrighted ears of the accused.

'No, no,' he cried; 'it is not so. Which of you, who are so boisterous and so bold in accusing me, will step forward, and, without a tremor, do this which I am required to perform? The guilty man may be among you, and he might most tremble, but still there is not one here present who would not shake as much as I.'

'The ordeal!' shrieked Alice. 'The ordeal!'

'Besides,' continued Sir Rupert, 'I knew him in life.'

'The ordeal!' cried every voice; 'he shrinks from the ordeal!'

'No, I do not; and now is my moment for triumph.'

He averted his head, and raised once more his right hand. By great effort of resolution, he placed it on the breast of the corpse, and there it lay as if its owner were possessed of the ague.

'I am innocent,' he said; 'I swear I am innocent! I call upon Heaven to make the red blood flow again, if any of its crimson stream has been shed by my hand.'

He had scarcely concluded these words, when he uttered a cry of horror; for fresh crimson blood bubbled up through his very fingers, crimsoning the snow-white sheet which was laid across the body, and becoming manifest to every one of the spectators near, or remote. He held up his hand, and the sanguinary fluid dropped from his fingers; then he reeled back upon his heels, and if he had not been caught by the priest, he would have fallen on the spot.

The effects of this result of the ordeal by touch upon Alice Hensman were overpowering; she tried to speak, but could not. She tried to move forward towards the bier, but her paralysed frame refused to aid her. She grasped at the air, as if endeavouring to clutch at something for support, and then fell in a state of total insensibility on the marble steps of the altar, where she lay, to all appearance, as lifeless as he was whom she so deeply lamented.

It would almost seem as if she could not have contemplated the result that had occurred, but, from the language she

had used, and from the vehemence of manner that had characterised her throughout the whole affair, it is scarcely possible to come to such a conclusion.

Possibly it might be, that the certainty so far transcended any effort of the imagination she might have made in depicting to herself the circumstances that had occurred, that it completely overcame her, producing insensibility instead of violent action upon the rush of feeling which ensued.

What she might have said, and what she might have done, if power and speech, and if will had remained to her, it is hard, indeed, to conjecture; but, yet, we can well conceive that in such excess there could be nothing but an extreme of one kind or the other. No medium could have depicted her feelings—she must either have transcended all she had hither be do or done, or have lapsed as she did into a state of perfect insensibility, leaving the issue of that fearful adventure to be decided by others.

But we have not yet spoken of the effect which that sudden gush of blood, fresh, and of its own rich and ensanguined colour, from the congealed veins of the dead, produced upon the minds of those whom we might call indifferent spectators.

Thousands of persons are superstitious, and yet the realisation of any one of their own superstitious dreams would at any time suffice to fill them with the profoundest terrors. How many persons believe in the existence of spiritual appearances who would be driven to the very confines of madness by the appearance to them of any one of those shadowy forms, whose existence they will not doubt.

And thus reasoning by analogy, we may suppose that the effect produced upon the crowd in the old cathedral was not the less great, because it had realised a superstition of their own; indeed, so various and conflicting were the sensations produced, that the scenes of chaotic confusion which ensued baffle description.

Some, with loud cries, denounced the murderer, calling aloud for justice—some wept—some prayed—and not a few rushed from the church, some to spread the tidings of the miracle which had been achieved, and some repaired to their own homes in tribulation of spirit to think that such things could be.

And perhaps it may be that the priests who looked upon the strange effect that was produced by the hand of Sir Rupert Brent being placed upon the corpse, were most surprised of all, familiar as they were with every description of holy cheating, and completely divested, as they must be by their very profession, of anything in the shape of pious superstition, they looked at each other, and at the dead body, with countenances of the deepest wonder; in truth, to them it was a marvel which their philosophy could not master.

They placed Sir Rupert Brent in a vacant chair by the side of their dead superior, and for many minutes not more dead did that aged man appear than the ruffian who had thought to gain a point by pandering to a popular superstition, but had found himself completely overwhelmed by its consequences.

One of the priests crept close to him and whispered in his ear. At first he seemed not to hear the amnesty of that zealous friend and partizan; but soon he listened, and he shewed by the expression of his countenance that he was not an unobserving or an uninterested listener.

'This is nothing,' said the priest, 'we care not that as issue is thus given to some of the disputes; but the king and the council—the right of sanctuary violated—will give his Holiness a good pretence for stirring all Christendom against the heretic that sits upon the English throne, and as for you, to avoid scandal and the damage of a great and holy cause, you must decide this matter personally by offering to assert in single combat your innocence, with any champion that the widow can produce.'

'That champion will be John Elkington,' whispered Sir Rupert.

'Be it so. You are cunning of fence, or should be, and means could be taken so to unnerve your opponent—so to destroy all vital energy within him—that you shall obtain an easy victory, and it shall seem as if Heaven itself had smitten him for waging war against you.'

'But this ordeal by touch, will not its results be spread far and wide?—Will not it even rise up against me as evidence of my guilt?'

'No! When this affair is over you are no longer Sir Rupert Brent, but the Jesuit.'

'Hush, hush! Breathe not my name.'

'Enough—you understand me; throw down your gauge and declare your willingness by a single combat to decide the question. I am superior here, since the death of Father Wyndcliff, and shall continue so until letters come from the Pope to depose or to confirm me—I know not how I stand with his Holiness—there have been some intrigues afoot, but long before I can be displaced this control will be over—be advised, and leave the issue to me.'

'I will, I will—how the people rave and shout. I did not think the blood would flow; and hark ye, I cannot tell that this John Elkington is no more than what he represents himself to be. He a humble follower of the Earl of Surrey, no, no—that man's a humble follower of no one. The Earl of Surrey may have Hensman, and no doubt he has, for he is deep in the intriguing policy of the king, but this man is not one of them.'

'It may not be so, inquiry shall be made. It was a foolish thing to do the deed.'

'No, I could not help it—it was a foolish thing to create the cause to do the deed, but a most wise thing to do it.'

'It may be so—hush—they speak again; I hear much, but say little.'

The priest left him and advanced toward John Elkington.

'Sir Rupert,' he says, 'still denies the crime imputed to him, and says that it is a well-known physiological fact that the heat of the hand will liquidate congealed blood in any of the superficial vessels, so that it will flow again, appearing fresh, and he further says, that the hand of an innocent man, of a warm and generous temperament, would produce the effect quicker than the hand of one who is cold and phlegmatic, though he were so deeply dyed in guilt as hell itself would visit him.'

The priest half closed his cunning-looking eyes as he spoke, and peered into the countenance of John Elkington, to note the effect his words had upon him.

'I know not,' said Elkington, fearlessly, 'and I care not for your physical deductions—what are they to me? Before this ordeal by touch took place, I expressed to you my opinion. Its failure to my mind would not have made the man less guilty—its success adds but a feeble link to the chain of evidence against him.'

'As you please, I dictate nothing—but merely suggest—do with him what you like, you have power here; the power of numbers, and of force. Break through the Church's sanctuary. We are men of peace, and cannot resist you. We can say, John Elkington did this, or that, and woe be to John Elkington, for he must take the fearful consequences.'

'I am willing to a just man, acting from his own just motives pursuing what he considers fair objects by fair means; there can be no fearful consequences, and I shall appeal—'

'To Rome?'

'No, from Rome.'

'To where?'

'To Rome's master; to Heaven!'

'The priest looked at him for a moment or two in silence,' then he turned upon his heel, as he muttered to himself:—

'Indeed, is it so? a score of such men scattered throughout Europe, and dogmatical religion grovels in the dust. He must die! the breath of such a man must be stopped, or it would soon taint the very air of the Vatican with heresy. He must die! he shall die! Aye, even if this hand should be compelled to strike the blow, and it will be a most acceptable service too'—he clasped his hands, and raised his eyes upward, but he lowered them again, and folded his arms in his cassock, as he added, in a lower tone, 'to the Catholic Church.'

Then he glided up to the altar, at which he knelt down as if in prayer.

It was now time for Sir Rupert Brent to carry out the advice that had been tendered to him. It was time that he should appear and make the attempt to save himself from criminal prosecution, by a voluntary offer to set himself in single combat against his accuser, or against any one who should come forward to be the champion of his accuser.

This was a course of proceeding at this period only just allowable. People were getting daily more and more enlightened, but still they could not altogether shake off old feelings, and old habits, besides it was the statute law of the land, that a man might demand trial by combat, and, consequently, when he did so demand it it, was generally awarded to him, when the proceedings against him were dropped entirely.

Sir Rupert still trembled as he rose from the chair, and advanced forward before the mass of people, who yelled, shouted, screamed, and execrated him. As he advanced, he appealed to them by gestures to hear him, but that effort would have been in vain, had not John Elkington have stepped forward and procured silence—then it was that Sir Rupert Brent spoke. His voice was hoarse and strange; and the sentences flowed not freely from his tongue, but the substance of what he said was this:—

'I am innocent—think you that a guilty man would do that which it is but foolish for an innocent one to undertake? I am well advised that this ordeal by touch is a complete delusion.'

A roar of execration followed this remark; and it was not until after considerable trouble that he could be heard speak again.

'I know,' he said, 'that I am speaking against the convictions of you all; but what man can do to prove his innocence, that will I, denying fully the imputation that is cast upon me, and believing, that although an accidental circumstance has seemed to condemn me. Heaven will yet protect me, and therefore, that I may prove to you how willing I am to assert that innocence even at my own risk, I here throw down the gauge to claim trial by battle; arm to arm, foot to foot, soul to soul, in proof of my guiltlessness.'

A breathless stillness pervaded the multitude, and then a voice cried—

'Shame upon the coward! Can a helpless woman fight him?'

'Hold,' cried John Elkington. 'Who is that man that supposes that an Englishman cannot be found to take the part of the widow and the fatherless.'

This was one of those speeches which was sure to produce a volley of applause, but somehow or another nobody stepped forward practically to carry out the sentiment. Mobs can act in masses; but no individual of the aggregate likes to be dragged out for the performance of anything special.

There was a slight appearance of contempt in the tone of John Elkington, as he then said—

'Do you suppose that I could act so meanly and so unworthily a part myself, after coming forward in the manner I have done, not to offer to become the champion of her who so much needs one? Sir Rupert Brent, I have to be upon your gauge, leaving you mine own in its stead, and if you shall make it appear that your rank is higher than mine, it shall be my business so to procure one who shall meet you upon equal terms, that you shall fight with none but your peer.'

'It is well you say,' replied Sir Rupert Brent, 'I will fight with none but my peer. I am a knight of Rome, and it is not probable I would meet in single combat any one of less degree.'

'You shall represent yourself as what you like, even inquiry shall then be made as to the truth of those representations, and then I will engage to find one every way your equal to meet you as the champion of Alice Hensman, in support of the accusation which has been brought against you.'

'Be it so, then,' said Sir Rupert, 'I am content, under those circumstances, to leave sanctuary.'

'Your memory fails you, sir,' remarked John Elkington, 'you have already denied that it is on account of this affair you seek sanctuary at all.'

Sir Rupert Brent bit his lips, and betrayed by his confusion that he had, indeed, for the moment forgotten the artfully constructed tale he had told concerning the reason that had induced him to fly to the cathedral for sanctuary. Then recovering himself, he looked up and said, audaciously—

'I have not forgotten; but it is well known that a man who has committed himself to trial of a combat is by common courtesy invariably unimpeded in carrying out that resolve.'

'It is so,' said the priest, 'Sir Rupert Brent speaks fairly.'

'I know not why or wherefore,' said John Elkington, 'it is that all you church officers seem so extremely intent upon screening this man, nor do I care; it is sufficient for me that he has proclaimed himself a knight of the holy empire, and that having announced trial by battle, he has engaged to find a champion who will meet him. So far as I, or any of the friends of Alice Hensman are concerned, he shall part from sanctuary without the slightest hindrance, always provided some one present, in whom credit can be placed, will substantiate the statement he has made respecting his rank.'

'That will I do,' said the priest. 'I know him to be a knight of the holy Roman empire, and as such he is not likely to retract the challenge he has given.'

'Enough!' said Elkington—'I am satisfied.'

'But that,' said Alice Hensman, who had but a few minutes before recovered from her swoon, and had the aspect of affairs explained to her, 'but that am not I. No, John Elkington, you shall not risk a life so precious as your own against such a man as that. Better that the murderer should go unpunished than that he should have an opportunity of making another victim. Who can calculate the chances of combat?'

'Nay, Alice Hensman, be easy upon that score; it is the right of the accused of such a crime as this to demand such by combat, and although legally speaking he might be placed upon his trial first—yet would it save all that trouble and annoyance to meet his defiance at once. I have accepted his challenge and will find the champion.'

'More bloodshed!' said the widow, wringing her hands. 'More bloodshed! Will this never end? Alas, alas! it is ever thus one crime becomes the harbinger of many more. John Elkington, you were my husband's friend. I would rather, much rather, now, that the guilty should escape all the punishment that is due to his crimes than that you by some possibility should meet with some mischance at his hands. Let him go; I will leave his punishment to Heaven!'

'Nay, now it is natural that you should feel thus. Let me conduct you from this sad scene. Take your little ones by the hand, and follow me, I will speak to the Lord Warden in your behalf. You shall not be left so desolate as you imagine. Come, come away at once; as much has been done here as can be done, and when those sad remains are placed in the tomb you shall receive due notice.'

She said no more, but raising the children from their knees, she followed John Elkington through the dense crowd to the door of the church. The people made way for her, and many a murmured benediction was uttered as she passed. Many a prayer too was uttered for Elkington's success in the combat to which he had pledged himself, and several more compassionate of the bystanders proffered at once a temporary home to the widow and the children.

Alice Hensman could not speak her thanks, but John Elkington replied courteously for her, saying—

'Good friends all, it will be better to see first of all what the Lord Warden will do in such a case as this. The deceased Ranulph Hensman was his secretary, and as such I can tell you of my knowledge he was highly esteemed. You will see, therefore, the policy as well as the justice of appealing first to the Lord Warden.'

This satisfied the people, and they knew not which more to admire, the determined courage of John Elkington or the wisdom that dictated his counsels. Numerous questions were asked from one to the other concerning him, but none knew more of him or his affairs than what he had chosen himself to state, viz.: that he was a follower of the Earl of Surrey,—he was a stranger in the city, but now, in consequence of the extraordinary circumstances that had occurred, no man was likely to be better known than he.

In fact, he bade fair to become a popular idol, such as had not been in the good city of Winchester for many a day. Whether such a state of things was likely to be agreeable to him or answerable to other objects which he might have in view, the progress of this narrative will quickly show; but whether such was the case or not it is more than likely that John Elkington pursued the course he had from a pure conviction of its justice, and not from any calculation whatever regarding its expediency or adaptation to other objects.

When he, with the widow and the children had left the church, the priests adopted the most prudent course they could. They took no further notice of the assembled multitude, but commenced chanting in a monotonous tone masses for the dead.

Sir Rupert Brent, too, passed out of the sacred edifice by the doorway, at which the priests had entered, and closed the heavy curtains behind him.

All attraction therefore had passed away, and in ten minutes more the cathedral was completely deserted to the priests and to the dead, while, to look upon the quiet solemnity that was about its cloistered walls, no one could have supposed it possible that such a scene of confusion could have there taken place.

CHAPTER IV.

The Secretary—The Messenger from London—The Warning— A Striking Contrast.

THREE months before the incidents we have recorded had taken place within the walls of the ancient cathedral of Winchester, Ranulph Hensman, whose murder we have said created such a sensation, was seated in a small apartment, in the mansion of the Lord Warden.

The rays of the setting sun were streaming in through the ancient large window of the room, and taking all sorts of fantastic colours from the stained glass through which it poured its beams, it became most beautiful, though dazzling to look upon.

The secretary arose for the purpose of getting out of the influence of such a flood of refulgent light. As he did so, the door of the apartment opened, and a tall, stately looking man, clad in a dress of black velvet, and whose countenance was dignified and expressive, entered.

It was the Lord Warden himself. In his hand he held an open letter, which he placed before the secretary, saying, in a deep and impressive voice :—

'Good master Ranulph, I have been more than once indebted to your skill and sagacity in matters of moment, can you explain to me this missive, it was brought to me by a lad belonging to the town, who said he received it, along with a silver coin for his trouble, from a mounted man, who immediately rode off at such speed as to baffle his endeavours to regard him sufficiently close to again know him.'

'I will do my best, my lord,' said Hensman, 'so far as my humble ability will let me, I will do you service.'

He then read the letter carefully through, and found it contained the following words :—

'A friend warns the Lord Warden of Winchester of danger. To-night a man will arrive, of specious and pleasant appearance ; he will represent that he comes with letters from Lord Norfolk, now in the low country. These letters he will refuse to deliver, except to the Lord Warden personally, and then he will attempt the Lord Warden's life.

'How, and in what manner the present attempt will be made, remains a mystery ; but it is one which may be explained, before practical experience has proved it, by Sir Rupert Brent, the honoured guest of the Lord Warden.

'The Church of Rome is alive to the danger of losing its supremacy in England. A secret conclave has drawn up a list of persons throughout Europe who are to die for the preservation of Catholicism. The Lord Warden of Winchester is one—King Henry the Eighth is another. Be warned, and believe this comes from a friend, although behind a
'MASK.'

Ranulph Hensman showed by the seriousness of his deportment, that he thought something of the letter which the Lord Warden had placed before him. And the importance which the latter placed upon his secretary's judgment was sufficiently evident from the manner in which he watched his countenance.

'Well, Hensman,' he said, 'what think you of it ?'

'My lord, it is anonymous.'

'True, that is much against it ; but yet, an anonymous warning, should not meet with the same contempt that we would regard an anonymous threat with.'

'A highly proper distinction, Hensman, and one which should well be considered ; besides, I am well aware of the absolute truth of some of the statements contained in the epistle. The king has already sufficiently declared the nature of his feelings towards the Church. The cardinals have already taken the alarm, and the experience of the past has told us that the emissaries of Rome will stop at nothing to accomplish their objects.

'The Jesuits are overrunning Europe. By the rules of their order, they are compelled to execute the command of a superior. If there be any such atrocious designs afloat as this letter would indicate, they would be carried out by Jesuits.'

'Of that there cannot be a doubt. I rejoice that you are disposed, Hensman, to view this letter in a friendly spirit ; my own feeling as regards it is a favourable one.'

'It is so with me, my lord. Besides, it asks you to do nothing, and its truth or falsehood will be quickly proved by the fact. I implore your lordship to allow me to be present at the interview you may have with this stranger, if ever any should come.'

'I will place you, at all events, in an adjoining apartment, so that you shall hear all that passes, while the stranger shall not have an opportunity of being aware that any one but myself is at all cognizant of his presence.'

'Let me pray you, my lord, to be upon your guard.'

'I will be so, you may rest assured ; I am forewarned and therefore forearmed. Fear nothing, good Hensman, we shall get the better of the knave, should he really make his appearance.'

Notwithstanding these assurances of the Lord Warden, that he would be cautious, Ranulph Hensman was in a state of great anxiety, as regarded the issue of the adventure. He well knew that the Lord Warden carried the high feeling of courage, he foresaw, to a most extravagant extent, and much he feared that any one bent upon assassination would find but little difficulty in accomplishing his object.

The only hope he had was that the design would be attempted to be executed by some trickery, rather than by an act of violence ; and against the former the Lord Warden was, no doubt, from the warning he had received, well capable of guarding.

There were apartments in the house well adapted, from the proximity to each other, for the interview which Ranulph Hensman fully expected was about to take place.

One of these apartments was lofty and spacious, the other was small, and communicated with it by a door, the upper part of which was glass. Now Hensman resolved that in the larger of these two apartments the interview between the Lord Warden and his visitors should take place, while he ensconced himself in the smaller, and kept a wary eye upon the stranger's movements.

He spoke to the Lord Warden, and desired him to say that he would make his visitor occupy a parlour chair, which he, Hensman, placed with its back exactly against the glass door which opened inwards in the smaller room.

These preparations being complete, he waited with considerable impatience the issue of the affair, and as the night wore on without any visitor appearing, he began to suspect that, after all, the writer of the letter might be misinformed.

Nine o'clock was solemnly pealed forth by the various church clocks, and the curfew bell sounded, while a page belonging to the household of the Lord Warden came into the apartment where Hensman was seated, and said to him :—

'There is a stranger in the court-yard below ; he says he has come from abroad and has letters for my lord.'

'Yes, yes,' cried Hensman eagerly, 'admit him instantly : yet stay a moment, boy—said he from whence he came?'

'Yes, from the low countries, sir ; and he states that he brings letters from Lord Norfolk.'

'The same, by Heaven !' exclaimed Hensman ; 'show him into this apartment, and I will let his lordship know of the fact of his arrival.'

The boy did as he was bid, and in a few moments ushered into the room a man well attired and of pleasant manner and address.

He seemed in the prime of life, and although English by his accent, the sun of foreign lands had sufficiently embrowned his complexion to make him look not a native of the country in which he now was.

He bowed courteously to Hensman, saying—

'Have I the honour of addressing the Lord Warden ?'

'No,' was the reply ; 'but if you wish to see him, I will inform him of your presence.'

'I am much beholden to you : I have travelled far with letters, and, as I made a promise to deliver them into his own hands, I would fain perform it, if he would honour me with an interview.'

'Most certainly : the Lord Warden is within, fortunately, and, no doubt, will see you on the moment. I pray you, sir, be seated.'

The stranger bowed again, and accepted a chair, but it was not that which Ranulph Hensman wished him to occupy. The only way in which he could be made to take possession of that would be by the Lord Warden sitting down immediately opposite to it, and so it had been arranged between his lordship and Hensman, that that important arrangement should be accomplished.

If the stranger really came with a sinister motive, that the anonymous letter was attributed to him, his presence of mind certainly, for a moment, did not desert him, nor did he betray the exultation of having succeeded so far in his design ; but, on the contrary, he waited with all the calmness of one who had nothing at all important on hand, the arrival of the Lord Warden

Ranulph Hensman, when he left the room, immediately hurried to his lordship, and informed him of the arrival of the man, indicated by the epistle that had been received. He then begged of him to exercise the greatest caution ; and, while he, the Lord Warden, walked to the apartment, Hensman, by a circuitous route, and another door-way, reached the room with the glass door, adjoining to which the stranger was seated.

Upon the entrance of the Lord Warden into the apartment, the stranger arose and addressed him in the blandest accents.

'I ought to apologize to your lordship,' he said, 'for personally troubling you ; but as the Lord Norfolk made me promise most particularly that I should not deliver certain letters with which he has entrusted me, into any hands but your lordship's, it becomes my duty thus rudely to persevere in my request to see you.'

'A messenger to the Lord Warden can never be blamed for performing his commission well. I hope his Grace of Norfolk is in health.'

'The most robust health, my lord; in fact, he is quite cultivating the graces abroad.'

'Indeed! you quite surprise me.'

During this brief conversation, the Lord Warden had contrived, by some tact, to bring his guest round to the two chairs which Hensman had placed in their proper position by the glass door. Then, with a courteous wave of the hand and a gracious smile upon his countenance, the Lord Warden sunk slowly into one of them and said—

'I pray you, sir, be seated.'

Now, there was no other place for the stranger to sit, where he could at all converse with the Lord Warden, but in the chair the back of which was against the back of the glass door, and so he took possession of that seat, probably without the least suspicion that he was running any risk by so doing.

The Lord Warden seemed completely at his ease—he looked stedfastly in the face of the stranger, and continued the conversation by saying—

'And so, my Lord Norfolk is perfectly well and studying the graces? He was apt to be rather more the rough soldier when last in England.'

'Doubtless, my lord, but foreign travel, together with the extremely different habits and manners of foreign countries, have produced a great effect. You will understand, my lord, that he has been, during the last twelve months, to most of the great continental cities, and at all the foreign courts he has been so caressed and admired, in consequence of his great reputation, both as a statesman and a soldier, that he could not help adopting some of his graces.'

'I am glad to hear it, so they be not foppish ones.'

'Well, I scarcely know, my lord: he makes a laugh of it himself; and it was but on the morning of my departure I saw him at his toilet, when he said to me—

'You will see the Lord Warden, and tell him that I am so much changed as to spend a larger sum in personal adornment in one month than I formerly expended in a year.'

'Indeed: perhaps, sir, now you will oblige me with the letters you mentioned.

'Oh, with pleasure, my lord; but really, when I come to consider what a fantastic thing it was to see my Lord Norfolk, once so rough a soldier, taking pains with his attire, I cannot do less than laugh. I did so when he spoke to me in such a manner, which he observing, produced a greater pleasantry in his mind than before; so that he took from his toilet table a bottle of rare and costly essence, of a most delicious scent, presented to him by a fair lady at Milan. "Take this," he said, "and give it to the Lord Warden as a proof of the change which time and trouble have made in me."'

'But the letters—'

'Yes, my lord, I am coming to the letters; but in proof of what a merry humour my Lord Norfolk was in, I brought away the essence—but fear I have lost it by the way.'

'It is of little consequence.'

'Nay, it was so small a bottle, I put it in some pocket, I am certain, and then forgot all about it until the present moment, which I regret, for it was a rare essence of most delicate perfume: you would have been pleased.'

The stranger felt in all his pockets with the most free and unconstrained air in the world, until at last, with an expression of satisfaction upon his countenance, he cried in a cheerful loud voice—

'And here it is: it would indeed have been hard to lose it after bringing it so many miles.'

As he spoke he took from a pocket a very minute but most exquisitely cut bottle, which he held out for the observation of the Lord Warden, adding—

'Here it is, my lord, in the very state that Norfolk gave it to me, and, as I shall be returning very shortly, I should like to be able to report to him how the perfume pleased you.'

The Lord Warden took the bottle in his hand, but at the moment Ranulph Hensman slowly and noiselessly opened the glass door and made a sign of caution, which the stranger could not perceive, in consequence of his position.

'The stopper unscrews, my lord; you will be delighted with the delicious fragrance, if you but smell it.'

The Lord Warden hesitated for a moment, and he thought Ranulph Hensman was too suspicious, for the stranger looked quite unarmed; besides, it was but a poor way of distracting a man's attention, to induce him to smell a bottle of perfume;

surely it would have been better to have given him some letter to read, which would have attracted much more of his attention, and so enable any sudden attack to be made upon him with greater effect.

Again Ranulph Hensman made a gesture of caution, but the Lord Warden, situated as he was right before the eyes of the stranger, could make no reply to it; and thinking it but a general caution, he proceeded, with some degree of curiosity, to unscrew the stopper from the bottle. Before, however, he could succeed in that object, Ranulph Hensman interfered most effectually.

Suddenly he stretched out his arms, and seized the stranger so firmly by each side of his head, getting such a grasp of his hair and ears, that he held him an effectual prisoner, filling my Lord Warden with surprise, and the pretended Duke of Norfolk's messenger with a terror that seemed perfectly overwhelming.

There he sat, transfixed, having no means whatever of knowing who his assailant was; but feeling as effectually in his power as a child in the grasp of a giant. Then Hensman spoke aloud, saying:

'My lord, no doubt that bottle contains some most rare essence—so rare that he who has brought it so great a distance deserves the first odour of its contents; let him have it, and, if he enjoy it, it will be time for your lordship to test its fragrance, and to praise my Lord Norfolk for his taste.'

Before the Lord Warden could make any reply to this, the stranger uttered a scream of horror, and it became evident he regarded the proposition that was made by Ranulph Hensman, with the greatest possible amount of dread.

'No, no,' he said, 'let me go; I will tell all—let me go. Mercy!—help—help! Who is it holds me thus? Let me go—let me go.'

He struggled violently as he spoke; and it was no small trouble for Ranulph Hensman to hold him, but, by tightening his grasp, he did succeed in doing it; so that the discomfited ruffian, who now the Lord Warden could not doubt was intent upon his murder, sat there, completely at the mercy of those whom he had endeavoured to betray.

No one can blame the Lord Warden for what he did. He spoke not a word, but rising from his chair, he approached the ruffian, while with both hands he held the phial, the glass-stopper of which he was unscrewing, as he came near.

A most frightful change took place upon the countenance of the pretended messenger; he looked like a man who felt that his last hour was come; his cheeks, and even his lips assumed a pallid hue, while his eyes seemed starting from their sockets.

'Have mercy upon me,' he cried; 'I am defeated; have mercy! My name is Rowcliff—I am a Jesuit. I will tell all—but spare my life.'

'Nay,' said the Lord Warden, 'a little harmless perfume from the essence bottle, presented to the Duke of Norfolk by the fair lady of Milan, can surely do you no harm?'

'No, no—it is deadly poison.'

'For the honour of human nature, I will not believe it; no man could play so villanous a part. You surely jest; the Duke of Norfolk would never keep such a deadly drug upon his toilet-table. Hold him, Ranulph—hold him fast.'

'I will, my lord.'

The Lord Warden had taken the stopper from the bottle, which he now held at arm's length from him; but he came sufficiently near to the defeated assassin to hold it exactly beneath his nostrils.

A strange, convulsive scream burst from his lips—a shudder pervaded his whole frame, and then his head sunk upon his breast, for Hensman released it from the hold he had taken of it; and all was still.

'Is he dead?' said the Lord Warden.

'It would seem so, my lord. I regret it not for his sake, though, for of all deaths it is the one to which he is justly entitled; but, had he lived, we might have got from him some useful information.'

'No,' said the Lord Warden, 'no, that would have been a vain hope, Hensman, from a Jesuit. Believe me, you would have got nothing from him but a tissue of falsehood; he has now met with a just retribution for the offence he tried to commit. Is it not monstrous, now, that a man, with whom I could have had no personal quarrel—a man, who never saw me in his life before—should come with such deep duplicity to take my life? I could not have supposed there were such potent poisons.'

'Yes, I have heard of them as being in possession of the Italian priesthood. Had you been alone, and incautiously inhaled any of the vapour from that poison, he, in all probability, would have called for assistance, and your death would have been ascribed to natural causes; no mark of violence would have appeared upon the body, and the most zealous medical examination would have discovered no trace of poison.'

'Just so; and thus I should have been, as he is now, a dead man; but look at the bottle, Hensman, it is perfectly empty, and can have contained nothing but a mere vapour.'

'I pray you do not trust in it; secure it again and place it away, my lord, where it is not likely to fall into incautious hands.'

'I will do so; and now let us search this knave, to find if he has about him any documents or letters that may lead to a discovery of the plot he has been so fortunately foiled in executing.'

An examination of the Jesuit's pockets brought to light several memoranda, but they were written in cypher, and without the key to them, could not be understood. There was, however, a letter, firmly sealed, and addressed to Sir Rupert Brent.

As that letter lay before them, the Lord Warden and his secretary looked at each other, as if they were anxious to ascertain what each thought upon the subject. The secretary was silent; he felt that it was not for him to offer a suggestion regarding one whom the Lord Warden called a friend, but probably the expression of his ingenuous countenance said as much as if he had clothed his thoughts in words.

'I can well perceive, Hensman, you consider that there is here matter for grave suspicion.'

'My lord, I have heard you say you know Sir Rupert Brent.'

'I thought I knew him well; I met him on my travels, and he appeared much altered; so much so, that I told him if ever he came to England again by no means to omit visiting me. He came, as you know, to me a short time since, and I gave him all the friendly acceptation that was in my power; but, wanting accommodation for him here—for, as you know, I am but a temporary sojourner in this house—I asked you, out of your affection for me, to provide for him suitable lodgings.'

'Which I was proud to do my best in my own house, the moment I heard the words pass your lips, that Sir Rupert Brent was a friend of yours.'

'Precisely so—I understand.'

'And since that time he has sojourned with us.'

'And you have had no fault to find with him?'

'Certainly none, although at times I have thought that Alice, my wife, has regarded him with an expression of fear and loathing I could not well account for. What will it please you, my lord, to have done with this letter?'

'It must be delivered to him as it is; let him have it, Ranulph, from your hands, and mark well his countenance as he receives it. Tell him a stranger brought it here, who came by a sudden death in one of the apartments of my house. Peruse his features well, good Ranulph, while thus you speak to him, and from their appearance you will learn much. It is frightful to suspect, so, to make even an attempt to remove suspicion, or convert it into certainty; go at once, and return to me with what tidings you can upon this most painful subject.'

'It is but yet ten o'clock, my lord, I shall be back to you before the midnight hour, if I can have a hope to find you stirring.'

'Be assured, Ranulph, I shall not sleep until we meet again; I shall expect you with all impatience. This matter is most serious; the king's name has been mentioned in it, and, when such deep designs of villany are afloat, we can trust no one except those who are well-tried in our confidence, and stand first in our esteem. Be careful of yourself, Ranulph Hensman, and return to me as quickly as you can, for I shall be most anxious.'

CHAPTER V.

Sir Rupert Brent's Expectations—The Impatience of a Bad Spirit—The Letter.

At the very time when this scene was passing at the temporary mansion occupied by the Lord Warden, Sir Rupert Brent was in his own apartment, in Ranulph Hensman's house.

Towards nightfall he proceeded homewards, and shut himself in. Something evidently had strongly agitated him; but it was more agitation of excitement than of fear.

He paced the large apartment, which was devoted to him as a private sitting-room, with rapid and unequal steps.

More than once he consulted a clock that hung upon one of the walls, and, as often as he did so, he would mutter, 'Not nine yet! not nine yet! how slowly the day lags along!'

Then he would resume his uneasy march to and fro in the room; and soon his thoughts assumed a more connected strain, and he uttered many of them audibly, although perchance not aware of that fact.

'Yes,' he said, 'to-night it will be accomplished. It will be certain to be done, for the device is as excellent a one as ever entered into the mind of man. How strange it is that, coming here upon public and political grounds, I should light upon the very person whom I hate the most, and likewise she whom I most love—she whom I love still, despite of time's changes.'

He was silent for a few moments, and walked more slowly, with his arms folded across his breast, as if his meditations were of a quieter and calmer character than they had been.

'Yes, I wooed her,' he said, 'and she is still beautiful! as beautiful as when I saw her a fair young novice, in that convent from whence I thought she would never emerge. I tempted her in vain, and thought it was the rigidity of virtue that resisted me. Then I learnt, too late for revenge, that it was personal dislike, and that when one whom she could love contrived, by bribery and finesse, to whisper to her words of tenderness, even within the cloistered shades to which she had retired with such seeming devotion, she was ready to come forth into the world again and enjoy all its gaieties, and all its frivolities and pleasures.

'This news came when I had abandoned all hope. Oh, what fires of rage and jealousy were then awakened in my breast! I swore to discover her retreat; I swore to be revenged on him who had deprived me of the consolation of feeling that if she did not live for me, no other would receive the consolation of a smile from her lips.

'But all my researches were in vain. I visited city after city, but I found her not. Armed with a written authority from the Inquisition, I could in any Catholic country have seized upon her, but three weary years passed away, and my hopes were all defeated, my warmest expectations merged into despair.

'And at length, by the merest accident—such an accident as at its first blush seemed an unlucky one—inasmuch as it deprived me of the opportunity of remaining in the same house with the Lord Warden—discovers to me, in the wife of this Ranulph Hensman, the long-lost novice whom I loved.

'And she, who never saw me but in a monastic garb, with the shaven crown of priesthood, knows me not when I appear in the ordinary vestments of the world, dressed as a cavalier, and with these long locks, moustache and beard, all of which alter so much the contour of the countenance.'

He paused, and glanced at himself in a mirror that hung upon one of the walls.

'Oh yes,' he added, 'I am altered; I am much altered; who would know me? and yet, at times, I have thought that as we sat together at meals, she has looked upon me furtively, as if endeavouring to call to her mind something of my features or my voice. I have seen her shudder, too, when I have suddenly spoken, as if some well-remembered tone had struck upon her ears.

'If she does suspect, her suspicion shall soon be verified. This night the Lord Warden dies: to-morrow, Ranulph Hensman is accused of his murder; and then, in the height of her grief and dismay, and while Hensman is rotting in a prison, I reveal myself to Alice, and show her what power I have to claim her in the name of the Church.'

His countenance as he spoke assumed an aspect that was perfectly demoniacal. His eyes flashed with unholy fire and passion, and at length he sunk into a seat as he heard nine o'clock strike, and felt that the hour of his vengeance was nigh at hand.

''Tis well,' he said; ''tis very well that I am thus enabled to fulfil my duty to my order as a Jesuit, at the same time that I am enabled to carry out my private revenge, and so satisfy the most secret purposes of my soul.

'Nine o'clock, that is the hour. We Jesuits are always punctual; we acquire power by being something which the world is not. The greatest affairs of this life are dependant frequently upon moments of time. Kingdoms have been lost and won : it is not so with us—we lose nothing; and, as surely as the sun will shine to-morrow, brightly or obscurely, as the case may be, but yet sufficiently to chase away the clouds of night, will all that I have pictured to myself come to pass.'

This extreme confidence of Sir Rupert Brent, the Jesuit, was really but very little more than what he was entitled to feel. His order had acquired an immense influence in the affairs of Europe.

The emissaries of the Jesuits were at every court, and no man could know unless some unusual circumstance occurred, to force a disclosure, on the part of some one of them, of who and what Brent really was.

They were supplied with the most abundant means to assume almost any rank in society; and as the Court of Rome had ample power to confirm titles, she awarded them at their pleasure, and thus was it that the Jesuit, Rupert Brent, called himself Sir Rupert, by the complete confidence in the fact that no one could dispute his title.

And he had every right to suppose, from former experience, that the plan which had been laid for the death of the Lord Warden would be successful, as doubtless it most certainly would have been but for the anonymous communication that had warned him of his danger.

He now sat for about ten minutes in deep thought, and then he started to his feet.

'Why need I delay? What is it deters me from proceeding with that which I have undertaken? By this time the Lord Warden is no more. To-morrow I shall be able to consign Hensman to a dungeon; and yet, perchance, I might make some better terms with Alice before than after the catastrophe. 'Tis worth the trial; she is in the house—the children have retired to rest. I heard her voice a short time since—that voice which I know so well—that voice which is such exquisite music to my ears. I will speak to her at once, I will not sleep without a knowledge of hope and encouragement concerning her.'

He walked to the door of his apartment, but there he stopped again, as if irresolution had taken possession of him.

'Why do I pause?' he muttered. 'Have I any doubts? Do I doubt that I love, or do I doubt that I hate? No, Alice, you are still beautiful—so beautiful that I would risk much for you! There was a time when I would have staked my life for a smile; and now, indeed, it seems to me that that time has come again.'

He no longer paused, but with a feeling of determination left the apartment, and descended the steep flight of stairs which led to the lower portion of the house.

It was a large, irregular-shaped mansion, in which Hensman resided, and a very small portion of it was occupied by him and his family. It had been a house at one time belonging to one who must have kept a large establishment and a great retinue, but some change of fortune, or possibly the caprice of fashion, had caused the old house to be deserted, so that Hensman got it as a place to dwell in, in all its vast extent, on as liberal terms as he could have procured a smaller dwelling.

What Sir Rupert Brent had said regarding Alice Hensman was strictly true. The cupidity of relatives had placed her in a convent at an early age; but not before she had attracted the observation of Ranulph Hensman. It might possibly be that some knowledge of his attachment to her influenced her friends to place her within walls unaccessible to mortal affection.

While there, she had been noticed by Rupert Brent, who, by virtue of his authority and privilege of his order, visited the convent; and a passion for the fair young novice, which not only set at naught all the vows he had himself made, but would have proved her destruction at once, fairly possessed him.

He had told fairly enough the tale of his disappointment; and now, after a time, he had been informed of the escape of the young woman with a lover, her choice—most probably to some foreign land, where they could not be traced—and most despairingly had he at length given up the search, which was now dictated by revenge as well as love.

Probably he would have let the whole affair rest as one of those slumbering passions in his bosom which it would be useless to awaken, had it not been by the command of his superiors he was placed in Winchester as a political agent, because he had declared he knew something of the Lord Warden abroad, and there, in the person of the wife of Ranulph Hensman, the confidential secretary, he discovered the object of his search.

And a most gratifying thing it was to him to discover. He had it, he believed, in his power to completely crush the husband, while, with the aid of the ecclesiastical authorities, he should be able to seize the wife and to lodge her in some place of security, where she could not hope to avoid his visits.

He well knew the bond of union which held all churchmen together in one common cause, to resist the laity in bringing a priest to justice for anything whatever, so that he had no compunctious visitings as to the consequences of what he purposed; but he viewed with the greatest complacency the prospect of full success that was before him.

Having thus placed the reader in full possession of all those facts which will enable him to understand the motives of the principal actors in our story, we can proceed with greater deliberation, and without the necessity of any digression, to depict the various scenes that occurred consequent upon the clashing of so many different passions and feelings.

And now let us take a glance at Alice Hensman, as she sits alone, awaiting the return of her husband from his duties at the Lord Warden's.

At sunset the children had retired to rest, and after feeling satisfied that sleep had closed their eyelids, Alice had crept gently from the room, and sat down to ruminate upon the past, much of which had been of a sad and stormy character, while she drew bright visions of the coming future.

And she might well be excused for anticipating that future with pleased attention—she might well be excused for supposing that in the love of such a man as Hensman she would be free from all harm, and that, considering the years that had elapsed since her escape from the convent, she had nothing to dread from that quarter.

She was aware, likewise, from what her husband had frequently told her of late, that great changes might be expected, and, in fact, the notion that some attempts would soon be made, by the king and his present advisers, to curb the licentiousness of the clergy, was extremely prevalent. The suppression of monasteries, too, was broadly intimated, and, if such were to be the case throughout England, of course Alice need be no more apprehensive of the fact becoming known, that she had escaped from monastic restraint and control.

The husband of Alice enjoyed the protection of the Lord Warden; her children were all that she could wish, and so Alice had indeed abundant cause for thankfulness, and abundant reason to draw from her imaginings bright visions of the future.

To be sure she had not been so happy since Sir Rupert Brent had resided in the house, for at times there would come over her a feeling which she could not define, as she looked into that man's countenance.

She certainly did not recollect him as the Jesuit who had annoyed her in the convent; but yet he never came into the apartment in which she was without a feeling of alarm taking possession of her, which she could not account for or conquer.

To be sure he had never intruded upon her in the absence of her husband, and had always, except now and then, when she caught his fiery glance upon her, behaved with the greatest decorum and respect.

What was her surprise now suddenly to see the door of her apartment opened, and Sir Rupert Brent making his much-dreaded appearance.

The very fact of his walking in without his going through the ceremony of knocking for admission, was startling, but alarm reached its height when she looked upon his face, and when she saw him turn the key in the inside of the lock of the door.

She was too terrified to scream for aid, but with clasped hands and blanched cheeks she gazed upon him as if he had been some spirit of evil, possessed of more than mortal power to work injury to the good and the beautiful.

And he was silent, for the fair form before him had never looked more beautiful, and he knew not whether at once passionately to avow his long-enduring affection, if to such a passion as his that word can be applied—or to commence by letting her understand how much her husband would soon be in his power.

His silence was of the most ominous character: it was more dreadful to Alice than anything he could have spoken, and she at length broke it herself by saying—

'Is this Sir Rupert Brent I see before me?'

'It is; your eyes do not deceive you, and now, Alice, look at me again: you have often, with a feeling as if you thought you ought to know me, gazed upon my face. Gaze upon it once more, and then call to mind where you have seen such a one.'

'It is true said Alice, trembling, 'that there have been times when I have thought we have met before: but I know you not.'

'Think again, Alice.'

'Nay, sir, my name is Mistress Hensman; it is somewhat strange that one with whom I have no acquaintance, nor wish to have any, should wish to speak with such familiarity. Leave me, sir; my husband is not within now, or this piece of presumption would not have occurred.'

'Leave you I will not: as to the presumption of calling you by your christian name, we are sufficient old acquaintances for me to presume so far. Do you hear me, Alice Hensman?—I say sufficient old acquaintance: have you any doubts upon that score? If you have, I will soon recall to your remembrance something of the history of the past which shall resolve them.'

Alice trembled, but yet she listened with the greatest intensity, in the hope of hearing some sound which should signify to her her husband's return: she feared to aggravate the bold, daring man, whose eyes were cast upon her with an expression she feared to translate.

She knew that she was in that large house alone, with the exception of the presence of the children, who might weep for her, but who could not aid her. Ranulph Hensman might return at once, or he might be hours. Sometimes he was with her days together—sometimes almost entirely absent for such a period, according as the Lord Warden required or not his services. But she knew he would come over that night, he had told her so, and she had waited for him with a pleasant expectation—now, so frightfully marred by the appearance of that man, the recollection of whom was momentarily dawning upon her soul.

'Well, Alice,' he said, after a long pause, 'do you know me yet, and recognise my right of old acquaintanceship to call you Alice?'

'I do not know you.'

'Duplicity! Look again, and fancy me divested of the moustachios—of these flowing locks—of this style of clothes. See me, Alice, in your mind's eye, invested with the ecclesiastical garb, looking as downcast and as pious as—as a monk who loves a woman of such wondrous charms, that she has weaned his soul from heaven.'

'No more—no more!' half-shrieked Alice.

'Ha! you know me now?'

'I do. I know you now, well—fiend that you are, I know you. Through all your disguises came a faint memory of the persecutions I had suffered from you—truly I know you now.'

'Yes, I knew you would; I was then called Father Georges. I loved you—but you despised me, and, with a pious hypocrisy you have since so fully proved, you pleaded the arguments of your novicate engagements, which you broke the moment that another, who awakened corresponding passions in your heart appeared. You fled from your convent with Ranulph Hensman.'

'And if I did, that Ranulph Hensman will soon be here, to your confusion, Sir Priest.'

'Yes, he will soon be here, but not to my confusion.'

'It will be so; and most mad were you to tell me what you are, that I may tell him you were my persecutor.'

'Indeed! I thought you knew that I was a Jesuit—I thought you knew that I was considered artful, cunning, and designing even beyond my order. Think you, then, that I have done so foolish a thing as, without motive and due reflection, to place myself in the way of a brawl with Ranulph Hensman? No, Alice, you know me better: do not insult me!'

'Begone! your presence here is the deepest insult that can be offered to suffering virtue. Each moment I expect to hear my husband's footsteps on the stairs; I know that he loves me, and that I have power to turn aside his wrath; but I know not that I shall use that power to save a truckling hypocrite, such as thou art, from the consequences of his anger,'

'Go on—I like to hear you; it matters not whether you be uttering words of kindness or of anger; the music of that voice still falls upon my heart, as the memory of my earliest dreams of love. You are so dear to me, that I have placed my soul in the balance against your affections; you need not listen for your husband's step—he will come, but not yet; you will hear him by-and-by, and, when he does appear, I shall have something, perchance, for his private ear that may make him tremble.'

Alice sunk into a chair, and betrayed great agitation.

'I know,' she said, 'that you are a Jesuit—I know that you belong to that powerful order which, in the pursuit of ambition or of revenge, knows no touch of human sympathy or kindness. You talk of love—is it a manifestation of that passion to strive with heart and soul to make wretched the thing you say you love?'

'What is your happiness to me, if I am wretched?' Thus spoke the selfish priest.

'Oh, Heaven,' exclaimed Alice, 'save me from this man! Georges, such scorn and such contempt as you can fancy my nature capable of feeling, I feel for thee; such abhorrence as I can entertain for anything human, I entertain for thee: you have your answer, now be gone!'

'I have an answer, but it is a premature one—you should have waited, fair lady, until you heard that which I have to say: listen—'

'No, no!—not to thee—not to thee.'

'Close the portals of your ears, if you can—escape if you can—the door is closed, the window shut—cry for assistance; those who come shall have a goodly tale to tell to Ranulph Hensman. Alice, you shall—you must hear me.'

She saw that it was useless to contend. She sat gazing at him for a time in speechless awe, while thus he spoke:—

'I have in my possession a document, which has never left me, night or day, for some years past—it is an authority from the Vatican, enjoining all good Catholics, all ecclesiastical and lay dignitaries, to assist me in claiming and taking possession of you, who in defiance of the holy ordinances you have outraged, broke from your convent; the conventual life you led was long enough to let you know the power of such a document. It bears the sign manual of Cardinal Lorme—you have heard of him! It empowers me to take you from your home, to tear you from your husband and your children, and to deliver you to the officers of the Inquisition, who will question you upon the fact of wedding with a heretic, as I hear this man Hensman is. Hold! I know what you would say—you defy all that; but I have so arranged that your husband shall be powerless to save you. He may not want the will, but he shall have the agony of wanting all the means.'

'Fiend! monster!'

'Aye, rail on, lady; those choice epithets convince me that I've made some impression on your fears. Think you I am alone in this city? think you I have not friends here and there, up and down, and about, who are watching well and carefully my movements? Breathe but a word of this that I have said to you to-night into your husband's ears, and he is a dead man, were he hidden in the very bowels of the earth, ere he be four-and-twenty hours older.'

'No, no.'

'But I say yes, and for proof of all this I only say to you, Alice, I'm a Jesuit and I know I need say no more.'

Alice shook, for she knew well the signification of those words. Immured for a time in the cloisters, she had heard much of monastic power, but still she rallied, and was determined that, for her husband's sake—for his name, reputation, and dignity, she would not let that bold, bad man see all the fears with which he had filled her.

'You may be a Jesuit,' she said, 'I know you are, but I will tell you, that a better spirit is abroad; the hours of priestly supremacy in England are numbered, and you know it.'

'They may be; I cannot say nay to the proposition. All things have an end, but dying institutions, like dying individuals, acquire often a preternatural power. Beware that you and all you love fall not a sacrifice to the vengeance of the Jesuits, even in their last days.'

'What is it you would do? what is it that you wish? I have told you! abhor you. Must I put the same sentiment in weaker terms, and say I cannot love you?'

'In the first instance, all that passes between us now must be kept profoundly secret. Breathe but a word of it to Hensman, and I shall hear it. He cannot keep such a secret—he would not, if he could. For a time I shall remain, trying to gain your love.'

'Must I brook that insult?'

'Aye, must you—and hark ye, Alice! if I succeed—if by showing you how truly I adore you, to what a height of rank and power I can raise you, although I may not bestow upon you my name, if I succeed in convincing you—that happiness here, and bliss hereafter——'

'Monster, do not profane sacred writ, and the promises of Heaven, by linking them to your worldly passions.'

'As you please, I am not particular upon that score—but if, by such perseverance as you cannot disapprove of, I win upon your regard sufficiently—that you shall feel something of an impression in my favour—I will present you with the document I have mentioned, that you may yourself destroy it. If I fail——'

'If you fail!'

'Hush! I hear a foot upon the stairs.'

'It is my husband—my husband!'

'It is—not a word! I tell you his destruction and your own rest upon your discretion.'

He walked to the door, and gently turned the key again in the lock, so that it might be freely opened, and then he sauntered up to one of the windows, and taking up a book, he assumed a musing attitude, while Alice sat in such a con-

fusion of thought, that it was doubtful what she might do or say when her husband should appear.

The step now came plainer upon their ears. It was a bold thing for Sir Rupert Brent to remain, for it would be the first time that Ranulph Hensman found him there, as he always made a point of returning to his own apartments when the secretary left home.

But Ranulph was not a jealous man; he would not have done Alice so frightful an injustice as to assume even the possibility of a thought of wrong-doing entering her pure breast; he therefore merely bowed when, upon entering the apartment, and casting a rapid glance around it, he observed Sir Rupert Brent by the window. Moreover, his mind was too full of the dreadful occurrence that had taken place at the Lord Warden's to enter minutely into more trifling circumstances. Indeed, a feeling of gratification came across him at the

moment that he had so readily found Sir Rupert Brent; and, therefore, could at once deliver to him the letter which had been found upon the dead body of the assassin

One glance of the cunning eye of the Jesuit upon the ingenuous countenance of Ranulph Hensman, seemed to assure him that all had happened at the Lord Warden's as he would wish it.

'She is mine,' he muttered to himself, 'she is mine; the Lord Warden is no more; the scheme prospers, and in four and-twenty hours Alice Hensman will be in my power.'

'Sir Rupert Brent, well met,' said Hensman; 'we've had fearful doings at the Lord Warden's.'

'Indeed, Master Secretary, how does the good Lord?'

'Excellent well.'

Sir Rupert retreated a step, and looked fixedly at Hensman. 'Well—well, did you say well —you—you mean—'

'Go on, Sir Rupert, we're plain folks here, and like to hear others speak their ِ.inds.'

'So do I. I'm glad to hear he's well; but you spoke of strange doings at the Lord Warden's. Are they such as may be told to a sympathising ear?'

'They are. This night at nine o'clock there came a man affecting to bring letters from the Duke of Norfolk.'

'Yes, yes.'

'But some strange fancy took him: before he could surrender those letters to the Lord Warden, he must needs get his lordship to give an opinion upon some exquisite perfume which it appears the Duke of Norfolk had taken such a liking for, he must send some to the Lord Warden in proof of its great excellence.'

'Really.'

'It was so: but the Lord Warden, not being fond of artificial scents and essences, and likewise not wishing to be outdone in civility by the Duke's messenger, prevailed upon him to inhale the odour first himself.'

'Damnation!'

'In all probability the man dropped dead, of course from excess of joy at such delicious perfume, steeping his senses in oblivion.'

Sir Rupert stepped back and plunged his hand into his breast, slightly withdrawing it, so that the handle of a poniard was visible—a precaution which he appeared to think necessary, although it was not so, for Ranulph Hensman had quite unconsciously placed his hand upon the hilt of his sword as he spoke. It was a mere habit he had, which Sir Rupert Brent might have noticed upon many a preceding occasion, but now his fears were so much aroused by the recital that had come from the lips of Ranulph, that he construed it into a menace, and was on his guard accordingly.

'You seem excited, Sir Rupert Brent.'

'I am; all men who hear of such deeds as these should feel excitement. I envy not him who is so vicious or so cold as to feel no indignation at such proceedings.'

'Well spoken, sir.'

'I thank you; what happened next?'

'The Lord Warden and myself searched the body which had died of such a delicious odour.'

'And you found —'

'Some memoranda, which we keep, and this letter addressed to you.'

'Addressed to me? How very strange—a letter addressed to me!—I am surprised. I pray you give it me, it must be for some bad purpose; why did you not break the seal and read it?'

'I am not in the habit of adopting such jesuitical proceedings.'

'Jesuitical! upon my word, now, I should not wonder if this assassin was a Jesuit; for that he intended assassination there can be little doubt: a bad fraternity, Master Hensman, a bad fraternity. Although I am a Catholic, I do not scruple to say so to you who are a Protestant, because I know that you are quite as liberal in your religion as I am in mine; I may, therefore, speak my mind to you freely—I do not like the Jesuits. But tell me what happened next.'

'You have shrewdly guessed what happened before, for he avowed himself a Jesuit, and, before his death, made a voluntary offer to tell all.'

'All?'

'Yes, implicating others, and exposing the ramifications of a plot as extensive as it was diabolical.'

'He told you all this?'

'No, he would have told it, but the odour of that rare essence interposed and he expired.'

Sir Rupert Brent drew a long breath, as if he felt an exquisite relief at being told of such an issue to the affair; then, with a side-long sort of bow to Alice, he said:—

'Perhaps I may be excused if I am sufficiently curious at once to open that letter found, addressed to me, in the pocket of that arrant knave.'

As he spoke, he broke the seals and opened the letter, which he at once affected to read aloud:—

"Beware, Sir Rupert Brent, you are a marked man, for you have incurred the hatred of the Jesuits; they never forgive, and, sooner or later, you will follow the fate of one whose death you will quickly hear of—namely, the Lord Warden of Winchester."

'An idle threat,' added Sir Rupert, as he crumbled the letter up in the form of a ball and thrust it into his pocket,

'an idle threat! I don't know how I have incurred the hatred of the Jesuits, but I do suppose that all liberal Catholics come under the ban of their displeasure in some way or another. It appears to me that they are making some great movement in this country. How infinitely rejoiced I am that my friend the Lord Warden has been saved from their machinations! In the morning I must call upon him, to tender him my congratulations; truly, I shall sleep all the easier to-night for a knowledge that he is saved.'

'I shall take pains to inform him of what you say, Sir Rupert, and, as I shall probably see him at a very early hour, you will perhaps allow me to show him the infamous threatening epistle you have received.'

'Certainly, certainly,' said Sir Rupert, and he put his hand in his pocket and half drew out the epistle, but then he returned it, adding:—

'Yet, now I think of it, I ought to show the letter myself to the Warden, that is the most respectful course, so I shall take especial pains to be with him very early on the morrow.

'As you please, Sir Rupert; and in the meantime, I much regret to say that it will be quite impossible for me to accommodate you longer in my house.'

'Not accommodate me! you have abundance of room here.'

'Exactly, and yet I regret to say I can no longer accommodate you in my house.'

'What do you mean by this continued reiteration? The bedroom I occupy, as well as the apartment in which I sit, were both of them, you told me, rooms you never used.'

'I thought that what I said was clear and distinct. When a man says he cannot accommodate another in his house, surely he speaks explicitly. I have a marvellous fancy myself to the room you sit in; and, as for your bed-chamber, it seems to me unsuited to one of your quality and condition. In fact, Sir Rupert Brent, I have made up my mind that you or I shall remove from here to-night; and, as it is more convenient for you to move than myself, I shall trouble you to take your departure with as much expedition as may tally with your convenience.'

This was rather too unequivocal a turn-out to be misunderstood. For a moment or two Sir Rupert Brent seemed upon the point of saying something very passionate, but cunning prevailed over anger, and, bowing profoundly, he replied,—

'I cannot help admiring the delicate tact which at length has become alive to the fact, that for a man of birth and rank to reside under the same roof with you, was a manifest infraction of his dignity. I discovered it some time since, and although one cannot expect that refinement of feeling among plebeians that belongs to the aristocracy, I did shrink from telling you my own impressions; but, since you have yourself mentioned it, I now do so no longer. I do feel, I have always felt that this place was not suited to a man of my rank and consequence; therefore I will leave it.'

'I am most grateful,' said Hensman; 'I did not bless the hour that you crossed its threshold as a guest, for I regarded the circumstance with too much indifference, either for a blessing or a malediction; but certainly now, when you do us the honour of leaving, I shall be extremely happy.'

'A philanthropic mind,' said Sir Rupert Brent, 'likes to see happiness beaming around it, even amongst the lowest and most despicable of human beings.'

'Ah! he must be a philosopher of the first water who considers any of God's creatures despicable, except they be stained with crimes.'

'Such as assassination,' said Sir Rupert Brent; 'I had that crime especially in my eye when I spoke.'

'Are you sure it was not in your heart, sir?'

'Quite certain. I have the honour of bidding you adieu. Madam, when you are a widow, I wish you a handsomer husband. Master Ranulph looks cadaverous; he won't live long!'

'He may live,' said Hensman, 'beyond the wishes of his friends. Do you see the door, Sir Rupert Brent? A fall from that window of about thirty feet might derange the delicate organization even of a Jesuit.'

'Ah! so it might, or even of a great man's favourite—a crawling sycophantic wretch, that smiles, and bows, and cringes to be allowed to pick up the crumbs that fall from the table of some rich Dives—one who speaks with humble and abated breath to his good Lord Warden, who praises God that made him such a master, and rubs his oily hands together with " a good sir, I am well aware what makes my service so acceptable. My wife is handsome, and I see nothing." Good night, Ranulph Hensman !'

' Villain !' cried Hensman, springing forward.

' Ha,' he said, ' the Jesuit wins at last. Why will such fools play with edged tools? You've cut your fingers—good night.'

Hensman would have rushed after him, but Alice clung to him.

' No, no,' she said; ' do not, do not—let him be, Ranulph; let him go. It is a happy hour when he leaves our roof; a bad man, Ranulph; a bold, bad man. Let him go at once. We cannot—do not want him here.'

' Nay, Alice, unhand me; let him say what he pleases to me, but insult to you I cannot, will not bear.'

' You shall not resist this. His object is clearly to force a quarrel with you. Ranulph, you are blind if you do not perceive it; let him go, and go in peace. I shall thank Heaven he no longer sleeps beneath our roof. Such a man should sleep beneath no roof where innocence reposes.'

' But, Alice, Alice.'

' Nay, Ranulph, Ranulph, to please me, let him go at once; it will be far better to do so. I implore you to let him go.'

' I yield, Alice; I yield to you, and perhaps it is better that he should leave this house without any act of violence. There has been an attempt upon the life of the Lord Warden. I cannot take upon myself to say for certain that it was planned exactly by this Sir Rupert Brent; but I can take upon myself to say, that he has had much to do with it—very much to do with it—for his name appears throughout the whole transaction under the worst of aspects.'

' But you will promise me to say nothing to him—to interfere no more with him.'

' I will, I do promise: cease this supplicating tone, Alice, I promise all that you can ask; let him go, since it is your wish; my anger is over, and I have no doubt, upon reflection, that you are right in supposing his object was to draw me into a quarrel; and if so, I am glad that he is disappointed, for such a man never attempts quarrelling except when he is certain the issue will be manifestly to his advantage. Let him go. I will not say, peace go with him, but I sincerely hope that we may never look upon his face again.'

' This is a happy moment,' said Alice, ' to me to be relieved from the presence of that man; there was something about him of a sinister and foreboding aspect that made me dread him; I am certain that he means evil.'

' It would seem so, and his connexion with the affairs you have heard me detail as having taken place at the Lord Warden's, convinced me at once that he was an unfit guest for us and made me resolve upon his expulsion.'

' But yet, dear Ranulph, you cannot say that the letter you brought him in any way criminated him.'

' The probability is that could we have seen that letter it would have criminated him abundantly.'

' You forget, Ranulph, he read it to us.'

' I do not forget, Alice, that he affected to read it to us; do you know so little of such a man as Brent, as not to suppose he has talent sufficient to hold a letter in his hand, containing certain statements which he may seem to read, and yet really not read one word it contains? you know not with what exceeding art he avoided placing that letter in my hands to show to the Lord Warden.'

' He did, Ranulph, he did indeed, and much as I thought I knew of the artifices of the Jesuits, this man's conduct transcends all that; I would have revenge, and now that he is gone, Ranulph, I have something to say to you concerning which, previously you must make to me a solemn promise, or else I dare not say it.'

' Dare not ?'

' No, I dare not, for your own safety sake, I dare not. I know well your impetuosity of temper; I know well that it would hurry you to something that would give your enemy great power over you.'

' I can guess what it is you have to say; the villain whom I have even now thrust from my house, has taken advantage towards you. I see clearly that that must have been the case; my sword. Alice, my sword—where is my sword? let me follow him.'

' Ranulph, Ranulph, this is what I feared; I can tell you nothing while you are in such a mood as this; be calm and

you shall know all; promise me that you will undertake nothing in this affair without my full and free consent, and then I can tell you something of this Sir Rupert Brent that may be most useful for even the Lord Warden to know of.'

' Speak, Alice, speak at once; keep me not in this torture and suspense.'

' I dare not—cannot speak, without your promise.'

Ranulph Hensman paced the room for some moments endeavouring to control the passion that had risen in his heart, then suddenly he cast himself into a seat, saying,—

' Be it so, Alice, be it so; you have my promise, and now let me implore you to speak freely, and tell me all without reserve.'

' I will do so, dear Ranulph : listen to me now, and listen with patience. When first, by the aid of a kind friend, and likewise a great personal risk to yourself, you met me in the garden of the convent, which had become my prison, I told you I was persecuted by a monk, named Georges.'

' You did, and that he belonged to the order of the Jesuits.'

' I did not tell you how much I had been insulted by his insolent addresses, because I know my own power of repelling them, at the same time I know my enemy's power of injuring you, if by a recital of my persecutions you were inflamed to take some violent step.'

' Go on, go on; I partly guess what you would say.'

' You may do so; in Sir Rupert Brent I have this night recognised the villain Georges.'

' Indeed ! did he declare himself to you?'

' Yes, and from the obscure hints he let fall, I am led to believe that he contemplated something was about to occur, to give such power as to render concealment unnecessary.'

' That feeling must have arisen from his fore-knowledge of the attempted assassination of the Lord Warden—an attempt which he considered, no doubt, had about it so many of the elements of success, that as the hour approached when he knew it must be made, he considered it as almost done. Truly, then, I should have lost my only protector, but Heaven averted such a blow, and the base agent of crime himself fell, as you have heard me relate, a victim to the man he had devised for the destruction of another. It almost becomes my duty, immediately to seek the Lord Warden, and give him this information.'

' Not to-night, Ranulph—not to-night; go not forth again to-night, you know not what danger may await you; the hour is late, the street dark and dismal.'

' I fear nothing.'

' That may be, but yet do not increase the danger; many a man, Ranulph, has died fearing nothing; it is such men that the dagger of the assassin most seeks. The Lord Warden has, in all likelihood, retired to rest; he could do nothing to-night with the information you would bring him, so go to him as early as you will on the morrow, when the sun is shining; but not to-night, Ranulph, oh! not to-night.'

' I will yield to you, Alice, and yet it grieves me much to see how this Jesuit has succeeded in awakening your fears. I do not think that there is any danger, but I will not go forth since my doing so would make you so unhappy; and now, dear Alice, that you perceive I am neither passionate nor headstrong in this affair, tell me all you have to tell me of this Georges, and how it was that, upon my return, I found him in this apartment.'

Alice Hensman had the promise of her husband that he would undertake nothing against the Jesuit, whose power, she had not without reason, so much dreaded, and, therefore, despite the denunciations which had been levelled at her head, if she should presume to make her husband acquainted with the interview that had taken place between herself and Georges, she told him all, and when she had concluded her narrative, she said :—

' And now, Ranulph, do you think it possible he possesses such an authority as he mentions? do you think that the Church of Rome would vest in an individual the power of hunting individuals in such a way ?'

' I do, indeed, Alice; it is the general course that is pursued with regard to broken monastic vows of any description. The Church authorities know well the outcry of making any public disturbance on such occasions, and, consequently, some zealous member of the priesthood is given such a power as Georges mentions, and is expected, like a blood-hound upon the scent, to track the victim from clime to clime, from city to city, aye even to the confines of the habitable world, until some opportunity arises to seize him or her with secrecy and safety. I have no doubt whatever that he possesses the document he mentions.'

Alice trembled.

'Why, Alice,' continued Ranulph Hensman, 'you surely are not afraid of the envious priest; these are not times when in England such a power can be exercised openly, as it is sometimes done in Spain and Italy; this is not a country in which a priest in the open streets can call upon the populace to aid him with a certainty that they will do so. No, Alice, you may banish your fears. That Georges possesses the document he speaks of is likely enough, but he knows well that these times are too ticklish ones for the clergy to hazard the use of it.'

'Your words give me fresh courage, and I feel now as if I could defy him.'

'Rest in peace, to-morrow I will have some conversation with the Lord Warden, with regard to Sir Rupert Brent, or Georges, as is his proper name, and he will advise what is best to be done in such a case. Probably a protection from the king under the royal sign manual could be obtained; they do say that his majesty is glad of an opportunity of doing any sovereign act that will place him in collision with the Church of Rome, for that he is casting about for legitimate means for widening the breach between him and the Pontiff; but let us speak of happier things, Alice, and believe me you may dismiss all thoughts of danger from such a man as Georges.'

'But when you are abroad, Ranulph, I shall be full of fears.'

'Nay, I will remain away for as short a period of time as possible, and likewise I will get my friend John Elkington, who you know resides so near at hand that from his domains he can see this house, to keep a wary eye upon it.'

'What a noble, brave spirit is John Elkington! I sometimes think it is impossible he can be of higher rank than what he now appears.'

'Rest content, Alice, with what you know of John Elkington, and believe that he may be most thoroughly and entirely trusted. There is a mystery connected with him which I have given my word shall not pass my lips, so therefore, Alice, to keep the very letter of my promise, even to thee, I must not mention it.'

'That is right, Ranulph,' said Alice, 'it is enough that you tell me to trust John Elkington, I will do so most freely; and without seeming to penetrate the mystery that envelopes him, I was certain he was not what he seemed to be as regards rank and condition.'

'He is not, and without a doubt with his own good tongue he will allow me to make a confidant of you.'

CHAPTER VI.

The Conference at the Lord Warden's.—The Messenger to London with the Missive to the King.

By the earliest dawn of the following morning, Ranulph Hensman rose and made his way to the lodgings occupied by John Elkington, which were in a slanting direction, almost immediately opposite his own house.

What passed between them consisted of but few words, for Elkington had received a communication from the Lord Warden requesting to see him at an early hour, and was, at the period of Ranulph Hensman's visit, ready to proceed to the Warden's mansion.

They therefore walked together, conversing in low tones as they went upon what had occurred at the Warden's on the preceding night, concerning which as yet Elkington had not received any authentic details.

He seemed much moved at the narrow escape which the Lord Warden had had, and insinuated his impression that the Catholic party was much more active than those who were interested in opposing it, as all imagined.

'Master Hensman,' he said, 'a feather will tell which way the wind blows; there are as clear and as far-sighted men with their interests completely bound up with the Church of Rome, as the whole world could produce. I have no doubt on earth but that they will perceive the storm that is brewing, and that they have decided upon making the most stupendous exertions to preserve their supremacy.'

Ranulph Hensman fully concurred in this view of the question, but as they had now arrived at the door of the Lord Warden's residence, further conversation upon the subject ceased, until they were in the presence of that nobleman.

In a private chamber of the mansion, so protected by double doors that it was quite impossible any of the conversation could be overheard, these three persons—the Lord Warden, John Elkington, and Ranulph Hensman—held a long and serious counsel.

It was fully agreed between them all, that Sir Rupert Brent must have been cognizant of the attempt upon the life of the Warden; although, certainly, there was not sufficient evidence thoroughly to convict him of the fact. They now regretted that they had not retained the letter addressed to him, which had been found in the pocket of the assassin, as that might have contained every necessary proof to connect him with the crime.

'But, even then,' said John Elkington, 'it would have been a difficult matter to have tracked him. He would have disowned any participation in the affair, simply saying, that he was not accountable for what another man might choose to write; so that, beyond our ignorance of who the writer of the letter was, we are as well acquainted with the Jesuit as if we had it, for we know him to be guilty.'

It was then decided among them, that a careful watch should be kept upon the proceedings of Brent, and that, in the meantime, an express messenger should be despatched to London, with a communication to the King, detailing all that had occurred, and asking his majesty's assistance and counsel.

That such a communication would find a hearty welcome from Henry VIII. at that period, there could be no doubt; and, as it was signed by both the Lord Warden and John Elkington, it would seem as if they knew that their joint names would amply vouch for the veracity of the communication.

There was a man in the household of the Lord Warden who had recently brought a boy, his son, to serve as page, and this lad, for his fearless spirit and his unrivalled skill as a horseman, had attracted the particular attention of the Warden; so that now, when the subject was mooted, as to who was to be the messenger to London, his lordship at once named this lad, as one who he thought it would be wise to send, and who, perhaps, would be less suspected of being the bearer of any important despatch than a man.

At first, John Elkington and Ranulph Hensman both started a little at the idea of sending a mere lad, whose age certainly did not exceed sixteen, upon an errand of so much importance; but they had sufficient faith, both of them, in the judgment of the Lord Warden, soon to become reconciled to the idea, and the boy was at once summoned to their presence.

He was an active-looking lad, small for his age, slim, but all bone and muscle; and, as he stood before the Lord Warden, he looked the very personification of an individual whom fatigue could not touch, and to whom the sentiment of fear was perfectly unknown.

His name was Reuben Clifton; and although he fixed his keen eyes upon the countenance of the Lord Warden, there was nothing disrespectful in the gaze. The Warden addressed him, saying,

'Reuben, do you think you could ride to London quickly, with a letter?'

'I know I could, my lord. Give me Altamount for the journey, and I will do it.'

'There may be danger, Reuben.'

'Yes!' said the boy.

'Your very life would be taken, if the errand you go on be suspected.'

'Good! I and Altamount will do our best.'

'It will be necessary, if you find yourself hard pressed, to destroy the letter, as well as this signet ring, which, if you reach London in safety, will admit you to the presence of the King.'

'It shall be done, my lord.'

'When you reach the palace at Westminster, if the King be there, you must ask to see one of the royal chamberlains; show him the ring, and he will conduct you to King Henry; but if the King be at Hampton, Windsor, or elsewhere, you must follow him; and now, how soon will you be ready, Reuben?'

'I am ready now, my lord;—as soon as Altamount is saddled.'

'There is the letter, then, Reuben. Remember, that some people's lives are dependant upon it. If it do not reach the King's hands, it must be hidden or destroyed—it matters little which. Take the signet ring, and here is a purse well stocked, for the exigencies of your journey.'

The boy took the letter, which he carefully concealed next to his breast, and then, as he held the purse in his hand, he said—

'My lord, a fourth of this amount will be sufficient—and to carry more will be but to afford a temptation to robbers, which I do not wish to do, for although I have no objection to fight in defence of the king's letter, I don't want to chance anything for the sake of a few gold nobles.'

'We dictate nothing to you,' said the Lord Warden; 'pray perform your journey in your own fashion; your reward, at its conclusion, shall be ample, you may depend; take from the purse whatever money you think you will require; but by all means be sure you take enough, and remember, you have the sustenance of your horse to look to as well as yourself.'

'Quite right, my lord,' said the boy, 'I have enough; and in ten minutes' time shall be upon the road.'

CHAPTER VII.

The perilous Journey of Reuben Clifton.—The Four Attempts at Murdering, and the Arrival in London.—The Halt by the Meadow for the Night.

THE boy was as good as his word; in five minutes he wa on the road, which for some distance was steep, but straight It was one of those roads which have remained ever since th time the Romans entered this country; and, when all othe remnants of their power have for ever passed away, these roads will remain till the end of time, to tell us who first entered the country with the sword. They were not on l powerful as warriors, but indefatigable workmen—capable of undertaking any vast design, and of finishing it too. These indomitable men, when no longer occupied with bloodshed, turned their weapons to good account, and the sinews that were once bent upon the destruction of their foes in battle, were now directed to the improvement of the country they had subjugated.

This road runs from Winchester to Basingstoke; it runs almost entirely straight, regardless of any natural impediment, running over one hill-top, straight down to the valley below, and then up again on the summit of the next hill—so that, whoever reached one hill-top, could see distinctly the whole road between that and the next hill; and if anyone were about to cross that hill-top too, he would be distinctly observable.

It was this road that Reuben Clifton took; and his good horse Altamount no sooner felt that he was on a road that led through an open country for many miles, than he met the country breeze with a snort, that told his rider he was eager for the road that led him away from the city.

'Now, my good steed, Altamount,' said Reuben, as he pressed the spurs close to the animal's side, so that they touched him in the gentlest manner possible, but enough to show him they were there, and then stroking his neck, and urging him with his voice—'show thy mettle, and allow nothing to touch thee on the road, for the journey may be perilous, and there may be some occasion for the speed and wind thou hast.'

Away, however, the good steed bounded, but was checked by the bridle of Clifton, who knowing he had a long road before him, determined he should not do the first part of it at such a speed that promised to exhaust the best horse that ever wore a saddle, before he came to the end of his journey.

There were some cottages on the road-side, and from one of these sprung a man, and he mounted a fleet horse and rode ahead of Reuben Clifton for some time, and then increasing his speed he disappeared over the next hill-top.

'What means that?' thought Reuben, 'it can't bode good, some ambush on the road—but, thank Heaven, the next hill-top will reveal the mystery, if any there be, but I will not hurry my good steed now; if occasion should happen, as I somehow or other think it will, I can, I believe, show them a little speed; a clean pair of heels will do more than all the cunning and strength in the world. Thank Heaven,' he exclaimed, 'I have a good horse, and intrusted with a letter to such a personage, I would dare more than I am likely to face upon this occasion.'

The road was good, but yet the hedges and trees were wild nd had grown to an extent not often seen on road-sides ine ahose days; it gave plenty of room for all sorts of ambuseades tand concealments, of various characters.

'I had not thought of that,' muttered the youth to himself

'I had not thought of that, how he disappeared! yet he could not have reached the next hill-top.'

He was almost inclined to stop and push across the open road, but that was objectionable in more than one way: he might miss the way, or meet with more impediments than h e anticipated, which might disable his horse.

He determined therefore to ride on, with his horse well in hand, so that he might be able to push on at a gallop were it needful, fer he was determined to seek safety rather than turn and face any danger, however it might promise a successful issue to an encounter with any one whatever.

But he saw no danger, but pushed on, and as he proceeded he saw the horseman he had noticed start before him crossing the ridge of the opposite hill.

'By Saint Andrew there he is—he has been creeping along under the shadow of the trees—it is well I had my eye on the hill, or he would have stolen away, 'tis well I have my foe before me, if foe he be.'

These words were scarcely muttered between his lips, when his attention was attracted by something in the road which he had not noticed—his eyes had been fixed on his horse's eet for some few yards, watching his motions with care; when he raised his eyes he beheld two men some fifty or eight yards a-head of him in the road, with bend ed cross-bows, which were raised towards him.

'Stratagem is worth something,' he muttered, 'when force won't do. If I could escape their bolts, which is not very likely, they would drag me off with their bows; and yet I would risk all about that, if I could be but sure of their missing me.'

'Stand like a true man,' shouted one of the fellows.

'What want you?' shouted Reuben Clifton, in reply, drawing his bridle, so as to halt at a distance.

'We want your purse.'

'To that you are welcome; but you must cast your bows on one side, and I will throw you my purse.'

'But we must search you.'

'You cannot do that.'

'We both can and will do so; so stand, and submit.'

'Well, then, I cannot count upon any chance against such odds as these, so I may reasonably give in.'

'You will find it to your advantage, my youth,' said one of the men, lowering his bow. 'Do you, Hickson, keep a good aim at him. He may give us trouble yet—there is no knowing the pranks these young gentlemen may play.'

'I have him at the end of my bow, about three barley-corns in advance, so that if he moves. I have him right through the heart, never trust my bow again.'

'Well, keep it so. Now, young messenger, dismount, and give me your bridle. I'll hold your horse—it's a mettlesome one, too, and will require a steady hand like mine.'

The youth now rode up leisurely until he came within about two horse-lengths of the man, when suddenly striking sharply the spur into his horse's side, he caused him to leap forward several yards. He struck over the man who was approaching to seize the bridle; at the same time the active man, seeing something about to happen, let fly his bolt.

The bolt struck the youth across the back, but it was only a graze, not even raising the skin, merely brushing the clothes on his back, and then made a catch at the bridle, as he, Reuben Clifton, passed him at full speed.

'Ha! ha!' said Reuben, as he rode by at full speed, 'you must be better men to catch me.'

'Curses on the young hell-hound,' said the first man, rising, and seizing his bow, which was yet bent, and, fixing a bolt in, he aimed it at the flying figure of Reuben. It was not a bad aim, considering the speed of the horse, for the bolt went right over the shoulder of Reuben, who kept on the same speed as before.

'You are a pleasant messenger,' he said, as he heard the bolt whistle by. 'I would sooner hear than feel you; but my time is not come yet. I would I were at Basingstoke! I think in the old town I could rest a few hours secure, for if I am to ride at this speed, I will stop there until the horse has rested himself, else he may fail me ere I get safely to London.'

He pushed on at a rapid pace, and in two hours, or thereabouts, he arrived at Basingstoke.

The reason for his going through Basingstoke was, there was less probability of his departure being noticed, and he was, if the design he had was suspected, less likely to be followed and set upon, for he would have been waited for on the dire t London road. However, he was in error on this occasion, for his enemies were as keen sighted s men could be, and moreover he could not now alter his course, but pushed ahead.

Once in the good town of Basingstoke he entered an inn, where he gave directions to the ostler to rub his horse down, and call him when he fed him.

These directions were complied with, and Reuben saw his horse well cared for before he himself sought a mouthful to refresh himself.

' I am so far safe on the road,' he said, ' and can have but little heed of the remainder of my journey. I should imagine that those two men were the only enemies I am at all likely to encounter, and yet that horseman, he's ahead, or was so. Where can he be, I wonder? He must be connected with that affair at the bottom of yon hill. I will be on my guard. The Jesuits are no mean enemies, and if I can but foil them, then I shall have some thanks for my service.'

He left the public room in which he had been sitting, but there were several persons seated there also, one of whom especially sat and gazed earnestly on his countenance.

' Friend,' said the stranger, ' art thee going to London? '

' And wherefore do you ask a traveller concerning his road? ' inquired the youth, with a keen glance of his eye, which, however, the other returned with a stedfast-stolid stare.

' I thought,' returned the traveller, ' that if you had been going that road, the company of an older man would have been a protection to thee, and also it might shorten the journey to thee and to me.'

' I shall get over my journey quicker than you can; my horse is a fast one, and it will outstrip every other on the road, so it would be but company for a short way.'

' As you please, young sir; but do not reckon too much upon your horse—I think mine may equal it; but it matters not; if you start now, you may see me before you reach London, that is, if you meet with no accident on the road.'

' I expect none, but that is as may be; yet, whatever character it may be, it will be met somehow or other, and of that, be assured, it will cost those who attempt it dear.'

' I hope such a gallant youth will meet his rewards,' said the stranger, as he gazed into the measure that stood before him, and Reuben Clifton soon after left the room.

He entered the stable where Altamount stood munching a few mouthfuls of hay after his corn; and looking round when he heard Clifton's step he stamped his fore-foot, and neighed

' Oh! Altamount, you and I must be on the road presently; we have no time to lose; you are as gay as a lark and as fresh as a young calf, this rest has done thee great good.'

He proceeded at once to saddle him, and to examine into the state of the harness, to see that no fault existed that would render his journey in any way troublesome.

' Fine horse that, sir,' said the groom, who now entered the stable; ' don't know that ever I saw his equal.'

' He is a good horse,' said Clifton, looking carefully at his feet, ' a better I never crossed; he is sound, too.'

' So I think; there's one in the next stall but one that's nearly as good though, I reckon.'

' Indeed, is there? '

' Yes, yes; at least he is a good horse for a long journey; he will last well, and goes fast.'

' You cannot say more for any horse; where is he? '

' Next stall but one, sir; this way, sir—you'll see him; he's quite quiet, I believe, at least he was with me.'

Reuben Clifton approached the horse, and at once recognised, or believed he recognised, the very horse he had seen the stranger mount from a cottage near Winchester; at least he strongly suspected it to be so, and turning to the groom, he said,—

' Yes, this is a powerful strong horse, and one, I should think, that could go a good journey.'

' Aye, at a good pace.'

' Whose horse is it? ' inquired Reuben.

' I don't know who the owner is; but he is up-stairs in the travellers' room— an elderly man.'

' Ah! I saw him.'

' He'll be down soon, I dare say; he talked of being on the road directly; he's going to London.'

' I dare say,' said Reuben Clifton, as he mounted his horse, and rode out of the inn-yard, and then trotted leisurely through the town of Basingstoke until he got to the outskirts, when he heard a bolt whiz through the air; and, on looking round, saw a man in a crouching attitude, with a cross-bow in his hand, making the best of his way round a low wall.

The first impulse of Clifton was to dart after him, and make him repent the dastardly attack, but second thoughts checked him; for he thought that, perhaps, the man was not alone, but aided by others who might be at hand, and who, as he dismounted, would show themselves, and overpower him, and take his letter from him.

This was a matter of paramount importance, and he therefore pushed on with speed to escape the vicinity of such dangers.

' Now, Altamount, put forth your speed, and see if we cannot give these evil people the road behind. Once in London, I do not care; if I can reach it by daylight I should be glad; but if not, I must do the best I can.'

He now paced along very rapidly: houses, trees, and gates all passed by him, the road changed, and the scene also with great speed; a moving panorama seemed to be before his eyes, and each moment he was presented with some new object, some new point in the scenery that was moving about him. He had travelled more than half an hour when he thought he heard the tramp of horse's feet behind him; he was at first inclined to pull up and listen, but then he thought that he should lose time and give any adverse party time to come up. He, therefore, kept on at the same speed; now and then, indeed, he turned his head backward to catch a glimpse of any one who might be behind him, but the road wound along, and the trees in the hedge-rows were wild and straggling, and all view of the road behind was screened from the position in which he happened to be placed, and he could see nothing.

' I can hear the sounds of the horse, too,' he muttered; ' and it seems to me to be gaining upon me.'

This caused him to feel uneasy, and to push his horse to yet greater exertion: the willing animal had already got over seven or eight and twenty miles of ground in a space of time not much over three hours, which, considering the stoppages he had made, was quick work, especially in those days. However, he now approached a little town called Hook, about seven miles a-head of Basingstoke, nearer London; he determined not to make any stoppage there, but by the first road-side house he met, a mile or two beyond, he would give his horse a drop of water and a moment's pause.

It was now towards the afternoon when he passed through the little country town, and, excepting the gaze of one or two idlers, he saw no one at all that was likely to disturb them; true it was that, just as he was getting out of the town, a drunken man reeled into the road and attempted to seize his bridle and unhorse him, but he struck him a blow with his riding-rod that laid him on the earth senseless.

' There, take that, you sot—a fit place for such as you! the King's highway is infested all along with thieves and vagrants of one kind and another.'

He now pushed on for about a mile and a half, when he came to a road-side house, where a large tree grew before the door, from a limb of which hung the sign-board.

' Here I will wait a few moments,' he said, as he rode up and dismounted, leading the horse up to the water-trough, and from which he permitted him to drink but sparingly.

' Here,' he said, to a man who came out, ' give him a little wet hay, but not much.'

He had scarcely turned round to examine the place, when he saw the horse that he had before seen in the stable; it would seem to him that he was completely haunted by this strange man, and, do what he would, he was compelled to abide his company, or rather his unseen vicinity. He sat down in the room, the public room, in a chair opposite to the window; but, at the same time, he became conscious that he was in the immediate vicinity of another party, and, on looking round, he saw the same person he had seen at Basingstoke.

' Friend youth,' said the stranger, ' I thought thee hadst ridden so hard there would have been no occasion of again meeting; but travellers are fellow-wayfarers, and right glad am I to see you safe so far, for the road has a bad name.'

' I think it has.'

' I started after you, and yet I am here. I have been here some minutes; how I could pass you, I cannot conceive; did you see me on the road? '

' No,' said Clifton.

' You are for London, I dare say? '

' Truly, we will not discourse upon the end of one's

journey—travellers go where they go without advertising which way they will go; is not that the way, sir traveller?'

'Yes, I believe it is; but company upon a long road is not the less desirable—it shortens the road and makes the way cheerful, and, moreover, it gives those who travel together greater security against attacks on the road :—it is safety that it ensures.'

'I have already passed through such dangers, and, therefore, I have no need of protection.'

'Then, valiant sir, will you grant me your protection Londonward? I am travelling that far, and will defray the expenses on the road for your continuous company.'

'I prefer travelling alone, and require no company.'

'You are saucy, boy.'

'If you intend a quarrel you cannot have a better beginning, but I fancy it matters not much how you commence so long as the end answers the purpose you have in view.'

The stranger made no reply, but suddenly seized Reuben Clifton by the throat, and placing a dagger at his breast, he said,—

'Give me the letter, or you are dead; quick, quick!' but, as if belying his intention of showing him any mercy, he raised his hand to give a heavy blow, when Reuben shifted his position, and parrying the blow, brought his own heavy riding-boot in sudden and quick contact with the sharp part of the stranger's shinbone, and, however undramatic it may seem, gave him exquisite anguish, and caused him for a moment to be perfectly powerless, and his eyes to swim.

That moment sufficed Reuben Clifton to release himself, and to seize his riding-rod and bring it down with all his weight and strength on the stranger's head. He fell with a groan upon the floor, without motion or sense, and after a moment's pause to gaze at the fallen man, he left the room, making the best of his way down-stairs.

Another minute and he was away on the road at a hard gallop for several miles, passing through many villages as he went along, but not drawing bridle for one minute until he entered Bagshot, and there he rested his horse for half-an-hour.

The animal, though full of fire and spirit, was not without some instinct of his journey, and had been ridden at a rapid pace over the ground, and was now in a foam with the exertion.

The first thing he ordered was a little water to wash the animal's mouth, and then to have him well cleaned, and a feed of good solid oats and some bread.

He entered the public room, himself somewhat fatigued, and glad to sit down.

Having called for refreshments, he partook of them hastily. There were several persons present, and two horsemen were conversing together; they had got their refreshments before them, and seemed to be well-armed men, who had travelled far.

They conversed freely and aloud, but upon indifferent subjects, and at the same time Reuben Clifton could not but think he had heard one of them before: his voice was much like that of the man he had the last encounter with, and yet he deemed it impossible.

However, he no sooner rested enough to give his horse time to eat his corn, than he quitted the room and proceeded to the stable, and having discharged his dues, he drew the horse out, and was about to mount, when the two strangers appeared.

The nearest made a cut at him with his sword, which narrowly missed cleaving his head in two, having cut off part of his bonnet. Reuben Clifton waited not to return the blow; having one foot in the stirrup, he vaulted into the saddle, and was out of the yard just as the other had brought two horses out ready saddled.

Reuben got the start of one or two hundred yards, and away he went, putting his good horse Altamount to his mettle.

'Now or never!' he said, 'I want your speed. I am beset by two who will not leave me while I live, and I have not means to defend myself sufficiently against two such men: on—on—my good Altamount!'

The noble steed, as if well aware of what was required of him, put forth his strength and fleetness, which was prodigious.

The strangers were well mounted, and proceeded in the chase with the determination of men who would not be baffled. For ten or fifteen miles did they keep their places

well, and even Altamount could not gain upon them until within a few miles of Staines, and then their steeds appeared to give way under the severity of the pace. He crossed the Thames, and pushed through Staines with his reeking steed, until he came within five miles of London.

It was now dark—quite dark, and his horse seemed much distressed; he looked around, saw no one near, and determined to turn the horse into the meadow; and dismounting, he threw himself beneath the protruding boughs of some trees and a thick hedge : he fell fast asleep on a dry bank, with Altamount grazing by his side. The dangerous journey had atoned for the nature of the difficulties opposing, and the short time in which it was completed.

CHAPTER VIII.

The Palace at Westminster.—The Chamberlain.—King Henry in his Closet.—The Page's Reward.

WITH a feeling, almost approaching to exultation of the most ecstatic character, Reuben Clifton saw the bright sun gleaming upon the numerous church spires and lofty buildings of what was then, although not one-half its present dimensions, the large City of London.

He shaded his eyes with his hands and looked long and earnestly at the mass of houses which seemed to fill up so large a space of the horizon.

'Now I have arrived!' he cried; 'and, after all these dangers, I have the king's letter and the king's signet safe. Now, Altamount, let us be up and jogging.'

The horse knew the lad's voice, and ceased copping the fresh green herbage of which he had made his morning meal. With the greatest docility he suffered himself to be again saddled and bridled by his young master, and the boy then springing upon his back, left the beautiful green meadow in which he had passed the night, and took a well beaten road towards the metropolis.

The steed had done the business gallantly and well, but when we come to consider the light weight of the boy, and the power and mettle of the horse, we shall feel no surprise at his travelling so great a distance in so short a space of time.

Indeed, his rider was as nothing to him, and only might be considered as accompanying him to cater for forrage, instead of being anything in the shape of an incumber.

The road which they now took was bounded on each side by a hedge-row, from which sprung up, here and there elm and lime trees, which in some places spread their luxuriant branches so far across the roadway as to make a complete leafy canopy, and leave that portion of Reuben Clifton's path in comparative darkness.

The hour was an early one, and with the exception of a few husbandmen going to different field employment, the boy met no one for a distance of three or four miles.

He had looked upon London from an eminence that had made it appear much nearer than it really was, and he was little surprised at the distance he had to go before he even entered the suburbs of the city. The bustle of the streets, however, and the variety of the houses, soon took much of his attention, and he paused at a little change-house, called the Lamb, to inquire his way to Westminster.

'Why, bless the boy,' said a woman, to whom he propounded his question, 'where are you now but at Westminster?'

'I am a stranger here, and know nothing of the city I have ridden for.'

'And whom seek you, if it is a fair question, my lad?'

'Oh, perfectly fair. I have come to see King Henry.'

'Take that,' said the woman, as she dealt him a blow on the side of the head; 'take that, for making sport of one who is nearly old enough to be your mother.'

'You are too modest,' said Reuben, 'and do yourself an injustice ; you are quite old enough to be my grandmother.'

After this he thought it prudent to leave, for he saw, by the gathering anger of the woman, that she considered what he said to be a very doubtful sort of compliment indeed.

He trotted Altamount down a long, narrow turning, and then meeting a man with a good-humoured expression of countenance, who stopped to gaze on the beauty and symmetry of the horse, he asked him his road to the palace; and was immediately directed to that building which is now no more, but which at one time was the favourite town-residence of the English monarchs.

If Reuben Clifton's appearance, dusty and travel-worn as it was, would have attracted but little notice, no one could refuse a glance of admiration at the horse he rode; and, as he drew up to the palace gates, the lazy throng of lackies and yeomen of the guard looked upon him with no small amount of curiosity.

He dismounted from his steed, and throwing the bridle across his arm he was about leading it into a court-yard that faced him, when one of the yeomen of the guard opposed his halbert to his progress, saying—

'What now, do you think the King's palace can be walked into like a road-side inn? be off, boy, and thank your stars you have come across a merciful man, who has not thought it proper to give you a crack of the skull for your impertinence.'

'Be wary of yourself, Master Yeoman, it is not worth my while to brawl with such a fool; I come on a special message to the king, and must see one of the royal chamberlains.'

The yeoman's face grew as red as his coat, and he made a blundering blow at Reuben, which took effect upon the thick skull of one of his companions, producing a hollow sort of sound that created much mirth among the lackies and pages who always profess to hold the bulky yeomen of the guard, and they were all men chosen for their size alone, in great contempt.

'Why,' cried one, 'should the boy be struck because he comes with a message to the King? we don't stand here to knock people on the head for such a cause as that. Do you really want to see a chamberlain, boy?'

'I do. I have travelled for it, and that is my errand. Long live King Henry! but God help him if he had not better friends around him than those bloated savages who I have heard do nothing but eat and drink.'

'In truth,' said the page, 'you have heard a right good character of them. I may not take you into the courtyard, nor is it likely a royal chamberlain will come to speak to you here; so then you see, boy, there is a difficulty which I must ask your own ingenuity to get over.'

'I have a ring,' said Reuben, 'which if you show to the chamberlain, and by him shown to the King, will procure me an audience.'

'Trust me with the ring, and I will perform your message.'

'I will trust you,' said Reuben; 'take it, I trust you freely with what I have risked my life to retain within my own hands. I have brought it far, but if it now answer my purpose I shall be abundantly satisfied to confide it to you.'

'You may do so with safety; wait patiently, I may be some time gone, courtiers will not be hurried.'

So saying, the page left Reuben Clifton waiting at the entrance of the old palace of Westminster, and gazing intently upon the ring which had been given him he proceeded into the kingly residence.

From the manner in which the question of the boy's reception had been entertained by the King's page, the yeomen of the guard began to suspect that there was something more in the matter than exactly met their eyes. He who had endeavoured to strike Reuben mumbled out some excuse about having mistaken him for some one else, and intimated that he considered a cup of canary an extremely good thing, even at that early hour of the merning.

Reuben, however, declined the proffered hospitality, and led Altamount gently to and fro before the palace gate; and waited most anxiously for the return of the page, whose absence, measured by his impatience, seemed long indeed.

At length, however, that official made his appearance, and beckoning to Reuben, he said—

'You are to leave your horse in charge of some of the grooms here, and follow me.'

'To the King.'

'Yes, all is right.'

When the yeomen of the guard heard this they shrunk back; and he who had behaved so roughly looked extremely rueful lest the circumstance should reach the ears of his royal master, for well he knew the stern, impatient temper of the King, and that he was rather fond, than otherwise, of showing his anger in trifles.

But Reuben Clifton's mind was by far too much occupied with felicitation as regarded the success of his mission thus far to cast a thought upon any of the little crosses that had interfered with his progress. Every thing within the palace was new and strange to him, for the Lord Warden, in whose ervice he was, was a man of such simple habits that although of ample means his mansion boasted of none of those allurements or fanciful diversions which the boy saw now around him in such abundance.

He was conducted across a courtyard, and then up a flight of marble steps into a spacious but low-roofed hall, where there were more of the yeomen guard, as well as pages and other officers of the household.

The only attention which these paid to Reuben consisted in a listless stare of curiosity as he passed onward, for they knew, by the chamberlain that preceded him, he was no intruder, and therefore they were not interested in his presence.

They all looked sleepy and wearied, likewise, for they were of those whose duty it was to keep watch and ward in the palace during the night, taking what necessary repose they wanted in the day-time, and their hour of relief was near at hand.

This hall conducted into an octagonal apartment hung with rich drapery, and from that apartment ascended a short flight of stairs, which brought them on to the principal floor of the palace. Here a most brilliant suite of rooms presented themselves to the bewildered gaze of the boy. Everything of a costly nature which the art and genius of the period could produce was there assembled, and as Reuben walked onward through that apparently interminable line of rooms, he was in danger of forgetting the great object of his mission.

Twice, however, he felt in his breast for the Lord Warden's letter, and was gratified to find he had it securely.

Suddenly the page paused in one of the apartments, and said to him—

'I can conduct you no further, you must remain here now until some one comes to you. Fear nothing, and what questions are put to you by the King answer boldly and fearlessly, and as shortly as possible.'

Reuben Clifton had scarcely time to thank the page when he withdrew, closing the door after him as he did so.

And now the boy was alone, and he looked around him with undisguised admiration at the splendour which surrounded him.

The walls were hung with such rich tapestries that Reuben could not take upon himself to say where the door was now by which the page had made his egress, or what other if any entrances to the apartment there might be.

There were two windows fitted with diamond-shaped panes of glass which looked into a garden laid out after the Italian fashion, and adorned here and there with statues and vases.

It was an exquisite scene, because there was such an air of repose about it, and the boy thought he could have thought upon that garden for ever, without at all tiring of the refreshing sight, so full of floral beauties was it, and in such admirable order did everything appear.

On one of the walls of the apartment hung an exquisite painting: it was a portrait of a lady, young, fair, and most beautiful; so life-like was it painted that, catching the eyes of the boy as he turned, fancying he heard a slight noise, he could not take his gaze from off it, but looked until he could almost fancy the exquisite resemblance of so much beauty was starting from the canvass full of life.

How long he gazed upon that face he knew not, but it was long enough for him never to forget the impression that it made upon him, and he was startled by a voice from behind him, saying:—

'Well, sir, when you have done contemplating that masterpiece of painting, you will state what you are wanting with the King.'

Reuben turned instantly, for it might be the monarch himself.

A single glance, however, sufficed to convince him that it was not so, and that in the thin, spare-looking person before him, there was no resemblance whatever to bluff King Hal, whose personal appearance was sufficiently well known to all his subjects.

'I have a letter,' said Reuben, 'from the Lord Warden of Winchester, and likewise from John Elkington. I was charged to deliver it myself into the hands of the King immediately, as it concerned matters of grave import.

'From John Elkington and the Lord Warden of Winchester! Give the letter to me, and here is a rose noble for your pains; you can go back and say you have done your errand.'

'How so, sir, if I give you the letter instead of the King?'

'What, do you mean to cavil with me?'

'I know not,' said Reuben bluntly, 'what you call cavilling, but I will not give you my letter for

'What if I force it from you?'

'Then you will have it! try to do so, and we shall see whether the arm which defended it for many a mile cannot defend it yet.'

'Boy, boy, you mistake me; I applaud you very much for your perseverance in getting here. Be assured your letter shall reach the King, and you shall not go unrewarded; here is a purse of gold, give me the letter.'

'Not while I have life to retain it.'

The stranger, who was attired in the most costly fashion, bit his lips, and his hand wandered to the hilt of a sword he wore upon which Reuben Clifton stepped back a pace and drew a small poniard from his girdle.

'Pooh, pooh!' said the stranger; 'I was only jesting with you, follow me and I will show you to the King.'

'You are old enough,' said Reuben, 'to know better.'

'A young viper!' muttered the chamberlain, as he strode before the boy. 'A young viper! that letter I'll be bound contains important truths, which it might have suited me well to suppress.'

He opened a door in the wall, which was so well concealed in the panelling that no ordinary observer would have observed it even after the rich hangings had been moved aside, and Reuben Clifton followed him into a much more spacious apartment, at the further end of which was another door, partly opened.

'What have we here?' cried a voice from the inner apartment. 'Ho! what have we here?'

The Chamberlain advanced respectfully, and standing upon the threshold of the door, he said,

'The boy, your majesty desired should be conducted to your gracious presence, is here.'

'Yes, the letter—give it to us, good master Chamberlain.'

'I won't let him have it, your majesty,' cried Reuben; 'I promised to give it into your own hands, and if you will not take it, I can return with it to the Lord Warden.'

'Ho!' cried the King; 'what is this? not give up the letter to our Chamberlain!'

'No, your majesty,' said the Chamberlain; 'it is a most obstinate and pestilent kind of youth; I have asked him for the letter in vain.'

'And very right he was not to give it you. Come in, boy; if you promised the Lord Warden not to part with the letter, except into our own hands, you have performed your duty well.'

Reuben Clifton at once stepped into the King's chamber, where he found Henry not yet up, for the hour was early, and there had been an entertainment on the preceding night at the palace which had dipped into the small hours of the night.

Reuben Clifton knelt one knee and handed the letter, which the monarch hastily broke open and perused; he knit his brows, and so fierce an expression came across his countenance that Reuben Clifton fully expected some sudden explosion of anger. As it was he sprang from his bed, and called in a loud tone—

'Master Wallis! Master Wallis! come hither. What ho! come hither, Master Wallis, I say.'

'I will seek him, your majesty,' said the chamberlain; 'he is in the palace.'

'Do so and at once, this is brave work truly; so these saints are throwing down the gauntlet in their own way. The assassins! I'll not leave one of them in merry England if I live to see this day twelvemonth; ourselves will not be safe from these knaves. Wait, boy, wait, can you ride back again to Winchester?'

'At once, if it please your majesty.'

'Then you shall carry our answer to the Lord Warden. We will let these knaves see we are a king. They shall not disturb the meanest subject in my realm; and as for their power over the inmates of the monasteries, we have a plan for the settling all that. Hand me that mantle, boy.'

Reuben Clifton took a rich gilted mantle, trimmed with ermine, from a chair, on which it had been flung carelessly, and brought it up to the King, he kept stretching out his arms for the boy to assist him on with it, which not being accustomed to that kind of service, he did so clumsily as to elicit two or three round oaths from the King that quite astonished him.

'Yes, indeed,' said Henry, conversing to himself; 'yes, these Jesuits shall have a taste of my quality; I have temporized with them long enough, they or I shall rule in England; I will have no divided power here. Let me consider, this is a fair ground of quarrel; this escaped novice shall be protected with a grant of protection under our sign-manual, addressed to the Lord Warden of Winchester, whose duty it will then be by force to resist the aggressions of these priests. Let it be so, this is one of those trifles that may shake a kingdom.'

He wrapped the robe round him, and then the Chamberlain returned to announce that Master Wallts, the King's private secretary had made his appearance.

The King immediately had him into the chamber, and first of all dictating a few words of greeting and approval to the Lord Warden, not forgetting John Elkington and Reuben Clifton, though there was a slight smile upon the King's face as he pronounced that name.

Then, lower down upon the same sheet of paper, he desired the secretary to draw up a formal and distinct pardon and protection to Alice Hensman, for all monastic vows broken or offences committed up to that date, whether ecclesiastical or civil, and calling upon all his officers, judges, justices, and magistrates whatsoever, to give effect to the instrument, and this he signed, and desired his secretary to affix his private seal thereto.

The whole was then carefully enveloped in an outward wrapper of fine linen, around which was wound some silk, and then the King handed it to Reuben, saying—

'Go back to Winchester, and give this to the Lord Warden; you must ask him for some recompense for bringing me the letter so safe, which he addressed to me, and tell him I think that recompense ought to be some of your own choosing; and if you take this, my letter, as safely to his hands as you brought his to mine, think of what you please to ask of us, and in reason you shall not be refused.'

'I humbly thank your majesty. Is it your pleasure that I take back the Lord Warden's ring, or leave it with your majesty?'

The King mused a little, and then replied—

'The Lord Warden is provided with such passports to our presence. You shall have it yourself, boy, in case again you want to see King Henry. Give him the ring, my Lord Chamberlain; give him the ring.'

The chamberlain, with not the best grace in the world, took the ring from off his own finger, where he thought it probable it might as well have remained, and handed it to Reuben, who was about to express his thanks to the King, when, upon glancing upon the trinket, he saw it was not the same.

'His lordship the chamberlain, said Reuben, 'is not only anxious to get possession of his master's letters, but his affection for the King is so great, that for his Majesty to mention any particular ring is quite sufficient to induce my Lord Chamberlain to keep it.'

'What do you mean, boy?' said Henry.

'Only, my lord, that this is not the ring I brought from the Lord Warden.'

'Ha?'

'Quite a mistake,' said the chamberlain; 'having two rings upon my finger, I gave the lad the wrong one. I trust your majesty will excuse the error?'

The King bent his brows upon him, and then, after a brief pause, he said—

'Beware of such mistakes, my lord; the business of our kingdom grows each day of more importance, and mistakes light in appearance may produce great consequences. I don't think, my lord, your turn of duty upon our person will come round again quickly.'

The chamberlain turned very pale, but he only bowed very low to the King, in answer to this observation, which really was almost tantamount to a dismissal. But, as Reuben Clifton left the room, he cast upon him such a look of deadly nature, that the boy might well suspect some mischief towards him was lurking in the mind of the irritated chamberlain, and probably that to the full as much danger would be certain on his return to Winchester, as on his journey to London.

He was escorted by the page to the palace gates, where he found his horse waiting for him, and, declining an invitation to partake of some refreshment in the mess-room of the yeomen of the guard, with thanks, for it was courteously enough given, he mounted Altamount, and trotted off through London.

His intention was to get clear out into the open country before he made a halt, and then he intended to give both himself and Altamount a few hours' repose.

CHAPTER IX.

The Proceedings at Winchester.—Alice's Danger.—The Fret of Elkington.

Turn we now to a consideration of what was happening at Winchester.

Notwithstanding what had been done with the Lord Warden on behalf of Alice, in consequence of the threats of Sir Rupert Brent, there was still much anxiety on the parts of Hensman, Elkington, and himself, concerning the present aspect of affairs.

Of necessity there must be some days elapse before any news could be had from London, even if Reuben Clifton was so fortunate as to fully succeed in getting there without personal hazard.

This fact, of course, must be as well known to Sir Rupert Brent as to the friends of Alice, and it seemed more than probable that if any attempt were really to be made against her liberty, it would be made at once, and before she could receive any extraneous assistance.

And, although Ranulph Hensman fully believed that any open attempt to seize Alice and place her in charge of any of the ecclesiastical authorities would be unsuccessful, because resisted by the people, yet he dreaded some deep-laid scheme which should quickly drag her from him.

He would have felt quite easy with the subject had the case been an ordinary one, for the Catholic party at Winchester certainly were not in a condition to risk the consequences of a collision with the rapidly-growing Protestant ascendancy; but it was the ungovernable passion of Sir Rupert Brent which made him believe something would be attempted under the pretence of carrying out his ecclesiastical mission.

The Lord Warden was well aware of what a load of anxiety must necessarily rest upon the mind of his secretary, and he absolved him from all his duties, except such as answering any correspondence which might come in from day to day.

To say that Hensman was grateful for such an indulgence would be to say little, but the fact was that the association between him and the Lord Warden was more that of friendship than anything else, and the most perfect understanding prevailed between them.

Hence was it that Hensman was always enabled to get to his own home before sun-set, after which time of course he considered that the danger of any attempt on the part of the Jesuits to force Alice from her home was much greater than it could possibly be in the day-time.

And when he was compelled to be absent, John Elkington kept a tolerable watch upon the house, so that nothing unusual could occur without his being aware of it.

Two days thus passed away without anything taking place to give rise to a suspicion that Sir Rupert Brent meditated any attack, and Ranulph Hensman began to breathe a little more freely, and to consider that after all the crafty

Jesuit's schemes, there would be too much danger in carrying out his threats.

On the evening of the second day after he had returned from the Lord Warden's, and had been at home about an hour, a message was brought him that he was wanted again, as some letters of importance had recently arrived.

Putting on his cap he hastened to comply with the request, bidding Alice to keep the door fast until his return, and admit no one on any pretence whatever but John Elkington, should he call.

This, although not expecting any danger, she promised to do, but after Hensman had departed, a feeling of insecurity, and a presentiment of some coming danger, crossed her mind.

The children had retired to rest, and she listened attentively without hearing the slightest noise in the house, and yet her alarm each moment increased, until she got into such a fever of anxiety, that she almost prayed for the return of her husband to assuage her terrors.

She sat in the same room where that interview had taken place between her and Sir Rupert Brent, during which he had avowed himself to be her old enemy the Jesuit priest, and as she stood there, listening to the throbbings of her own heart, and counting the weary minutes as they winged their leaden flight, she suddenly heard a heavy knock upon the outer door. She felt convinced that this was not Hensman or John Elkington. In the first place her husband had not been gone long enough to get to the Lord Warden's and back again, if he had not stayed one minute at the house when he arrived, so that it could not be him. Bearing in mind the injunction that had been given her not to open the door to any one, she crept down to the passage only to listen, but not to betray the fact of her presence; she listened attentively at the street door, but all was still. Whoever had knocked appeared to have taken the disappointment of not being admitted quite calmly, and to have gone away again, for, after waiting a much longer time than any one's patience could possibly have extended to who meant to knock again, Alice crept up-stairs, feeling convinced that it was a matter neither of importance nor of danger.

She found, to her surprise, when she reached the room she had so recently left, that the lamp which had been burning was extinguished, and it took her some trouble to procure a light and re-illuminate.

But what was her terror and surprise, when its rays again shot across the apartment, to see, sitting in the chair she had herself so lately occupied, no other than Sir Rupert Brent.

A sense of terror and danger at the moment completely overpowered her faculties, and she stood looking at him as if he had been some vision from another world rather than a living reality of this.

And he glanced at her as though he enjoyed the confusion of mind into which he had thrown her, and was determined to wait until she first broke the silence that was maintained for several minutes between them.

'Georges' she exclaimed, at last, 'Georges, can I believe my eyes?'

'It is true,' he said, 'I am Georges; I have come to ask you if, upon reflection, you will return a more favourable answer to my suit?'

'Insolent intruder!'

'Indeed! still in the same vein. I shall be compelled by your own obstinacy to exercise the authority which is vested in me; you will become more complacent in a dungeon; but I see you are surprised at my presence here; I can tell you that my power in this city over you and all that belongs to you, and all that will raise a hand for your protection, is only limited by my inclination. I do not wish to behave harshly to you; I love you. Consent to receive a visit from me, in perfect safety, as I can so arrange them out occasionally, and you are free, and Ranulph Hensman shall be rather protected from danger than exposed to it.'

'You think me defenceless,' said Alice; 'you think, because no man is here, you may venture upon these insults, but, Sir Priest, you will find yourself mistaken; and, until my husband's sword can avenge the insult you have cast upon me, I have a weapon here that can protect me against a ruffian.'

As she spoke, she from a corner snatched an arquebus, a clumsy imitation of the modern carbine, which Ranulph Hensman had had from the Lord Warden but the evening before, and showed Alice, more in jest than earnest, how to use it.

Sir Rupert Brent was doubtless more surprised than pleased to perceive so formidable a weapon held by Alice in a manner which gave him a strong suspicion it might be dangerous in her hands. There was something, too, about her manner of holding the arquebus which made him suspect she had been tutored well concerning the use of it, and that it might be loaded. If it were, his, Sir Rupert Brent's, life, was in her hands.

'What do you mean, Alice Hensman?' he said, as he rose and strove to throw off the careless, mocking manner in which he had conducted the interview. 'What do you mean by this violence or show of violence? I have given you no cause to suppose that you had aught to dread from me that could require such an answer as that.'

'Keep off, Sir Rupert Brent! you may be bold, but I hold your life in my hands; approach another step nearer to me, and you will reap the consequences of your folly.'

'Nay, nay, Alice Hensman, I know better; the weapon you hold is but so much wood and iron: it is not loaded—I see it is an arquebus; but I have had some experience even with such weapons as those—we Jesuits should know every thing, but certainly one thing that I do know is, that that weapon is unloaded.'

'Will you chance that fact?' said Alice, as she presented it to his head and drew back the lock.

'Pshaw! this is folly,' he cried, as he sprung aside. 'I have but once to ask you your determination on a matter merely of sufficient moment to warrant me in so doing, and you make this attempt upon my life. Give me your answer and I leave you; can I speak fairer?'

'You cannot, because you speak under the influence of fear; you have my answer, it is the same you had before. I hold you in special abhorrence and most unmitigated contempt. Now, leave me.'

'I will do so; but we shall meet again.'

He moved towards the door, and Alice made no reply to him, but kept the mouth of the arquebus towards him, and watched his eye most steadily; for he was just the man to make a sudden rush, and endeavour to dispossess her of the weapon to which, no doubt, she was indebted for her safety.

She could well perceive that a storm of angry passions was raging at his heart; but most certainly, among the rest of the accomplishments taught to the Jesuits, self-control was one, and, feeling most acutely and particularly the danger to which his life was exposed, he thought it prudent to beat a retreat while he could in safety.

'I bid you good-night, Alice Hensman,' he said; 'my departure has not been accelerated from the fact that you are armed. I should despise myself were it so.'

'You could not despise yourself more than I despise you, recreant and coward as you are, and I am rejoiced at length that I have found the means of making your guilty soul tremble. This, Sir Rupert Brent, is the last visit I shall endure from you; you're a dead man if you again have the audacity to venture hither. I will take my own part, sparing my husband the danger of an encounter with you, and the malevolence of your companions should he overcome you.

'Beauteous Alice, how ill do those stern words become so beautiful a countenance; you do but jest after all, you know the arquebus is not loaded!'

'Sir Rupert Brent, another moment and I lose all patience; for I condemn and almost despise myself for parleying with you—it is not, of course, in the nature of woman not to regret taking a life, even if it should be that of her bitterest foe; do not, then, I implore you, force me to lay you dead upon the threshold of this house.'

'I force you: you know not what you say—I, your own good friend, whom you admitted might call you Alice—you admitted it by implication; but tell me, Alice, while protecting yourself, as you imagine, by an unloaded arquebus, where are your children?'

A half-shriek burst from Alice's lips, and the wily Jesuit now saw that he had hit upon a subject that moved her strongly.

'Yes,' he continued, 'what has become of your children? Is it quite a new thing for the Church to seize upon the children of heretics—heretics who have once been good Catholics, but who have strayed from the flock of the faithful, in order that those little ones should be educated in believing, and not in the despicable doctrines of those to whom they belong?'

' My children! my children! if you be human let me pass, —let me seek them, and be assured I have them still.'

' You have them not. Harkye, Alice, I'll make a condition with you: I will exchange your children for yourself. Come with me now, at once, to where they have been conveyed. You saw them sleeping two hours since—you find me here when least expected. I told you that I had power in Winchester—the power of confederation—come with me, at once, and your children shall be released, while for one kind word from those lips you shall purchase your own release.'

' Fiend! Monster! Can you be man? Is it possible there can live such a heart? Return me those little ones, and I'll forgive the past; nay, I will pray for you, I will assuage the anger of my husband, and the memory of that one deed shall much avail you, when all else that remembrance may present shall wear the aspect of despair.'

' Their fate is in your own hands, not in mine.'

In the eagerness with which she spoke, and the intense agony with which she listened, poor Alice forgot the defence which had availed her, and the arquebus, before so firmly pointed at the intruder, hung listlessly from her hands, while her eyes were blinded with tears, and all her mother's agony sat brooding at her heart.

This was the moment that Sir Rupert Brent chose to dash forward and lay a hand upon the weapon, turning it completely from him, so that, were it discharged even, there could be no danger to him from its contents, and then Alice gave him abundant proof—more proof than he wanted, that it was loaded, for in the agitation of the moment, as she uttered a scream, likewise of terror, she pulled the trigger.

A report ensued which awakened every echo within the large mansion, and a couple of bullets, which had far better have found a home in the politic brain of the Jesuit, dashed through the window, out into the street.

' What folly is this!' he cried, as he clutched her by the arm; 'Alice, do you consider that I am so wretched a fool that a woman, let her be armed as she might, could conquer me?'

' Unhand me, ruffian!'

' Not until I have kissed away those tears.'

' Hush! hush!' cried Alice, as she clasped her hands, and let the arquebus fall to her feet; ' hush, yet a moment,—those sounds—those joyful tones—my children—I hear them call upon me; the report of the arquebus has awakened them, they are here—they are here.'

' Yes! it was a delusion; but it has answered its purpose, and your children are here; they may cry to you, nay, may cry to me, but no one now shall force you from me. Within my call—within sound of a whistle of peculiar tone, I have so strong a force of the agents of ecclesiastical authority, that resistance will be madness. Your husband will not return for hours, I have sent him on a false message, and as for your other great friend John Elkington—'

' He is here,' said a voice, and the door of the apartment was flung open by John Elkington, who entered, sword in hand. ' Well met, Sir Rupert Brent, the parting may not be so easy.'

' Curses!' said the Jesuit, as he released Alice from his grasp, and staggered backward to the wall.

' Yes,' said John Elkington. ' curses! that is ever a priestly resource, whenever anything goes amiss; but curse away, you are now in the toils.'

' No, by Heaven! it is you are in them.'

As he spoke he raised the whistle to his lips, but ere he could emit a sound, John Elkington stepped up to him, and placed his sword within an inch of his body, saying :—

' Sound that whistle, and by the God that made me I swear to run you through Your friends may come and find you, but it shall be pinned against the wainscot where you now stand, by a rapier.'

The whistle dropped from the hands of the Jesuit.

' You speak bravely,' he said.

' I do, for I am in the habit of keeping my word, and now Sir Priest, Father Georges, alias Sir Rupert Brent, and alias Heaven knows what besides, I arrest you in the King's name.'

' Arrest me!'

' Truly so, having authority from the Lord Warden of Winchester under his hand and seal to arrest suspicious per-

sons. I must say, on my soul, I never saw a man so suspicious as yourself.'

He placed his hand on Sir Rupert Brent's shoulders as he spoke, and the Jesuit regarded him with a look of unfeigned astonishment.

' Arrest me!' he said again. ' This is a sorry jest.'

' I'm glad you think it one—my time is precious; for although I do not expect to have the good fortune to make another such capture, I am anxious to secure the one I have made; so, come along, Sir Rupert.'

' And whither, pray?'

' To the castle. We'll find some stronghold that'll do for the cowardly spy, the villanous Jesuit, who has the gross hypocrisy to persecute an honourable woman on the pretence of making vows she never made, while he himself is most deeply perjured in the eyes of both man and woman.'

' It is well, since it must be so. Come on, then, let us to the open street.'

' Oh! beware of him, John Elkington,' cried Alice Hensman, ' beware of him, I pray you. He has friends abroad, and when you gain the streets, you will be overpowered by numbers.'

' Not so,' said John Elkington; ' Sir Rupert Brent shall walk with me the greatest appearance of contentment, and he shall smile as Jesuits can only smile, when anger and hatred are at their hearts instead of mirthfulness, so shall his friends not molest us; and should he object to these terms, should he be content to sacrifice himself and die a martyr to this adventure, he may do so, for my first impulse shall be to cut him down the moment any one, with even a seeming hostile intention, comes within a sword's length of him. Now, Sir Rupert, you know the conditions. Let us, as you say, gain the street.'

The countenance of Sir Rupert Brent looked livid with anger. He saw that he was completely in the power of his calm, collected, and athletic antagonist, who, from the firmness with which he spoke, he had not the remotest doubt on earth would carry out fully his intention precisely as he had expressed it.

He looked around him like some wild animal at bay; then, as John Elkington pointed to the door with his sword, he felt himself compelled to leave, but still, before he did so, he summoned up some of his old effrontery, and, turning to Alice Hensman, he said—

' Good night, sweet one; it seems as if our little delightful meetings should even end with some commotion, as if the gods were envious of our deep affection—a sad thing, very! but we shall meet again—farewell.'

John Elkington had scarcely patience to let him finish these words, and it required all the presence of mind he was master of to keep him from giving him a gentle hint in the back with the point of his sword, that such extreme courtesy was not required.

He moved from the room, closely followed by Elkington, who merely cast upon Alice before he left a glance of encouragement, while she murmured blessings on his head for the effective aid which he had rendered her at a moment when despair seemed to be taking possession of her heart, and the Jesuit had her in his power.

The fact had been that John Elkington was passing down the street when he heard a crash of glass, and a couple of shots came whizzing past his ears. Upon looking about in great indignation to see whence they came, he perceived that a window was broken in Ranulph Hensman's house, and, with no small amount of trouble, he had effected an entrance to it by getting the people at the next door to admit him on the plea that he feared some mischief was going on, and then scrambling over a garden-wall, so that he got in at the back of the mansion, arrived in time to render such effectual service.

He had overheard the last few words of the Jesuit, so that he was enabled to take his measures accordingly, and he resolved upon arresting him, and carrying him at once to the castle, under a general warrant from the Lord Warden, who had received, in common with other persons invested with high authority in the different counties, orders from the king in council to cast into prison such persons as there were reasonable grounds for believing entertained views inimical to the well-being of the government.

This was an immense and arbitrary power to place in the hands of any person, but such cases can only be judged upon their individual merits, and when we come to consider the

England was at the time on the eve of a very great moral revolution, and that the party opposed to that progress of opinion was disposed to adopt any means whatever for the purpose of thwarting it, therefore it became almost justifiable to resort to measures that under any circumstances a lover of his country would have reprobated in the highest degree.

We give no credit whatever to his bluff majesty King Henry VIII. for the war that he waged against monasticism, because it is well known that his motives were quite of a private and personal nature, and that he was as incapable as a broomstick of any nobler elevating principle.

Like most of our monarchs, he partook of something of the brute, and something of the fool; and gross sensuality being the load-star of all his actions, as has likewise been the case with most of our monarchs, he was willing to play any game with the institutions of the country that favoured his own private views.

It was a mere matter of good fortune that because Henry quarrelled with the priesthood he threw himself into the arms of the reformed religion, and waged war upon the immense revenue of the Church, as well as throwing open the gates of the monastic institutions of the country.

But it so happened that by this course of conduct he became a favourite for a time with a number of men of the most liberal and enlightened views, such men as the Lord Warden of Winchester, John Elkington, and the like, to whom any arbitrary power might be entrusted with great safety, inasmuch as they were incapable of abusing it.

When John Elkington reached the street along with his enforced companion, he did not sheath his sword, but he held it down by his side in such a manner that in the darkness it was not visible, and he whispered low to Sir Rupert Brent:—

'I am perfectly serious; it is seldom that I use any asseveration to strengthen my words. I have done so in this instance, however, upon the impulse of the moment, and I swear to you, Georges, for I believe that to be your real name, that you shall not live another moment, unless you walk with me, and comport yourself in such a manner that it shall appear you are doing so with perfect willingness.'

The Jesuit did not entertain the remotest doubt on earth of John Elkington's sincerity, and it was singular indeed to see the manner in which he adapted himself to the circumstances in which he was placed.

There was something positively ludicrous about the smile that his countenance wore, and with what a degree of feverish anxiety he strove to look pleased, in case those who were really waiting without should fancy he was in durance, and make some effort to save him, which, like the good-tempered bear who fractured his master's skull by brushing a fly off his cheek, would be productive of his instant destruction.

John Elkington, as well as the priest, observed that they were followed in their progress towards the castle by at least half-a-dozen men, and it must have been a sore trial of temper for the Jesuit to feel that he had such a force at hand, and yet dare not make the slightest effort to render it available.

Then he had his own doubts likewise as to the fact of his continued detention. He knew that as yet no overt act could be brought home to him, and although there might be abundance of suspicion, he had too good an opinion of the Lord Warden to believe that he would detain him on that score.

'Your friends,' whispered John Elkington, 'press hard upon your heels; be so good as to remark in an agreeable and pleasant manner, that it is a fine night, and do it loud enough for them to hear.'

'A thousand curses!' muttered the Jesuit, and then he said aloud, 'this is a delightful night.'

'Very,' said Elkington, loud enough for any one to hear, 'and so you give up your enterprise until some more convenient occasion; say yes, certainly, will you?'

'Damnation! certainly, yes,' said the Jesuit.

'Add, that your good friends may go home with the blessing of Heaven.'

Sir Rupert groaned, but he had no resource; therefore he said, with as good a grace as he could,—

'My friends may go home, and be damned to them all, as quick as they like.'

The men who were following laid their heads together in consultation at this, and they, no doubt, came to some very wise conclusion; for, after nodding their heads a number of times, they all turned and went into the nearest change-house above, with, probably, some portion of a handsome gratuity that had been presented to them by the discomfited Jesuit, they soon got into a very glorious state of intoxication.

When Sir Rupert Brent saw that his party had gone, and imagining that there was no further occasion for a concealment of his real feelings, he turned to his captor and said,—

'Master Elkington, I presume that you have now succeeded in your object. By a combination of circumstances, that gave you many advantages, you have defeated me; be it so, I cannot help it, and freely own it—so now, I presume, I may bid you good-night?'

'I am surprised,' said John Elington, 'at you, a man of the world, talking in such a way; you really cannot mean what you say! Did I not tell you that I had made you prisoner by virtue of a general warrant to apprehend suspicious persons? Did I not tell you that I thought you an extremely suspicious person, and apprehended you accordingly?'

'Nay, you are jesting.'

'Jesting, indeed: very far from it. And here we are, just by the castle; I intend, Sir Jesuit, to surrender you into legal custody.'

'In the name of the devil, who are you?'

'John Elkington.'

'I know that; but you are something else than John Elkington, or I am much mistaken.'

'Well, you Jesuits are sagacious men, and I see no reason why you should not employ that sagacity in making the discovery, if it so please you, of who I really am. But now, allow me to state that we must part, for here we are at the castle postern; and, mind you, I still keep my word: attempt to escape, and you are a dead man.'

John Elkington tapped at the postern-gate of the ancient castle; and, when it was opened, he gave a private signal and was instantly admitted within its precincts.

Two men at once advanced; and, in obedience to an order from Elkington, which they received with an amount of respect that much astonished the Jesuit, and increased his suspicions that his captor was indeed something more than he pretended to be, instead of being, as is too commonly the case with human nature, something less—they laid hands upon his prisoner, and at once conveyed him into a guard-room.

There was but a dim light in this apartment; and there he was left for a few minutes, with a sentinel who looked so grimly at him that it was pretty evident there were orders to keep a sharp eye upon his movements.

Then a couple of halberdiers, bearing lights, entered the place, followed by a man of stately mien and aspect, who was not at first recognised by Sir Rupert Brent, but who, as he approached, he perceived to be the Lord Warden, who certainly had so pretty a quarrel with him if he chose to pick it.

It was astonishing how the effrontery of the Jesuit bore him up; he rose at once, and confronting the Warden, he said,—

'My lord, I rejoice at having met with one who can understand and appreciate the feelings of gentlemen. It seems to me that, without the shadow of a pretence, I have been arrested and brought hither; what I am pretended to be guilty of I know not.'

'In the pockets, Sir Rupert Brent,' said the Lord Warden, 'in the pockets of the incautious man who came to murder me were found some papers, written in cypher; a learned individual, of the name of Clarke, residing in Winchester, has partially deciphered those papers.'

'The idiot!'

'Do you mean the learned scribe or the assassin, Sir Rupert?'

'Go on, go on! what then?'

'He states that those papers contain some interesting particulars of a plot most dangerous to the state.'

'But what is that to me?'

'Your name is mentioned.'

'The name of Brent?'

'No; the name of Georges. I would not do you an injustice, but these are sufficient grounds to warrant me in your detention, and therefore detain you I must.'

'Till when? for how long?'

'Till the King in council decides what shall be done in the affair. I have only power of detention, not of trial. If the latter be determined upon, you will be sent to London under an escort; if the former, I shall have the honour of opening the prison-gates for you, and setting you free. Guards, remove him !'

The Jesuit for a few moments appeared to be upon the point of speaking, but probably, upon a second thought, he considered that the less he said the better, and, folding his arms, he lapsed into a gloomy silence.

A couple of the halberdiers marched in front of him, while two others followed closely behind; and thus was Sir Rupert Brent, for the present at all events, placed in safe custody, and out of the power of doing further harm to any one in whom the reader entertains a kindly interest.

CHAPTER X.

The mysterious Meeting in the Vaulted Chamber.

WINCHESTER CATHEDRAL was a very ancient building, but it was composed of what might be considered two distinct portions.

There had been a little old Norman church on the site of the cathedral, which was afterwards erected during the middle ages with all those elaborate architectural adornments which characterised that period.

The ancient building had fallen into serious decay, and but little of it remained; what there was, however, of it adjoined the new structure, and presented a remarkable difference in style and formation. It was generally supposed that this ancient portion of Winchester cathedral was totally unused; and, indeed, great care had been taken to stop any means of entrance to it, except through the new building.

But this, to persons who at all reflected upon the subject, would rather seem to intimate that the priests required that part of the building for some purposes of their own, than that it was wholly and entirely deserted.

It is to that portion of Winchester cathedral that we are now about to introduce our readers.

Twelve o'clock had just sounded when one of the officers of the sacred building might have been seen traversing a narrow and gloomy passage which led from the Gothic cathedral to that Norman portion of the building which we have described.

He carried a lamp, and strolled along like one accustomed to the place, and only about to perform some very ordinary duty. The distance he had to go was considerable, and at the extremity of the passage, which he was moving along, there appeared a door of considerable thickness, that he opened with a key, which he took from his girdle.

Through this door was another and much shorter passage, but of very similar aspect and appearance to the one he had recently left. A short distance down it he opened another door, and that conducted him at once into a large vaulted chamber, from the centre of the ceiling of which hung a bronze lamp, of fine workmanship, and great strength and solidity of structure.

His object in reaching that vaulted chamber seemed to be to light the lamp, and to prepare the place otherwise for some expected guests. He ranged a number of seats around a massive oaken table, which was in the centre of the vault, and upon which he had stood to ignite the lamp. After completing these arrangements he drew one of the chairs towards the door at which he had himself entered, and sat down, as if with the resolution of awaiting the arrival of some one.

And now let us look at what is going on in the cathedral. All is as still as the very grave; the candles are burning upon the high altar, shedding but a faint ray for a few feet around them; the rest of the church is completely enveloped in gloom. The doors are open as usual; so that any one might enter the sacred edifice for prayer, and now and then some midnight wanderer did prostrate himself at the altar's foot, mutter his orisons, and then depart again.

A woman, too, stole in, and filled a bottle with holy water from the font that was near to the entrance; it was to sprinkle upon the bed of the sick, and wonderful must have been the efficacy thereof—but imagination does wonders, and, at all events, that superstition is a tolerably harmless one.

Then, about five minutes after the hour of twelve, a man entered the cathedral, enveloped in a large cloak; he neither stopped to pray, nor did he, as was the custom with all other comers, cross himself, in signification of his faith, as he entered the sacred place. Perhaps he had no faith to signify so that crossing himself would have been an idle ceremony especially as, by a glance around him, he saw that he was alone.

He crossed the church and strode directly up to a remote corner, where a very attentive observer might have seen that there was a door. Another glance of caution around him seemed to assure him that he had nothing to fear, and then, with a small key, which he selected from several others which he took from his pocket, he opened the door, and passed from the cathedral, shutting it sharply behind him, in order that the lock might fall into its place by a spring, which it immediately did.

Scarcely had this man thus entered, and thus left Winchester cathedral, when two others arrived, and after taking the same precaution as the former had done, to be convinced that no one was listening, they opened the little door, and likewise passed through it.

This same manœuvre was carried on by about twelve persons, and then a long period elapsed before any one arrived, so that, in preference to watching in the cathedral, we will conduct our readers at once again to the vaulted chamber, where he will find the whole of those persons assembled who had passed through the small door, and used so much caution in doing so.

The man who had lit the lamp and placed the seats had evidently acted as a kind of door-keeper to the party, for now that all were assembled, or nearly so, he removed his chair to the outside of the room instead of the in, and sat down to keep guard, thus showing that he had nothing to do with the deliberations that were going on, except in an official capacity.

The mysterious guests were all seated in the vaulted apartment, and, after a pause of some minutes' duration, one of them spoke, saying :—

'We are all assembled, excepting two of our number: it does not surprise me that one of those is absent, for although a zealous and highly esteemed member of this our convocation, we have never been able to depend upon his punctuality.'

There was a slight smile upon the countenances of some of the others, and one of them said :—

'That is true; we have certainly never been able to compliment Stephen Ratcliff upon his punctuality, but what can have come of Father Georges? hitherto he has always been the first arrival.'

'That is what surprises me,' added he who had first spoken; 'I hope that no mischance has befallen him.'

'It would be a serious thing for our cause to lose him,' said another; 'he is bold and resolute, so much so, indeed, that I almost fear, from his non-appearance here to-night, that he has attempted something of too great importance for the performance of one man.'

'We must proceed to business,' remarked another: 'it is half an-hour past midnight, and the sun at this season rises early.'

This was accordingly done: one of the number, by general consent, was elected president for the evening, and he opened the proceedings by saying—

My friends,—We have met here to-night, especially, to consult upon what was next to be done in Winchester, after the death of the Lord Warden, but it is known to you all, probably, that that person still lives, and consequently the attempt upon his life must by some mismanagement or accident have entirely failed.'

'It would seem so,' said another; 'and if any one could have given us information respecting the causes of such failure, it would have been Sir Rupert Brent, as he chooses to call himself in Winchester.'

'Hush, he comes. I hear a footstep—no, it's Father Ratcliff.'

The individual who was always expected to be late now made his appearance, and there was a look of deep anxiety upon his countenance, which at once convinced his companions that he had something of a disastrous character to tell. They were all silent as he approached the table, and when he reached it he said—

'I have bad news: Georges is a prisoner to the Lord Warden.'

They all rose, and for a few minutes the greatest confusion prevailed among them; several spoke at once in an exclamatory manner, and it required all the exertions of him who acted as president to allay the commotion that Ratcliff's words had excited. When, however, something like order was restored, Ratcliff was asked to give what further authentic particulars he could concerning the capture of Georges, and the causes which had produced such a result.

'I know nothing,' said Ratcliff, 'further, than that I was informed by one of his men, of the fact, that two persons, of whom he was one, had entered the castle by the small eastern postern. I made inquiry of a sentinel, who, for a small bribe, informed me that one of these men was a prisoner to the other, although which was which he knew not, nor either of their names.'

'That is quite sufficient evidence for us,' said the president. 'Georges has no prisoner to take, and if he had, the castle would not be his place of destination. He himself was the prisoner, and the person accompanying him his captor.'

'His absence this night,' remarked one, 'is proof positive of his apprehension; what is to be done? we know not our own danger; possibly we may be all standing upon a precipice, down which a single incautious action may plunge us.'

These words created considerable consternation, and the members of the Jesuitical convocation, for such it was, rose from their seats again, each of them feeling intensely alarmed for his personal safety. 'I see no danger,' said the president, 'and if there be any real peril it cannot but be greatly increased by anything like precipitation. Let us deliberate calmly upon what is to be done. For my own part, I am more inclined to believe that this is only some private affair of Georges, than that concerns us at all publicly. I do not think it has anything to do with the failure of the attempt upon the Lord Warden's life.'

These words, spoken with an air of great authority and decision, evidently produced a great effect upon those who heard them, and went far towards restoring tranquillity to the meeting.

One who had not spoken; now addressed his brethren, saying:—

'It is quite clear that in the present aspect of affairs we can resolve upon nothing—it is information that we want, and therefore I suggest that we should adjourn our present meeting until an early date, and in the meantime, let each individual use all the means that may suggest themselves to him to discover upon what plea Georges is arrested, and under what circumstances the attempt on the life of the Lord Warden has failed.'

'That is well,' said the president, 'as regards some of the objects of the meeting to-night, but not, I think, as regards them all. We have advices for London that our friend Sir John Harrington is chamberlain to the King for the next month; if Henry is to be got rid of, let it be within that period of time.'

'Yes,' said one; 'and we were to draw lots who was to go to London to place himself under the direction of Harrington, in case accident should develop any circumstances that would present a fair opportunity of removing the King.'

'It was so,' said the president; 'and I see no reason why that should still not be done.'

'There can be none, I am willing to take my chance; let the name of each man present be placed in a cap, the president can draw one, and let that be the individual chosen for the enterprise.'

No one made any objection to the arrangement, which after some more conversation among them of an indifferent character, was agreed to, and the names were written, each upon a small slip of paper. These were then placed in a hat, belonging to one of the number, and well shaken, so that they became sufficiently mingled together to make it a matter of entire chance which name should be drawn. There was an appearance of considerable anxiety upon the faces of that small party of Jesuits as the president dipped his hand into the hat, and drew forth one of the small folded pieces of paper. He deliberately spread it out, and read upon it the name of Leoni.

All eyes were now turned upon the man on whom it had fallen to execute so perilous an enterprise. He was a small man, of extremely spare habit, and his olive complexion, and dark restless eye, sufficiently proclaimed his Italian origin, if his name had not done so. He looked just the man for an assassin, although wofully deficient in physical power to accomplish anything in which that would have been a desideratum.

He spoke at once, and, as he did so, his eyes flashed with excitement.

'I do not regret,' he said, ' that this choice has fallen upon me. I am willing to perform the duty and to fail in the attempt,

if it must be so, or after, if it must be so likewise. I hate this King; he is the greatest enemy the Catholic faith ever had; if England under his auspices shake off the papal supremacy, we shall feel the consequences throughout the whole continent of Europe, and although we may retain among the people the outward semblance of the Catholic faith, that which we care much more for, namely, the power of the priesthood, will be greatly shaken.'

These observations met with general assent, and it would seem, by the increased spirits of the party, that the task which had fallen to the duty of Leoni to execute had been by no means a pleasant or popular one to reflect upon, but something very desirable to avoid, if possible, and which nobody regretted it had not fallen to his share.

It was now nearly two o'clock, and as, in another hour or two, some of the more early rising or devout of the community would begin to make their appearance within the church, it was desirable that the jesuitical combination should think of separating in order to avoid observation, as they passed out through the cathedral.

It was agreed, that on the seventh night from that time they should meet again, and during that period it was hoped by them all that some change for the better in the aspect of their affairs would ensue.

They went out by degrees, some singly, and in no instance more than two together, until at last the vault was entirely clear. Then the man who had kept watch and ward on the outside again entered it.

In quite a business-like manner he removed the chairs from around the table, placing them again up against one of the walls, in a formal row. He then extinguished the light and left the place, but instead of returning to the cathedral he pursued the passage for some distance to the right, and opening another door, he stood at the head of a flight of dark stairs.

'Griffiths,' he cried, 'Griffiths.'

'Aye, aye,' said a voice from below.

'Have you the key of the cellar?'

'Yes, to be sure; I can't come up, for I have just bored a comfortable hole into a cask of rare Malmsey, and when I end drinking, I am forced to keep my thumb upon it.'

'Well, what a fool you must be not to have provided yourself with a plug of wood!'

'I did not think of it; there are some laying about in the cellar; but if I leave the cask to look for one, the wine leaks. Come down yourself and look for one.'

'I'm coming, I'm coming. Griffiths—Griffiths, your brains will never save you from hanging, whatever your heels may do, for the fact is, good Griffiths, you are rather a fool than otherwise.'

This man descended the staircase into the cellar, where the monks stored their choice wine, and he and Griffiths were soon deep in the contents of the Malmsey butt.

CHAPTER XI.

The Return of the Lord Warden's Messenger.—The supposed Murder.—The Recovery of the King's Letter.

To escape the perils of one journey seemed but the forerunner of others in another; and as human events are uncertain, the like success is not always attainable, and though Reuben Clifton had been successful in baffling foes of no ordinary character and daring, yet he was not so regardless of the past, but he was aware the like might happen on his return to Winchester as happened on his journey up.

It is difficult to say how long we may escape the shafts that fate may aim at us; we may do so now and then, but we shall be hurt in the long-run. Youth and high spirits joined to success, however, are not always safe; as to the probabilities of success or failure, they engender but little fear; and even precaution is often disdained by those who stand most in need of it. Reuben Clifton had been successful; he knew it, and it was a great thing for a youth of sixteen to escape the dangers of such a journey—to have baffled crafty and designing men,—to have seen the King, and to have delivered his letter safely; and, moreover, he was now entrusted with the answer in return to the Lord Warden of Winchester's letter. If the letter to the King was of so much consequence that he was so beset, and his life attempted four different times, the answer must likewise be of importance, and it might be that he would be again beset by his enemies.

'I will not return by exactly the same route that I took," he muttered, 'in coming up. I will strike off to the left below Staines, and then proceed towards the road that leads to Farnham.'

He quitted the suburbs of the metropolis, then entirely detached from the city, and proceeded on his journey with something like speed, for his good horse was now refreshed, and his spirits seemed to equal those of his rider.

'I must rest myself somewhere on the road; I will push on, and when I come near the first house that promises quiet and rest, then I will halt and there pass the night, or so much of it as may serve for myself and horse, for I cannot ride all night without a halt; besides, I might meet more dangers on the road than can be well met; unpremeditated enemies I may encounter, who might be willing to cut my throat for the value of my buttons.'

He touched his horse with his wand and started onwards with an increased speed, and he soon was some miles distant from London. The sun was setting behind some clouds—the shadows were falling fast and thick, and he became aware that he must soon take the first place that offered, or else he must be content to travel all night, for no one would take him in after dark, or at least, he ran some risk. About an hour's riding brought him to a road-side hostel, one which, from its extent and size, promised good quarters, and, by the bustle connected with the house, it seemed that there were many visitors stopping there.

'It may be that I shall not succeed in obtaining a bed, but that is no great evil; I can sleep beneath the manger, Altamount will then be my guardian; we can sleep together; such a night's rest has been a boon to many a better man—but—I will remain if I can.'

The house was a large place—more rooms and places kept as store-rooms than were inhabited, but there was ample room where he could expect accommodation. He rode up to the door, and called loudly for the house, and in another minute a man appeared, who turned out to be the landlord.

'Here,' said the host, 'here I am; who wants me?'

'Can I have accommodation for myself and horse?' said Reuben Clifton.

'You can, young sir; and though I don't boast of what I can do, yet if a soft bed and good feed both for you and your animal will satisfy you, I think I can accommodate you better than any other man in the three kingdoms.'

'That is saying a good deal,' said Reuben, dismounting.

'But not more than I can perform, young sir: you shall be the judge of that, my good sir. Here, you Will, come and see to the gentleman's horse; come quick, you lazy clown, or I'll soon see reason why you are not more attentive. Will, Will! where are you? come here.'

'Here I am,' said a deep, gruff voice.

They both turned round, and saw the ostler rising from off a heap of straw close by them.

'Here I am, here I am.'

'You lazy, idle hound, what do you mean by laying about here all day? you ought to be made a hewer of wood and drawer of water, you ought, you sot.'

'Ah! it's all very well, master. As for a hewer of wood, that is, I reckon, a much better trade than mine; and as for drawing of water, why that I have a pretty good turn of; and as for lying about all day, why that I can hardly do at night; and as for sottishness, why I can only get the water I draw.'

'Oh! you are always grumbling. Come, attend to the horse.'

'Yes, my good fellow, do your duty by him, and I will not forget you,' said Reuben Clifton.

'Will you walk in, sir?'

'Yes, when I have seen my horse accommodated, for then I can afford to look after myself.'

So saying, Reuben followed the ostler from the space in front of the house through a gate to a stone, enclosed yard, where there were sheds and stables all around of one character, and another for various purposes connected with the inn, for in those times men's goods required the protection of high walls to secure the owners in possession of their goods, and even that, at times, was but a poor and inefficient barrier to the stronger arm of those who could plunder with weapons in their hands.

The stables were a long low range, but had lofts above, and into one of these the ostler led Altamount, followed by Reuben, who surveyed the place with a scrutinizing eye.

'This, then, is the stable.'

'Yes, young sir, it is; and I guess there arn't better stables between here and London, nor as far on the other side of the road as one that lets a good bed for you and your nag; though old hunks, the landlord himself, says so, he's not far wrong, but he's plaguy short-handed with those who, like myself, have to serve him.'

'And the horse's feed—when will you do that?'

'I'll come and let you know, sir; you may depend upon me—I will come, sir. I always cares for the guest as cares for me; and as for the old curmudgeon as is landlord, I don't valley his good opinion a brass button.'

Reuben Clifton left the stables and entered the house. 'Twas a public room, in which were many men, apparently arquebusiers, for they were all armed with that weapon.

He sat down at a table that was unoccupied, and having ordered some refreshments, which was the usual custom, want it or not, for the good of the house it must be ordered; and there, in silence and unnoticed, he sat for some time.

The guests were laughing and joking among themselves, though now and then they cast a look towards him, but that was a thing he could not feel alarmed at, as the same thing was done by himself towards them; yet what he had encountered caused him to be cautious and suspicious to a degree.

However, he saw nothing to justify any alarm whatever, and when the host came in he said—

'Which is to be my sleeping-room?'

'There is no choice to-night, sir; but one that overlooks the yard is yours—it is small, but there is a good bed, and a traveller may go farther and fare worse, even where there is a choice.'

'I am content, so that I can sleep quiet, and rise early, for I am on the road by day break.'

'As you will, sir.'

'Please, sir,' said the ostler, 'the feeding time is come.'

'I will go with you,' said Reuben Clifton, and he arose and left the room to follow the ostler to the stable, where he saw Altamount fairly fed and sorted down for the night, and then, before leaving the stable, he said to the ostler—

'Feed him again before daylight, as I shall be off by the earliest dawn. If this be done honestly, you shall have your reward for your trouble.'

'I will do it, young sir,' said the ostler, as he closed the stable-door; 'and now, unless any new arrivals come, I have done my labours for to-day, at least I hope so.'

Reuben returned to the inn, but by some mistake he took the wrong passage, or opened the wrong door, which led him into a small room. He was about to retire, when, to his surprise, he heard his own name mentioned by some one in the next room, who appeared to be speaking to several others.

He closed the door and advanced towards the wainscoating, through which he had heard the sounds proceed. There was a little window, before which hung a dusky, dirty curtain.

Drawing this curtain a little on one side he looked into a room, where several men were seated, drinking, round some tables. A second glance convinced him it was the public room, which he had just left to attend to his horse.

What could they mean? His own name sounded distinctly enough upon his ears. If any one there was aware of his name, he was also acquainted with his errand, that boded him no good.

He listened, and he distinctly heard the men who had crowded together converse, and upon a subject that was of the most vital importance to him.

'I know him; there can be no mistake about that matter, none at all. I followed him all the way to London, but how to get at it is the difficulty.'

'The letter is delivered.'

'We know that well enough, and, after having missed intercepting the letter, to intercept answering, is of importance; he has the King's letter about him.'

'But where abouts is it concealed?'

'In his jacket; I am sure of that, for, if you noticed him, you might see he was continually putting his hand to his pocket, which proves to me there the letter is concealed.'

'I saw no signs of a pocket.'

'Perhaps not; nor did I, but yet he has no doubt a secret pocket, or something of the same sort. However, he took no care of any other part of his dress as he did that.'

'Well, well, I dare say you are right; the plan, then, will be to get his jacket away from him.'

'Which can only be peaceably done when he is asleep.'

'He will sleep like a cat, with one eye open. You may depend upon it he will never be caught napping, and then comes all the clumsy expedients of groping about in the dark, and getting foiled after all one's care and trouble.'

'Granted; but who thinks it necessary to go to all that bother? Wait till he has put himself in such a position that we can give him the contents of an arquebus.'

'Pshaw! and then the jacket and letter will be riddled with shot, and, what is worse, saturated with blood.'

'Wait until he is gone to bed, and when he has taken off his jacket, then fire at him. He is sure to fall, and one of us can run in and carry off jacket and all.'

'That is a very good plan, a very good plan, I reckon;

but who's to fire at him? and where are you to fire from? You must fire in the dark, and you may miss him.'

'If I should, I will undertake to go in and finish him with the butt end of my arquebus; but there are enough here to help me if it should not turn out as we expect, besides, the room he sleeps in is commanded from several points, within half-shot considerably. What more could be desired than to wait for him, then pour the contents in upon him, and rush in and carry off the prize? That done, we may expect to be well paid for our part of the business.'

'That is very smoothly laid down, and I do not see any reason why we should fail.'

'None under heaven, unless he escape before he be shot at; besides which, there is no other accident that is at all likely to foil us in our plan.'

'He cannot escape every window—every alley will receive

its appropriate sentinel. We shall have our posts; so that he cannot escape, and, should he attempt it, butcher him at once.'

'A very good plan.'

'He cannot escape; we are too numerous and too well armed; besides, we have sworn his destruction. I fear that we shall have him, too, easily; he will not show the fun I might have expected of him. He's cooped up, and having no chance, it will take all the courage out of him.'

'So it will; but I don't know, if we shoot him suddenly, there will be no room for any display.'

'Nor any need; he is safe, and will be more so by-and-by, and that's all we need care. I have seen his bed-room—I will fire into it, and then rush into the room, carry off the jacket, and then, when we find we have got the letter, I will

start for London as fast as my legs will let me. You know our rendezvous?'

'Agreed, agreed! in the mean time, we hold possession of the house until my youngster is disposed of.'

'The exact state of the case; but if he attempt to make any escape, you may stab or shoot him, no matter which, so long as he is disposed of; but shooting him in his room, with his jacket off, has the preference and advantage.'

* * * * * *

'The murderous villains!' muttered Clifton; 'if I can baffle them yet I will. I will endeavour to find a way out, seek safety with my good horse, and then they may catch me, if they can; but it will be of no use to attempt to get out by force—I may have more shot in my carcase than I shall ever have leisure to pick out.'

34   ORDEAL BY TOUCH.

He left the room, intending to go by the front door to the one that went into the yard, but he had taken the wrong door. There were two in the little room, which led him round to the back of the house, and near the back entrance were stationed two arquebusiers, who were in conversation.

These men no sooner saw Clifton than they handled their arms as if preparing for an immediate attempt, but in a manner as little ostentatious as possible, and Clifton saw it was useless to attempt an escape by them, for they were well prepared for him, and it would only end in his death and the capture of the letter.

He found the other doors in the same state, and beneath the windows were arquebusiers, lounging about.

'I am fairly beleaguered this time,' he muttered ; ' I must see what I can do up-stairs. I will go to my bed-room. When I pull off my jacket, that is to be the signal for my death—ah, well ! that is news of some import, too.'

He entered the common room, and there he saw the man who had undertaken to shoot him. He had just examined the loading and priming of his weapon, and, feeling that it was as it should be, placed it against the wall by itself.

Reuben sat down at the table next to the weapon, and the others then went out, while his executioner went to sleep. While he dosed Reuben contrived to extract the balls from the weapon, and place them in his own pocket, and replaced the arquebus.

He had a very narrow escape from detection, for the man, partially roused up from his nap, but seeing Reuben sitting and eating some of his victuals, he thought all was right, and slept again.

'Now,' thought Reuben, 'if I can persuade them I am dead when he discharges his weapon at me, then he will have the letter—that I cannot avoid, but I may recover it ; if not, the news that it has been taken will be enough.'

He sat for some time, and then walking to the window and seeing it was quite dark, and the moon rising, he walked up to his sleeping-room. When he opened the door, he pondered for a few moments, and then he took his jacket off, as if he were going to sleep, but had only done so when the thundering report of the arquebus came upon his ear, and the crashing of some glass and splintering of wood, and the place was filled with smoke.

Reuben uttered a loud cry, and fell to the floor, where he seemed to be in a death-struggle, and at that moment the arquebusier entered the apartment, stepped over his prostrate body, seizing the jacket, which he crushed in his hand to ascertain if it contained the letter.

'I have it now,' he muttered ; 'and hey for London !'

He left the room and quitted the house, and Reuben saw by the moonlight that he and his companions parted company in the road, and he started on the London-road with all the speed imaginable, having no companion with him.

'That is fortunate,' muttered Clifton to himself, as he quitted the room. 'Now for my good Altamount—we will soon overtake that cowardly fellow, and see if I cannot repossess myself of the letter.'

So saying, he quietly made his way through the house, until he got into the yard, when he made his way to the stable, which was fastened, but he soon tore open the door by wrenching off the staple that held the lock, and then he was not long in finding out Altamount's stall, for his neigh directed him to it.

It took but little time to put saddle and bridle on, and leading him to the stable door, and then looking about for a weapon of some sort, he seized upon a short bludgeon, or rod of some kind, that lay by the stable-door, and then proceeded to examine the gate, and he found he was unable to force that—it was secure beyond any force he could exert.

Suddenly, however, he made up his mind, and, mounting his horse, he walked him gently up to the gate ; the sagacious animal rested his under-jaw upon the top bar a moment, and then he turned back ten or fifteen paces, and pressing his heels near the horse's flanks, he cantered up to the gate and leaped clean over into the space that faced the inn.

'Now,' he muttered, 'I am free of this place, I will soon overtake that rascal. He is more than an hour a-head of me, and will be an hour-and a-half's journey a-head before I can reach him, about seven miles, if he has no horse, which I think he has not ; but if he has I will overtake him before he reaches London, though two hours' ride bring me there.'

The moon was up, and the road lay through a beautiful, wild, and picturesque country, and by the light of the moon ;

but he pushed on, regardless of all that, at a rapid pace. The scene changed continually ; the rate he was travelling at gave him no time to notice one scene before another was present.

After a half hour's ride or less, he came up with a man, who appeared to be walking towards London at a quick step. He turned round as Reuben came up, as if apprehensive of an attack, but, seeing only one man, he pursued his way again.

Dismounting he fastened his horse to a tree, and then strode after the man with a hasty step, that in less than five minutes brought him up to the man's side.

Hearing a noise the fellow turned round, and seeing Reuben without his jacket, he staggered ; but when the moon's rays fell upon his features, they gave him a peculiar and ghastly look, and then he gave a deep groan, and crossed himself, for he believed himself beset with the spirit of the murdered messenger.

'The letter,' murmured Reuben, holding out his hand, and speaking in a hollow voice, ' the letter.'

'Ave Maria ! Pater Noster !' muttered the man, endeavouring to recollect some prayers, and reeling side ways from Reuben, as if he dreaded to be touched by anything superhuman.

Reuben, seeing the man's terror, determined to take advantage of it, and dealt him a heavy blow on the head with the staff that he had in his hand ; but, thanks to the fellow's steel cap, it saved his life on that occasion.

However, he reeled, and nearly fell to the earth, but it awakened him to a real sense of his danger, and he arose and rushed at Reuben for the purpose of grappling with him ; but the latter, not doubting the man's strength superior to his own, met him with a repetition of the first blow, which fell upon his arm, and nearly disabled him. Then Reuben was compelled to grapple with the ruffian.

After a desperate struggle of some minutes he threw the assassin down, and as he fell he struck his head on a large stone that lay by the wayside, and they parted. Reuben sprang to his feet, seized his staff, and beat the fellow till he neither moved hand nor foot.

Then, with the quickness of thought, he repossessed himself of the letter and his jacket, which the fellow had secured as a memento of his exploit in shooting Reuben, putting it on, and restoring the letter to its place as well as he could, for it had been ripped open to get at it.

Taking a last look at the man who yet lay motionless on the road, Reuben turned from the spot, and walked to the place where he had fastened Altamount.

'Now, my good steed,' he said, 'we have nearly fifty miles of country before us. We must now push on till we reach Winchester ; neither rest nor stop must now be ours.'

The good steed seemed to be well aware of what was said to him, and he started off at a speed that showed his willingness to return homewards.

'There will be no pursuit,' thought Reuben, as he travelled along, and had passed through Alton, 'especially if that fellow rises not from the earth, and, if he do, there will be but little chance of his communicating with his fellows for many hours at least. I expect I shall be at Winchester before they know of it.'

*   *   *   *   *

After some hours of hard riding the towers of Winchester rose to view, and the cathedral itself could be seen from the road. It was not long after this ere the gates of Winchester itself opened to receive him, after his perilous journey had been completed.

CHAPTER XII.

The Lord Warden's Anxiety.—The Question to Sir Rupert Brent.—The Welcome Announcement.

As day after day elapsed, and Reuben Clifton came not, the Lord Warden of Winchester became extremely anxious as to what had befallen him.

Over and over again he regretted that he had sent so young a person on an errand fraught with so much danger. He accused himself with precipitancy ; and, with all the bitterness of regret, he told John Elkington that, if anything happened to the boy, he should never cease accusing himself of rashness for exposing him to so much danger.

'He has been gone now,' he said, 'more than ample time for his progress to London, as well as his return ; but still he comes not, nor have we the remotest knowledge of his fate.'

This remark was made to John Elkington as they sat together in that same apartment which had witnessed the signal defeat of the assassin.

'I am not so much disposed,' said Elkington, 'as you seem yourself, to regard the boy's absence in a gloomy light; the fact is, that many things might occur in such a journey to delay him, if not altogether to impede his progress for a few days. From what I have seen of him I have great faith in his skill and judgment; and although I must confess to you, at the first blush of the affair, I did not like the idea of employing one so young, yet, after a time, I became reconciled to it.'

'I am glad to hear you say so.'

'It is my genuine opinion: I think the boy more likely to escape the dangers of the road and the perils of such an enterprise than a man.'

'Well, that was my own impression.'

'And an impression you might well entertain; for it is easy to perceive, that although having but the stature and appearance of the boy, that youth possessed the matured intellect of a man.'

'So I thought, or I should not have employed him. Besides, fully hoping and expecting that he would be successful, the pleasure of rewarding him was no small aid to my anticipations. If he do not return to-night, I shall begin to entertain the most serious apprehensions regarding him.'

'And I likewise, I must confess; but now that we have this Jesuit, Sir Rupert Brent, in safe keeping for some time, do you not think it possible enough that his insolent spirit may be tamed sufficiently to enable us to get some information from him?'

'I doubt that much; you do not seem to be aware of what these Jesuits really are. The specimens you have seen of them at court were by no means the most wily and cunning of the tribe. Those who appear openly are selected from among those of the fraternity who are not considered talented enough to work in secret.'

'It may be so.'

'And yet, if it please you to ask any questions of Brent, he is, of course, at your disposal.'

'I think that I should like to do so. That he is capable of being terrified I have already proved, and that he loves himself so well that he would do anything to escape personal injury, I am well aware. It is from these feelings and motives that I am induced to believe I could accomplish something.'

'Be it so; I will order him to be brought into the guard-room for examination.'

This was done, and in a few minutes the Lord Warden and John Elkington walked towards that same apartment, where the Jesuit, when he was first brought in a prisoner, was placed previous to being consigned to a dungeon.

They found it guarded, and an oil lamp burning upon the table, by the side of which stood Sir Rupert Brent, looking somewhat pale after his incarceration, and probably not a little anxious to know what was about to be done with him.

When he saw John Elkington and the Lord Warden he strove to put on a look of defiance; but yet it was easy to perceive, through the mask of such a feeling, that he was but ill at ease.

Elkington advanced and stood opposite the prisoner, while the Lord Warden seated himself.

'Father Georges,' he said, 'it is the wish of the Lord Warden that I should communicate to you a decision upon your case.'

'I presume,' said the Jesuit, 'that you are now convinced that you have no grounds whatever for detaining me; but what compensation am I to have? and what excuses can be made to me for the inconvenience I have suffered?'

'You are premature in these remarks; it is not intended to offer you compensation, nor is it intended to release you. At the discretion of the Lord Warden you are to be removed to London, there to be lodged in the Tower, or remain here in more easy confinement, according as you answer or not the questions that may be put to you.'

'The Tower of London?'

'Yes, and the transition from that to the block is, as you well know, short and simple.'

Georges evidently trembled.

'I am perfectly innocent,' he said, 'of any offence of a political nature. As regards my private quarrel with Ranulph Hensman, I do not see what that has to do with consigning me to the Tower of London, and besides, it is over. I had authority,

certainly, to be a serious annoyance to him, but you have taken that authority from me by depriving me of the document which enabled me to call upon the ecclesiastical authorities to aid me in seizing upon his wife, who committed the offence of breaking from a convent and uniting herself with a heretic.'

'It is true that in your attempts against the peace of mind of Ranulph Hensman you have been foiled, that is strictly true; but the present are dangerous times, and it is more than suspected that the Jesuits have some designs on foot which it is the duty of those connected with the administration of the laws to prevent.'

'I know of no such designs.'

'Father Georges, you are a clever, politic, intriguing man; your own conduct has shown that you are evidently selfish; you are unscrupulous, and care nothing for party or association except so far as your own interest is concerned. You are the last man that I should think would be willing to die for any cause, provided you could live for your own advantage.'

'This is bold language, and somewhat ungracious to a prisoner in the power of his enemies.'

'You are much mistaken if you suppose that it owes any of its boldness to that circumstance. It would be precisely the same were you free and I the prisoner.'

'It may be so. I do not call myself in a condition to deny such an asserted fact, and therefore do I say it may be so, but that makes not the ungraciousness of the remark less to one who really is a prisoner. I know not what more you want of me than what you have already obtained.'

'These are mere words,' said John Elkington, 'they are not the medium by which you tell us what you think, but they are the means by which you conceal your real thoughts and intentions; and now listen to me, Georges, you are in a good position if you please to make yourself a martyr to the cause which you espouse. If it suit your purpose to covet the crown of martyrdom, I am aware it will be useless to attempt to turn you from it; but I do not think that such is your intention.'

'What then?'

'On the other hand, if you will give such information to what I may call the King's party as will enable them to defeat the Jesuitical attempts that are now making, I can assure you oblivion for the past and a rich reward for the future. You shall have a free pardon for every thing you have done or may have projected doing, and by continuing to reside in England you can be perfectly safe, and be assured of a large, independent income.'

Sir Rupert Brent was silent for several moments, and then he said, in a low tone—

'We have so many instances of prisoners being entrapped by such promises as these, to make statements, which afterwards have been used greatly to their detriment. Without pledging myself to a moment's favourable consideration of your proposals, I wish to ask you what means you have of assuring me of their sincerity?'

This was a question which both the Lord Warden and John Elkington probably might have answered, if they had liked, in such a manner as to convince the Jesuit they had the power, if they chose, to make such terms; but then such a declaration upon their part would have involved a confidence in Sir Rupert Brent they had not the remotest idea of bestowing upon him.

After some hesitation the Lord Warden spoke, saying—

'You know me, my rank and my station. You know that I never have had other than a reputation for keeping my word, and I now pledge myself that whatever John Elkington promises I will see performed.'

'That is well enough,' said the Jesuit; 'I will give twenty-four hours' consideration to the question, but if I am again consigned to the dungeon from which I have been now brought, I will give it no consideration whatever. Place me in more comfortable lodgings, and it may be the better for your own purposes.'

'Have you any objection to that, my Lord Warden?' said John Elkington.

'None whatever. I can see no rational objection. I am not one who considers that the security of a prisoner depends so much upon his dungeon as upon his guards. You shall remain here, Sir Rupert Brent, in this guard-room, if it will suit you better.'

'It is preferable to the hole in which I have been confined, and much more likely to forward your own designs. Come to me again when twenty-four hours have elapsed, and I shall

...e in a condition to return you an answer to the proposal you have made me.'

This was a state of things which could not be very well objected to, and both the Lord Warden and John Elkington left the Jesuit, with a firm impression that he would accept the terms that had been offered to him.

They did not come to this conclusion from reasoning upon the fact that he was a Jesuit, but they arrived at it from a knowledge of him as an individual. They knew that, as an order, the Jesuits were a powerful body, and that it was considered so infamous as well as so dangerous among them for any one of their number to betray the secret resolves of the fraternity, that it would have been quite hopeless to make the proposal they did to Sir Rupert Brent, had they not had a full conviction of what an unscrupulous ruffian he was, and a strong idea that he cared much more for himself and for the carrying out of his own ambitious projects, than he did for the whole Jesuitical fraternity, or for any odium that might attach to his own personal character.

Certainly John Elkington was more sanguine of the results than was the Lord Warden, who was a better judge of the fraternity of Jesuits than he; but still he considered there was a hope of a favourable result—if only a hope.

A sentinel was placed over Sir Rupert Brent, with orders not to spare him, if he should make any attempt to escape; and, in order to make assurance doubly sure, the door of the guard-room was left unlocked, and the sentinel was ordered to march into it about every quarter of an hour, in order to see what the prisoner was about.

Twice during the progress of his guard had he obeyed these directions, and appeared before the eyes of the prisoner. A third time the Jesuit spoke to him.

'I hope,' he said, 'I have a good Catholic on guard over me.'

'I hope so too,' said the soldier, as he crossed himself.

'I am a priest,' said the Jesuit, 'and as such, at all events, entitled to some respect from you.'

'A priest?'

'Yes, most certainly. Why should you be surprised?'

'It is enough to surprise anyone to see a priest with moustaches of a cavalier, and in such a costume as you wear.'

'The interests of the holy Catholic Church sometimes require that her servants should disguise themselves.'

'Well, that may be.'

'This imprisonment is nothing to me, because I am an innocent man, and were it not for something else that grievously troubles me, I should be content.'

'And what may that be— is it a secret, holy sir?'

'To heretic ears it would be; but not to you, who tell me you are a good Catholic. I have promised this night to say some masses for the soul of one departed.'

'And you cannot say them?'

'I cannot here, for my spirit is too much troubled. What I wish is, that some other priest of Winchester cathedral may say them for me. Could you provide me a messenger, who would be handsomely rewarded for carrying a line or two, addressed to one of the fathers of the cathedral?'

The soldier shook his head as he said—

'Why not apply to the Lord Warden? such a simple request, I am sure, he would grant.'

'No, I have shown too much indignation at my imprisonment to ask any favour of the Lord Warden, otherwise I would, and of course he would grant it; but, as it is, I would rather some honest fellow like yourself made a few gold pieces by the transaction, than I would ask a favour of anyone. Will you do it?'

The soldier was silent for a few minutes, and then he said, in a low tone,—

'I shall be off guard in another hour, and, as you say there is no harm in it, write what you wish, and I will take it for you, and bring you back an answer.'

'You will?'

'Most assuredly I will.'

There were writing materials in the guard-room, and Sir Rupert Brent wrote upon a small piece of paper the one word, 'No.'

This he addressed to 'Father Redell, Winchester Cathedral.'

'Take this,' he said, to the soldier, 'and when you see Father Redell, ask him for five gold pieces as your reward.'

'I will, holy sir.'

The Jesuit looked so much elated at the success of this manœuvre, that he paced the guard-room to and fro, muttering his congratulations to himself.

'They will understand,' he said, 'well the meaning of that one word which I have written—it is preconcerted; it means much, and is far superior to writing in cypher. They will understand how I am situated, and what kind of exertions to make for my release. Who would have supposed I should have so easily outwitted the Lord Warden?'

When the soldier's two hours' guard was over he gave a significant nod to Sir Rupert Brent, as much as to say that he fully remembered what he had to do, and then, as deliberately as possible, he walked to the room in which Ranulph Hensman, the Lord Warden's secretary, sat, and handed him the note, saying—

'The prisoner wants this taken to Winchester cathedral. You are a better judge than I, Master Hensman, whether it ought to go or not; and if you were not a better judge, it is my duty to bring it to you, so there it is.'

'You have done quite right, indeed you could not have done better; it is your duty, as you say, but you shall lose nothing by vigilant performance of it. Had you any special instructions with this letter?'

'None, further than to go to the cathedral and ask Father Redell for five gold pieces, for bringing him the letter, and then, I suppose, if he had given me an answer, I was to have brought that back.'

''Tis well; I will speak to the Lord Warden upon the subject—you shall hear more of it to-morrow.'

Ranulph Hensman at once proceeded to the Warden, and showed him the mysterious little word which had been written by the prisoner. Of course they could make nothing of it in the way of reading. The one word, 'no,' was perfectly enigmatical; but that it contained some hidden meaning, which was intended to be a warning to the Jesuitical party at Winchester, there could be no doubt.

The question of what was to be done under such circumstances, was easier asked than answered, but when the Lord Warden had stated that he could not think of a judicious course to pursue, Ranulph Hensman spoke, saying—

'If it please you, my lord, I should like much to go to the cathedral, not with this letter but with one exactly like it, and see this Father Redell, to whom it is addressed.'

'I do not like your running any risks, Ranulph.'

'There would be little or none. I think I can copy the Jesuit's hand, pretty well.'

'What would you say in it?'

'Why instead of no, I would write yes. If no give them a correct information, yes must lead them astray, so that no harm can result from the correspondence.'

'I must confess,' said the Warden, 'I like the idea of endeavouring to get an answer from this Father Redell. It is in these matters diamond-cut diamond, and we must take all the advantages we can. Go, Ranulph, if you will, and I will wait for your return.'

Thus empowered to set out upon his mission, the secretary prepared a note in imitation of the one which the Jesuit had written, only with the essential difference of the word 'yes' being in it instead of the word 'no,' and took his way, with rapid steps, towards the cathedral.

As the hour was already past that which he usually returned home, he thought of making a round, on his way to the cathedral, in order to call at home, and tell Alice not to expect him for some time, but, upon second thoughts, he abandoned this idea, for he not only considered she was perfectly safe, since the imprisonment of the Jesuit, but he thought, and justly so, that it would be establishing a bad precedent for him to do so, as another time he might be detained without power of giving her intimation of the fact.

So he decided upon going directly onward to the cathedral.

CHAPTER XIII.

Ranulph Hensman's Adventure—Father Redell's Answer to the Letter.—Reuben and Altamount.

THE distance was not very great, and Hensman soon reached the cathedral porch. He passed into the church, which he found deserted, and he began to consider how he could fulfil his mission.

But, before he could resolve on any plan, he saw a boy in the white surplice of a chorister walking down one of the aisles, and him he instantly accosted.

'Can you tell me, boy, if Father Redell is within the building?'

'Yes, certainly,' said the boy, 'he is now in the refectory, if you wish to see him.'

'But how can I get there?'

'Oh! you can't get there at all—no strangers are allowed; but I will tell him he is wanted, and he will come out.'

'Thank you, I will wait for him on this spot.'

The boy passed out of the church by a small door at the side of the altar, leaving Ranulph Hensman waiting for him, not without considerable anxiety as to the result of the adventure in which he had engaged.

In about five minutes the boy returned and informed him that the priest was coming, and presently an ecclesiastic of venerable appearance came into the church.

He looked inquiringly around him, and when he saw Hensman, he fixed a pair of piercing eyes upon him, as if he would read his very soul. Hensman saluted him respectfully, and then said—

'Holy sir, if you be Father Redell, I have a letter for you from one who is so anxious to have it delivered that he bade me ask you for five gold pieces for my trouble.'

'Indeed, my son, that seems a large demand merely for the carriage of a letter, but if its contents will justify so much you shall not go without your reward.'

'I thank you, holy sir; there is the letter; I will trust entirely to your judgment concerning its contents.'

The priest opened the letter and then started slightly.

'Young man,' he said, 'you bring this from Sir Rupert Brent?'

'I do,' said Hensman.

'Wait here awhile and you shall have your answer and your gold pieces.'

Father Redell hastily disappeared by the same door that he had entered, and, believing that he might possibly be some time, Ranulph Hensman sat down in a confessional to rest himself.

He had not been there many minutes, when a man entered the church and sauntered up and down close to where he was, as if waiting for some one, and presently another appeared enveloped in a cloak, who said to the first one—

'Who holds the key?'

'Saint Peter,' said the other.

Then they linked themselves arm-in-arm, and walked along the aisle.

As they passed the confessional one said—

'You will attend our adjourned meeting to-night in the vault.'

'Most certainly.'

'And I hope we shall hear some news of Georges; it is an unlucky circumstance.'

Then they glanced around them carefully, and one taking a small key from his pocket, opened the concealed door which we have before mentioned to the reader, and then they both passed through it, closing it carefully behind them.

Ranulph Hensman was well pleased with the amount of information he had gained, small though it was. At all events it let him know that something was going on which it would be well to watch, and his possession now of the watchword of the confederates was a great point, inasmuch as it would enable him, probably without danger, to make inquiries, and perhaps to listen to their very counsels.

He had not much time, however, left him for thought, as Father Redell now returned, bearing in his hand a small note, which he gave to Hensman, who advanced to meet him, saying—

'You will take this back to the person from whom you brought the note addressed to me, and give it faithfully into his own hands. Here are the five gold pieces you were promised. Be faithful and discreet, and you will earn the good wishes and prayers of the Church.'

Ranulph Hensman put on a demure countenance, as if he really set some good value upon 'the prayers and good wishes of the Church;' and then, with what he hoped was an answer in full to Sir Rupert Brent's letter, he made the best of his way to the Lord Warden's.

Upon his arrival there, although the hour was getting late, he found that he was anxiously expected by both John Elkington and the Warden, for the latter had sent for him to give his advice upon the occasion.

The note given to Ranulph Hensman by Father Redell—unlike the one of which he had been the bearer from Sir Rupert Brent—was carefully sealed, so that the expectation, that it contained something particular, was wound up to the highest point.

The Lord Warden opened it; and then, to their great disappointment, they found only the word 'occasionally' written in it. They looked at each other for some moments with silence, and then the Warden could not forbear laughing, as he said—

'Now really, this is too bad. These Jesuits are determined not to give us a chance of understanding them. What, on earth, can we make of 'no,' and 'occasionally?''

'This is some secret mode,' said John Elkington, 'of carrying on a correspondence; it is quite useless to attempt to unravel it; but, from what Ranulph Hensman has intimated, I think he has done something more than bring this enigmatic letter from Father Redell.'

'I am happy to say I have,' was Hensman's reply: 'I have certainly acquired some information—I hope of more importance than this.'

He then related to his well-pleased listeners what he had overheard while concealed in the confessional; and concluded by saying—

'I am certainly strongly of opinion that the Jesuits are holding secret meetings for some desperate object, about the church. I have their watchword; and I shall have no fear in venturing among them.'

'Nay,' said the Lord Warden, 'to that I must oppose my interdict: it must not be. By the use of their watchword you might get among them; but, you may depend they know each other too well not soon to detect the fact that you are a stranger. We will do what we can, and shrink from no general or ordinary risks, but we will not attempt impossibilities.'

'I must, of course, bow to your decision,' said Hensman; 'but I should like again to go and hang about the church, with a hope of being able, by the use of the signal I know, to get some valuable information.'

'Do that, Hensman, but be careful. Go well armed, and most specially guard yourself against being decoyed to any place where your life might be taken by power of numbers.'

At this moment it was announced to the Lord Warden by John Elkington, who, upon hearing a knocking at the door of the apartment, had gone to see who it was, that one of his attendants wished to speak to him.

The man was desired to enter the room; and then his exultation at the tidings he brought almost overpowered his habitual respect for his master, and he said aloud—

'My lord, my lord—good news! Altamount, whom we all thought lost, has come back again.'

'Altamount—the horse!—Good Heavens, what can have become of Reuben Clifton?'

'Oh!—young Reuben, my lord—I forgot to mention him—he is on Altamount's back, my lord.'

'You scoundrel,' cried the Warden, 'I suppose you think more of the horse than the boy; but, thank Heaven, we shall look upon him once again. What a great relief this is to my mind! Show him up at once.'

'Altamount, my lord? He will never come up the stairs.'

'No, you villain!—Reuben Clifton. You know well what I mean.'

CHAPTER XIV.

Alice alone—The Manuscript—The Night Alarm.

ALICE HENSMAN sat alone, waiting for the return of her husband, who was engaged in the manner we have described to the reader, and who suffered no less anxiety than she did to return to the bosom of his family.

After finding that he did not arrive at his usual time, she began to be doubtful as to when he would come; and although these doubts were certainly not unmingled without some fear, she had been so particularly enjoined by Hensman not to augur anything ill from an unexpectedly prolonged absence on his part, that she was not so alarmed as she otherwise might have been.

Besides, it was something to know that her arch enemy, the Jesuit Georges, was not in a position to cause her any uneasiness, and there was no one else whom she considered that she had any cause to dread.

She knew that in those ticklish and feverish times something might very well happen to detain Hensman at the

Lord Warden's, and therefore she would not allow herself to feel such an amount of alarm as perhaps really might have been justifiable, and perhaps which really was struggling with other feelings at her heart.

'He will return soon,' she said, 'and I will be calm until he does. Of course the Lord Warden has need of his services, or he would be here. The only man whom I have cause to dread, is not in a situation to harm me. The Jesuit is a prisoner; myself and my children are alike safe. Wherefore should I then feel these sensations of alarm, merely because Ranulph Hensman is beyond his time!'

At the thought of her little ones, Alice rose, and taking a lamp in her hand, she proceeded across a small passage, which led to the apartment in which the children were reposing.

Treading so lightly as not to endanger the awaking of them from their innocent sleep, she gazed upon them for some time with an expression of rapturous affection beaming from her eyes.

'Sleep on,' she said, 'and may your repose be ever as calm and placid as it now is—may you never know the dread and persecution to which I have been exposed!'

She shaded the lamp with her hand so that its rays might not disturb the little sleepers; and after gazing at them for a time, she turned and left the apartment, casting behind her many a lingering look of affection ere she closed the door, and again sought the solitude of her own apartment.

This visit to the children had awakened better and happier feelings in her mind. She was more composed, and sat down to think of the past, and to dream of the future, much more serenely and calmly than she had done before.

She hoped that those troublous times would soon pass away, and that, by the expulsion of the Jesuits from England, (a measure which she had no doubt would soon ensue,) peace would be restored to the distracted land, and none of those fears which now beset her, despite herself, would find a home in her heart.

But now again, as she heard the midnight hour strike, and no appearance of Ranulph Hensman's return was manifest, her fears began again to assume a strong ascendancy over her.

She went upon the staircase and listened attentively, but not the slightest sound met her ears—all was still and calm as the very grave itself.

'All is hushed,' she said, and that, at all events, speaks of safety. I am alone, and that is all. I can have nothing to fear—nothing, nothing! I should indeed, if that violent man, that bad-passioned and demoniac priest were free, have cause for alarm, but now I have none—none whatever; but I would that Hensman had returned! He may have other enemies besides the villain Georges the Jesuit.'

With a shudder to think that this might be the case, she sat down and drew towards her, her work-box. A glance at its contents reminded her that Ranulph had put into her hands on the preceding evening a few sheets of paper, which he had found in the library of the Lord Warden, and with the contents of which he had told her to entertain herself, if he should ever be absent late.

This was a great resource in her present state of mind, for although she could not get rid of her fears, she felt at the same time that they were but imaginary, and that, could she occupy herself in any way, they would soon be dissipated. Upon opening the manuscript she found it to contain a regular narrative, in which she soon became deeply interested.

It commenced as follows, and contained a most true picture of the times:—

'Holy brother,' said the friar, 'as times go now we are more likely to become beggars and outcasts in this world than rise in our profession—in our holy calling, I should have said.'

'Yes, brother, as you say, there is more probability of our becoming the seekers of that charity which we have been the bestowers upon our fellow-creatures. It seems hard, after so many hundreds of years that we have held our rights, that we should be deprived of them because his Holiness the Pope should refuse to do that which the great man in this country should desire.'

'Aye, but it is unlawful.'

'Yes, undoubtedly; his Holiness would never have refused so great a monarch as his Majesty, if he had not been outraged both in honour and justice. But, brother, if they should proceed with this unholy work of destroying our monasteries and abbeys, enriching themselves with the spoils thereof, as they have in many monasteries already—'

'Brother, I can foresee the ruin of all: not one of us will be saved; every one of the holy houses are doomed to fall before the rapacious hands of this great man.'

'But bad man.'

'Aye, brother, aye, he is a bad man, a very bad man; and, if the blackness of his heart could be made apparent in his face, he would become an Ethiopian.'

'Thou sayest truly; but, brother, there are some of our own order who do not altogether bear that sanctity of character in their cells that they bear out-of-doors before men.'

'Alas, alas! brother, we are but men.'

'Thou sayest truly, brother; and though we be men of God yet we cannot change our nature, and where God wills we shall do so we become saints, and then we are held up as examples to men. It is a hard thing to become a saint, brother.'

'So it is; the body requires rest and nourishment, and we have our passions, as other men.'

'Have you heard of the Abbot Englefield—how he was deceived, and how he has become a beggar and a wanderer from the place where he was once the ruler?'

'Alas, alas, poor man! what has happened to him? I knew him very well. He was a merry, harmless soul—a good man and a learned clerk, and what would they have more?'

'I do not know, indeed.'

'But stop a minute, brother—you must be a-hungred—you have travelled far, and the traveller we are enjoined to cherish, and you are sinking: our larder is not furnished as it was of old; we do not now obtain the respect of the common people, as we used; when the higher authorities place themselves above us, and, despise us the lower are sure to follow their example.'

'No doubt! no doubt!'

'But though we are not what we used to be, yet I can contrive to find you a little snack and a drop of something pure.'

'Brother, a crust of bread and a drop from the spring becomes the pilgrim—give me such, and it is all I ask.'

'Yes, good brother; but we live in evil times, and we must strengthen the body to resist such attacks upon us; sit down here, I will myself seek what I may find for our comfort and strength, and as our brothers have all gone to bed, we will, with all humility, wait upon ourselves and feed in secret.'

'As you please, brother.'

This conversation took place between a superior of a small monastery or religious establishment, where the news of the destruction of the religious establishments was first carried by a wandering friar, who was well known to the superior and with whom there had long been some familiarity, on the score of old friendship.

The room was a snug one, and one that was well furnished with all that could add to conveniences as well as luxuries that were in character with those times.

The friar sat still and looked about him. He was a stout, stalwart man about forty, and one that appeared to be in the habit of enjoying the good things of this life, notwithstanding the show of humility he made use of in dress and language.

'Indeed, brother,' he muttered to himself, 'you are sure to be unhoused in a very short time—but it matters little, the people of this country will always receive me; I have the art of making myself agreeable where he would hardly be received.'

In another minute the prior returned laden with a tray and a small basket, which he laid down, saying—

'Brother, I am unused to these things; that is, to the placing them rightly on the table; but, as the things are here, we may eat of what we will: here is some venison pastry—some chicken pie—some ham—some roast goose.'

'We can manage to recruit exhausted nature,' said the friar, looking with an admiring eye upon the eatables.

'With God's assistance, brother, we will try.'

'And, I dare say, the moisture which one imbibes in the vicinity of such a larder will have the qualities most calculated, under Divine blessing, to cause a good digestion and an easy repose—two things of great importance in the animal economy of all human beings.'

'So it is—so it is.'

'And we will essay to accomplish this purpose, if there be any virtue in venison or chicken pie.'

'So we will, brother.'

'And what is in the basket yonder?'

'Some generous wine, brother: the best we can procure from the south of France—from Italy, and from Spain.'

'Brother, you do me more honour than I, abject sinner that I am, deserve at such hands.'

'It is no more than our duty to be charitable—to comfort the wayfarer now, and, men will not do so to us, we must do so to one another—to at least such as we know to be true and willing to do the same to us.'

'Of course, brother, it would be a great scandal to the order to throw open the doors of God's house for the purpose of entertaining the idle and wicked.'

'You put it in its right light, brother; but allow me to help you to some of the chicken—here is a fine breast.'

'Aye, a breast, did you say? I am very fond of the breast—the tender, white morsels are delicious.'

'So it is, brother.'

'Is it not a great piece of goodness in Providence to send us such food? If we came not to eat it, of course it would not have been sent to us; that is my theory of the designs of Providence. People say that they are mysterious—to me they seem very plain;—what is given, is given for our use.'

'You have expounded my own private opinions; and yet, if we were to teach that openly, there would be no knowing the excess people would run into, and men would be drunk as with too much knowledge; they would, in fact, brother, have got hold of the daubed end of the crosier.'

'Ha! ha! ha! brother, brother, you will impede my digestion; I never laughed so much at a joke before. Ho! ho! he! ha! ha! well, I declare, sinner that I am—'

'Bourdeaux or Burgundy, brother,' said the superior, taking out a couple of bottles, and placing them on the table.

'Burgundy, brother.'

Then, pouring out a large drinking-cup full, holding about half a pint, he said—

'That is generous liquor, brother, and will cherish the blood; but you promised me some news about the Prior of Englefield.'

'I did; and I will redeem my promise after the business of the platter is ended; my mind will be disturbed by having two objects before it, and so will yours.'

'Yes, brother, certainly.'

'And moreover, it will not be such a one as would increase your appetite; indeed, it would be a serious sin to spoil so good a supper.'

'It would—will you taste some of this goose? it is young, tender, and juicy; some of the breast of that.'

'Yes, I prefer the breast to all other parts of winged animals; the limbs are always tough, having more sinews in them, despite all that people may say concerning flavour, and so forth.'

'Well, I begin to think with you on that subject, and yet I would sooner have the wing of a tender subject than the breast of one that is gone in years.'

'Most undoubtedly—the most despised part of a young bird in preference to the most choice of the old bird.'

'Exactly.'

'And now, brother, as I see you have done, and I have finished, why, with your permission, I will relate to you what happened to Father Mathew, of Englefield Priory.'

'Aye, good brother, do; I am dying to hear what could have befallen so good a man.'

'You shall hear. Have you ever spent a night with Father Mathew—I mean in privacy, as you and I are now, when we fully confess our faults as men?'

'Yes, I have once or twice—albeit, he can chant a merrie lay, and has an eye to female beauty.'

'Yes, he has; and much more than that, they have a secret admittance to their private ball, when a certain number of brothers known only to the prior, admit a certain number of nuns known only to the prioress. So that there is nothing but what is fair—one and one—and no advantage taken.'

'Did brother Mathew do this thing?'

'Yes, surely.'

'But he never permitted them to associate so openly as that whilst I was there—I never saw that.'

'Perhaps brother Mathew feared your sanctity too much—he thought you were not an advocate of the doctrine, that, churchman or layman, the necessities are the same.'

'I believe in it,' said the prior.

'And so do most men who have any brains. Well, to return to our father of Englefield. He used to shrive all the nuns himself and confess them, and consequently he ran no danger of ever having any unpleasant discoveries, and when it was necessary to confess to any one else, he gave them a dispensation upon certain points connected with their confession; so they were by no means liable to discovery.'

'Upon my word, a good plan!'

'Well, there was a traveller who came down: he was a fat, jolly man, after the prior's own heart, and they laughed and joked together, and drank as well as sang songs together.'

'As may be imagined they grew into great friendship, and the prior spoke to him concerning several matters connected with the pleasures of the monastic life, when the other declared that since they had banished from their society women—'

'Aye'—said Prior Mathew, 'brother, brother, you know not the secrets of the secluded.'

'Secrets, brother, secrets—you have none that can interest me. I am what Nature made me. If that be wrong blame Nature not me; and as for you, who pretend to be more than or above Nature, to be, in fact, supernatural—you must lead horrible lives—I can hardly believe that men can, with any pretensions to brains, debar themselves the pleasures they were made for.'

'Nor do we, brother.'

'Pshaw! Do my constructions of your association show it?'

'Yes, to the vulgar it does seem so—those who are educated in the ways of the world require something more than ordinary to fix their minds to certain matters, and we must enchain them by an appearance of superiority in some matter or other.'

'Then why chance that?'

'Because people will scarce submit to such a privation as that; hence it creates the greatest difference between us.'

'But what you gain does not, in my opinion, pay for what you lose. You have no compensation adequate to the wants you must surely feel, and the separation between you and society.'

'You don't know all,' said Father Mathew; 'we have our moments of weakness, I assure you.'

'Nonsense,' said the guest, 'you are not going to make me believe that you who have no thoughts of that kind are ever given to an occasional indulgence?'

'I ought not to admit that it is otherwise,' said the prior; 'but you are a man capable of understanding the wants and wishes of men. I will admit you to see one of our conclave meetings if you will consent to swear never to reveal what you shall see to any human being under any circumstances whatever.'

'I will,' he replied.

He took the oath, and the next evening after the vesper bell had been rung, and the prayers of the priory said, and the hymns chanted, the prior came to his guest and said—

'When the monks have retired for the night, there will be some who remain; with these we will retire to the secret hall, where we hold our feasts and revelries.'

'I shall be happy to be there, I assure you,' said the guest, 'and shall be happy to take my part, if permitted.'

'You are welcome, most heartily welcome,' said the prior. 'At ten to-night I shall come to you; and then I will introduce you to what I have before said.'

* * * * *

The prior was as good as his word. About half-past ten he came to his guest and said—

'Now, you see, all are gone to bed, and are safely locked in their cells, and no fear of interruption can be experienced.'

'But what, however, of them?'

'Oh, you must know that every community must have a certain amount of fools, else it would never last: fools are to wise men what mortar is to bricks, only folly exceeds the usual proportion of mortar—it binds together the whole.'

'That is very good, Sir Prior. I have now some hopes of being agreeably deceived.'

'You will find yourself quite astonished, I assure you,' returned the prior:—'but as I was saying, we have only a chosen body who partake of these orgies—for the rest are mere neophytes, who are not likely to become full-blown flowers of godliness.'

'I see—I see; the infatuated, the enthusiastic — all are induced to carry everything to extremes.'

'Just so,' said the prior.

They both proceeded to the room in which they all were to assemble that evening. It led through several passages, until they came to a double door, which the prior opened by a pass-key.

In they went, and the guest was really astonished at what he saw there. There was a long table, with plenty of the best viands, meats and drinks, and then there were plenty of lights. The place presented an imposing, not to say magnificent spectacle; but coming, as they did, out of the dark, he was very much indeed surprised and amazed.

He was quite staggered, and he appeared confused.

On one side of the room were a number of monks, waiting apparently for something, while just at that moment, on the oppsite side, a door opened, and in came a number of nuns, who walked into the hall, with considerable *sang froid*, and appeared to know the place well, and its different ways.

They had lain aside their head-dresses, but appeared in their tunics or frocks, and presented a charming appearance.

'You may imagine, holy brother, what feelings such a scene would engender. By St. Dunstan, the monks and nuns pair off like twin brothers and sisters.'

'Well,' said our guest, 'this seems natural enough, but I haven't seen the evening out yet.'

'You shall do so with pleasure.'

The prior then advanced towards the table, and took his place, presenting his guest to them, saying—

'This is a brother, but one who will not take orders—he can keep any and every counsel.'

'He is doubly welcome,' said the monks, and at the same time a very pretty nun came round the table, and placed herself next to him, at the same time smiling most bewitchingly in his face.

'By St. John the Evangelist, prior,' he said, 'you have the advantage of us laymen; we only reach happiness by detail—you at once; what you can have every day, we but find only once or twice in our lives. I had no idea you enjoyed yourselves so.'

'Yes; and our king would destroy such happiness,' said the monk; 'that is the only thing we care for—all the rest is nothing.'

'That is very true.'

The evening went on very harmoniously; songs and music and many jokes and *bon mots* were uttered; so much laughter and good-will, that the hours went by most happily.

'I must beg you will let me retire,' said the guest.

'Retire!' said the astonished prior, 'I let you retire; indeed, I shall take it as an affront if you attempt it.'

'But I feel so very ill, I am not able to tell you how I feel. I am very sick; one half-hour up in the cloisters, and I shall be able to return.'

'What is it, think you?'

'I don't know,' said the guest; 'but I suspect your wine and the warmth of the place has got the better of me. If I remain now, I shall not be able to see the evening out comfortably.'

'Well, well, if you will return, we will excuse you, but mind you do return to us.'

'I will pledge my word that I will return in an hour; will you give me the keys of the cloisters, that I may get into them without any one hearing me?'

'Oh, that is a very good thought of yours—a very good thought. I tell you what, though, you had better take the bunch, for I can't very well see the ring upon which they are hanging, my eye-sight is so bad at night.'

'I will take heed of what you say.'

The guest had departed, and there was no lack of joy and uproarious mirth, when, lo! suddenly the door opened, and in walked a train of soldiers. The guest had been gone about half an hour—he was one of King Henry's men—the soldiers and others who came in with them formed all in a row, posting sentinels at the doors, so that no one could escape.

There was scarce such a scene in the world; each one stood there in the attitude in which he had been surprised; but at the same time the guest appeared, saying—

'This monastery must be dissolved. I take possession of all; and as for you, thieves and harlots, you must hence and away—obtain your living according to your vocation.'

'The poor brother Englefield has been suddenly turned out for indulging in a saturnalia—eh?'

'Yes, poor man, I am very sorry for him, for a better man never lived, and a kinder one, too, never shrived a poor soul.'

'I can bear testimony to that. Well, we shall all have to bend to the blast that comes from the throne.'

'You may safely say that; but no matter, it all comes in one's life-time, and forms a part, though a very disagreeable portion, it must be admitted; but come, brother, sorrow is dry, and if we must sip the cup of bitterness, let us enjoy as much of the sweets as we can. I am of opinion we had better take care of ourselves, for our day will come.'

'You are right—the storm blows over the whole kingdom —no part will be safe from its visitation, and in the meantime we must gain strength, with what speed we may.'

The friar and prior both sat late, and pledged each other in choice wines till the matin bell called them to prayer.

*   *   *   *   *

The perusal of the manuscript entirely absorbed the attention of Alice Hensman, and created a train of reflections in her mind of the most unbounded astonishment — for, although indeed she had novitiated, assuredly her pure mind never for an instant fancied scenes like those described above.

And, certainly, the picture was not too highly coloured— creating to the mind's eye a vivid portraiture of men and women, who, under the guise of the most consummate hypocrisy, and clothed with the sacred mantle of Religion herself, abandoned themselves to licentiousness, drunkenness, and gluttony, at those magnificent monastic orgies, so often depicted by the ecclesiastical historian, and which, in our own times, excite in the well-regulated mind unmitigated disgust, horror, and pity.

The lamp, however, at length began to flicker, and the coldness of the morning air cast a shiver over the fair form of the delicate, yet energetic and high-minded Alice, and induced her to rise from her seat, to which she had for so long a time been attentively riveted; but, as she did so, she heard, or fancied she heard footsteps outside her dwelling, and the well-known knock of Ranulph on the street-door.

CHAPTER XV.

The Attempted Abduction—The Fight—The Dungeon of the Convent.

So certain did Alice feel that the knock she heard was that of her husband, that, without a moment's hesitation, she proceeded down stairs with speed, and, flinging open the street door, exclaimed—

'Ranulph, dear Ranulph, how anxiously have I expected you!'

Some one immediately stepped into the passage, and then, before for a moment she could think of flying from the intruder, a violent grasp was laid upon her waist, and the door was slammed close.

She had laid the lamp on the stair-head, and now, as it cast its feeble rays downward, it fell upon that countenance which of all others was most hateful to her—the countenance of Sir Rupert Brent.

How he, whom she thought was securely confined in prison, and completely at the mercy of the Lord Warden, came to be there, was a matter of the profoundest mystery to her. She could not think—she could only feel the horror of his presence.

A shriek burst from her lips, and then she glared wildly in his countenance.

'Aye,' he said, 'look at me. Am I not changed? Am I not different, indeed, to what I was when last we met? This is the effect of imprisonment, Alice—the effect of a dungeon to which I have been consigned for your sake, although under pretence of a different motive. My death might have sealed my devotion to your charms, but I have escaped—look at me!'

It would have required one, indeed, who well knew Sir Rupert Brent, to have now recognised him.

His appearance was completely altered, for not only did his countenance bear evident traces of deep anxiety, and not only had he lost the faint colour which previously could be traced in his cheeks, in consequence of want of air and exercise, but he was attired in a fashion so different from that which she had ever seen him wear, that only her vivid recollection of his countenance enabled her to recognise him.

He wore the costume of a private soldier of the Lord Warden's guard, and, had her own private griefs allowed her time for reflection, she would have come to a conclusion then that that costume afforded a clue to the means by which he had effected his escape.

But such was her agony of mind that she could think of nothing but that he was there, and that his cold and vice-like grasp was upon her arm.

He soon perceived and profited by the state of mental confusion into which he had thrown her.

'Alice,' he said, 'I have threatened you. Had you known me better you would have known that I am a man who never makes a threat in vain. It is rare that I make any; actions and not threats belong to me; but I was subdued by your charms, and I paused,' in order that you might have an opportunity, if you chose, of escaping a doom which otherwise I had it in my power to inflict upon you. It is true that in the progress of this affair I have been taken prisoner, and for a time consigned to a dungeon; but think you that has damped either my affections or my energies—think you that has placed me in a worse position for action than I have been? No! you are mine.'

'Never, never,' she cried. 'Help, help! Strangers will rise up and defend me—I will alarm the citizens. Sir Rupert Brent, you shall not hold me!'

She struggled to free herself from him. It might have been that he was weakened by his imprisonment, or that he really was solicitous not to hurt her, but certainly he allowed her to wrench herself from his embrace; and, when she had done so, she rushed up the staircase again to get possession

of the arquebus which had done her such good service on a former occasion, and see if she could not, as before, defend herself by its means from the machinations of the Jesuit.

But he seemed to be aware of her intention; and, although she had got from him, he rushed after her with a speed that soon brought him up to her, and he detained her by a grasp of her garments.

Rendered desperate then by the imminent peril in which she was, Alice turned upon him, and, by great good fortune, as she did so her hand fell across the hilt of his sword that hung by his side.

Nerved by despair, she drew it on the instant, and aimed a blow at him which, had it taken effect, would have finished at once his earthly career; but it did not do so, for he, with greater agility than we could have given him credit for, upon perceiving the descending blade, immediately sprang backward the whole height of the staircase, probably calculating that a fall to the passage of the house could not be productive of the bad consequences of such a desperate wound as that he might have received from Alice.

Had she retained her station upon the staircase she might have defended herself well, for her position would have been almost impregnable, but she thought she was following up an advantage by pursuing the Jesuit.

Accordingly she rushed down after him into the passage, wishing to drive him from the house, which, to all appearance, she was doing, for he opened the street-door precipitately, and darted out on to the step.

'Begone!' she cried, 'and for the second time begone, defeated by a woman's hand.'

In her eagerness, with the sword in her grasp, she stood in the doorway, and did not notice that a slim, dark figure glided behind her.

'Insolent priest,' she added, ' I know not what insanity has goaded you to add another to the numerous insults rankling in my husband's mind against you, but the day will come when I shall want both inclination and ability to turn aside his wrath from you.'

'You are my prisoner,' said the Jesuit, ' and I shall convey you to the convent of the Benedictine Sisters, where you shall be immured in a far worse dungeon than that from which I have escaped, until you abjure your errors, and learn to look with a little more favour upon one who, by force, is restoring you to the arms of the Church, and who, by foul means, still hopes to hold you in his own.'

'Foul priest! stain to your calling, blotch upon the Church, and disgrace to everything sacred—I defy you from my soul, utterly and entirely do I defy you!'

The Jesuit smiled scornfully, and made a sign with his hand, and then the man who was behind Alice, being well prepared to do so, threw a thick black veil completely over her head and face, and then, flinging his arms around her, he kept it close, so that she could not move, and the stifled cries she uttered would not have been heard at the distance of half a dozen yards.

'Remove her,' said Sir Rupert Brent, quickly. 'Where are your companions?'

'Close at hand,' said the man who had captured her, and he gave a shrill whistle.

In an instant five other men stepped up from different doorways. They lifted Alice from the ground among them, as if her weight had been nothing, and, preceded by Sir Rupert Brent, who had picked up his sword, which she had dropped upon the door-step, they hurried down the street.

About the outskirts of Winchester, to the southward, was the celebrated monastery of Benedictine Nuns. Its superior was well known to be a woman of the most despotic and arbitrary disposition. She ruled with an iron hand all who submitted to her sway, exercising the most sovereign authority, and showing no mercy whatever to those who strayed from what she called faith.

Poor Alice could not be placed in the custody of one who would be more likely to exercise her trust with rigour than this haughty and unmerciful abbess.

By the route which her captors took it seemed tolerably evident, that for once in his life Sir Rupert Brent had spoken the truth, and that he really intended to do what he asserted — namely, place Alice Hensman in a Benedictine convent.

Probably, had he had his own wish, some private asylum would have suited him better; but the only terms upon which he could procure the assistance so efficiently rendered to him by his associates, consisted in a proof of his authority from the Church.

And although, upon his imprisonment occurring, he had been deprived of that authority, yet, as these six men were the same who had before acted for him, they had once seen it, and were inclined to believe he had it still.

Consequently, it was upon this assumption that they acted, and consequently it was that he was obliged to keep up the character of the transaction, by placing his prisoner in a convent.

It was a great gratification to Sir Rupert Brent doubtless to find that now, after all the crosses he had experienced, after all the difficulties that he had encountered, and the power and determination with which he had been resisted, that he was at length successful.

He forgot his fatigues—he forgot the lassitude which his imprisonment had brought upon him—he forgot every thing but his revenge, and he exulted over the fact that he had thus obtained its first instalment by getting possession of Alice Hensman in spite of her husband, in spite of the Lord Warden, and in spite of John Elkington, all of whom had thought their victory over him so complete.

This mode of carrying Alice to the convent was much quicker and better than if they had brought any conveyance for her, and the party went on at an extremely rapid rate, pausing not a moment, but following Sir Rupert Brent, who, although at such an hour as that it was not likely they would meet any party stronger than themselves, took the least frequented route he could towards the convent.

The dress which he wore, no doubt, had he encountered any one inclined to be curious with regard to its owner, would have greatly facilitated any explanation he might offer, for the costume was perfectly well known as that of the Lord Warden's guard, as it was called, and therefore an air of authority was given to the whole proceeding, which otherwise it would much have wanted.

No doubt Alice endured the greatest agony of mind to find herself thus hurried on in darkness, she knew not whither, and that, too, at a moment when she had fondly imagined she had gained another victory over her despicable opponent.

More than once she tried to speak, but the thick folds of the veil in which she was enveloped checked her voice, and it was with the greatest difficulty she succeeded in drawing breath sufficient for existence.

About twenty minutes thus elapsed, when the men halted, and she heard the sound of a heavy bell; then a gate creaked upon its hinges, and she felt assured that she was in some prison-house, from which, unless by the bounty of Heaven she was freed, she might in vain sigh for a release.

One despairing effort she made to scream, and she did succeed in uttering a faint sound of that description, but it was more calculated to delight than to annoy her captors.

She found that she was placed upon her feet, and then that she was propelled forward so sharply, that, had she not walked she must have fallen, so she had no resource but to move onward at the pace those around her chose.

Not a word was spoken, until a voice cried—

'There are stairs!' and then she felt that she was descending to some region below the earth, for the cold and damp air made itself evident to her, even through the thick folds of the veil in which she was enveloped.

She thought that the voice which spoke to her was a female one, although harsh and ungracious to the ear, and she gathered no hope from it whatever.

She felt suddenly that the staircase had ceased and that she was treading upon earth.

'I am being conducted to a dungeon,' she thought; 'my fate is sealed—I shall never again look upon the blessed light of day—I have gazed my last upon the sweet faces of my children, and never again will my husband's voice sound like music to my ears.'

Such a sudden gush of despair came over her that on the instant she fainted, and had she not been supported by some of the Benedictine nuns that were around her, she would have fallen to the earth.

Sir Rupert Brent and his followers had parted from her at the gate.

Before his own captivity he had had an interview with the abbess of the convent, and secured her effectual co-operation in the captivity of poor Alice.

Of course he had asserted to her that it was purely upon stern religious grounds that Alice, as an escaped novice, was to be placed under arrest.

Indeed, he went so far as to affect some concern that he had been picked out as the humble instrument for carrying the resolution into effect; but he considered it, as he told the abbess, his duty, and therefore he must do it.

She had warmly coincided in his views; the idea of having anybody to persecute for religious motives was to her so delightful an idea that she was not at all too curious in inquiring into the circumstances of the case.

To her it was quite sufficient that Alice had been a novice —that she had left her convent to commit the heinous offence of matrimony, and that too with a heretic, with whom she was so comfortable, that it was quite a savage satisfaction to disturb her.

And hence was it that Sir Rupert had found a great ally in this woman, and one who was disposed in every way to stretch her authority to the utmost for the purpose of seconding his designs of a persecuting nature. It was an understood thing, too, between them, that in his spiritual capacity Father Georges should visit Alice whenever he pleased; so that he now could have ample opportunity of urging his suit without his victim being able to escape from the toils by which she was surrounded.

When Alice had thus fainted in the arms of the Benedictine nuns, they were a little alarmed at the consequences which might ensue from the close manner in which she was enveloped in the veil, which they hastily removed, in order to allow some fresh air to visit her cheeks.

All but the flinty-hearted abbess were struck with her beauty, and did not wonder at the heretic having the good taste to take from her convent one possessed of such abundant charms.

But if anything could have added to the aggravation which the abbess had at all people who left their convents and got married, it was to observe the exquisite charms of her victim.

She at once ordered her to be conveyed into a cell; and when she saw that the nuns were about to convey her into one which boasted of some ordinary comforts, she reproved them for so doing, and peremptorily ordered that she should be put into the worst which the convent afforded.

Thither, then, she was carried; for no one dared to dispute the savage commands of the superior.

Indeed, it was with great difficulty she was prevailed upon to allow one of the nuns to remain with her and attempt her restoration; so disposed was she to visit her with all the evil consequences she could for her most venial offence, if indeed offence it could be called at all.

But she did consent to this, rather than that her victim should die; for if such were to occur she would be deprived of the glorious privilege of tormenting her—a privilege which she would not give up readily, and which promised her in the course of time some of the most exquisite enjoyment.

Desiring, then, the nun who remained to leave as quickly as possible, and to be sure to lock the prisoner in the cell, so that she might taste as many of the delights of solitude as possible, she with the other nuns ascended again to the upper air, leaving poor Alice still in a state of utter insensibility.

CHAPTER XVI.

The Recovery.—Unavailing Sympathy.—The Promise, and the Appeal.

THE nun who had been left with Alice, in what might be called a small dungeon, for it was little else, had not had her heart so entirely indurated by her residence in a cloister as not to feel something for the distressed and wretched.

She looked upon the fair form that lay before her, with all the insignia of death about it, with deep compassion.

'Alas!' she said; 'was it a crime to love? I have sworn that my own heart shall be dead to all such emotions; the only one with whom I could have trodden with joy life's thorny path is now, alas! no more; but had that one lived I too, like this poor creature—but hush, hush! this is sinful. These remembrances ought to form no part of my daily meditations. I must repeat many an ave for thus allowing memory, even for a moment, to thus fly back to the sinful world.'

She supported the head of Alice on her knees, and gently sprinkling some cold water upon her face, she had the pleasure, in a short time, of seeing her open her eyes and look up with an expression of amazement.

Then she uttered a deep sigh, and the compassionate nun, bending over her, spoke gently, saying,—

'Be at peace, sister; at all events, there is none here now who will harm you. Learn to bear with a resigned spirit the will of Heaven.'

Alice looked bewildered for a moment or two; and then, as a full tide of memory rushed upon her, the hideous present as compared with the happy past presented itself to her in all its vivid reality.

'Oh! save me, save me!' she cried. 'Save me from this doom, worse than death itself! To thee, Heaven, do I appeal for justice—I ask not mercy, God of Heaven! I ask but justice.'

The nun shuddered and spoke gently,—

'Sister, sister, this is sinful. Is that the way to address Heaven, whose holy will it must be that you are in your present circumstances? Heaven is ever just. You cannot tell, and do not know, but that this trial—severe though it seem—may be for your ultimate benefit. Do not, therefore, I implore you, in such a manner impugn the wisdom of that Providence which governs all things.'

'Listen to me,' said Alice: 'have you a husband whom you love?'

'No, no! I have no earthly tie.'

'Children who are so dear to your affection, who are so entwined around your heart of hearts, that to pluck them from it is to break it?'

'No, no, no!'

'Did you ever love?'

'No more, I beseech you, no more! Speak of yourself—complain of the past and of the present—picture to yourself the future how you will, but ask not such questions as these of one who has suffered—aye, suffered more than she chooses to relate. You have said enough—you have said enough.'

'Where am I.'

'In the convent of Benedictine nuns.'

'Alas, alas! I have heard of such a place. Is not your abbess celebrated for her religious fanaticism?'

'I dare not say so: she is my superior. Do not ask me.'

'I am answered. The Jesuit for a time has triumphed; but surely Heaven will aid me yet.'

'Heaven will always aid the just; but is it true that you have turned aside from our holy religion? Can it be true you are thus benighted?'

'Religion is an opinion. Be tolerant.'

'An opinion! Are you a heretic?'

'What is heresy?'

The nun was silenced. Although poor Alice was in no mood for a controversy, she saw that there was much kindness in the poor creature's face, and that her limited perceptions were more owing to education and habit than to any real narrowness of soul.

'I know that you will aid me,' she said; 'I am certain that you will; there is kindness in your every look and every tone. Listen, while I unfold to you a tale that shall rend your very heart-strings, and convince you I am unfortunate, as I trust I am, and not guilty.'

'I will hear you, sister, but not now; I will visit you again, and my visits, although tolerably frequent, must be brief ones; the abbess would be angry were I to remain longer with you.'

'And yet she is religious?'

'A very pattern of holiness and piety.'

'Alas, alas! what religion can that be which refuses aid to the afflicted—the common, ordinary aid of friendly sympathy?'

'Do not speak to me upon these points, I dare not answer you. I do not wish that the serenity of a life I care not how soon closes, should be disturbed. Let me be in peace! Receive such sympathy as I can offer to you, and such good as I can do to you, but say no more to me of such a character. I will soon return to you and bring you some refreshments.'

Alice was extremely gratified, even for the amount of sympathy which the kind-hearted nun tendered to her. In fact, a moment's thought convinced her that it was as much as she fairly ought to expect. Although, as might naturally be expected, poor Alice was much overcome by this sudden and violent change in her fortunes, hers was not a disposition long to cherish thoughts of despair; but, on the contrary, she possessed sufficient resolution soon to enable her mind to recover from the first shock of her altered circumstances.

She took a careful review of what had occurred, and then she set about with better hopes, asking herself what could be done to relieve her from her present painful state.

Her former residence in a convent had enabled her to know quite enough of the species of life which was passed in such places to come to an accurate conclusion of her chances of escape.

She knew well that it would be a disputed point as to whether she, having been only a novice at the time she left her convent, and really not having taken the veil, could be subject to anything more than ordinary ecclesiastical censure and disapproval.

But that was not a circumstance to gather much hope from; for she well knew, if she were to be kept imprisoned until the Church of Rome came to some decision in her favour, that such imprisonment would be likely to last for the whole of her existence.

The only benefit likely to accrue from such a fact would be, that she might probably succeed in convincing some one of the justice of her cause, who from that conviction might aid and assist her in escaping from the tyranny to which she was subjected.

And if any one were likely to do so much for her, it would probably be the compassionate nun who had already expressed sympathy with her distresses.

While she was thus calculating her chances of escape

from the prison-house to which she had been conveyed, Alice contrived to keep her mind in a state of tolerable serenity. It was only when she reverted back to thoughts of her husband and her children, that her courage seemed to fail her; then would the bitterness of her anguish almost entirely overcome her resolution, and it required her to call up all the strength of mind she was mistress of to divert her thoughts into some other channel.

Thus alternately hoping and desponding, Alice passed the weary time until the compassionate nun returned to her, bearing a small basket, which contained provisions.

She apologised to Alice for the simplicity of the fare she brought to her.

'No doubt,' she said, 'your residence in the world has accustomed you to much more sumptuous fare than a convent can afford, but still what I now bring you is contrary to the orders of the abbess.'

'Bring me what you please,' said Alice, 'I shall be content; and more than content shall I be, if you can bring me any hope of again revisiting that world from which I am now shut out by these cruel walls.'

'I know nothing,' said the nun, 'which can enable me to give you such a hope; I can only pray for you, and that I will do most truly and devoutly.'

Alice was doubtful as to whether it would be quite safe at once to let the nun know that she wished to interest her in the subject of her escape; and she said to her,

'If you tell me that I may speak to you with perfect confidence I will do so, but if you think it your duty to report anything I may say to the abbess, tell me so at once, that I may not commit the error of making a mistaken confidence.'

'You may speak freely to me, I will report nothing; it would be a sad thing, indeed, if the unfortunate were to be exposed to the still further evil of having spies set upon them. I do not say that such will not be the case, even as regards you, but I can say that I am not one, nor would I accept such an office.'

'Then you will tell me your candid opinion. I was but a novice in the convent. I left to obey the impulse of the best and most beautiful feeling which Heaven has implanted in our natures. I had taken no vows to devote myself to the cloister, therefore is my imprisonment most unjust.'

'It is said,' replied the nun, 'that a novice leaving the cloister so clandestinely, commits a great sin; it may be so, I cannot tell, but do not ask me to aid you in escape; I dare not do so.'

'You dare do what you consider right.'

'I cannot reason with you upon this subject, but yet, I pray you, do not ask me.'

The nun was so evidently distressed at the idea of being, even by her sense of justice of her sympathies, drawn into such an undertaking, that Alice most reluctantly felt that she had nothing to expect in the way of active assistance from that quarter, although she did not dread anything like opposition.

'I am speaking very freely to you, indeed,' she said to the nun, 'when I tell you that my thoughts by day and my dreams by night, in this place, will all tend to the one subject, viz. as to how I can best escape from it. The only thing that will make separation from those whom I hold dear at all bearable, will consist in constantly nourishing the hope of a speedy re-union with them.'

The nun was evidently in a most wavering state of mind; she was swayed strongly in Alice's favour personally, and yet all her prejudices and course of education took the opposite side in the contest, so that, probably, if she were to consent to do anything that would seem to favour Alice's designs, it would be done in a vacillating manner that might defeat the object it was intended to promote.

Alice was again alone. The nun had told her to expect no visitors for many an hour, so that she was completely abandoned to her own reflections.

'What,' she exclaimed, 'oh! what will be Ranulph Hensman's feelings when he reaches his home and finds it thus deserted? By this time, perchance, he has given way to all those ideas of despair which will first arise in his bosom ere he begins to reflect and to hope.'

As Alice pursued this train of reflection she arrived, at all events, to one important conclusion, which was, that Ranulph Hensman would be certain to guess what had befallen her; and, coupling the fact of the Jesuit's escape from prison with her abduction from her home, he could come to no other conclusion than that the latter circumstance was dependent upon the former, and consequently that she was in the hands of the Jesuit.

From this she gathered hope, because it would direct her husband's exertions to discover her to the right quarter, and, knowing his energy, and the powerful friends by which he was surrounded, surely she had everything to hope, and but little to fear, beyond the temporary inconvenience of the confinement to which she was subjected.

'Oh! if I could but think of some means,' she exclaimed, 'of letting him know precisely where I am, so as to spare him the pain of an useless search, all would surely be well again!'

She hoped that she might be permitted to walk in the convent garden, in which case she thought she might surely manage to give some indication of her presence to some one who would take the news to Hensman; but if she was still to be confined to the convent-cell in which she now was, she could have but little hope.

It was in the midst of these reflections that sleep gently stole upon her, and the refreshing slumber of some hours' duration gave her strength to bear up against what might be the severe trials of the coming day.

But a faint streak of daylight, when even the sun was at its highest, visited that gloomy cell; but still, as contrasted with the darkness of the night, it was light if not cheerful, and she could gaze around her upon the scanty accommodation it afforded.

A miserable pallet bed, a wooden crucifix nailed against the wall, and rough chair and table, such as would have disgraced the cottage of the humblest peasant, completed the whole furnishing of Alice's cell, if we except a brown pitcher with water, which stood in one corner of it.

She was gazing upon these scanty accommodations when she heard the sound of footsteps, and became aware that some one was rapidly approaching the cell-door.

Full of hope that it was the compassionate nun, she rose to receive her, but to her disappointment it was another, and that one a more elderly person and of much more austere aspect.

'Follow me,' she said, 'the abbess commands your presence.'

'And what if I refuse?' said Alice.

The idea of any one refusing a command of the abbess seemed to take the nun so completely by surprise, that for some moments she could hardly reply to the extravagant proposition.

'Refuse!' she said, 'the abbess waits!'

'Let her wait,' said Alice; 'I am here a prisoner, and not of my own free will: I, therefore, do not owe common courtesy to your abbess.'

The nun crossed herself repeatedly and muttered a prayer, as if it were quite necessary to do so in consequence of Alice's dreadful wickedness, and then she said,—

'The holy Father Georges must come and reason with you.'

'Georges—Georges the Jesuit, call him not holy! I will not see him here; surely, surely, the cell of a convent ought to be sacred against the intrusions of that meddling priest. If his presence is to be the penalty of not attending your abbess's order, I will follow you.'

The nun made no remark, but preceded Alice along the gloomy passages and up the flight of stairs which have been previously noticed.

After some distance a door was opened, which revealed a much more habitable portion of the convent, and finally, the nun tapped at the entrance of an apartment, which Alice rightly conjectured to be the private parlour of the abbess, and the moment she caught sight of its interior she was convinced that was the fact, although her heart sank within her for a moment to perceive that Sir Rupert Brent sat in the apartment, with an ecclesiastical habit thrown over his ordinary costume, and which contrasted strangely with the black moustache that was upon his upper lip.

CHAPTER XVII.

Ranulph Hensman's Proceedings in the Cathedral.—The Conspirators.—Ranulph in Danger.

WE left Ranulph Hensman, John Elkington, and the Lord Warden together, at the moment when the gratifying intelligence reached them of the return of Reuben Clifton.

The Lord Warden had desired his instant presence, and he welcome which the lad received must have been such as to amply compensate him for the many dangers he had passed.

'You are most welcome, Reuben,' said the Warden; 'we had began to entertain the most serious apprehensions for your safety.'

'We are all glad to see you,' said John Elkington; 'you shall tell us at greater leisure what has detained you, and your adventures on the road; but, in a word, have you performed your mission?'

'Yes,' replied the boy.

'Did you see the King?' said the Lord Warden.

'I did; and here is his answer.'

He handed to the Warden King Henry's letter, which was eagerly opened, and read aloud.

'We could not desire more than that,' said John Elkington; 'you perceive, Ranulph Hensman, that here is such an ample protection to your wife that the Lord Warden will not scruple to use force against the Jesuits should they attempt to interfere with her.'

'Under this authority,' said the Lord Warden, 'I will act. So long as the King admitted the Court of Rome to be a higher authority, as regards the life and liberty of any of his subjects, than his own, I was bound to obey that authority; but he is the King of England, and my master. The authority that he assumes I will carry out; and if all the priests in Winchester were to surround Alice Hensman, my sword should clear a passage through them.'

Ranulph Hensman's eyes glistened with satisfaction as the Lord Warden thus spoke.

'I cannot thank you sufficiently, my lord,' he said, 'nor can I ever sufficiently show my gratitude to his Majesty for this timely assistance.'

'The King,' said John Elkington, 'has done what is right; but at the same time, Hensman, bear in mind that in so doing he is only carrying out a settled policy.'

'That is quite correct,' said the Lord Warden.

'He has no objection whatever to a quarrel with the Jesuits: there could not be a better occasion for it than such an attempted act of tyranny as that which Father Georges has contemplated.'

'It matters little to me,' said Hensman, 'whose policy this is—I am satisfied: may I, my lord, take the protection of the King with me?'

'Most certainly, it may be of use to you at any moment that we may least suspect, although I dare say the imprisonment of Georges will have the effect of considerably damping the energies of those who otherwise would have interfered with you.'

'Of that I have no doubt, my lord. So long as Georges continues a prisoner, I can have but few apprehensions, for no one but he is interested by private motives to assail the liberty of Alice; and now, with your good permission, I will fain go back to the cathedral and endeavour to make some use of the watchword I have obtained.'

'Do so, Ranulph, but run into no unnecessary risks; and as for you, Reuben Clifton, before we say another word to you, or you to us, I insist upon your having some repose. In the morning, you shall tell us your adventures, but not at present.'

'Reuben retired at the same time that Ranulph Hensman did, the former to repose, and the latter to the cathedral, where he yet hoped to obtain some information of importance to what now may be fairly called the King's cause, now Henry had so far committed himself to it.'

The hour was now such an one that Ranulph felt convinced that Alice must have given him up for the night, so he hurried on to the cathedral, more than once muttering—

'All is safe, for Georges is a prisoner in the castle.'

With this agreeable conviction on his mind he reached the church, and wrapping closely round him a cloak which he had brought with him from the Lord Warden's, he walked slowly up to that corner of the sacred edifice where he had seen the two persons from whom he had got the watchword open a door.

He determined to linger about there for a time until some one should approach upon whom he could try the efficacy of the words he had heard.

He had not long to wait, for presently a man came in hurriedly, and scarcely casting the slightest glance around him, he walked up to the secret door of the cathedral.

Then he saw Ranulph Hensman, and hesitated, but the latter slipped up to him and said in a low tone,—

'Who holds the key?'

The stranger hesitated a moment and then replied, 'St. Peter;' and then he added, 'How is it that you are not at the conclave? I fear I am myself too late.'

'I have mislaid the key of this door,' said Ranulph.

'Oh, if that is all, I can admit you here with mine.'

Hensman knew not what danger he might be plunging into, but to retreat now would be at once to proclaim that he was an impostor. He shrank from the idea of such a proceeding, for up to that point he could not be said to have acquired any new information whatever.

'I thank you,' he said, 'I will accompany you.'

The stranger opened the door, and Ranulph Hensman, freeing his arm as much as possible from the incumbrance of his cloak, loosened his sword in its sheath, and kept his hand upon it still, to be ready for any emergency that might ensue.

A man of clearer or sounder judgment than Hensman to conduct such an affair could not have been found. There was no hurry or confusion about him, and nothing was likely to escape him that would at all tend to the furtherance of his object and his own preservation.

A glance at the other side of the door showed him that there was no fastening except the lock, and that on that side it required no key to open it, there being a handle, which turned it at once.

Gratified somewhat by this state of things, inasmuch as to secure a good retreat in an emergency was a matter of great importance, he followed his companion along the narrow passage before noticed, until they reached the door of the vault where the Jesuits held their secret meetings.

And there sat the man who on the last occasion had solaced himself, after the fatigue of acting as door-keeper, in the wine-cellar of the priest, along with his companion Griffiths.

He opened the door of the vaulted apartment without the slightest hesitation; but not before Ranulph Hensman had had time to see that there was a massive bolt upon its outside, with a bar of iron at right angles to it, fitting into a projecting loop, so that the whole might be secured by a padlock, if necessary.

In another moment he was in the vaulted chamber. There were ten or eleven persons present, and luckily, at the time of Ranulph's entrance, one of the number was speaking, upon whom much attention was fixed; so that Hensman, without difficulty, could glide into a chair and there remain an unobserved spectator of what was proceeding.

He took good care to keep as near the door as possible, and the words he heard the speaker utter were these,—

'It is necessary that the blow should be struck now; and since I have been chosen to rid the world of the only crowned head that can be dangerous in his opposition to our Church, I shall proceed towards London by the earliest morning's dawn.'

'It will be a great object,' said another, 'to expedite the business. I am of Father Leoni's opinion, that the sooner it is done the better, and highly applaud his resolution of proceeding to London immediately.'

'And I! and I!' cried several.

'That seems then the concurrent opinion,' said Leoni, 'and I can only much regret the absence of Father Georges, whose aid and counsel have always been of so much service to us.'

'We all regret it,' said the president. 'A letter has been received from him by Father Redell, which informs us that we must use our best endeavours to expedite our cause, and that nothing whatever is suspected. Father Redell sent him an appropriate answer, and since then we have heard nothing of him.'

'When was that?' said one.

'This evening.'

'Indeed, so lately! it is a sad thing this imprisonment of his—it keeps us not only in a state of constant terror respecting its causes, but at the same time it deprives us of his active assistance.'

The door at this moment opened, and a figure appeared which spread so much alarm among the Jesuits that each instantly sprang to his feet. The figure was that of a soldier in the well-known uniform of the Lord Warden's guard. But if surprise and alarm produced a great effect upon the Jesuits, the former feeling at least took, for a few moments, entire possession of Ranulph Hensman; for, in the figure before him, he at a glance recognised Sir Rupert Brent.

That he had escaped in that disguise from the guard-room of the castle was evident, and Ranulph Hensman felt that now, unless he speedily got out of the vaulted chamber, his own fate would be sealed; as, let him make what resistance he would, he must be overpowered by numbers.

He arose upon the instant, and had taken one step towards the door, when his eyes met those of Sir Rupert Brent.

'Ranulph Hensman!' shouted the latter, 'the Lord Warden's secretary here! we are betrayed—seize him!'

Two or three flung themselves between Ranulph and the door; but drawing his sword, he cleared space in a moment, and dashing past Sir Rupert Brent, he reached the passage. To turn then and bolt the door of the vaulted chamber on the outside was the work of a moment; but then, before he could defend himself, the man who had charge of the entrance made a fierce lunge at him with a sword, which was nearly finishing his career, for, had he not turned at the moment, it must have passed completely through him.

As it was it went through his apparel, grazing the skin across his breast, but inflicting no other serious wound.

Self-defence compelled him to do as he did. He ran the man through in a moment; and, as the body fell with a groan, he heard the Jesuits in the vaulted chamber making furious and frantic efforts to burst the door.

Springing forward then, he reached the church, and carrying his sword in his grasp, to the consternation of a priest, whom he met in his progress, he rushed into the street, and with frantic eagerness took his way towards his own home.

The knowledge that Georges had been at liberty, perhaps for some hours, and that Alice was unprotected, was agony to him; and those who met him rushing onward with the sword in his grasp, shrank from him and hid themselves in door-ways as he passed, for they thought he must be some madman who in his indiscriminate rage would slaughter all he met.

Thus, then, he pursued his way, nearly distracted by his fears, until he reached his own home.

The first glance he got of the state of things there served to confirm his fears. The door swung idly on its hinges, a nearly expiring lamp was upon the staircase. A faintness came over him, as he now felt certain that, before coming to the convocation of Jesuits, the much-dreaded Georges had paid a visit to his home.

For several moments he could not cross the threshold; but then, mustering up all his resolution, he dashed in and ascended the staircase, crying aloud—

'Alice, Alice! speak if you be here! speak if you be here, Alice, or this suspense will kill me!'

He reached the room in which she ordinarily sat. A glance showed him that it was forsaken; but in the work-box of Alice, and the papers that lay upon the table, he saw signs of recent occupation. There was still a hope she might have retired to rest.

Another minute brought him to the chamber-door; and if she were not within that apartment he knew that his worst fears were confirmed. No wonder he dreaded so to confirm them, and that he paused a moment and trembled ere he opened the door. But it must be done—joy or despair awaited him; and so, with the fading lamp in his hand, which scarcely gave so much light as the faint early dawn which was breaking, he walked into the chamber. It was empty.

Ranulph Hensman sunk into a seat. The appearance of the bed was that it had not been slept upon, and now he knew the worst—Alice had been torn from him. No, not the worst—the children—were the children safe? He staggered into the next apartment, which was theirs, and found them sleeping soundly, little dreaming of the deprivation they had suffered.

'Thank Heaven!' he said, 'for that much mercy; the villain has not made war against these little ones—but oh! Alice, Alice! what is become of thee? where am I to search for you, and how am I to recover you from the hands of the villain Georges?'

He remained for some time almost in a kind of stupor; but then slowly the energy of his spirit returned to him, and he felt that that was a period of action, and not one in which he ought to sit and give way to idle grief.

He sprang to his feet. 'I will procure,' he said, 'some one to attend to the children, and then I will to the Lord Warden at once, and claim his promised assistance and advice. Alice, Alice! what may you not be suffering even now!'

With a heavy heart he left his own house and knocked at the door of a neighbour, between whom and Alice he knew some civilities had been interchanged, and where he thought it likely he should be able to procure the assistance he wanted as regarded the children.

He found these people stirring, although the hour was so early, and from them he learnt, they had heard some disturbance at his house some hours before, but that being females they were fearful of interfering, and consequently were compelled to be mere spectators, where they would gladly, if possible, have interfered as protectors.

'The disturbance you heard,' said Hensman, sorrowfully, 'was the abduction of my wife from her home by the Jesuits, under the pretence that she had made herself amenable to their jurisdiction, by leaving her convent when a novice, to wed with me.'

The women expressed their sympathy and their willingness to use all their power to aid him in such an extremity of his fortunes. He told them of the unprotected state of the children, and how necessary it was for him to be absent from home at once, in order to take measures for the recovery of Alice.

'If,' he added, 'any one could be found who will take care of them in my house, I shall be able, with some degree of ease of mind and satisfaction, to devote all my energies to a discovery where my wife has been secreted.'

'They shall be brought into this house,' said one of the women, 'where they will be safer, for if you and Mistress Hensman have enemies, your children may have enemies likewise, so that they had better not remain in the house where they now are.'

This was a suggestion which the reason of Hensman at once approved, and after he had seen the children safely in the care of his compassionate neighbours, he set off for the Lord Warden's with a lighter heart, and better hope of before long succeeding in overcoming the Jesuits.

*   *   *   *   *   *

Had Ranulph Hensman delayed his departure for the Lord Warden's another quarter of an hour, when he went to seek adventures in the cathedral, he would have been apprised of the escape of Sir Rupert Brent; for, upon a party of soldiers going to change the guard, what had happened was discovered, and immediately communicated to the Lord Warden.

Vexed to the greatest possible degree at such an occurrence, for which the Warden blamed himself, because he thought that, if he had insisted upon Sir Rupert Brent remaining in the dungeon where he was originally cast, it would not have occurred, he sent messengers and escorts in all directions in search of him.

Such, however, had been the rapidity of the Jesuit's movements, that he had not only got possession of Alice, and lodged her in the convent of Benedictine Nuns, but he had hastened himself to the cathedral, where, as we know, he encountered Ranulph Hensman at a time when it was so dangerous to the latter to be recognised.

Those whom the Lord Warden sent out in search of the prisoner were completely unsuccessful, and it was not until Ranulph himself made his appearance, that any authentic news of Sir Rupert Brent could be got. He briefly explained what had occurred at the church, and then, with a manly sorrow, alluded to his private grievances.

'The villain Georges,' he said, 'has succeeded for a time, and Alice is in his power.'

'It shall not be so long,' said the Warden; 'let him have hidden her where he will, armed with the King's authority, I will by force wrest her from him; every possible exertion shall be used to discover where he has concealed her, and I do hope, Ranulph, before twenty-four hours are over, that you will again have her in your home.'

'I pray, my lord, that it may be so; and now that I have made such a report to you as it was my duty at once to make, I trust I may be excused for leaving hastily, in order that I may engage myself in an endeavour to discover Georges' retreat.'

'Consider your time,' said the Lord Warden, 'at your own disposal. Under the present circumstances I make no call upon it, but a messenger must be instantly despatched to London with the news of this outrage, and of the designs of the Jesuits to the King. Do but bring me word, Ranulph, that you have found where Georges has hidden Alice, and such a force shall be at your disposal to tear her from him as shall overcome all opposition.'

'Thanks, my good lord,' said Hensman, as he left the chamber; 'soon do I hope to be enabled to avail myself of such an offer.'

'How well he battles with his grief!' said John Elkington, when Hensman had gone: 'he feels this flow of evil fortune far more keenly than he will allow any one to observe.'

'It is a most monstrous outrage,' said the Warden, 'such a one, indeed, as I can scarcely trust myself to speak of; but this audacious priest shall suffer yet severely for it. I cannot but pity for Hensman with all my heart; his is truly a noble spirit, and it is a thousand pities to see it thus depressed by misfortune it is so far from deserving.'

'His wife,' said John Elkington, as he rose, 'shall be rescued from these Jesuits, or England shall shake for it from one end to the other. Besides, the very reputation of the King is staked to protect her.'

'And he will do it, you may rest assured. Whither go you?'

'To assist, I hope, in the discovery of the Jesuit. I will see what can be done by careful inquiry, for I think a stranger more likely to succeed than Hensman himself, whose feelings are so largely interested in the result.'

'That is true. I wish you all imaginable success. The proceedings of Sir Rupert Brent are an insult to us all, and we are individually and collectively bound to do everything in our power to assist Ranulph.'

'And in doing so, my Lord Warden, you may depend we shall achieve a great political purpose; and from this little circumstance of Sir Rupert Brent consulting only the dictates of his ungovernable passions, we may perhaps date the expulsion of the Jesuits from England.'

John Elkington left the Lord Warden's house as he spoke, and probably in a more wary and collective manner than the state of mental distress which Ranulph must be suffering made it possible for him to exert, he commenced his inquiries.

His first object was to discover what sort of party had taken possession of Alice, and by pursuing diligent inquiries from house to house, for it was now morning, he discovered several persons who had seen from their windows six or eight men at the door of Ranulph Hensman's abode.

He likewise had no difficulty in finding the route they took, until he traced the party so near to the convent of Benedictine Nuns, that, knowing the character of that establishment, and that its abbess was ever ready to lend herself to any act of religious oppression, he came to the conclusion that it was there that Alice was held a prisoner.

It was necessary, however, to be quite certain, before taking any steps in the affair; so he went to a shop in the town and purchased a small lace scarf, and, with it in his hand, he proceeded to the gate of the convent.

He rang boldly, and, when the portress appeared, he said,

'This scarf was dropped by the prisoner who was brought in here last night. Father Georges thought I had better bring it; so here it is.'

'Very good,' said the portress.

'I suppose she is as obstinate as ever?'

'Oh, I don't know anything about her; don't trouble me with your questions; it is quite bother enough to have the convent made a place to bring heretics to. For my part, I don't see why they can't burn them at once.'

'A very pious idea. But heretics are so obstinate, that you may depend they would object.'

'Go along with you,' said the portress, and she closed the wicket.

'She is here, then,' said John Elkington, as he walked away; 'and if I could but find Ranulph Hensman, I should be able to spare him the trouble of further search. However, I will to the Lord Warden at once, and leave him to take such measures as he may consider necessary for accomplishing Alice's rescue.

With that he hurried towards the castle, and at once communicated the intelligence he had gained.

'That is sufficient, then,' said the Warden; 'I will but wait for Ranulph himself, and then, with such a force as shall amply suffice, I will proceed to the convent, and, under authority from the King, which I consider we have sufficiently, rescue the prisoner.'

'And now, as we have shown, under two situations, Sir Rupert Brent as having escaped from the castle, it is necessary that we should describe briefly the manner in which he accomplished that object, which at first sight would appear so difficult.

CHAPTER XVIII.

The Escape of Sir Rupert Brent from Winchester Castle Guard-room.

The prisoner confined in Winchester Castle was placed in the guard-room, or rather in a small room adjoining, there to await further inquiries and examinations that might, or might not, be agreeable to the prisoner, as the case might be.

Sir Rupert Brent gazed about him and saw but little comfort in the strong walls, high windows, and iron bars, that guarded, what appeared inaccessible to him, without even any other assistance than what he could procure.

He threw himself into a settle to rest and brood over the security in which he found himself placed. There was no room for escape; the windows were high and narrow, and, moreover, were strongly secured by iron bars, that presented an impenetrable barrier, and there was but one door, and that was strong, defended by bolts and locks on the outside, and, as if the demon of ill-fortune for him had thought that not enough, the door opened into the guard-room, where there were many men waiting their turn of duty, on the walls of the castle and the different parts of the walls where it was usual to post them.

The voices of the men reached him as they were conversing upon matters, that were most at home in, they joked and laughed and seemed light-hearted enough, while Sir Rupert Brent sat still and listened to them with something like sullen contempt, but, at the same time, his thoughts seemed active, for, now and then, he cast a look at the door and listened more attentively than before to the sounds that came from the guard-room.

'At what hour are you going on duty?' demanded one of the men of another.

'At midnight,' said the other, 'and then I shall remain till the light of morning comes to relieve the dulness of night.'

'Well, I would much sooner you be there than I.'

'Why so? your post is none of the best, I should imagine,' said the other.

'It may not be, but inside of stone walls with a good seat and a warm corner is far preferable to the walls and a bleak wind. Don't tell me to the contrary of that, for I won't believe it, so that's the truth.'

'You may fancy your berth all very comfortable, but I can tell you I wouldn't take the office of keeping the guard-room all night for all your pay.'

'Why not?'

'Because, in the first place, you have nothing but the four walls round you, no comrades to speak to, and you pass several hours here together with nobody.'

'Aye—but in the dead of night I sleep.'

'Aye, after a fashion, sitting bolt upright against a prop, or a wall—a pretty sort of rest that! why, it's as bad as an extra drill, to be sure.'

'Indeed! a soldier ought to be able to sleep anywhere, and that is no hardship; but I am more comfortable than that, I can lie down at all hours, and I have no extra drills, which you have very seldom to do; and as for being alone, I am not the man to be frightened at my own shadow.'

'Then you have a thundering cavalier in your care, with a moustache as fierce as a Normandy bear, and looks as if he would eat you up at a meal.'

'He! why, I'd throttle him in two minutes. He's no man to stand against me, not he.'

'You are afraid of him, at all events, and dare not go in, if we were not here to back you.'

'If I had occasion I would, but if not I shan't to please anybody, and there's an end of it. I am not going to play any game with my prisoner and be laughed at for a fool.'

'That is often your case, old man; but never mind; fortune betide you another time.'

'How goes the time?' inquired another.

'Oh, not time to mount guard yet awhile, never fear; you don't want to be cooling yourself there on the walls for any purpose, it ain't so agreeable, I reckon, as you would desire to make it appear. You don't make it quite so smooth as all that, I know well enough you'd sooner be in your bed than looking for owls on Winchester walls.'

'There's no treason in saying I should, I hope, and no bad

exchange—a good bed and warm quarters, for a moonlight walk upon the ramparts, with nothing to do but to walk to and fro till the moon looks the colour of a Jesuit's cap.'

'I think you are about right there,' said the jailor, 'but, without joking, the hour for relief will soon be here, and then there will be but a short time before the guard turns in again, I suppose, and then they will soon be off to their sleeping-rooms.'

'You may well say that,' said the man, 'they have had a long drill of it, but it will be an hour before they are all back. It takes that to relieve all the different posts.'

'Ah, I see; they'll be back, I suppose, as usual, and that's all about it. How do they manage about the posting of men down at the bridge, the river is not deep?'

'No; but I think there's no danger apprehended from that quarter at any time, and there are but few sentinels posted there; but hark, I hear the challenge of the sentry.'

A drum was now heard along the vaulted passages, and men were running to and fro and collecting in masses and answering to the roll and muster. The guard-room was in an instant deserted, and the jailor comfortably reposed in his chair just to get the right position, so that his bones came against no sharp points.

'Now,' thought Sir Rupert Brent, 'I have hope. Alone in that room, none else with him, I may escape yet—one man—only one man—I can secure him; but how to get at him? that is the question; he may not come in, and to make a noise would be to attract disagreeable attention.'

His brows contracted as some dark thought crossed his mind, but he thought of nothing else, save his escape and the deeds he might do if he were once outside of that door.

He listened for the slightest sound, but could only hear the mustering of the men-at-arms and the clang of their weapons, the words of command, and then the tramp of men trained to war; they came on and on till they neared the door and entered the guard-room; the doors were opened, and the relief passed out to set the watch for the night until morning.

Sir Rupert Brent listened to all these sounds with some anxiety, and for nearly ten minutes he scarce moved from his seat or breathed; he listened so intensely that his very soul appeared bent upon catching the slightest sound.

None came, and Sir Rupert Brent became satisfied, for a grim smile came over his countenance as he thought there would be no one to interrupt him in his struggle with his jailor, who promised to give him work, for he was a powerfully made man.

He was about to rise, when the jailor suddenly started up. 'I had forgotten to look to my prisoner before I went to sleep,' he muttered, 'but will do so now, while I think of it.'

He approached the door, and opened it, thrusting his head in; he held a light above his head as he said—

'Oh! you are safe, are you?'

'Quite,' replied Sir Rupert. 'Will you give me a glass of water? I am dry; your courtesy shall not be lost.'

'You have a pitcher full beside you. Confound it, man alive, can't you see?'

'I tell you what, villain,' said Sir Rupert, in apparent wrath, 'if I were other than a prisoner here, I would reward thy merits as they deserve, but, as I am, I may not. An empty pitcher is good for no man's thirst, and I cannot drink from it.'

'In God's truth, an' that be the case, Sir Cavalier, you have some reason to be angry with me, though I could have sworn upon the four evangelists that I had filled the pitcher with my own hands, and I cannot understand it now.'

'Look, and be convinced.'

'I will,' said the jailor, who, however, took the precaution of locking the door on the inside, and taking out the key before he quitted it, as a proper precaution. He then advanced towards the pitcher, which was close beside Sir Rupert Brent.

'I recollect very well filling it, and, if it be empty, why the devil or you, Sir Rupert, must have drunk it up.'

'Not I, my good fellow,' replied Sir Rupert, rising and pointing to the pitcher, and as for the other individual whom you name so irreverently, he wouldn't come here for a draught of water.'

The man was in the act of stooping as Sir Rupert spoke, but the nature of the speech caused him to look up, and, as he did so, he perceived his prisoner about to throw himself upon him, and before he could change his position to defend himself, he found Sir Rupert had executed the manœuvre, and

he was seized by the throat, and a desperate death-struggle ensued.

When two powerful men struggle for life in the manner these two did, without any witness—without any hope of aid—without any hope of mercy on either side, the struggle is desperate indeed, and a more determined one than that now going on between Sir Rupert and the guardsman has seldom taken place.

Though Sir Rupert had the advantage of the attack, and placed his adversary in a position not at all calculated to aid him in his struggle, yet the man, by dint of a most violent effort, threw off his assailant, yet it brought himself upon his knees, and before he could rise, Sir Rupert had again seized him with a giant's grasp round the throat.

The unfortunate man felt his strength giving way; the pressure at his throat was so great, that he could scarcely breathe. His face became distorted, and his lips purple; the blood seemed to swell out into his head, while his eyes protruded.

He tried to gasp for mercy, but utterance was denied him. He tried by violent efforts to shake himself off; he struck Sir Rupert violent blows on the head, but the latter gave no way, but held tightly.

The jailor then tried to kick Sir Rupert, and succeeded in doing so; one or two dreadful buffets, and then Sir Rupert took advantage of the man's shifting his position to throw him down, and fall upon him.

The fall completed the struggle, for the man's head came with a dreadful crash upon the stone flooring.

In an instant the man's face was covered with blood, which gushed from his ears and mouth in a copious stream, and he ceased to breathe any more.

'So far success has attended my exertions,' muttered Sir Rupert, as he rose up off the floor. 'By Heavens! the fellow was harder to kill than I could have believed.'

He seized upon the pitcher, which stood close beside him, and applied it to his lips; he was thirsty and heated by the violence of the exertion he had gone through.

'Now I have overcome one danger, and shall find many more beset me; but I will overcome them, too, or there is no virtue in cunning.'

He immediately began stripping himself and the dead man, exchanging such garments as he thought necessary and needful to enable him to escape detection.

'Now,' he muttered, 'if I can but succeed in preventing the discovery of my flight but an hour or two, I think my escape certain. I will lock this man in here, and they will not be able to get in for some time, for they will not suspect what has happened, because the door will be fastened, the jailor absent, and the keys not to be found.'

He was completely dressed like one of the guard, and he now took the keys from the jailor's person, and turning him over with his foot to ascertain if there were any life remaining in him, but there appeared none, upon which he quitted his cell, and locking the guard-room door, he stood in the guard-room itself.

All was still—no sound met his ear, and he paused before he should take the last step that would place him in the streets of Winchester, free, but sought after.

'They cannot be very long before they are back, and if I be found here, I shall be secured, that is certain, and have the death of the jailor to answer for. No, no, that will not do, I will escape if there be any means under heaven of doing so; and as I can gain nothing by staying here, I will encounter what danger I may have to face at once, before the guard returns.'

He carefully and cautiously opened the guard-room door, and then stepped into the street.

'Hilloa, Stangroom!' shouted a drunken soldier, reeling up—'let us in—there's a good fellow. I shall have a damned hard drill to-morrow if I'm found out.'

'Well—'

'It is, and will lead to ill if you report me;—come, that's a good fellow, let me in, and I'll tumble into bed in no time; you are a good chap, and would help a fellow out of a scrape, if you could. Now, I know they are all out, and you will be safe enough;— open the door, and let me in.'

'Go in, and I will say nothing about it,' said Sir Rupert, in an assumed voice—'say nothing about it. What's the pass-word—I've forgotten it?'

'One good deserves its fellow—'St. George for England,' is the word, Stangroom. Good night, my boy !'

Sir Rupert opened the door, and pushed the man in, and then shut and locked it, taking the keys with him : he walked away, for though he had the pass-word, yet at the gateway he thought the jailor would be familiar with all, and question him why he wanted to leave the city at that hour.

Indeed, it was clear that the pass-word was of no value to enable him to get out of the town, because he would be stopped on suspicion, unless he had some authority, as none of the soldiery had any authority for being out at that hour, much less to go out—and he could produce none.

It would be of use, certainly, if he were stopped by any of the parties in the town, and at places he might, accidentally, approach in the dark. The moon was rising, but there were clouds about that seemed to indicate a storm, and yet they were not heavy enough to promise a speedy change.

Ever and anon, as some of these clouds crossed the face of the moon, the good town was enveloped in darkness; but even then there was a reflected light that enabled any one to see and avoid aught they desired.

He walked along for some little distance, determined to make for that part near the little river, over which was a bridge; there he thought he should run less risk of detection, or, at all events, he would meet with less opposition—such as he could have a better chance of contending against.

However, he walked onward cautiously enough, until he came near the Cross, and then he met an officer and two men, who were returning to the guard-room.

'Who goes there ?' was the challenge.

'A friend to the good city—one of the guard.'

'The word !'

'St. George for England.'

"What brings you out at this hour at night, my man ? inquired the officer.

'I am on special business for the governor.'

'Where are you going to ?'

'To the cathedral.'

'Pass on,' said the officer, and Sir Rupert immediately did so, but could see very well that he was regarded with suspicion, for the officer looked after him for some distance; and he, to avoid giving further cause for it, immediately continued in the direction of the cathedral, until the darkness rendered either invisible to the other.

Then he pushed on at a rapid pace towards that part of the wall running beside the river, but here he was compelled to turn out of his path, for he met another party returning, and not being desirous of being questioned again, he concealed himself until they had all passed by.

'They will find it all out presently, and then there will be a pursuit. I shall be chased—I must push on, by Saint Gregory ! and that pretty sharply.'

'Who goes there ?' again said a voice; and in another moment the form of the guard came upon his view.

'A friend !' he said hastily.

'Well, friend, what brings you out at this hour ? You are out after hours—you must return to the barracks, and there report yourself.'

'Very well; but I am on special business for the governor.'

'Indeed ! And how comes it that the governor had no other messenger than a guardsman ? Where is your pass ?'

' I have none.'

' No letter—no sign?'

' None save the pass-word,' replied Sir Rupert.

' Then you must come back to the barracks. Come, Sir Guardsman, stand out in the moonlight, and let us see who and what you are.'

Sir Rupert obeyed and stood out in the moonlight, thinking the man might fail to detect him, but he was mistaken.

' Well—ah! there's none in our company with such a moustache as that! No, no, you must come back to the guard-room with me, as I think something is wrong.'

Sir Rupert Brent saw there was no chance of getting off without discovery, and so, without thinking any more about the matter, he drew his dagger and stabbed the officer to the heart; he fell to the earth with a groan, and in falling his arms clashed loudly on the stones.

Fearful the sound would cause some one to come up to the spot, he immediately hastened onward with all the speed he could make, but the tramp of men again stopped him, and he was not desirous of being again questioned by any party he might encounter, and this one, by the sound, appeared to be a more formidable party than he had yet seen.

' If I can escape them—and it can be no difficult matter—I shall soon be near the wall.' This was so very near that he could almost see it, but the party was near at hand, and the necessity for immediate concealment was great. A doorway seemed the only chance that was afforded him, and into this he pushed himself with haste.

The door, however, was not secure, but opened as soon as he pressed himself against it. This was fortunate, for the doorway did not offer the same facility for hiding as he had anticipated, but the sudden opening of the door was an incident of a favourable character.

He immediately stepped into the passage and stood there for a moment, and heard the party approach gradually, and step by step, until they reached the door, and then they passed by.

' So far safe,' he muttered, and was about to open the door, when he heard some one approach, and then stop.

' Confound thee!' muttered Sir Rupert; ' what, must thou come here? So I am to be met at every turn by one enemy and another to-night! The very air teems with adventure.'

The person who stopped pushed against the door; he seemed to mutter to himself, and expect to see it open, but was disappointed at finding the door secured.

There was a pause of about a minute, and then a key was inserted into the lock, and the door gently opened by a man, who stepped inside and closed the door.

Sir Rupert Brent stept back a pace or two to allow the man to come in. The opening of the door was an event he had not thought of, and had not provided for.

When the door was shut again another door was opened. A strong light issued from the room into which the door opened, and fell full upon the form of Sir Rupert; and the man who entered it, turning round to look at him, gave a start.

' What do you here? Help! help!'

' Another word, and you die.'

' Help!' shouted the man, and he attempted to draw his sword, but Sir Rupert Brent had planted his dagger in hi- heart, and he, reeling backwards, fell to the floor.

However, the house was alarmed, and he heard people rushing about and calling to one another, and he could even hear some one coming down the stairs. Finding he was likely to be beset on all hands, he gently opened the door, and closed it after him.

He now made the best of his way towards that part of the wall which he knew was the lowest and least guarded, and arrived there without any further impediment; but there was a difficulty yet to be overcome—that of mounting the walls unseen by the sentinel, who was walking to and fro in the moonlight.

After waiting some time in deep thought he determined upon a step that, if it succeeded at all, would give him egress, without any further trouble.

He ascended the steps that led to the sentinel's post, and the moon was obscured, and he was silent in all his motions; he succeeded in reaching him unseen and unheard; drawing his broad sword, he gave the man a thrust below the shoulder blade. He fell, and in doing so he discharged his arquebus.

',By Heaven, they'll be here soon enough now!' muttered Sir Rupert, as he leaped from the wall to the earth on the outside. ' There is no time to spare.'

So saying he got on his feet, for his leap had thrown him down and had shaken him. As may be imagined he stopped for nothing, but pushed onwards till he came to a road. He knew the way well—it was the London road; then, with a hasty tread, he traversed the path that lay before him, taking care to keep as much under the cover of the trees as possible, and, where it was possible, he crossed the meadows, keeping out of the main track, presenting less chance of being seen by any stray traveller, and so, by making a detour, he got gradually round to Winchester, and executed the feats which we have recorded.

CHAPTER XIX.

The Consternation among the Jesuits.— The Determination.

ONE may well imagine that when Ranulph Hensman left the meeting of the Jesuits in the manner we have described, and had been compelled, for the preservation of his own existence, most reluctantly, as we know, to take the life of the man who acted as their door keeper, the state of alarm and consternation in which he left them must have been of the most serious character.

That such men as these should fall into such a serious piece of trouble, and have their secret meetings invaded by one whom they could not consider but as their very worst foe, was enough of itself to drive them almost frantic with rage, if we put aside altogether the consideration of the imminent danger in which it involved them and their cause.

There was not a man among them but was armed, and the flashing of the swords, as they were all drawn, had a singular and imposing effect among the assemblage.

The rush made to the door had something tremendous about it, for they entertained no doubt in the world of overtaking the rash intruder, and sacrificing him to their vengeance.

But when they found the door fast—that door which they themselves had been so careful to have made of prodigious strength for their own defence—when they found that fast, and that they were thus cheated of the hope of sacrificing a man whose life at any time, they would gladly have taken —positive yells of rage burst from them, and they showed an amount of demoniac fury which one would scarcely have expected from men educated, as they were, in all the wily arts of priestcraft, and to take an extensive part, by stratagem and deceit, in the politics of Europe.

Several of them flung themselves against the powerful door with shouts of execration, and three or four were seriously hurt in the frantic endeavours they made to pass that strong and iron-bound entrance.

And then, as moment after moment passed away, and he whom they had placed as their trusty sentinel and doorkeeper moved not aside the bar which kept them in the vaulted chamber, they began to think—what from their knowledge of him on any other occasion they would have been slow to imagine— namely, that he was the traitor who had not only introduced the spy into their councils, but who now, by devilish ingenuity, cheated them of their revenge.

Oh! could they but for a moment have encountered him— could they but have had the satisfaction of sheathing their swords in his heart—it would have surely been some satisfaction for the wrong which they believed he had done them.

Cries of revenge echoed through the vaulted chamber— oaths, shouts, and execrations were upon every tongue; but such a war of words surely must soon cease, and considerations of personal safety speedily suggested that some means of exit must be found, lest the next circumstance that occurred should be an armed force coming to arrest them in the name of the King.

A feeling of self-preservation collected them again in solemn counsel round the table; and now the sole object of that conclave was to devise means how to leave the place they had themselves made so secure. Sir Rupert Brent was the man who spoke.

' We have no time to lose,' he said. ' There is but one entrance to this place, and that is evidently so secure that we can have no hope of breaking through it; but we are in a ruinous part of the ancient cathedral. The wall opposite the door is but of flimsy material, and may be hewn down by our swords : it is our only chance. Come on, and let us attack at once our own fortress.'

With his drawn sword in his hand—for he had never sheathed it—Sir Rupert Brent rushed on, and, accompanied by half-a-dozen of the others, who had the strongest weapons, he commenced an attack upon the wall which soon yielded to their united efforts, and began to crumble away. An orifice or breach was soon effected, but all looked dark as the grave beyond it.

'Fear not,' cried Brent; 'it only looks farther into the vaults, from which there is many an outlet. Come on; at least, we shall be personally free from the consequences of this most direful misadventure.'

Under such circumstances as these, any man of cool and temperate judgment who takes the lead is sure to maintain it for a time; and so it was, that almost whatever Brent said was acceded to, and the Jesuits, one and all, followed him through the breach in the wall to the gloomy vaults adjoining the most ancient part of the cathedral.

The most profound darkness was before them, and they had forgotten to bring with them a lamp from the vaulted chamber. One of the number, however, with difficulty found his way back, and procured that important agent to their proceedings, so that in a few moments more they were, at all events, enabled to see where they were.

'This way,' said Sir Rupert, 'this way; follow me and the light. Are you mad that you hesitate? Know you not the implacable character of the Lord Warden; and that, backed as he is by an apostate King, he is ready for any act which may be calculated to strike a blow against Catholicism? Come on, and come quickly!'

Thus urged—not that they needed much urging—they pushed onward, making their way with what expedition they could amid huge fragments of broken stones and other rubbish, which from time to time had been collected in that ruinous part of the cathedral.

A strange and excited group they looked—attired partly ecclesiastically and partly in lay habits, but all armed to the very teeth, and looking as desperate as men could do who were engaged in the desperate cause that animated them.

It was clear, from the anxious glances that they cast behind them from time to time, that they were in expectation of pursuit; but when they found that there was no sign of any enemies being upon their track, they somewhat slackened their speed, and finally arriving at an open space, which had been devoted to sepulchre, they paused to take breath and consult concerning their present position.

By common consent—as is always the case under circumstances of peril and of personal danger—they gathered round the boldest spirit among them, and that one was Father Georges, *alias* Sir Rupert Brent.

He stood in the centre of that excited throng, and all was still, awaiting what view he would take of the circumstances in which they were placed.

'This night,' he said, 'has been productive of some of the strangest accidents and coincidences that ever I have encountered. You all know how I became a prisoner to the Lord Warden, and how unjustifiably he detained me under an authority from the King, which carries with it such an abundance of latitude, that the liberty of no man is safe for one moment.'

'It is aimed at us, of course,' said one, 'and is intended to be an instrument of persecution.'

'Disgraceful!' said another; 'as if we ever persecuted.'

'John Clement,' said Brent, 'may spare his sneers. We do persecute, and we will persecute while we have the power to do so. Our mission is of a mixed nature, political and theological.'

'And for once,' said John Clement, 'I am bolder than you, Sir Rupert Brent, for I avow that the supremacy of the Romish Church, and the political influence of its members, is highly delightful, because it brings with it pleasant personal consequences.'

'Be it so, be it so,' said Brent, impatiently, 'but this is no time to indulge in idle conversation. I say the history of this night's proceedings is most curious. We have either been betrayed by him who kept our door, or some accident revealed to Ranulph Hensman, the detestable secretary of the Lord Warden, the secret signal which enabled him to be present at our conference; but I have accomplished that to-night which, as regards him, is enough to drive his very soul to madness.'

'You allude to his wife.'

'I do. She is in the power of the Abbess of the Benedictine nuns.'

'Indeed,' said John Clement; 'that hawk will look well after the chicken. By heavens! I'd rather encounter a man clad in complete steel, with weapons aiming at my life, than the devout Abbess of the holy Benedictines.'

'As a matter of course,' now continued Sir Rupert Brent, 'all that has passed here to-night will be communicated to the Lord Warden, and from him reach the ears of the King. You know best whether there was much or little danger in what was said and done before my arrival; but it is quite clear that, unless we are most cautious, Winchester will not hold us.'

'We must separate,' said one. 'The Lord Warden is a man to take prompt measures.'

'Yes! and Ranulph Hensman, with his private wrong to back him, will stir heaven and earth against us. Oh! if we could but have killed him—if we could but have taken his life—what a glorious circumstance his prying into our camp would have been! What a notable adventure would it have been for us to have deprived the state and accursed Protestantism of such a servant! Believe me, my friends, we shall scarcely meet with such another chance.'

'It was scarce a chance,' said one, 'for we knew him not; and I here at once avow to you that I introduced him.'

A dozen swords were in a moment turned towards the speaker.

'What folly is this!' he said. 'Could I not have kept my own secret if I'd pleased, and so incurred no danger? but I think it for the general weal that we should know not only how he obtained admission, but at what precise moment he obtained it.'

The sword-points were lowered, and Sir Rupert Brent said—

'That is quite correct—perfectly correct. If even our friend here made an error of judgment, he can do nothing now better than regret it, and tell us all about it.'

'I did admit him,' continued the speaker. 'He accosted me in the church with our own watchword ready on his lips, and I made the agreed-upon reply; upon which, pointing to the secret door, for he knew it well, he told me he had mislaid his key, and was compelled to wait until some of us arrived. I had no suspicion of him—I believed what he said. Where he got our watchword from, Heaven only knows. He came in with me; and so you have the whole account.'

'Our friend,' said Sir Rupert Brent, 'stands almost acquitted of indiscretion. We must adopt some other place of meeting. Suppose we separate now at once; and, if you will leave it to me to find some secure spot on which we may hold our next appointment, I will do so, and the information shall be open to every one by a slip of paper placed in the hollow of the old elm-tree by the Abbey gardens. There are twenty-two of us who require the information. Let each who gets it mark the figure 1 on the slip of paper, so that the last comer may know that he is entitled to destroy it; and he will do so accordingly, for the shortest possible time it remains in existence the better.'

'Agreed, agreed!' they said.

'Then let us separate at once. We are in the open air, and surrounded but by a few crumbling walls of what was once the old cathedral.'

'But let us, before we separate to-night,' said one, 'ascertain, beyond dispute, if he who kept watch for us at the door of our council-chamber was true or false.'

'It will be a dangerous task, perchance.'

'Not at all,' said Sir Rupert. 'Wait for me, and I will execute it: some of you lend me a cloak, for I am but in a strange mongrel garb, having been compelled to adopt a disguise, in effecting my escape, which sits but ill upon me. I feel so convinced that Ranulph Hensman's presence was but an experiment, and that he has no force to back him, that I believe there is no risk in traversing the secret passage. Wait for me; I shall be with you ere many minutes have elapsed.'

He darted off, and, making the turn of the cathedral, he entered at the great gates. The interior of the sacred edifice appeared to be completely deserted, but it was only a very casual glance that Sir Rupert cast around him, and then he strode on towards the secret door.

A man more versed in all the cunning which was requisite to carry out an enterprise with success could not be found than this wily Jesuit.

He knew that if parties were secreted in the church, watching the secret door, probably they were too well concealed for him to discover them, and that his only chance of escape, if such were the case, consisted in the rapidity of his movements.

He paused not, but, carrying a key in his hand, he made for the secret door, at once opened it and passed through, securing it on the inside with such celerity, that no one could have stopped him.

'So,' he said, 'if any one was watching, he has learnt nothing but what he knew before, namely, that there was a door—a key to fit its lock, and that a man might pass through it when opened.'

He saw the faint glimmer of a light, and, upon closely approaching, he saw that it was the lamp belonging to the man whose duty it was to take charge of the door.

It was overturned, but the light still burnt upon the ground with a dull and sickly lustre.

His sword was drawn in his hand, for though he anticipated no danger, he thought it best to be prepared against any contingency, and so he advanced, guided by that light, until he came to the dead body of the door-keeper, lying upon its face.

Sir Rupert Brent turned over the corpse with his foot, and then he saw that it was lying in a pool of blood, and that the fixed and horrible stare of death was upon the convulsed features.

'Ah!' he said, 'the man was faithful. Very good! Ranulph Hensman's sword has done this deed. We shall see if we cannot requite him by-and-by—perchance we may. How true it is that there is always a day for him who treasures up a wrong or a revenge! They are the same to me. I have been crossed, and that I will not forget. No one yet ever foiled me for a time that did not meet death as his ultimate reward; and I do not intend that Ranulph Hensman should become an exception to such a goodly rule.'

He then passed on, taking the same route which he and his companions had done so short a time before. He informed them of the discovery he had made of the faithfulness of the door-keeper.

'He has sealed with his blood his good faith,' said Sir Rupert; 'and so far we are obliged to him. These subordinates should always die at proper times.'

The Jesuits then parted for the night, each taking a different route; and in a few minutes a silence, as of the very grave, reigned in and about that ancient portion of Winchester cathedral.

CHAPTER XX.
The Attack upon the Convent.

PASSING over some preliminary thoughts and feelings, which the reader may well imagine possessed poor Ranulph Hensman as hour after hour flew by, and he was deprived of the sweet society of her who had become the solace and the principal pleasure of his existence, we will conduct the reader to that small audience-chamber in the castle where the Lord Warden usually received guests unknown to him.

That individual himself was in the apartment, as were likewise Ranulph Hensman and John Elkington.

Hensman was evidently combating with his grief; and although the Lord Warden and John Elkington both had given him every possible reason to be hopeful of such an immediate result as should restore Alice to his arms, his mind was full of the most dreadful surmises as regarded the amount of persecution she might endure before the attempt to rescue her could be carried out. With great difficulty, after receiving the information from John Elkington that Alice was a prisoner in the convent of the Benedictine nuns, he had refrained from alone rushing to that building and demanding admittance in the name of Heaven and of justice. But if Ranulph Hensman, in an impulse such as we have described, felt inclined to do a desperate act, his better reason soon came to his aid, and he was able to exercise a patience which had all the appearance of resignation, if it wanted that faculty in reality.

'Hensman,' said the Lord Warden, 'take comfort in the assurance that John Elkington and I will lose sight of all other considerations until Alice is rescued. Be assured that nothing shall stir us from that purpose, and that before you separate from us now you shall find that we have concocted a plan of operations that will insure success.'

'Certainly,' said Elkington; 'it must not be an attempt that we make, but the thing itself must be done; and I recommend you, my Lord Warden, by authority of the King's protection to this lady—a protection which, if it did not in express terms call upon all in the service of his Majesty to give effect to it, fully and virtually implies so much—'

'I am of that opinion,' said the Warden, 'likewise; and moreover it is more consonant to my own views and feelings to do such an act as this boldly and at once, than to falter over it in the slightest degree.'

'I advise, then, that we take a sufficient force to overcome all possible opposition, and proceed at once in the open face of day to the Benedictine convent, and demand the person of Alice Hensman in the name of the King and by virtue of his authority.'

'Oh!' cried Hensman, 'if such a course as that be determined upon my heart will leap for joy to be the first to scale those convent walls. It is a bold plan and a worthy one; and believe me, when I say so, I do not speak because my private wrong weighs heavily on my soul; no, far from it, but I look upon it that, in the person of Alice Hensman, the rights of all England are attacked, and the King's power set at nought.'

'It is so,' said the Warden; 'it is most unquestionably so; and I feel, for one, that Winchester is doomed to be the scene of one of the first important public acts of the monarch against the Jesuits. It has ever thus been the case with great political and moral convulsions. Some private wrong, perhaps insignificant in itself, has fanned up the slumbering embers of popular commotion, and given an impetus to thought and action which has been felt throughout the length and breadth of a mighty empire.'

The Lord Warden rang a small hand-bell as he spoke, and the summons was answered by one of his pages.

'Send hither Capt. Angerstein,' he said, 'of the castle guard.'

'Yes, my lord.'

In a few moments a rough, war-beaten looking officer made his appearance.

'Captain Angerstein,' said the Warden, 'how many disposable men do you think you could bring effectively into the field, so as yet to leave a sufficient force to maintain the garrison?'

'For a few hours, my lord,' said the officer, 'while no entire change of sentinels is required, I can muster one hundred and fifty men.'

'Let them be ready, and well armed and appointed, as quickly as possible. We have to do something by express order of the King, and it is a something which, if done well, his Majesty will not feel inclined to forget the actors in. Let my charger be ready at the Castle-gate, and a couple of horses for these gentlemen; and if John Martin, the herald, be not drunk, as usual, bid him don his official costume, and take with him his silver trumpet, for, as I tell you, what we have to do is to be done in the name of the King, and shall be done by us, who are the servants of his Majesty, with all the pomp and circumstance as if Henry himself led the way.'

'In ten minutes, my lord,' said the officer, 'all shall be ready;' and he immediately left the apartment.

'Now, Hensman,' said the Lord Warden, 'you shall find that we are not tardy in doing you justice. If the King's warrant succeed in inducing the Abbess of the Benedictine convent to deliver up her prisoner, a great point will be gained, for the supremacy of the King over the liberty of his subjects will be acknowledged as superior to that of the Court of Rome.'

'And if she refuse, my lord?'

'Were it necessary, Ranulph Hensman, not one stone should stand upon another to mark the site of the Benedictine convent, or enable a future historian to say that there it stood.'

'My boundless thanks,' said Ranulph Hensman, 'my utmost gratitude is yours; and all I ask is, that if there be a fray I may be first and foremost in it.'

'You shall; and as second to myself in command of the troops, which I here at once appoint you—for Master Elkington comes with us as a volunteer—you will have abundant opportunity for action.'

'Alice! Alice!' said Hensman, 'I shall behold thee once again. For the second time I shall rescue thee from those cloisters in which monkish superstition immured thee; thou shalt be mine, Alice, once more, and, with the halo thrown around thee of the protection of higher power than priestcraft can exert, I shall indeed feel that you are safe.'

At this moment it was announced that the troop was ready; and the Lord Warden, making some slight alteration in his costume which gave it a more warlike character, girded on his sword, and led the way to the esplanade in front of the castle.

It was quite clear that Captain Angerstein had become impressed with an idea of the importance of the service on which the troops were about to proceed, for each man was armed as efficiently as the service would enable him to be, and attired in his best and gayest costume.

Three superb chargers in rich trappings were pawing the earth, and awaiting the appearance of their riders, while lounging idly about in his glittering official costume was a royal herald, whose big, burly appearance and bloated countenance fully justified the remark which the Lord Warden had made of him.

The troops were all on foot, but there was a led horse for the herald, and a couple of pages, one to run on each side of it, not to give undue importance to John Martin, but to do proper homage to the important office he held, which, although sometimes filled by but commonplace personages, was considered on of great consequence throughout all Europe.

'What's in the wind now, John Martin?' said one of the troopers; 'by the mass we've not had such a turn-out as this for many a long day.'

'Oh, it's only some royal proclamation to be read at the High Cross, I'll be bound, or they wouldn't want me.'

'I'll take my oath,' said the soldier, 'it's something more, or Captain Angerstein wouldn't come upon it; and, by the mass, Master Martin——'

'Nay, now, Solomon Digby, you swear by the mass, as if that were pleasant in the ears of the Lord Warden; but times are altered, and it was but yesterday se'nnight I heard Ranulph Hensman say that for the common people to swear by the mass would ere long be so rare a thing that he would be jibed and jeered at who used the phrase.'

'And why Master Martin—only answer me that—why?'

'Marry, then, because there'd be no mass to swear by.'

'Then the world is turning upside down, and by the mass——'

'By the mass thou art a fool, and know not what thou sayest. But peace, peace! Here comes the Lord Warden; and now, indeed, I do bethink me it's something more than a proclamation, for there is a look upon his face as if there were serious work to do. And behold, there is Ranulph Hensman—armed, too, to the teeth, and Master John Elkington, the Earl of Surrey's man. Depend on't there'll be hard knocks, Solomon Digby, and you're wrong—you are—in saying that it was nothing but a proclamation.'

'Now, by my faith! you said so yourself.'

'Ah! giv'st thou me the lie? Solomon Digby, I'll have revenge of thee another time.'

'A groat for your revenge!'

Further colloquy was stopped by the Lord Warden, accompanied by Ranulph Hensman and John Elkington, riding to the head of the compact little body of troops. The herald fell into his place, immediately behind the Warden; and then the latter giving the word to march, the cavalcade proceeded through the streets of Winchester, having a most imposing effect, and much astonishing the citizens by its force.

In a few minutes all the idle and disorderly persons in the city congregated and followed the troop, every member of which was busy in speculating as to what was to be their place of destination.

The greater number of them were decidedly of the opinion expressed by the herald, namely, that some proclamation of the King's was to be read with all due ceremony at the High Cross; and this apparently bore some probability, as the procession moved onwards in that direction; but then, when the Lord Warden turned his horse's head towards a street which led to the outskirts of the city, the whole affair became involved in mystery and a fertile field for conjecture.

Speedily the mob which now followed the little cavalcade doubled in number, and the Lord Warden whispered to John Elkington—

'This will be not the least important day in the history of England. It will be thoroughly seen now how far the wishes and feelings of the people go with the priesthood. For them to give up Alice Hensman without a struggle would be such a confession of weakness as I can hardly expect from the Catholic party; and, as our force is so strong that they can have nothing available to resist it, they can only give us some trouble by an appeal to the feelings and passions of the multitude.'

'And they will do so, be assured; and highly probable is it that this disorderly mass of persons now following us will be called upon to aid actually in preserving monkish supremacy over their liberties, by resisting what will be called our violation of the sanctity of a convent.'

'For my own part,' said the Warden, 'I have no objection to people immuring themselves in any particular building, if it takes their fancy so to do; and I should be quite willing to hold that building, as I would hold the house of any individual, sacred, but not in a religious point of view. When, however, a convent is converted into a prison, it most lamentably loses its inviolability.'

'It does so, indeed; but do you not see the throng is thickening around us?'

'Yes,' remarked Hensman, 'and, if you look closely, you will see that some men are among them of a different description to the remainder.'

'Indeed!' said the Warden; 'if, Ranulph Hensman, you can identify any one as having been present at the meeting in the vaulted chamber by the cathedral, we will arrest him at once.'

Hensman turned upon his horse and looked curiously at a man who was whispering intently into the ear of a stalwart mechanic, whose excited features showed that what was said to him, whether it was true or false, was taking a powerful hold of his imagination.

'There is one of them,' said Hensman; 'I know him by a peculiar habit he has of elevating his brows as he speaks. Have I your licence, my Lord Warden, for taking him?'

'Most unquestionably; order his arrest at once, and send him to the castle under charge of a file of men.'

Ranulph Hensman turned his horse's head in the direction where the priest whom he had recognised was instilling the subtle poison, most probably, of deceit and lies, into the ears of his unsuspecting listener.

Half-a-dozen bounds of the powerful steed which Hensman bestrode brought him to the spot, and, stooping from the saddle, he seized the man with such a powerful grasp, that to escape from him was impossible, and, flinging him among the soldiery, he cried—

'A prisoner for the castle, by the order of my Lord Warden. Let a file of men take him, Captain Angerstein.'

'Of what am I accused?' said the man, when he recovered a little from the astonishment the sudden attack had thrown him into.

'Ask your conscience,' said Hensman, 'and it will reply, High treason.'

Having thus executed the Warden's commands, Hensman trotted his horse back to its former station, and while a file of men proceeded to the castle with their prisoner, the calvacade went on, still followed, however, by the mob, into which some sort of awe appeared to have been struck by the manner in which the arrest had been executed.

'Sacrilege!' cried a voice in the throng, and then all was still.

'Heard you that?' whispered the Warden to Elkington; 'there spoke a priest.'

'Unquestionably; it will be sad if we have to take the blood of people whose ignorance and long habits of blind obedience to priestcraft will drive them into dangerous acts.'

Five minutes more of progress brought them within sight of the ancient convent of Benedictine nuns, and the Lord Warden slackened his speed a moment, in order that he might give some directions to the herald, and at the same time he handed him the King's written protection for Alice Hensman.

The herald bowed, and then trotted on a little in advance towards the convent gate, which, to the intense surprise of the mob as well as the soldiery, was now evidently the place of destination.

Two or three minutes more sufficed to prove this beyond a doubt; for the troop halted by command of the Warden at the convent portal, the gloomy walls of which appeared so sad and silent that one could hardly suppose it possible as many as two hundred human souls, which was actually the case, resided there, isolated from the great world, fancying that, by thus subverting the order of nature, they must be doing something peculiarly acceptable to its Author.

The herald shrank a little as he placed his hand upon the handle of the convent bell; but a glance at the Lord Warden's face showed him that the affair was no jest, and he rang a tremendous peal.

A few minutes elapsed, and then a wicket was opened, and a woman's face appeared, and she demanded, in high, cracked tones, what was wanted.

'In the name of Henry,' said the herald, 'by the grace of God King of these realms, you are commanded forthwith to surrender unto the Most Noble the Lord Warden of Winchester the person of Alice Hensman, confined within the walls of this convent.'

No answer was vouchsafed, but the wicket gate was closed sharply.

A dead silence reigned throughout the multitude for a few seconds, and then those who had been most forward and caught the herald's words repeated them to the others; and, in a very short time, the whole multitude was aware of the demand that had been made, and various speculations and surmises concerning it became apparent.

Then again, before the full buz of amazement had reached its height, the same voice that had before spoken cried aloud 'Sacrilege!' and several of the mob echoed the cry.

'Shall we take no notice,' said Hensman, 'of this interruption?'

'None whatever,' said the Warden; 'we'd better hear nothing and see nothing unless we are actually impeded in our progress. We need not presume that that cry of sacrilege applies to our movements.'

'Be it so, my lord; but I think we are treated with scant courtesy to be refused even an answer at the convent gate.'

At a motion from the Lord Warden the herald rang again; and then, as before, that small wicket opened, and a human face appeared at the grating, but it was not the one that had shown itself on the previous occasion.

'What is this?' demanded the new portress; 'what is this that breaks the peace of this sacred spot—on what pretence do armed men approach these walls?'

'In the name of the King,' said the herald, 'Alice Hensman is demanded.'

'And that demand,' cried the Lord Warden, 'will be enforced under the sign manual of his Majesty. A free and unconditional protection against all proceedings, ecclesiastical or otherwise, has been granted to Alice Hensman : you will do well to consult your convent's interest, by acceding peaceably to a demand which, if you do not, will be enforced, to the great scandal of your establishment.'

'And how dare any one,' cried the woman, who the Lord Warden shrewdly suspected was the abbess herself, 'how dare any one presume to think that the name of any mortal monarch will have power here? We are the servants of the King of kings, and the Church of Rome yields authority to no crowned head!'

'This is an answer,' said the Warden, 'which I will not say I did not expect; but yet it is a foolish one. Herald, again demand in the King's name the restitution of the prisoner.'

The herald placed his silver trumpet to his lips, and blew a blast long and loud. It was certainly one of the accomplishments of Master Martin that he could do such a feat, and, probably, that was the one which had succeeded in installing him in so important a situation. And then, ere the echoes of the sound had died away, he repeated the demand in due form, at the end of which the same voice that had before cried 'Sacrilege,' apparently emboldened by the impunity with which it had before spoken, shouted the word with a yelling emphasis, that was highly calculated to produce great excitement in the multitude.

The wicket gate remained open, and for a few moments the Lord Warden leant eagerly forward from his horse, to hear what reply should be now vouchsafed to his demand.

The abbess—far it was indeed that individual, who herself had come to answer the intruders—spoke, and it was evident, from the tone in which she did so, that all the bitterness of her nature was aroused by the demand that had been made for the restitution of a prisoner she had so recently had possession of, and had gloried in the notion of having time and opportunity amply to persecute.

'You can tell your master,' she said, 'the apostate infidel, this, that not while one stone remains upon another of these walls—not while one drop of blood circulates in these veins—shall any one imprisoned here by order of the Church of Rome be relinquished to mortal hands. The curse of outraged sanctity and of offended Heaven fall upon your heads!'

These words were spoken with such a bitterness and such a loud shrieking emphasis, that they reached the ears of every one present; and when the wicket gate was again closed, which it was with vehemence, a great confusion of voices arose among the people, and the soldiery were pressed closely upon, from the eager curiosity of those behind to see what turn the affair was likely to take.

Then again the voice shouted 'Sacrilege,' and this time an arm was upheld among the crowd, holding a small ebony cross.

'This will not do,' said the Lord Warden, and, wheeling his horse round as he spoke, he dashed in among the people. But he who had held up the cross suddenly withdrew his arm, and mingled so much with the crowd, that it was impossible to identify him. But a new ally suddenly sprang forward for the cause of virtue and for reformation.

An old man, with white hair streaming down his shoulders, raised his voice among the people.

'The time has come—the time has come,' he cried, 'when Babylon shall fall; the time has come when stone walls shall no longer be deemed sacred depositories of corruption; the time has come when God's holiest ordinances will not be outraged, and when the young, the good, and the beautiful shall no longer be offered up at the shrine of avarice or priestly lust. It is a husband here who seeks his wife—she whom Heaven has blessed with children : shall the mother be torn from her babes, because she differs in opinion from a crafty priest?'

These words had a great effect upon the wavering multitude, and seemed to place the affair in rather a new light; but it so happened that the aged man who spoke thus was close to him who had shouted 'Sacrilege,' and raised aloft the emblem of that which should be universal Christianity, but which had become sadly perverted to the exclusive use of Catholicism.

This individual might have thought that he was striking a bold blow, and one which would take with the multitude; but he was mistaken, as we shall see.

With his clenched hand, in which likewise was the crucifix, he struck the old man upon the forehead, inflicting a gashing wound with that emblem of peace to all men, exclaiming as he did so—

'Down, Satan, down!'

A yell of rage came from the multitude; the Jesuit was seized, and tossed from hand to hand; blows fell upon him like hail, and had not the troops, by the order of the Lord Warden, made a sudden movement, and saved him, he must in a few moments have been a mangled corpse.

As it was, he presented but a melancholy spectacle, being unable to stand or speak, so the soldiers propped him up against the convent-wall, and there he sat, glaring, with a world of hatred and malice in his eyes, upon those who had saved his life.

It was evident now to the Lord Warden and his companions that they had with them the popular voice, and, after a brief consultation, it was determined that the convent gate should be forced by the men-at-arms, and while as little violence was resorted to as possible not a nook or corner of the edifice should be left unsearched for Alice.

CHAPTER XXI.

Alice in the Convent.—The dreadful Interview.

THE precarious situation of Alice Hensman in the convent when we left her, induces us now to return to her for a brief space, and this is the more necessary, because we require an opportunity of detailing to the reader what took place within the convent, contingent upon the attack which was meditated, and which was now being so ably carried out by the Lord Warden and his followers.

And although Alice was, of course, well aware that something would be done, and that, too, of an energetic character, in order to rescue her from the trammels which surrounded her, she had no means of becoming acquainted with the precise mode of action that the wisdom of the Lord Warden might suggest as the best under the circumstances.

When she was conducted from her cell, where she had passed so gloomy a night, into the abbess's parlour, she fully expected a violent interview with that personage, but she was scarcely prepared to meet Sir Rupert Brent.

And now we may suppose ourselves present in a small apartment richly furnished, according to the taste of the times, and adorned with some works of art, all of which, however, partook of an ecclesiastical character, while Alice's eyes were fixed upon those of the daring and licentious man who had caused her so much uneasiness, and who seemed determined to inflict upon her a yet larger amount of persecution.

For some few moments they regarded each other in silence—a situation which was at last broken by the priest, who said, in tones of ill-concealed exultation—

'Alice Hensman, you must feel that you have forced me to take the present step; it is one which duty compels me to take, and you may now perceive that the power you scorned and slighted has been more than sufficient to accomplish all that it proposes. You are now a prisoner to those who have power to detain you, and who will not scruple to exercise that power to the utmost.'

'Yet,' said Alice, 'I am unsubdued, and the boasted exercise of the fancied power which has enabled you for a brief space thus to encroach upon my liberty, will soon discover its inefficiency.'

'Its inefficiency! Alice Hensman, are you not here, and a prisoner? Is not your very life in our hands?'

'It is; and although there may not be power to rescue me, there will be ample to avenge me.'

'The Church and its ministers heed little what the secular arm can do against them. Armed with that authority, which you know is higher than that which any king can boast of, we defy that feeling which you call vengeance.'

'The power you allude to is that of Rome; but the power of those who will avenge my wrongs is the power of Heaven, because it is based upon immutable justice.'

'Alice, Alice, this is idle talking; you know, and you must feel, that you are mine. Of what avail now are all your boasted friends? Are you not surrounded by walls they dare not scale? You are a prisoner in a building so sanctified, that were Ranulph Hensman, or the bold, audacious Warden himself, to attempt to enter it, I could call successfully, in the name of Religion, upon the populace to overpower them.'

'No, Sir Rupert Brent, no; priests like yourself may fancy that they know something of popular feeling, but I am certain there is scarcely an arm in Winchester that would not be raised for my defence.'

'Discard that delusion, Alice, and feel that you are in the power of one whose fiat of life or death will be uttered for or against you, as you shall yourself please. We are alone; and I care not to tell you at once, that, so little am I enamoured with prejudices, that you might have left a convent, and outraged all the oaths that were ever uttered, and every ordinance of that religion which I profess, and I should have viewed the act with perfect indifference, but that I love you, and then it became necessary that I should arm myself with a power greater than my mere passion could give me to make you mine.'

'These explanations,' said Alice, 'are needless. I fully understand the villany which has placed me in my present position. You need say no more: I understand you, and defy you.'

'That defiance is most rashly spoken. I have absolute authority here. I can compel you to receive my visits at all times and at all seasons, and no one will question my right. Beware lest you presume too far upon an affection which you may turn to hatred—a passion now of love, which you might turn into one of vengeance.'

''Tis you who should beware,' said Alice, 'for you have laid up for yourself a retribution which will be certain to overtake you. Do you for a moment think that those who call themselves my friends, and are such in reality, will idly leave me to pine here as your prisoner?'

'They may be as active as they please; they have first of all to find out the place of your concealment, and then they have to acquire the necessary power to take you from it.'

'Both of which will be done. As I have trust in Heaven, I believe both will be done.'

'You speak with a foolish tongue,' said Sir Rupert Brent; 'humbleness and submission would best become one who, like yourself, can have no hope but in my clemency. There are dungeons in this place where, before now, those who have braved the power of the Church have pined and died; nor are there wanting arms which would not scruple to inflict a speedier doom, if it were necessary, upon such as thou art. You may save yourself; but it must be by becoming mine. Give me now, Alice, but one word of encouraging kindness, and the convent-gates are open for you, leaving you free again to repair to your home, where your children cry in vain for a mother!'

'That word shall never be spoken,' said Alice.

'Indeed! and is this your boasted affection for your children—is this the feeling which prompted you so much to bewail your departure from your home? Why, you will not utter one word to restore yourself, to enable them again to know a mother's tenderness.'

'Most monstrous fiend!' said Alice; 'is it for such as thou art to talk of such feelings? No; you may fancy that with a diabolical ingenuity a mother's tenderness may be arrayed against a wife's honour, but the weak device was transparent as your own wicked heart. I scorn it, and still defy you!'

'Then,' said the priest, rising and seizing her by the wrist with a grasp that was painful in its tightness, 'then are you more bold than prudent, Alice Hensman, for I swear it, you shall be mine!'

'Never! I will raise my voice, and there are women here, who have sworn to lead a life of sanctity and of devotion, who will protect me from you.'

'Nay, Alice, the more I look upon you the more I wonder that such harsh expressions can come from lips made for love.'

'Unhand me, villain, or my cries shall rouse the convent. Help! help!'

A door opened, and the abbess appeared upon the threshold.

'You are welcome, holy sister,' said Sir Rupert Brent; 'this heretic still refuses the mercy of the Church, and when I implored and conjured her to confess her past iniquity, and seek by prayer and penance to atone for it, she cried for help. Truly, it must be the fiend of heresy that is within her which so speaks.'

'Nay, hear me,' said Alice, turning to the abbess; 'you are a woman, and whatever may be your religious opinions and prejudices, they should at least enable you to venerate virtue. I appeal to you, not against the religious exhortations of this man, but I appeal to you for protection against his libertinism and his vices.'

'You hear her,' said Sir Rupert; 'that is one of the devices of Satan. Can you, for one moment, believe anything so monstrous?'

'It is quite impossible,' said the abbess; 'surrender to me, Father Georges, this piece of iniquity, and by such means as we have in our power, such means as the holy power has given us, we will contrive to bend her stubborn nature; and if she shall resist all the exhortations that you and I can use, it will be fitting that some punishment be inflicted upon her commensurate with her deep offences.'

'It must be so.'

'Once,' continued the abbess, as she bent her eyes upon Alice, to note what effect her words had upon her, 'once during the history of this convent a cell has been closed upon a nun who forsook her vows, and was by great exertion arrested and brought hither. Being obdurate, she was left to die that miserable death.'

'You fix your eyes upon me,' said Alice, 'as if you thought that I should tremble at such a doom; but you are mistaken, for I tell you boldly, although I can well conceive such an act to have been once committed here, you dare not now repeat it.'

'Dare not!' said the abbess.

'I repeat the words, you dare not. The time is now arrived when such a thing would bring down upon the heads of its perpetrators the vengeance of a whole population. You seek to terrify me by threats, but it is you who ought to feel terrified, for I tell you most distinctly, that by this proceeding you have not only endangered your personal safety but the stability of that cause which you affect to have so much at heart.'

'You hear her, you hear her!' cried Sir Rupert Brent.

'I do, indeed,' cried the abbess; 'and a more fit subject for the rigours of the Church I never knew.'

Sir Rupert Brent was about to speak, when suddenly the loud ringing blast of a trumpet came upon their ears, and Alice, springing to her feet, exclaimed—

'They come, they come! Without a foreknowledge of what would be attempted, I know that I shall be rescued. Hark, there again, the trumpet sounds! I shall be free!'

Again every echo in and about the convent was awakened by the loud blast of the herald's trumpet, and before any remark could be made by the Jesuit or the abbess upon the subject, there came into the apartment, with trembling eagerness, the woman who acted as portress of the convent.

'There are armed men,' she cried, 'at the gate, some mounted and some on foot, but all armed, and they demand—

'Peace!' cried Sir Rupert Brent; 'reserve your errand until there are none but friendly ears to listen to it.'

The woman shrank back abashed; but Alice had heard enough to convince her that the armed host talked of came to rescue her from the state of thraldom into which she was thrown.

'I have heard enough,' she cried, 'enough to know that I am not deserted, and that my freedom is near at hand; that trumpet-sound heralds me to life and liberty. The armed host you talk of comes to set me free. Where, now, is your boasted power? and of what avail will the affected sanctity of your walls be against the bold, brave hearts that even now are crowding to my rescue?'

'They dare not,' said the Jesuit, 'they dare not storm these walls.'

'They will dare,' said Alice, 'all that the bravest and the best may dare.'

'This place is holy,' said the abbess.

'Not so; it is holy deeds that can alone sanctify us, and this is accursed and atrocious, because you have yourself avowed that atrocious deeds have been enacted in it; it has no sanctity to recommend it; and, once more, I defy you and all your boasted power.'

The rage that was depicted on the countenance of the abbess defies all description. All the worst passions of humanity seemed to be struggling together in her heart, and for the space of about a minute anger choked her utterance. When she did speak, her voice was high and cracked with passion, and she presented a melancholy example of how little the religion she professed could do towards allaying the worst feelings of human nature.

'You may defy us with your tongue,' she said; 'you may fancy that we are powerless, because some armed men are at our gates; but you shall find that such is not the case, for even should the enemies of our religion be so bold as to break into these sacred limits, be assured that before they can accomplish such a purpose your doom shall be complete.'

'Ay!' cried Sir Rupert Brent, 'and so you will perceive, Alice, that this advance of your friends, which you consider so propitious, only hastens your destruction.'

The abbess rang a bell, and several of the more aged nuns made their appearance.

'The heretic,' she said, 'must be removed to one of the sepulchre cells.'

'Oh! holy mother abbess,' said one of them, 'the convent is beleaguered; there are armed men, and they demand Alice Hensman; we heard them at the postern.'

'Enough, enough,' said Sir Rupert; 'we know all. The vengeance of Heaven will light upon them, and they have but insured the destruction of her whom they fancy they have the power to save.'

'These threats,' said Alice, 'do not affect me; for your own safety's sake you dare not take my life; the deed would be discovered, and such a retribution would fall upon you that even you might well tremble to encounter.'

'You reason badly,' whispered the Jesuit to her; 'of course I know full well that Ranulph Hensman would take my life even for what has already been accomplished: I cannot and do not blind myself to that fact; and what more can he do than that? so, when you strive to awaken any fears in me, you strive in vain, as I am prepared for the worst that anger can do, and know my own resources to resist it.'

'I will to the postern gate,' said the abbess, 'and then, ascertaining thoroughly what it is that these bold intruders require, I will, at least, gain time, while you place our prisoner in security.'

'Be it so,' said Sir Rupert; 'and now let those who know the way to these cells in which the living may be entombed lead me to one of them, so that I may place this prisoner in a position to convince her that the power she has braved is yet strong enough for her destruction.'

It is doubtful now whether rage had not become a more prominent feeling in the breast of Sir Rupert Brent than even his wild, ungovernable passion for the beauteous Alice, for he grasped her arm with such force as to be extremely painful to her, and, motioning the old nuns who had answered the abbess's summons to lead the way, he dragged her from the apartment.

The aged females who preceded him had for so many years made themselves the victims of gloomy superstition, that they never for one moment thought it improper to aid in the destruction of Alice Hensman, according to the means which had been suggested.

From the earliest periods of existence they had been taught to believe that a want of faith in the doctrines inculcated by the Romish Church was one of the greatest sins that could possibly be committed, and, such being the case, no punishment could be too severe.

They crossed themselves as they went, and affected to feel pity for her whom they would not make the least effort to save from the dreadful fate which they were aiding and assisting to bring her to.

Thus was it that superstition got the better of all the kindly feelings of humanity, converting even women into positive furies, and making them capable, in the name of Religion, of perpetrating the most frightful cruelty.

Alice felt that it would be madness, and would only entail upon her worse consequences, were she to attempt to resist the powerful grasp of Sir Rupert Brent; she therefore yielded to a necessity she could not hope to control, and allowed herself to be conducted down a steep staircase and along a number of passages leading to the subterranean portion of the convent.

A massive door was unlocked by one of the nuns, and as it creaked upon its hinges a damp and fetid odour, as if coming from some charnel house, came upon their senses, and they all involuntarily drew back, until, by an admixture with the not much purer air of the passages they had traversed, it was rendered more endurable.

After a few moments, Sir Rupert, with his disengaged hand, forced the door wide open, and disclosed an extremely dark and narrow passage, apparently running right and left. One of the nuns who carried a lamp slowly advanced, and, by its light, Alice saw that the passage was extremely short, and that it terminated each way at about eight or ten feet from the door at which they had entered by a stone wall.

Immediately in front of where the party now stood with their prisoner were three small arched doors, and Sir Rupert Brent, pointing to one of them, which was made fast by a heavy iron bar placed across it, said—

'Remove the bar if these be the cells we seek, and we shall see if the courage of this heretic is proof against the horrors of death by starvation.'

'No, no,' said one of the aged nuns, 'not that door, not that door; there are three cells, but that one is tenanted'

'Indeed!' said Sir Rupert; 'but now I remember me, the abbess did remark that once before it had been found necessary to use one of the sepulchre cells.'

'It was many years ago,' said the nun; 'and this place has never been opened since—the other cells are free.'

It appeared that there were no locks upon these cell-doors, but that the fastening relied upon consisted solely of the massive bar of iron which was across the one that already contained a victim.

The others yielded to a touch, and, one being opened, the Jesuit turned to Alice, and, pointing into the gloomy recess, he said—

'Do you doubt my power now, when I can make this your coffin? Do you not already feel something of the pangs of such a death as here awaits you steal across your heart?'

She shrieked and drew back; human nature, for a moment, was not proof against the terrors of such a place; and the Jesuit began to think that after all he should conquer. Bending his mouth close to her ear, he whispered so low that the nuns could not catch the purport of his remarks—

'Alice, I can yet save you; say that you will be mine—say that, forgetting the past, I may hope for some token of affection from you, and I will yet save you from the terrific death which else awaits you.'

The momentary dread, however, of the dreadful fate that might be hers had passed away, and that maturer courage and energy which she possessed had come back to her, enabling her, even at that awful moment, to defy all that was evil, and to put her trust and faith in that Heaven which surely would not desert her in so direful an extremity.

'Never, never!' she cried; 'I will never yield; and even now I tell you, Sir Priest, that you have my contempt and abhorrence to an extent which I thought I never could have felt for any human being.'

''Tis well,' he said, 'I am answered; go to your doom, and take with you my most inveterate curse!'

By a sudden movement of his arm, he hurled her with

brutal violence into the cell, which had been opened, and while the terrified nuns crossed themselves with the very mockery of devotion, and muttered prayers to that Deity whose ordinances they were outraging, the Jesuit flung the bar across the door, and Alice was alone in the dismal prison to which his evil passions, aided by bigotry, had consigned her.

For a few minutes he lingered, with the hope that some cry for mercy—some sigh, which should show him that he had conquered at last—would come from the cell; but he was disappointed—all was still; there came no sound whatever from the gloomy place, and he strolled away, muttering—

'Let her die, let her die, if she will not be mine. No one else shall ever look upon her face; and if my love be disappointed, my revenge, at least, shall be complete.'

He was followed from those subterranean passages by the trembling nuns, and as they reached the upper part of the building, a crashing sound came upon their ears, followed by a loud shout, as if from a multitude of demons.

'They come!' muttered the priest, 'they come! and if I can but sheathe my sword in Ranulph Hensman's heart, I shall have achieved all that I desire, and my revenge will be most perfect.'

CHAPTER XXII.
The Attack and the Defence of the Convent.

AND now that the reader is aware of what is going on within the walls of that edifice devoted to monkish superstition, we will turn our attention to the besiegers, who, it will be

recollected, had determined upon at once proceeding to the attack, and if necessary to the demolition of the convent.

The gates were strong and massive, and the walls high, so that, had there been anything like an efficient force within, those who sought admission might have been kept long at bay, but that there was not; and although the gates were kept closed and every fastening applied to them that they possessed, there was no personal resistance, and the only difficulty seemed to be, to procure some heavy weapon with which to batter in an entrance.

After a time this was obtained from a forge at a short distance, and two of the soldiery, armed with massive hammers, commenced such a determined attack upon the lock of the gate, that it was evident it must soon yield to the ringing blows that were levelled upon it.

The mob was quiet while these proceedings were going on, but from the expression of their countenances it was evident

that there was great excitement among the people, and that the strange spectacle of a convent gate being forced open by armed men was making a deep impression.

Probably but a short time before these very persons would have fully believed that some signal judgment from Heaven would at once light upon the heads of any who were audacious enough to take part in such an enterprise.

The non-resistance from the convent likewise, and the complete stillness which reigned within its walls, added much to the strange effect of the scene, and for nearly five minutes nothing was heard but the repeated blows of the hammers.

The old gates shook at each stroke that was given to them, and at length with a loud crash they yielded, and opened a short distance.

It was at that moment that the mob raised a loud shout—the same that had reached the ears of Sir Rupert Brent after he had, in the manner related, committed Alice Hensman to one of the sepulchre cells of the convent.

'Advance! cried the Lord Warden, 'advance!' and, accompanied by Hensman and John Elkington, he galloped into the court-yard of the convent, followed by the escort, of whom a small party was left to guard the entrance.

All remained still at the convent—not a sound came from it, nor did a human being appear at any of its windows.

'We must dismount,' said the Warden; 'and I think, if we take with us a small number of picked men from the troop, we shall be able to search the convent.'

'They will hide her, of course,' said Hensman; 'and Heaven knows what facilities they may have for so doing.

'Fear nothing,' said the Lord Warden; 'I have said, that if it be necessary to level the convent to the ground it shall be done. There shall not one stone of it stand upon another until we have discovered Alice.'

Ranulph Hensman dismounted quickly from his horse, and almost at the very instant that he did so there was a loud report as of some fire-arm being discharged, and a number of bullets passed over his head, one of which slightly wounded him, and nearly the whole of which must have lodged in his body, had he still remained upon the horse.

'That shot,' he said calmly, 'came from Sir Rupert Brent. I am well pleased to find the villain is here; and in recovering Alice, which I trust in Heaven I shall do, it will likewise be in my power to punish him who has torn her from me.'

'We must put a stop to this at once,' said the Lord Warden. 'Soldiers, advance! Burst open every door that opposes you, and make prisoners of any man that you can see.'

It was a kind of half court yard, half-garden, in which they now were, and it separated the actual building from the wall to the extent of about a hundred feet. A flight of stone steps led to the convent-door, and it seemed as if the shot which had been fired at Ranulph Hensman had proceeded from a window at the right-hand side of the entrance.

This act of hostility was just what of all others was calculated to irritate the soldiery, who, at once conceiving that they were set upon by concealed foes, lost the quiet demeanour which had characterised them, and became furious.

The convent door was closed, but the attack upon it was so sudden and fierce, that it at once opened, and the Lord Warden with his two companions, having relinquished their horses, at once walked into the building, which, for the first time, had thus been visited by the profane step of a man not belonging to the priesthood, since it was built.

They found themselves in a large and handsome room, but not a soul was to be seen, nor could they discover any traces, although they looked eagerly enough for them, of the individual who had fired at Ranulph Hensman.

'We must beware,' said John Elkington, 'of falling into an ambuscade, for these nuns are decidedly warlike.'

'What sounds are these?' said the Lord Warden. 'Listen!'

It was a solemn and beautiful strain of music that came upon their ears, and, after a minute or two, it ceased, and human voices took up the strain of swelling harmony which now resounded through the building.

'The nuns are at their devotions,' said Hensman.

'They may be,' said the Warden, 'but I wonder what part of their devotional exercise the firing a loaded arquebus at you constituted! We must put a stop to these ill-timed devotions, for that they are intended to put a stop to our proceedings I cannot doubt. Come on, the sound will lead us.'

The route to the chapel of the convent was easy: they had but to walk forward and to descend a few steps, when two doors presented themselves, which, upon being opened, disclosed at once the interior of the convent chapel.

The nuns were all kneeling and engaged in earnest prayer, and the entrance of the invaders of the sacred precincts had no other effect than causing a number of them to cross themselves more devoutly, while some of the most aged uttered deep groans of, no doubt, genuine mental anguish that that place should be so desecrated.

The Lord Warden paused a moment and glanced around him, and then he perceived upon a raised place, and kneeling by a chair of costly velvet, the abbess.

Without the hesitation of a moment he marched up to her, his spurs making a clank upon the marble pavement as he went, no doubt to the utter consternation of the nuns, and when he neared the abbess he spoke, saying—

'Madam, when I saw you at your postern-gate we exchanged some words of defiance, therefore it cannot be said that this visit has interrupted you in your devotions, for you should not have commenced them at such a time.'

The abbess sprang to her feet, and holding up a cross in her hand, she cried—

'Impious wretch! I call down upon your head the vengeance of offended Heaven.'

'You may call, madam, but will it come? You perceive that, notwithstanding your denunciation, I am much the same; and now, to explain again my errand, I demand of you, in the King's name, Alice Hensman.'

'In the name of a higher power than the King's I refuse her to you.'

'As you please; we have come prepared for such a refusal, and would rather hear it at once from your lips than a more evasive answer. We must and will have her, and therefore you will have yourself to thank that your convent will be searched from its foundation-stone to its topmost pinnacle.'

'Search,' said the abbess furiously, 'and find your minion if you can!'

'I have another question to put,' said the Lord Warden. 'I wish to know who fired a shot upon us from the house; 'tis better in such a case to tell the truth, lest I hang the wrong person.'

'Hang!'

'Yes, it was an act of treachery, and in defiance of the King's authority, which was fully expressed at the commencement of these proceedings, and I declare my intention of hanging upon one of the trees in the court-yard the man who fired that shot.'

'And what if it were a woman?'

'I do not entertain the supposition: it was a man; and from the victim that was picked out I have good reason to believe it was Father Georges, the infamous Jesuit. By surrendering him and Alice Hensman at once, you will spare yourself and your convent much inconvenience. By refusing, you accomplish nothing, for the place is well guarded, so that none may escape, and the search shall be so vigorous that we shall be certain to find those whom we want.'

'You talk to me in vain,' said the abbess; 'the consequences of your wickedness and your profanity be upon your own head!'

'Be it so; I am entirely willing to take those consequences. Commence your search, soldiers, and leave no secret nook or corner unexplored; and woe be to you, my lady abbess, if it be discovered that you have committed any personal violence, or connived at its commission, against her whom we seek.'

'Outcast of Heaven,' said the abbess, 'I despise your threats, and I hold my life as cheap compared with the punishment of heresy.'

'Woman,' said John Elkington, 'you have the appearance of one possessing intellect, and yet you talk like a fool! What is this heresy of which you talk so much but a mere difference of opinion with yourself? She of whom you speak might with equal reason call you heretic because you differ from her in faith.'

'I hold no argument,' said the abbess, 'with such as thou art; but I denounce you still, as the bitterest enemies of Heaven.'

'You have more of my pity than my anger,' said Elkington.

At this moment the Lord Warden felt something gently touch his hand, and upon glancing round he saw one of the kneeling nuns holding up to him a small slip of paper. She pressed her finger upon her lips at the same moment to impress silence and secrecy upon him.

He understood the sign, and while Elkington and the abbess were still exchanging some words he turned, and read upon the scrap of paper as follows :—

'Seek the prisoner in the sepulchre cells, and force me to show you the way to them.'

This was a most welcome piece of intelligence, and the Warden, after concealing the scrap of paper, and casting a glance of intelligence and approval upon the nun who had given it to him, said aloud, to the great surprise of the abbess as well as of his own companions—

'I will seek Alice Hensman in the sepulchre cells, where I

have no doubt she is confined, and I ask some one here present t show me the route to those places.'

The abbess started and glared around her with eyes of fire; as though she would have said, 'Who is there here present that has betrayed that secret?'

'I shall insist,' continued the Lord Warden, 'upon one of the nuns showing me the place, upon pain of death for refusal; and as I have no choice, I select her who is nearest to me.'

'So saying, he turned to the nun who had given him the paper, but before any reply could be made the abbess spoke, saying—

'Defy him; that which he threatens he dares not perform, nor does he dream for one moment of performing it—defy him, I say, defy him!'

'I will keep my word,' said the Lord Warden.

'I am not ready for death,' said the nun, 'and must yield.'

The abbess bent upon her a glance of fury and hatred. 'Idiot,' she cried, 'can you imagine for one moment that your life is in danger from such an idle threat?'

'I do not see,' said the Lord Warden, 'why we heretics should not be as fully capable of doing an atrocious deed for a good purpose, as you Catholics for a bad one. Surely there cannot be so much virtue in me, whom you have thought deserving of the bitterest curse you could level at my head. On pain of death, then, I insist upon this nun accompanying me.'

'She braves you,' said the abbess, 'and holds your threat in scorn and defiance.'

'Nay,' said the nun, as she gently rose from her knees, 'I am not prepared to die; and, therefore, I must needs obey the will of those who threaten me. Follow me, sir, and I will show you to the sepulchre cells.'

'What!' shrieked the abbess, 'is this one of the Benedictine sisterhood that yields so tamely?'

'I cannot choose but do so,' said the nun, 'and if it be a sin, I must seek pardon of Heaven for committing it.

'Then die,' said the abbess, 'the death which you so much dread!'

As she spoke, she drew from beneath her robes a small poniard, and made a rush upon the nun. She would unquestionably have sheathed it in her bosom, had not the Lord Warden interposed, and the thin blade of the weapon broke off close to the hilt against the coat of mail which he wore.

'Peace, woman, peace!' he said, 'these are no toys for such as you; how dare you call yourself a minister of religion, and yet carry about with you such a weapon? These are strange times, indeed, when the abbess of a convent maintains her authority at the dagger's point! Away, away!'

He flung the discomfited abbess from him, and she sank upon the velvet chair by which she had been kneeling, with a shriek of mortification and anger, while some of the aged nuns gathered round her to console her for the great slight that had been put upon her authority, and to assure her that ere long some signal judgment of Providence must overtake the Lord Warden and his party.

One, indeed, intimated that Heaven was only looking on quietly to see how far the impious wretches would go before it pounced upon them, and make them the objects of a terrific retribution. But these consolations utterly failed with the abbess, who was much too clever a woman to give any weight to them; and she knew that if she waited till Providence did anything to the Lord Warden and his followers, she would wait long enough, so she silenced the nuns peremptorily, and waited in gloomy and angry meditation what should next ensue.

The nun who had given the valuable information to the Lord Warden preceded him, Ranulph Hensman, and John Eckington, from the chapel, and, as she considered their own force would be sufficient, they left the soldiery behind them.

Hensman was all amazement at what had fallen from the Lord Warden; and it was not until the latter informed him in a whisper, as they went, of the little mysterious scrap of paper which had been handed to him by the nun, that he at all comprehended the nature of the movement. Hope then beamed forth in every feature of his face, and, stepping up to the nun, he took her hand, saying—

'Oh! how can I sufficiently thank you for this generous service? you are risking much, I am confident, to rescue the innocent; but you weep, when you should rather smile that Heaven has given you power to do such an action.'

'I weep because my doom is fixed; they will kill me.'

'By heavens, no!' said the Lord Warden; 'we will see to that—but lead on now, I pray you, as quickly as you can, to these sepulchre cells, which, as their very name implies, are no doubt full of horrors.'

'Horrors indeed!' said the nun; 'this way—quick, quick, for each passing moment to the poor prisoner must surely seem an age of anguish.'

The distance was not great to those who knew the most direct route, and they soon reached that massive door which we have before noticed, and which now hung idly on its hinges; for, in the excitement of the moment, the nun who had carried the key on the occasion of Alice's incarceration, had forgotten to close and lock that door behind her. There was no obstacle, therefore, whatever; and as the nun who acted as a guide to the party in whose fortunes we are interested, took with her a light which had been burning in a niche close to the entrance of those subterraneous passages, they saw at once the three little doors which led to those wretched cells so appropriately named sepulchres.

'She is here,' said the nun, 'she is here!' and she hastily removed the iron bar which closed the door.

'Alice, Alice!' cried Hensman; 'you are free! know you not my voice? It is your husband calls to you.'

There was no answer, and, snatching the lamp from the hands of the nun, he rushed at once into the cell.

One glance was sufficient to show him that it was perfectly empty.

'Alice,' he cried again, 'where are you? Speak! Alas! I am deceived; and the flame of hope which was lighted in my breast is extinguished again for ever.'

CHAPTER XXIII.

The unrequited Search.

RANULPH HENSMAN tottered despairingly from the cell; and had not the Lord Warden taken the lamp hastily from his nerveless grasp, he would have dropped it, and they would have been in darkness.

'She is not there, she is not there!' he cried; 'it is a delusion! Heaven forgive you, who have deceived us!'

'If I had deceived you,' said the nun, 'I should scarce have conscience to call on Heaven to forgive me; but, as Heaven is my judge, I saw her placed in there and left to die by a Jesuit priest.'

'His name, his name!' cried Hensman; 'was it Brent—Sir Rupert Brent?'

'No,' said the nun; 'his name is Georges.'

'It is the same; you know him not by his other designation. Oh! my Alice, my Alice! whither has this fiend in human shape conveyed you?'

'I believe,' said the Lord Warden, 'that this nun has acted most faithfully to us; we will examine all these cells, and then at once proceed to the upper portion of the convent. The search shall be conducted rigorously; and remember, Ranulph Hensman, that, although you are now smarting under a second disappointment, we have all our energies about us, and ample reason to believe that Alice still must be concealed beneath the convent roof.'

The slightest examination of the cells was sufficient to show that they had no living occupant; although in one of them was a pestiferous hideous mass, which bore frightful evidence to the testimony made by the abbess, that already, since the convent's formation, one poor victim had paid the penalty of broken vows by her life.

'And this,' said Ranulph Hensman, with a cry of indignation, 'this is the death to which my Alice would have been consigned! Oh! my Lord Warden, let us at once commence our search. Let my afflicted heart take you at your word, and show me that no hole or corner in this building shall remain unexplored.'

'I pity you,' said the nun, 'and would fain assist you; and such aid as I now can render, in pointing out the secret places in the convent, shall be freely yours.'

'I am too full of grief,' said Hensman, 'to thank you as I ought; the villain Georges has, no doubt, removed Alice to some other place of security, but still I think she must be within these walls; and oh, what a debt of vengeance shall I not owe to that crafty Jesuit when we meet again!'

'He must be found and arrested,' said the Lord Warden; 'I am bound to have him again on public as well as upon private grounds; so cheer up, Hensman; and although your fate looks now clouded and lowering, never fear but it will shine again, and all will be well. Remember that your wife is no ordinary, weak, vacillating woman, but that she has an intellect to plan resolutions and a firmness to carry them out.'

By this time they had reached the chapel again, and it was quite clear that by some means or another the abbess had become aware of the ill success of their search for Alice Hensman, for a look of triumph was upon her face, and her eyes flashed with the fire of a guilty exultation.

''Tis well,' she said; 'a convent is henceforth no longer sacred; on a vague and base suspicion its gates are forced, and the sanctity of its holiest portions violated.'

Hensman was about to speak, but the Lord Warden touched him on the arm, saying, 'Exchange no words with her, but let the search commence.'

He then ordered the soldiers to go three together, and to disperse themselves over the entire building, leaving no door unopened and no place unsearched, into which, by fair means or foul, they could effect an entrance.

Some he sent down the staircase which led to the sub-terranean portion of the building, while the others dispersed themselves over the remainder; and he implored Hensman, as the best possible plan, to remain with him and John Elkington in the chapel, establishing there a kind of head quarters, from whence they could receive reports from the different parties they sent to search the place, and who had general orders to take possession of and bring to the chapel any one, male or female, whom they might find concealed.

The nuns, with their long veils over their faces, retired to a distant part of the chapel, leaving the abbess sitting in her chair of authority, and looking defiance upon the armed men who had invaded that place which she had so long ruled with despotic sway. And occasionally she uttered taunts indicative of a strong opinion that the search would be fruitless—a fact which the Lord Warden began to suspect, for he knew that some of those ancient religious edifices had such well-planned places of concealment, as well as underground places of ingress and egress, that it became not at all an improbable thing that he would have to fulfil his pledge to the letter, and pull the convent down, before he could have any hope of dis-covering where Alice had been hidden.

Half an hour thus elapsed, and then the small parties of soldiery began by degrees to return, each with a notice of the ill success of the enterprise; and it became painfully evident to Ranulph Hensman that the rescuing of Alice from the hands of her enemies was by no means so easy a matter as at first it had appeared.

Rendered then almost frantic by disappointment, he, sword in hand, and followed closely by John Elkington, who would not leave him, rushed wildly through the building, calling loudly upon Alice by name, beseeching her to answer him, and now and then pausing to listen, with such intense anxiety depicted upon his countenance that John Elkington was beyond expression pained to see him in such a state, and finally led him back to the chapel almost in a state of ex-haustion.

'Be composed,' he said, 'I pray you be composed. This disappointment you ought to have felt was possible from the first.'

'Yes, yes,' said Hensman; 'but believe me, it is none the less bitter or severe—it is maddening. I begin now to think that we have lost all clue to her, and that she has indeed left this building.'

'Hush! let us speak low, and consult with the Lord Warden.'

They then held a brief council at some distance from where the abbess sat, the result of which was, that they should leave the place, but post a guard at the gates, and on the morrow, unless some information reached them of a favour-able nature from some other quarter, the Lord Warden dis-tinctly pledged himself to commence the actual demolition of the convent.

With this, of course, agonised as his feelings were, Ranulph Hensman could not but be content, and with a scornful laugh from the abbess ringing in their ears, they walked to the chapel door, but before they could pass out of it they heard a shriek, and, upon turning to see what could have occasioned it, they perceived the nun who had aided them in their ex-amination of the convent being forcibly dragged from the chapel, apparently by the orders of the abbess.

The Lord Warden stepped forward.

'I had forgotten,' he said, 'most criminally forgotten you. You shall not remain here to be punished for your hu-manity.'

'They will kill me,' said the nun, 'they will kill me.'

'They shall not have the power. Come away at once, and in Winchester Castle you shall be safe, if all the power of Rome was leagued against you.'

The nun trembled and clung to him: the love of life was strong upon her, much stronger than her monastic vows, and while deep sobs came from her labouring breast, she crossed the threshold of that place which had been her home for many a year, where she thought to have died in peace, but it was not so to be, for she never again looked upon its walls.

In the court-yard the Lord Warden and his two associates mounted their horses, and leaving a guard of twenty-five men with orders to arrest every one who should come to the premises, and allow no one to leave them, they passed through the broken gates, and were received with loud cheers from the populace without, who, when they saw the nun coming forth so willingly along with the soldiers, at once imagined that she must have been the object of the search.

'This is a delusion,' whispered the Lord Warden to John Elkington; 'but it is one that may just as well continue, for the populace had better think us successful than otherwise.'

Acting upon this impression then, nothing was said or done to undeceive the people, and the cavalcade, at a rapid pace, made for the castle, from whence they had now been absent for a considerable period.

When they reached there the nun recounted all that had occurred upon Alice Hensman being first brought to the convent, for she was the same who had originally taken com-passion upon her, and how she had promised to aid her as far as lay in her power.

These circumstances, conjoined with the imperative public duty which called upon the Lord Warden to secure, if possi-ble, the conspirators who had met and matured their design for assassinating the king, formed ample food for reflection and materials for action. A trusty messenger was despatched to London with the particulars of what had occurred at the convent of Benedictine nuns. The Lord Warden would not send the same lad who had gone before, as he considered that not only had he gone through quite sufficient danger, but that he could not be sufficiently recovered from his previous fatigues to undertake again such an enterprise.

And so once again, without having made much progress in that matter which concerned Ranulph Hensman so nearly, and in which John Elkington and the Lord Warden so fully sympathised, they again sat in council to deliberate upon the wisest and boldest course to pursue.

They felt quite confident that it would be useless to attempt to gain any authentic information by examining the Jesuit who had been pointed out by Hensman and captured in the crowd, so the Lord Warden merely gave orders that he should be kept in close custody, and told that he had better prepare himself for death, so that, if he should be a man upon whom thoughts of personal danger were likely to have a great effect, he might ask an interview of the Lord Warden, and seek his life by making a full confession of the designs of the Jesuits.

But this was a very forlorn hope indeed, and not one at all likely to be realized.

'I will go forth,' said Hensman, 'and still occupy myself in the double object of attempting to discover where my wife is hidden, and the designs of those who are conspiring against the person of the king.'

'Be more careful, Hensman, than hitherto,' said the Warden; 'you are too rash and headstrong. Who but your-self would have ventured into that vault where the Jesuits held their meeting? I look upon your escape from that place with life as little short of an absolute miracle.'

'Nay, my lord,' said Hensman, 'I think there is safety to be found, in that boldness, and I would defy any one to be long in your service and not acquire some of your own bold scorn of danger and habit of endeavouring to bend circum-stances to your will rather than allowing yourself to be the slave of them.'

'You will do as you please, Hensman, of course,' said the Lord Warden; 'you know that my reliance upon you is great, and I have only to ask of you to let me see you fre-quently, and not to let more than a few hours intervene between the times that I do so.'

Hensman made the required promise, and then left the

castle. His first object was to visit his children, whom he had not seen now for many hours, and finding them perfectly safe and well in the care of the kind neighbours who had taken charge of them, he felt that with a freer heart he could proceed to make those necessary inquiries which he had a faint hope might lead him to some knowledge of Alice's place of concealment.

He visited the guard that had been stationed at the convent, and from them he ascertained that no one had come forth, and that no one had visited the place excepting an old man, who was reputed to be a fortune-teller or an astrologer, residing in the vicinity, and whom, in pursuance of the orders they had received to detain any one who came, they had made a prisoner and now held in custody.

Ranulph Hensman reflected for a moment or two, and then he desired to see this old man, who was at once brought to him, and who began to inveigh loudly against the injustice of detaining him, and to ask on what possible pretence it was that he was made a prisoner.

'It was a general order,' said Hensman; 'but of course, as it cannot intend to apply to you, you can go at once.'

Hensman said this so carelessly that the man walked off without a word, and never once looked behind him; but the secretary dogged his footsteps, and found that, after going some distance, he took another turning which brought him back again to a part of the convent walls, and then he commenced casting small pebbles over, evidently with a view of attracting attention, but after awhile, finding that none was paid to him, he made a gesture of impatience and walked away towards the town at a rapid pace.

Ranulph watched his footsteps until he came to a mean house in a narrow street, the door of which he opened with a key which he took from his pocket, and into which he then went at once.

There was but slender foundation to go upon in the supposition that this man had anything to do connected with the affair of the abduction of Alice Hensman; but Ranulph was so determined that nothing should escape him, but that he would sift thoroughly and entirely even the most trivial circumstance which afforded the least clue to a discovery, that he resolved at once to make some inquiry respecting this man.

For this purpose he went into a shop in the immediate vicinity, and asked if he was known.

'Yes,' said a woman who was in the place; 'he is a fortune-teller, and all he says is quite sure to come true.'

'Indeed; and I suppose the mere fact of his saying it is the cause of that phenomenon?'

'Well, sir, I cannot take upon myself to say. Perhaps it is and perhaps it is not: but all I know is that he is a most wonderful man.'

'Do you happen to know if he will receive chance visitors?'

'I really don't know, sir, upon my word; but, at all events, it would be of no use for you to call upon him now.'

'Wherefore?'

'Because he has just passed my window wrapped up in the sad-coloured cloak I see him often go out of a night in, and——Well, I never! what a very impatient man that is to be sure! Why, he is off like a shot before one can finish one half of what one has to say. I suppose that's what he calls good manners; but I can tell him, and I only wish he was here to hear me, that I call it bad manners.'

The fact was that Ranulph Hensman was so anxious to follow the fortune-teller, that the moment he heard the woman of the shop make the announcement that he had gone, the secretary left the shop without any ceremony, and, darting into the street, was only just in time to see the astrologer, if such he was, turn a corner.

It was a great gratification to Hensman to find that the man went towards the castle again from whence he had come, but he diverged considerably on the way, and sought an open space, at some distance from which were some remarkably fine aged trees, that seemed as if they must have been co-existent with the first formation of the city.

Hensman watched him intently, and was surprised to see him proceed up to one of these trees and appear to be examining its trunk closely, after which he walked away more briskly than before.

Hensman did hesitate, but it was not above a moment, whether he should follow the man or proceed to examine the tree, but he decided upon the former course of action, and after looking sufficiently at the tree to make sure that he should know it again without any difficulty, he still continued to dog the footsteps of the fortune-teller.

This man had evidently not the remotest suspicion in the world that any one was following him—he walked on now with the freest and most unconcerned air in the world.

Ranulph Hensman, however, notwithstanding the apparent want of caution on the part of this man, would not himself give the least opportunity of being discovered. Having been so recently seen by him at the convent, he of course had every reason to believe that he should be at once recognised when seen, and then a suspicion of why he had been so readily released would be sure to come over his mind.

This was a consideration which involved the greatest caution, and Hensman took care, if possible, always to keep some intervening object so much between him and the man that, in the event of the latter looking round suddenly, he might quickly get out of the way, and so, at all events, avoid a close scrutiny, which was a thing not at all to be desired.

Moreover, as he looked at him and observed his gait, Ranulph Hensman could not but come to an opinion that when he seemed so aged he was playing a part, for now, instead of walking slightly bent and with unsteady steps, which he had done before, his action was bold, rapid, and erect, and the manner in which he flung about him the cloak that he wore had in it something of pride and consequence, extremely different indeed from what one would have expected would have been the habit of such a man as the reputed astrologer appeared at the convent gate.

But these were gratifying observations to Hensman, because they tended more and more at each instant to convince him that he was upon the right scent, and that the art and chicanery of the Jesuits were at work, and this man, to all intents and purposes, was an agent, if not a principal, in their nefarious transactions and designs.

If he had proceeded direct to the convent, it was the full intention of Ranulph Hensman to have captured him, for, although he did not recognise him as one of those who had been present in the vaulted chamber, he could not hope to retain a vivid perception of all their features, and therefore he did not doubt but that such was really the case, and that in getting possession of him he should, at all events, have captured another of that number of men who had been deputed by their general fraternity to work such woe and mischief in England.

There could be no doubt but that at that period the Jesuits had a faction strong in secret purposes and resolves in every capital of Europe, and the mere accident that in England they had pitched upon Winchester instead of the metropolis as their centre of action, probably arose from some circumstances of a personal character connected with their enterprises.

The mysterious and evidently disguised man stopped at a few straggling houses in the immediate vicinity of the convent, and, pushing aside a gate, with the air of a man who knew his way well, he passed by a private pathway which conducted to some house situated back from the line of road, and which consequently required some entrance of the sort peculiar to itself.

There was a gate at the entrance of this private roadway, which, when the stranger had passed through it, closed of itself with a clanging sound; but when Hensman followed him, which he did, he took care that nothing of that description should betray his approach. He let the gate close as softly as possible, and then with rapid but light footsteps followed the man along a gravel path of considerable extent until he came to a house.

Then Hensman paused and hid himself behind some trees, and as the evening was creeping on, and the long shadows of twilight were wrapping in obscurity all objects, the secretary congratulated himself upon the favourable time at which this adventure had occurred.

He could see the stranger ring at the bell of the house, and then a small square place in the door only was opened, and some few whispered words were uttered, after which he was admitted. Ranulph then had no hesitation in walking up to the house and reconnoitring it. It could not be deemed to be other than a handsome building, although rather ecclesiastical in its character. It looked as if at one time it must have belonged to the convent, or to some persons dependent upon this religious establishment.

Ivy grew nearly over the whole face of it, thus proclaiming it to be far from modern in its construction, and some stately trees towered upon its roof, making a melancholy but pleasant moaning in the wind, which, as the day declined, began to blow gently from the south-west, stirring the trees and flowers into fantastic shapes of beauty, and making the latter give forth their most delicious odour to that evening breeze.

As Hensman looked he saw a light appear in one of the windows, and then, almost before he could conceal himself, two men came from the house, and, conversing earnestly and mysteriously together, they walked down the gravel path which led to the open roadway.

Hensman followed them as closely as caution would permit him; but when he reached the gate, which only seemed to him to have closed a moment before with its usual clanging sound, he was mortified to find that the men were gone, and in what direction he knew not, and yet it seemed impossible they could have got out of his sight so rapidly, and he was forced to come to the conclusion that they had hidden themselves somewhere else, and that all he had discovered was a place of meeting in order that they might proceed together elsewhere.

This was mortifying, but still it might be but the delay of a few short hours, and perchance he might get admission even to the house, and, while no one was there, ascertain something of its interior, and so perchance come to a conclusion regarding the purposes for which it was used.

Acting upon this feeling, he went up to the street door to see what kind of fastening there was, and, as he did so, his hand touched the handle of the bell, producing a slight sound, but one which yet seemed sufficient to alarm the vigilance of some one within.

The little square opening of the door was at once released from its fastening, and a face appeared.

Of course, there was a dead silence, for Hensman knew not what to say; and the individual who thus appeared evidently waited for some signal which should justify the intruder in demanding admittance, and, as that did not come, the small square opening was immediately closed again, and Ranulph found that, instead of making any advance, he had rather retarded his ultimate object.

His information was not sufficiently correct or extensive regarding the place to justify him in adopting any violent measures, so he determined upon going to examine the tree which he had seen attract so much attention from the astrologer, in the hope that some sign, or perchance something cut upon its bark, might enlighten him as to the mystery of that individual's conduct.

'My poor Alice,' he said, 'as he walked along in rather a desponding vein, ' my poor Alice, I may as well consume the weary hours of the coming night in seeking for whatever adventure chance or destiny may throw within my way, for I shall know no rest till once again I have you in these circling arms, and feel assured that you are safe and pressed to the heart which beats alone for you.

So saying, he hurried from the solitary house towards the clump of trees which we have before mentioned.

Then placing himself in the same position from whence he had watched the stranger, he soon ascertained the precise tree, and, walking up to it, he saw that it was a magnificent elm, which, although much of its trunk had become hollowed by age, still presented in its vegetation a luxuriant aspect.

Ranulph Hensman walked twice round the tree, but could notice nothing peculiar which should attract his attention, and he was about to leave the spot disappointed at the result of his examination, when he heard the rapid footstep of some one approaching, and he concealed himself at a short distance in order to observe the movements of whoever it might be that was making his way towards that lonely spot.

He saw a man pause a few paces from the tree and look anxiously about him, and then, when he thought no one was observing him, he plunged his arm deep into the hollow of the aged trunk, and, to the great mortification of Ranulph Hensman, who saw in a moment what he had missed, drew forth a scrap of paper which the stranger anxiously perused.

Then taking a pencil from his pocket, he seemed to be adding something to the contents of the paper, after which he replaced it in the cavity of the tree, and glided from the spot.

Ranulph Hensman only waited until he was far enough off to prevent the likelihood of his sudden return, and then carting up to the tree he at once possessed himself of the written document which had been there left.

It was but a small scrap of paper, and by holding it up to the dim, fading light for a few seconds, and fixing his eyes intently upon it, Ranulph succeeded in reading the following words:—

' At the Well-house; midnight, to-morrow, September 16;' and then followed a number of marks or strokes upon the paper to the extent of nineteen, of which he could make nothing.

Nor could he, in fact, be said to have acquired any information from the paper itself, inasmuch as he knew not where the Well-house which was there named was situated.

He debated for a time whether he should replace the paper or keep possession of it; but at length he decided upon the former course, because, after all, it was valueless in itself, and if it referred to any meeting of Jesuits or others conspiring against the government or against his private peace, it was better - far better—that he should let it take place, and bend his exertions towards discovering where the Well-house was situated that was so mysteriously mentioned.

He accordingly carefully replaced the paper, and then, walking rapidly into the town, he called at the house where his children were placed, with an intention of asking its inhabitants—for he knew that they had resided in Winchester many a year—if they had ever heard of the Well-house.

The reply was immediate and distinct:—'Oh, yes! heard of it, certainly!' They knew it well. It was a house the front of which was covered with ivy, situated not above three or four hundred yards from the back of the convent of the Benedictine nuns, and it was called the Well-house on account of a well being in its grounds, the waters of which were said to have been blessed at their source, a long way off, by the holy St. Jude, and ever since had been possessed of miraculous power in effecting the cure of diseases.

' And who resides in the house?' he asked.

' No one,' was the reply, ' except occasionally. It belongs to the convent specially; and sometimes lay sisters and visitors are accommodated in it.'

Not wishing to invite questions in return from people whom he respected, Ranulph Hensman thought it best to say no more, but suspecting more and more, from the ascertained connexion of the house with the convent, that, by following up the train of circumstances he had hit upon concerning it, he should be able to ascertain something of vital interest to his own affairs, he left, and proceeded to the Lord Warden.

It was not so late in the evening as he had frequently taken less important intelligence to the castle; and when he had narrated all he knew to the Warden and to John Elkington, who happened to be there, they both agreed with him that, in all human probability, this fortunate train of circumstances had been the means of discovering the next place of meeting of the Jesuits since they had been hunted so completely from the vaults of the old cathedral.

The question which now propounded itself to their minds had reference wholly to what was the most eligible mode of taking advantage of the information, and finally it was agreed that, as that was the 17th, and consequently the night on which the evidently secret meeting was to be held, the most prompt and energetic measures should be taken.

' You perceive, Ranulph,' said the Lord Warden, 'that circumstances have so turned out as to mix up your private affairs completely with those of the state.'

' Most true,' said John Elkington; 'a compound plot is proceeding, the prime mover in which is Sir Rupert Brent. He is, as the accredited agent and principal man of the Jesuits in England, plotting and planning for the Church of Rome '

' It is so,' chimed in the Warden, ' and at the same time, likewise, he makes use of all his influence of name and party to carry out his own infamous private designs, so that you perceive, Hensman, that if he be carrying on a double purpose in so far as he is successful in one object he will be in the other, and at the same time if we foil him in one we foil him in both.'

' I do perceive well,' said Hensman, ' that such is precisely the case; but at the same time believe me, my Lord Warden, that I should never forget my public duties, even although my heart were ten times more impressed than it is with sensations of private wrong.'

' Of that I am well aware, Hensman, and I merely use it as a subject of congratulation to you that it should happen your public duty and your private duty go together.'

Some more conversation ensued between them, which resulted in a plan that they were to carry out that night as regarded the meeting at the Well House; but as this plan will show itself better in its execution than in preparatory description, we shall leave it to exhibit itself to the reader in its own proper shape.

CHAPTER XXIV.

Alice's new Prison.—The mysterious Transit.

WE scarcely dare hope to be able, in the faintest manner, to portray to our readers the feelings which came over poor Alice Hensman when the door of that frightful cell closed upon her—that cell which bore, not inaptly, the name of a sepulchre, and which, no doubt, was fully intended to be the grave of her who had done no wrong, but who, while she was beautiful, dared likewise to be virtuous.

The shriek which Sir Rupert Brent vainly paused to listen for did rise from her heart nearly to her lips, but she smothered its utterance, for she would not give that triumph to her enemy; and sinking to her knees upon the damp floor of that miserable cell, she wrung her hands and wept for a while despairingly.

' Oh, Heaven !' she cried; ' am I then forsaken? shall I never again look upon the cheering light of day—never again see the sweet sunshine amid the trees and flowers—never again hear the melody of a human voice, or look upon the face of him who is all the world to me? Shall I never again see those dear little ones that have made up so much of the sum of my happiness and of my anxieties?'

' Then again, as her face dropped upon her knees, a smothered cry burst from her lips, and for many minutes she gave herself up to all the agony of despairing reflection.

But Alice Hensman's was not a mind long to nourish such feelings of utter helplessness. She prayed—prayed long and fervently to that Being who at one time had given her such a world of happiness in the dearest relations of social life, to restore her again to that sunny part of her existence, and yet to let her children feel the pressure of a mother's kiss, and her husband smile with joy to look upon the happiness that he had wrought.

And then she became more calm and composed; but still it was something like the calm of hopelessness, the composure of despair—that appearance of serenity which will frequently arise and sit like death upon the countenance in periods of the heart's bitterest anguish, when the grief lies far too deep for tears, when no language will suffice to give utterance to a thousandth part of what the heart and brain are suffering.

And what a solemn stillness reigns around—the stillness of the tomb, in which she alone was a living thing, but, alas! too soon to change the garb of mortality for that which is eternal, passing through the gates of death—and that so horrible a death too—to another realm which she was all unprepared to enter, inasmuch as her best and dearest affections yet held a share in the world she inhabited. She stretched out her arms, and she found that either way she could reach the walls of that dismal prison-house.

They were damp and reeking with moisture, and then she held her hand above her head, and the roof she felt was so close upon her that she no longer wondered at the oppression on her chest, and that she drew her breath with intense labour and difficulty.

Suddenly that silence is broken in turn, and when it was, a strange subdued sound, as of a bell at an immense distance, came upon her ear, and muffled and low, like a wail of the dead, as it was, she could not help telling herself that it was her funeral knell, and accepting it as a kind of omen that she was hovering on the confines of the world to come.

' Oh, is it not horrible,' she exclaimed, ' to be thus entombed alive! why did they not kill me?—why did they not put me to some violent death, which I could have seen in the open face of day and met with such an amount of courage as I could have called to my aid?'

Then the bell sounded again.

' To die here in darkness and in solitude, to feel the pangs of want, and to pine away by degrees in all the frightful sickness and agony of exhausted animation. Oh, it is horrible—most horrible!'

The bell tolled again.

' Oh, for light—light and liberty, if it be but for a moment! Let me once again hear a human voice, even if it be that of my betrayer and destroyer: let me look upon the form of something living—take me from this my coffin—take me from this pestiferous air which clings around me like a shroud.'

The bell tolled again.

" Madness will take possession of me!—the hot blood runs riot through my brain!—husband!—children!—Ranulph—Ranulph Hensman! where are you now?—my breath comes short and thick.—Ranulph, Ranulph, will you leave me here to die?'

' The bell tolled again.

She shrieked, and, entangling her hands among the massive folds of her raven hair, she sank upon her knees.

' Save me—save me, Heaven! fiends are gnawing at my heart; I cannot breathe!'

*　　*　　*　　*　　*　　*

At this moment the door of the sepulchre cell was thrown wide open, and a broad glare of light came into it, making clear and perceptable, probably the first time for many a year, those rugged walls and that frightfully cheerless abode.

The sudden transition from intense darkness to such a full glare of light was at first bewildering in the highest degree, and Alice could almost have supposed she had already passed through the gates of death, and awakened in some other realm than any of this world. She sprang to her feet, exclaiming—

" Lights, lights—dazzling lights ; where am I?—oh, where am I now?'

Then, as the sudden confusion of her intellect passed away, she saw that she still inhabited that dreary cell, but that she was no longer alone, for on its threshold and in the passage beyond were several human forms, some holding torches, and some apparently looking on upon the proceedings of the others, and waiting to take their part in something that was to be achieved.

Among them too, and placed close to the door of the sepulchre cell, was a large odd-looking chest, and what it had been brought there for Alice could not conceive.

She had, however, but a short time for speculation, inasmuch as her whole attention became, in a few moments, riveted upon one person, and that was Sir Rupert Brent, who, with a most demoniac expression of countenance, and a world of angry passion struggling at his heart, advanced and stood just within the precincts of the sepulchre cell.

' Alice, has not your confinement here, short though it may have been, yet subdued the obstinacy of your heart?'

It was a moment or two before Alice could reply, for although it was the hateful form of Sir Rupert Brent, and although it was his voice that rang in her ears, yet it was a grateful change to her from the circumstances in which she had been to feel enabled to look upon anything human, and she felt that maddening impression which had been making such havoc at her heart and brain slowly fading away.

Then came back her old spirit of resistance against the tyranny of that man who had so cruelly oppressed her, and who certainly was the greatest enemy that virtue ever had.

' No, Sir Rupert Brent,' she said, ' I am not yet subdued; I may suffer, even to the verge of madness, for the terror of death must sensibly affect me, or I should be something more than human. Life is dear to me, as it is to all created beings, but there are things dearer still, and one of them is honour, so I tell you I am not yet subdued.'

' Be it so,' said Sir Rupert Brent, fiercely, ' be it so.' Then, turning to those who were with him, he added—

' Do your duty.'

Alice looked on with mingled feelings of terror and amazement. What the duty might be that they were required to perform baffled conjecture, and she could only look upon the proceedings that were taking place with a hope of acquiring speedy information.

The large chest was brought forward and opened, but, to her surprise, she found that it was empty, for, without having any particular reason for so doing, she had imagined that it must surely contain something which was put there to terrify or to injure her.

There appeared to be a kind of reluctance on the part of those who were with Sir Rupert Brent to proceed further, and he cried, with a voice half choked with passion—

' Do your duty, I say, do your duty!'

Thus urged on, they suddenly stepped into the sepulchre cell, and before Alice could be aware of what was intended, one of the heavy, thick black veils, such as were worn by the nuns, was cast completely over her head and face.

In vain she struggled, in vain she cried for aid, in vain she implored for mercy. Those who were persecuting her knew no gentle touch of such a human feeling, and she found herself in the powerful grasp of men against whom resistance was futile.

She was lifted from the floor, and she was conscious of being carried a few paces, and then she felt assured that she had been placed within the large chest, and the frightful idea that it was intended to be made her coffin, and that such a refined torment was intended for her in preference to the lingering death which she must have suffered in the sepulchre cell, came with a frightful feeling of probability across her mind.

She felt conscious that her voice must be muffled considerably by the closeness with which the veil enveloped her, but still, in that last dreadful extremity of her fortunes, she spoke.—

'Kill me, Sir Rupert Brent, kill me at once. If you are resolved to take my life, take it at once and boldly, and I can almost forgive the deed; but, oh! do not torture me thus.'

She heard a voice close to her ear; it spoke in a hissing whisper, and she knew that it was the voice of the Jesuit.

'Alice,' he said, 'do you yield now, or are you still obdurate? Say but the word, and I can yet save you from a death more horrible than any you have yet considered Are you content that it should be so, or not?'

'Heaven help me! I must die.'

'In another moment,' he continued, whispering, 'in another moment the lid of this chest, which may be well called a coffin, will be closed upon you. It shuts you out from the world for ever. Think again, Alice Hensman, think again; you may yet save yourself by an utterance of four of the shortest words language can dictate to you.'

'And those, and those,' she gasped, 'those four words are—'

'"I will love you." Say but those words, and you are free.'

'Never, never.'

With a sudden sound the lid of the box was closed, and at the same moment Alice felt the pulsations of her heart almost cease, and she gave herself up to despair and death.

She felt that the box was lifted from the earth, and carried slowly along, and, as it was, so she became conscious of a cool current of air coming into it through some perforations in its side.

'I am to die,' she thought, 'from starvation here, but not, as I first thought, from suffocation. This is but an exchange from the sepulchre cell to a yet smaller one, which merits the same name.'

Not a word was spoken by the bearers of the box, but they moved onward, carrying it for a long distance in those subterraneous passages beneath the convent, and then at length they halted, and she heard a whispered consultation: not one word, however, met her ears sufficiently distinctly to enable her to understand fully what it meant.

The chest was placed upon the floor for a few minutes, and then she did distinctly hear a voice say—

'Is she dead?'

Feeling that probably this was uttered with the view of inducing some expression from her, she determined that she would not speak, and then again the whispered consultation ensued, and after a time the chest was lifted, and, from the irregular movements of those who carried it, she felt certain that she was being lifted up a staircase.

Many minutes of this kind of progression ensued, the staircase seeming perfectly interminable, until at length the peculiar motion ceased, and the chest was placed down.

From the sound that it made she now felt conscious that it no longer rested on the bare earth, but was placed upon a wooden flooring, and then for a few moments all was still—a stillness which was only broken at length by some one distinctly tapping upon the top of the box with his hand.

'Alice, Alice Hensman,' said the voice of Sir Rupert Brent, 'you and I are alone here now, and I may speak freely; you are doomed, if it be my will and pleasure, to remain and rot where you now are. I am one who will have revenge or love. Once more, and for the last time, I ask you will you be free?'

She would not answer him, but preserved the most profound stillness, so that he could have no precise notion whether she were among the living or the dead.

'Alice,' he said, 'this criminal obstinacy will not avail you. Answer me, are you determined upon death?'

till no sound met his ears, and after a pause of some minutes' duration he muttered to himself,—

'Can it be possible that she is really dead? Is it so, indeed—and am I at last foiled? Well, well, better dead than ever again in the arms of him whom I so hate.'

Alice had an expectation that the lid of the chest would be raised, in order that Sir Rupert Brent might satisfy himself of the truth, or otherwise, of his conjecture concerning her decease, and she was not disappointed, for in a few moments she heard that some fastenings were being undone, when, just at the moment that she expected the lid to be raised, a hasty footstep of some one advancing came upon her ears, and a loud voice exclaimed,—

'Father Georges! Father Georges! the abbess desires your instant presence; the convent-gates are yielding to the blows of hammers, and the multitude without take the part of the besiegers instead of the besieged.'

'Curses on such fickle spirits!' cried Sir Rupert; 'I come—I come at once.'

Without, then, waiting to ascertain the fact of the life or death of the much-persecuted Alice Hensman, he rushed from the place.

His retreating footsteps fell fainter and fainter on the ears of Alice, until at last, dying completely away, the most profound, and to her the most agonizing, stillness reigned in that place of despair.

CHAPTER XXV.

The King's Danger.—Events in London.—The Attempted Assassination.

WHILE these affairs were in progress at Winchester, Henry the Eighth had left London for Windsor, where for a time he intended to remain, giving rein to such scenes of luxury and pleasure as the Court of England was wont to indulge in. The vast hall and apartments of the castle were filled with attendants, and gay courtiers, and haughty statesmen—haughty enough to all the world, save to one who set the whole in motion, namely Henry himself.

The castle afforded ample scope for such a man as Henry. There the state apartments were fitted up in a style befitting the time and the person of the king. Costly, indeed, was all that appertained to the monarch, who used to wander from apartment to apartment, and over the towers and embattled walls, which commanded views of the surrounding country of a pleasing and beautiful character.

The lordly park stretched out before the castle windows—the country beyond and around for miles was of a very different description to what it is now. The lordly monarchs of the forest stood thick—where now the blades of corn grow and ripen, there once stood Herne's Oak.

There for many a mile did the monarchs of England chase the wild deer—there, in splendid leisure, did they enjoy all that life was capable of producing.

Henry the Eighth was not a man to remain idle, something was always present to his mind, and that usually the pursuit of some new pleasure; a something his mind craved after or coveted, and yet there was little that such a monarch as Henry might not have obtained—he was too despotic to bear with opposition, and there were none who durst refuse him.

But powerful and despotic as he was, and pliant as were his ministers, yet he had his enemies, as the reader is by this time well aware, and men of great daring and power—powerful because of the manner in which they worked—powerful because of their union, numbers, and fanaticism, and the persevering energy with which they pursued an object.

Yes; and these men worked for their object in secret, and they were by no means despicable enemies, for men who are willing to do such deeds, and sacrifice themselves, must be fearful enemies to contend against, especially when assassination was the weapon with which they eventually decided upon fighting their battles.

Leoni, finding the king had gone to Windsor, there followed him, and determined to watch him until he should have a fair opportunity of killing Henry.

With this view he took a lodging at a peasant's house, where he could remain and wander about without being noticed by any human being. He gave out that he was an invalid, and had come there to recruit his health. To this the peasant and his wife were ill qualified to object, seeing it was by no means an extraordinary case; on the contrary, it was a very common one indeed, especially when the court was in that neighbourhood.

There was, no doubt, a means of hiding himself, but he did not wish to draw down upon himself or his order the eyes of the emissaries of Henry, who were numerous enough, and who, if they once obtained the least inkling of his design, would not hesitate to sacrifice him to even a suspicion.

There was something favourable in his coming to Windsor; Leoni thought there would be a better chance for his life if he succeeded in killing the king, of which he had not the smallest doubt, if he once got the opportunity to strike a blow.

'It must go hard, indeed,' he muttered, 'when a Jesuit's dagger and his arguments both fail. Henry, no doubt, will be walking about in the castle unattended, or he will be enjoying the hunt, and I must take my measures accordingly. The more alone, the further from his attendants and the castle,

the better for me. Killed the king shall be; but if I can save my own life too, I shall be satisfied; it will be the better for me, and I shall be alive to enjoy the reward and the reputation for so great and glorious a deed—the destruction of the Church's greatest and most powerful enemy.'

Thus thought Leoni, and determined to sacrifice himself, should it be absolutely required for the completion of his object, rather than not make the attempt.

Henry, who was unconscious of the danger that hovered near him, and whose disposition was by no means a fearful one, sought not to secure himself from secret enemies, or from those whom he might suppose would be unscrupulous of the means which they used to rid themselves of so formidable a foe in religious matters.

The festivities were as usual in the castle; the sumptuous entertainments common to royalty were never neglected by

any of the attendants round his person, and the hospitality of the castle was kept up.

What was to be expected in the way of facility for the attempt upon the king's life seemed not likely to happen, for Henry was surrounded by many courtiers who attended, as well as by some foreigners of distinction, ambassadors and envoys, who seemed to make an impenetrable barrier between the king and his secret enemy.

At length Leoni became impatient of delay, and determined to ascertain if it were possible to commit the deed in the castle itself. There would be, he thought, good hiding-places within those walls, and perhaps better than if he were to make the attempt outside in the forest, during a hunt.

With this view, Leoni made a visit to the castle, and approached towards the gate, where he encountered one of the attendants, who was hurrying back to the castle.

'Where, so fast, my good friend?' inquired the Jesuit.

'To the castle,' was the reply.

'What castle is this, then?' he inquired, in seeming ignorance of the locality in which he was at that moment standing.

'What!' said the man; 'do you not know that this is Windsor Castle, the residence of the King?'

'Is the King there now, good friend?'

'Yes, that is, at the castle. You are a stranger in these

parts; you don't seem to have heard of Windsor Castle or of our great king.'

I have heard of both, but I knew not exactly I was so near to either. What would I not give to see your king! I could tell you some things that would amaze you.'

'Tell me what?'

'Ay, I could tell you a little of futurity; I have more knowledge than most men.'

'And yet you knew not that this was Windsor Castle. Come, sir stranger, you cannot get over me in that way; I am a simple man.'

'Will you permit me to whisper in your ear; I will tell you something you believe to be known only to yourself.'

'Ay,' said the man, 'ay to be sure.'

He inclined his ear towards the stranger, who whispered some words in his ear. The effect was so great, and the man staggered back with staring eyes and gaping mouth. He looked at Leoni for some moments, and then he paused to look down at his feet. Leoni smiled mildly and nodded to the castle servitor.

'Come, come, sir servitor; come, are you a sceptic now, or do you believe in what I have told you, that I have more than ordinary knowledge?'

'Yes, yes,' said the man, 'whatever you are, you know more than most men. How you came by it I know not, but you know that which I believed known but to two persons in the world, myself and another.'

'I know that now, friend; do not judge from what I do not know, but from what I do.'

'I am satisfied.'

'And now,' resumed the Jesuit, 'I am a stranger in these parts, and can obtain no lodging to-night. Will you put me in some place in yonder castle so that I can get a night's lodging and see the king?'

'I dare not let you see the king.'

'Cannot you place me somewhere where I can obtain a good view of his majesty? I do not desire he should see me or any one else, but I wish to have a view of him. I have heard so much of the king that I desire to see him. Will you aid me?'

'I can help you to a lodging in the castle, but no more; I have told you you must not see the king. I dare not do it, therefore ask me no more.'

'Well, well,' said the Jesuit, 'I shall see the castle, and that will be something to talk about.'

'It will.'

'And a night's lodging will be a boon I most require: I will accept it, and thank thee for that.'

'Follow me; and say what I say if you be asked any questions. The king is here, and they are particular as to who comes near the castle, lest any improper characters, such as Jesuits and people who have no conscience, should get in.'

The Jesuit followed in silence until they came near the castle, when they were challenged by the sentinel, and replied to by the servitor, who accounted for the presence of the Jesuit by saying he was required to aid in the castle, certain preparations for a feast then in progress, and that more aid was required.

Thus the Jesuit was hurried into the castle—the very residence of the monarch he was about to assassinate. The murderer chuckled at the anticipation of the idea that he was lucky in having such facilities placed in his way for the completion of his offence.

'He is a doomed man,' he muttered. 'I am within the castle, and he will surely die.'

They now entered that part of the castle set apart for the servants who were engaged in that necessary part of attendance upon royalty, the management of the menial duties.

'There,' said the serving-man to the Jesuit, 'what have you ever seen like this before?'

'Nothing,' said the Jesuit.

'Well, what can be more pleasant than a bit of a sirloin? Come, come, neighbour, do justice to the good fare before thee; and as to ale, why there is nothing like it between here and London, I promise you."

'I do admire your cheer, and have partaken of it plentifully, besides which, I am so filled with wonder and astonishment at what I see, that it in part takes away my appetite.'

'I thought you hadn't seen the equal of this.'

'Indeed, I have not. How I should like to see the state apartments, they must be beautiful!'

'They are.'

'Is there no way in which I could unobserved visit them, and see what I may never have such a chance of seeing again. I would give thee something for thy trouble.'

'I will endeavour to do so, I will try and gratify thy curiosity,' said the serving-man; 'but you must be cautious, and say you are a traveller who have missed your way, and have begged a night's lodging at the castle.'

'I will,' he answered; 'and it is the truth.'

'Then if you have done your supper, we will go and see them at once; the king is engaged now, and will not leave his apartment for some time.'

'I have done.'

'Follow me,' said the servitor, and he arose and led the way to the state apartments, through which they traversed, one after another, until they came to one in which they paused several moments.

'This is a splendid room,' said the Jesuit; 'how often does the king come here?'

'Usually about this time; we must be gone, else we shall be caught to a certainty, and that would be more than my place is worth, perhaps my head too.'

'Is he revengeful?'

'He will not have any neglect, and will punish harshly, but not readily condemn any one; but we are obliged to be careful of what we are about, for such a place as this is not a bad place for a man to keep.'

'I dare say not.'

At that moment there was a momentary bustle and sound of some one coming, and his conductor said,—

'The king! the king!'

'Who?' said the Jesuit, as the man endeavoured to pull him away from the spot.

'The king!—fast! come away, unless you want to cause me to lose my place because I have obliged you and acted the part of the good Samaritan.'

'I will conceal myself behind the curtain yonder,' said Leoni; 'I will go there, and he will be none the wiser and you none the worse. Come, I shall be safe.'

'By all the saints in the calendar you shall suffer for this! What a fool I have been, to be sure, to have anything to do with a stranger! they may sleep in the ditches for aught I care for the future; I'll not endanger my place for the best of you that ever slept under cover.'

So saying, he walked after Leoni, and concealed himself behind the curtain also, and at the same time he took him by the right wrist and by the neck, whispering in his ear at the same time,—

'If thou darest to move when the king shall pass, be assured I will plunge my dagger in thy breast, and that too before the slightest offer of aid can be made; indeed, I doubt not if I should not be doing good service if I were to kill you at once upon the spot.'

There was no time to return any answer; for Henry himself entered immediately, and slowly pursued his way through the apartment, passing close by the curtains, which even some part of his dress brushed, that concealed them from him; at the same time, had he not been deeply thinking upon some one object or other, he must have found them out by the breathing which must have been heard.

Henry, however, appeared to be deep in thought, and walked slowly away.

The rage of Leoni knew no bounds, but he dared not show it; to have struggled to free himself from the grasp of the menial would have been madness, and would also have given the king notice of his danger. but had he been free the days of 'Old Harry' would have been cut short—as it was, he was unconscious of it all.

There was a silence of a few moments, during which the menial and the Jesuit spoke not; at the same time the latter regretted he had not made the attempt.

'Now,' said the serving-man, 'you have seen the king.'

'I have.'

'But you would have ruined me to satisfy your curiosity. You would not follow my instructions, and now you shall leave the castle.'

'There was no need of holding me, I was not going to leave my place of concealment.'

'That might have been; but you may depend upon it I would not trust you if you desired it ever so; no, no, out of the castle you go.'

'You promised me a lodging?'

'And you have forfeited that promise. You shall go out.

Your conduct is a sufficient answer to that part of our compact. You go out, so say no more about it.'

' I will raise the castle.'

' If you do, you will be worse off than you imagine.'

' They will not refuse me the poor boon of a lodging and food, and, as for my being here, if there be any harm in it, or mischief befall any one for it, you will be the one to bear the burden.'

' I shall, indeed, sir stranger. You reason like a clock, but you will get a lodging certainly, for you will be placed in the dungeons below as a sorcerer.'

The Jesuit was silenced for a moment, but he still thought if he could only remain in the castle that night he would be able to effect his purpose in the dead of the night, and then he would try to overcome the serving-man, and he determined to try his strength with him.'

' You must come,' said the man.

' Must! You will do wrong to lay hands upon me. I will resist you.'

' You must be stronger than I if you won't come when I tell you. Come on!'

As he spoke he pulled him forcibly by the throat, and then a struggle commenced, which at once proved the inferiority of the Jesuit in a personal struggle with the menial, for he was thrown down and dragged from the room, and thence through several passages, until he felt the cool air upon his features, which told him that he was near some of the court-yards, and he struggled desperately to free himself, but could not do so notwithstanding his strength.

' Now you will know how to conduct yourself when you are in a king's residence again,' said the serving-man, as he dragged him down the steps, and tumbled him into the open grounds.

' There, you may go yonder, and make your way through the guards if you can; if not you'll get imprisoned, and visited with punishment. I shall deny all connexion with you, so hasten off.'

Leoni felt himself free, but did not very well know what to do, so rose and walked away as well as he could, and proceeded towards the wood which lay before him, and pursued his walk for some distance from the castle, until he, fortunately for himself, reached the wood, which served to protect him from the inquiring glances of the sentinels.

Having walked till he had proceeded some distance, and to a spot where he believed himself free from all observation, he threw himself upon the earth fatigued and vexed.

' Curses upon that fellow!' he muttered: 'through him, as good a plot as ever was made has miscarried. Henry would have been no more. I should have killed him, and the palace and all the castle might have afforded me good shelter until I could get clear away; or perhaps I might have got off first, and been the first to carry the news of my own exploit to our head quarters, and received the congratulations of my order, who would not be slow to reward either merit or danger.'

As he reasoned thus within himself, he lay there a prey to rage and disappointment; and the moon now rose overhead, and there was not the remotest chance of his obtaining any shelter that night; all he could do would be to remain where he was until morning.

' I will remain here,' he muttered, ' I will remain here, and when daylight comes I shall be better able to find out where I am. The king and court must occasionally take their way through the forest, and there hunt the stag. Yes, yes, and Henry has too much of the Norman blood in him, though he cares but little for the sport, he will be here safe enough. I shall have yet a chance of prosecuting my resolution.'

He arose and threw himself beneath the spreading branches of an immense oak which overshadowed the spot and there among the smaller growth, he screened himself from the night air, and there fell, after some time spent in deep thought, asleep.

*   *   *   *   *

The sun had risen high before the Jesuit arose from his forest couch, and then he started up and listened to hear if any sounds met his ear, but none came. He was certain he had wandered some distance from the castle, for he could not see the huge flag that floated above the castle to denote the presence of royalty.

However he pushed onwards, directed in some measure by the rising sun, which shone from one point, and about two hours after daylight he came upon a peasant's hut—he was a wood-cutter

The Jesuit entered the cottage with a benison; the family were at breakfast, and there appeared plenty on the board—

' Good people,' he said, ' have you the means to show hospitality to a stranger? I have been benighted in these parts, and have slept in the open air. I will pay you for your trouble.'

' Stranger,' said the woodman, ' we do not keep open house, but we can afford to give a meal to a stranger without taking a reward for it.'

' Your hospitality,' said the Jesuit, ' will be most acceptable, for I am hungry and fatigued. This is a large tract of country; and to get once out of your tract would, indeed, have been worse than it is but for the appearance of your house.'

' Well, it certainly might have been worse, and much worse, for had you gone past this cottage you would have got into the wilds, from which you could not have got out very readily, for there are no paths such as a stranger can find or distinguish when he sees.'

' I am fortunate.'

' You are especially so as there will be a royal hunt to-day in the forest, and there is no saying which way the stag will go.'

' A royal hunt?'

' Ay, stranger, ay, there will be a royal hunt to-day. But sit down, stranger, sit down and eat; ours is coarse fare, but it is wholesome, and there is no stint either.'

' Thank you,' said the Jesuit, ' thank you. So there is to be a royal hunt, eh? I never saw such a thing in my life. I should much like to witness this hunt.'

' Well, if you chuse to stay here for a few hours, and considering that you have been in the forest all night, you had better remain where you are.'

' Thank you. If I may trespass upon you for so much, I will. To tell the truth, I feel but little refreshed by the night air in which I have slept.'

' Then let it be so. We shall consider you our guest until you choose to depart.'

' I suppose the king will be present?'

' Yes, surely; he always rides out when he is here at the castle. There would be no hunt without him; he is sure to be well forward in the chace—they never, indeed, go before; but he rides well, they say.'

' Does he? and is he a fearless horseman?'

' Yes, yes; as stanch as a big man can be.'

' Does the king often traverse the forest or any part of the grounds by himself, unattended by any one?'

' Not often now; but it is always uncertain; if he ever does, it is always at some time that nobody expects, but it would be of little use for any poor body meeting him; nor is it likely he would attend to any one; and should he be taken for any private person, he would not be taken much aback, because he would be ready to take his own part.'

' Is there,' said the stranger, ' no sure place of meeting with him, should one feel inclined to see so great a monarch? I wish to see him very much.'

' You cannot be better placed than you are here. You will stand a very good chance of seeing him, unless indeed you were to go to the castle; but if you are a stranger, which you say you are, you would most probably be interfered with: since the Jesuits have been the king's enemies, they are not allowed to go nearer the royal person than is consistent with safety, and I reckon that is a long way off.'

' Indeed! and are they such enemies?'

' Yes, surely; they would kill the king, no doubt, if they had a chance. They are like to be losers, and therefore they are the aggressors; and since the king has defied the Pope, these monks would think killing the king a very meritorious deed.'

' You are too harsh.'

' Not a bit, sir stranger; we have had to give a good deal to these few busy people.'

' You only change the burden,' replied the Jesuit; ' if you give it not to one, you will find you will have to pay it to another. You only shift the load from one shoulder to the other.'

' Well,' said the woodman, ' you know the relief we feel in doing this. You never carried a burthen, else you would know the truth of it; but I tell you we may shift some of the burdens upon the shoulders of those who are better able to bear them than we are.'

'You will find your mistake out; but there will be time, enough for that.'

'I hope so,' said the peasant: 'in the mean time we will enjoy what we have got, and let them fight it out between them who are the great gainers; our King's at home and the Pope's abroad—he's a long way off.'

'But he is your spiritual pastor.'

'He wouldn't be so if he got nothing by it, and it's hardly worth while paying two for that, for it is pretty sure we shall have to pay somebody, and that which is paid at home is more sure to be spent at home, so we shall be gainers by it in the end.'

'It is not for me to complain,' said the Jesuit. 'I am but one of the nation, and what men shall think fit, will do for me; but how goes the day.'

'About noon.'

'Past,' said the Jesuit, 'the sun is on the declension, you see there is a shadow.'

'True, true, but see, we have a storm a-brewing in the west; see how the clouds are sailing up almost without wind: those dark purple masses which now float in the air will give us some thunder.'

'There is a storm brewing, surely; if the hunt is begun the weather will hardly spare the King.'

'Not it,' said the woodman. 'Hark, I can hear the sound of the horn, and there is a clap of thunder to accompany it. Ha! and the rain, see how it comes down.'

'Yes, it does rain—the earth seems to smoke.'

'Ay, what will they do in the hunt? they cannot escape it; even Herne's oak would not shelter them, and that's the largest in the forest.'

'And would be dangerous besides.'

'It would. Hark, hark! do you not hear the sounds of the horn becoming more and more distinct?'

'Yes, I do.'

'They come this way, there—there is a flash of lightning as vivid as it can be—enough to scorch one's eye-balls out of one's head—I can't see at all.'

'And I scarcely.'

There was a pause now, and they spoke not, for the thunder now leaped and crashed through the skies with such overwhelming sounds that they could not hear themselves speak, but at that moment some horsemen dressed in gorgeous liveries rode up to the door.

They all crowded round one portly-looking person, and without ceremony he walked into the cottage and took a seat that was at hand.

'Good fellow,' said the king, 'we crave the shelter of thy roof tree from the storm. I wish I had been nearer to it when the storm commenced.'

'Great sir,' replied the peasant, humbly, for he had some notion it must be the king; 'most gracious sir, I wish it had been; but to such as I have, you are most heartily welcome. I would I were more than I am, that I might befittingly entertain you. But I am as many more are.'

'Good fellow, you talk like a courtier, but cease—the storm will soon blow over, and then we can resume our chace, or if not we can return to the castle.'

There was a pause for some moments, when the king, for it was he who had taken shelter, suddenly turned round and perceived Leoni was stealing up towards him.

'How now, sirrah! what means this? know you not your distance? dost belong to this place?'

'No; I am a traveller.'

'Then, sir traveller, know your place.'

'I am here for shelter the same as you, and I know not by what right you assume you are exclusively entitled to the shelter.'

'Ha! dost know who thou art speaking too? Dog! if thou sayest another word thou shalt be speared.'

'Tyrant,' said the Jesuit, 'thy time is come! thy race is run, and thy minutes are numbered! Thy life I will take—make thy peace—or rather thou shalt die in thy guilt!'

As he spoke he drew his dagger, and rushed headlong on the king, who, wheeling round, took the upraised arm of the assassin above the elbow, swung the Jesuit quite round, and before he could strike a blow he was knocked down and secured by the attendants, who immediately seized the traitor, by all means they had at hand.

Being bound hand and foot, he spoke not nor murmured one word, but sat still and listened to all that was said to him, and the jeers that were made against him.

In a short time the air was again serene. After a time the king rewarded the peasant who had thrown himself upon the Jesuit; and then, mounting again, the whole party rode off—the Jesuit being led to the castle vaults, after the most signal and complete failure of his attempt upon the king's life.

CHAPTER XXVI.

The Attack upon the Well House, and its Consequences.

WE have stated that the plans of the Lord Warden and his gallant associates for attacking the Well House were matured, and that they would best exhibit themselves to our readers in action; we shall, therefore, now proceed to state what ensued upon the information that Ranulph Hensman had so strangely obtained concerning the place of meeting of the Jesuits.

This information, it will be recollected, taught the Lord Warden and his friends to expect that at midnight, on that 17th of September, the same violent party of Jesuitical conspirators who had been, in consequence of the hazardous adventure of Ranulph Hensman, driven from their place of meeting in the vaults of the cathedral, were about to resume their deliberations at the Well House.

It was hoped, then, that here was an opportunity of at once arresting the whole of the captious and desperately wicked spirits who opposed themselves to the greatest reform which England had ever known since the signing of the Charter which had been forced from the truculent and base King John at Runnymede.

At about ten o'clock on the evening in question, the Lord Warden got everything in readiness for the enterprise he meditated.

Forty picked men-at-arms were taken from the castle guard and placed under the command of Captain Angerstein, who had received his precise instructions from the Lord Warden.

Ranulph Hensman and John Elkington accompanied the party; but they were not so indiscreet as to go in a body to the spot, which would have had the effect, in all probability, of arousing the worst suspicions of the Jesuits, and inducing them at once to change their intentions.

On the contrary, the Lord Warden, accompanied only by Hensman, John Elkington, and Captain Angerstein, walked down to the place of meeting, and instead of passing up the narrow private road-way which led to the Well House, they knocked at one of the front mansions, the back windows of which must be so situated as to command a partial view of the Well House.

The Lord Warden asked to see the proprietor or occupier of this house at which he knocked, and, informing that individual who he was, he added that for a few hours it became important that his house should be made into a military post.

He enjoined him to secrecy, and then Captain Angerstein departed to the castle to arrange the manner in which his men were to reach this place.

This was done by sending two and sometimes three at a time, so that by degrees they all reached the house without exciting any particular attention, for it was a common enough thing for those soldiers of the castle guard who happened to be off duty to be strolling about the streets of Winchester in couples.

When this was all arranged, they were placed in a lower apartment ready for immediate service, while their leaders took up a station at a back window, which commanded a view of the entrance to the Well House.

They waited there until half-past eleven before any one came, but then three men at once walked up to the door, and tapping at it, gave some watch-word to the man who opened the small square orifice that was in it, and were admitted.

After this the arrivals were numerous, until the Lord Warden and those who were with him counted twenty-five as having entered the house.

After this, although they waited in anxious expectation for half-an-hour, no more came, and consequently they considered that the whole of the conspirators had assembled.

It was in vain that Ranulph Hensman looked scrutinisingly at every one who approached for Sir Rupert Brent. Either he did not come, or in the darkness he could not be recognised.

'We have them all now,' said the Lord Warden, without a doubt, 'and I shall proceed at once to surround the house with the soldiers, so that none may escape.'

The garden-wall of the Well House was clear and defined, so that there was no difficulty whatever in placing sentinels, in such a position that no one could leave without being observed.

The soldiers were armed well, and they were all tried men, not at all likely to shrink from their duty, however arduous the task might be. They were placed in couples, had strict orders to make prisoner of any one leaving the house, and, if resistance was offered, to cut him down at once rather than allow him the chance of escape.

'I would rather,' said the Lord Warden, 'not take one of them than not take them all; we must and will succeed in thoroughly uprooting this nest of traitors to their country and their king.'

The distribution of the force in the way we have related, left but eight men at the disposal of the Lord Warden, and with these, at half-past twelve, he and his two associates marched silently up the gravel path towards the Well House.

John Elkington had been pitched upon as the one to make application for admission; and he, with his usual boldness and decision of character, had made up his mind to a most peculiar course upon the occasion, a course which few would have thought of, but which from its singularity and boldness fully deserved success.

While the others waited, he advanced alone and rang boldly at the bell, the summons of which had always produced so immediate an answer.

The sound had scarcely ceased to vibrate upon the ears of those who heard it, when the little square wicket was opened in the door, and a man's face appeared.

The moment that it did so, John Elkington, who was fully prepared for the occasion, doubled his fist, and, striking right in with tremendous force, he hit the man so fair and terrific a blow that he fell backward as if he had been shot, and lay in the passage of the house totally incapable of making the least movement or of in any way alarming the conspirators who were there assembled.

Without uttering a remark, John Elkington then reached his arm as far as he could in at the square office, and felt carefully about for the fastening of the door.

A key was sticking in the inner portion of the lock, and when he turned it the door yielded at once, and Elkington pushed it wide open.

Then he beckoned to the Lord Warden and Hensman, who had been waiting the success of this bold plan of getting into the house, and they at once advanced with the soldiers.

Two more out of the eight were now despatched back to the house which had been made a temporary garrison of, with the man who had been knocked down by John Elkington. Their orders were to dispose of him as quickly as they could where he could be locked up securely, and then themselves return to the Well-house.

'We must now search,' said the Warden, in a whisper, 'the lower rooms, for it is more than likely that in one of them we shall find the objects of our enterprise.'

A couple of torches were lighted, and, with their weapons in their hands ready for immediate use, the party, which was now certainly a small one, commenced their task.

They entered all the rooms on the ground floor without discovering any signs of the presence of those whom they had seen enter the house, and who they knew must be concealed somewhere within its precincts.

'We must find them,' said the Lord Warden, 'for this is a house too small to admit of any facilities for concealment, and the plan of it is too evident.'

'Besides,' said Elkington, 'the number of men we are looking for cannot get into a very small space. Come on, I will lead the way myself up the staircase.'

He bounded up the stairs, closely followed by Hensman and the Warden, the whole three ready for immediate action, while the soldiers brought up the rear with steadiness and precision.

A very suspicious stillness reigned in the place—a kind of stillness which seemed to imply the probability of an ambuscade, for they well knew the violence of character of the Jesuits, and likewise that they would be perfectly unscrupulous as to how they accomplished the destruction of their foes, so long as they did accomplish it.

It was a narrow and intricate staircase, and had that been a period when the use of fire-arms was as well understood as it is now, a most vigorous defence might have been made on that staircase against almost any number of assailants, but such was not the case; and although they scarcely expected to reach the landing without some

demonstration of opposition, they nevertheless did so; and to their surprise not only saw no one, but did not even hear the slightest indication of the presence of a human being.

'This is very strange!' whispered the Warden to Hensman, 'they either know we are here, or they do not; if the latter, why are they so still and quiet that we cannot even hear the faintest murmur of their presence? and, if they do know of our presence, it seems a species of insanity on their parts to make no sort of resistance whatever.'

'I cannot understand it,' said Hensman: 'it is impossible we should be all deceived; we saw them ourselves enter this house, and our sentinels we know we can depend upon, so that having entered it it is impossible that they could leave it.'

'Certainly,' said the Warden; 'they might at some particular point have made a determined effort, but we must have heard something of it.'

They walked into room after room until they had examined all the upper apartments, which were five in number, without discovering anything beyond the bare walls, and a few indifferent and ancient pieces of furniture, which were covered with dust, and had evidently been a long time neglected.

'This is as surprising as it is annoying,' said the Warden, 'and there is but one other place we have to examine, and that is the garden—light some more torches, and let us proceed thither at once.'

This was done, and without any caution now, for it was unnecessary. They proceeded into the garden of the house, which was a square plot of ground covered with rich and luxuriant grass, and shadowed by tall trees, the leaves of which were gently shivering in the wind, and presented a strange appearance as the light of the torches fell upon them.

It did not require two minutes' search to convince the Lord Warden that no one was hidden in the garden. In fact, there was not a shadow of a hiding-place for any one to get into; and now, with a feeling of great mortification at their thorough and complete disappointment, they stood beneath the shadow of one of the trees to consult upon what it was possible for them to do next.

No wonder that for some moments there was a silence among them, for so unexpected had been the whole affair that it completely baffled conjecture; and, as regarded the soldiery, it was evident that they looked with a superstitious awe upon the house and grounds into which some of them had seen twenty-five men enter, and yet within which not a single individual was to be found.

'By Heavens!' said the Warden, 'this is the most extraordinary thing I have ever encountered. It is quite clear that a number of men came into this house, but how they got out of it again is certainly to me one of the greatest of mysteries.'

'Are there cellars,' said John Elkington, 'into which they might have crept?'

'There may be; thank Heaven for any suggestion. That presents a possibility of clearing up this mysterious affair. Take the whole of the troop with you that we have at our disposal, and I will remain here keeping guard in the garden.'

The ordinary cellarage was soon found, and an attentive examination of the walls strongly convinced Hensman that there was no place of concealment, and he returned with that report to the Warden, who, during his absence, had communicated by voice with the sentinels on the other side of the wall, and ascertained from them that all had been quiet, and no one had endeavoured to disturb their post.

'We have searched everywhere,' said Elkington, 'but in the well.'

The Warden shook his head, as he said—

'That search would be the vainest one we have yet undertaken, for if it were perfectly dry even, it would not hold the number of persons that we are in pursuit of, unless, indeed, they stood upon each other's heads.'

'We will see for all that,' said Elkington; and he picked up from the garden a large stone, which was so massive that it took his two hands to lift it, and walked towards the well.

The orifice of the well was a circular one, and only just sufficient to allow the buckets to ascend and descend from the windlass which was above, but for about three feet beyond that in a circle stout planking was laid down, upon which

John Elkington stood and dashed the stone the which opening.

A tremendous splash in the water immediately succeeded, proving, beyond a doubt, that the well could be no place of concealment; and thus was it that, completely foiled, and unable to form the slightest idea of what had become of the twenty-five Jesuits, the Lord Warden was compelled to draw off his force with the bitterest feelings of disappointment, and depart from the place.

The sentinels were called in, and they all stated, in answer to repeated questions, their absolute certainty that no one had crossed the garden wall, nor had they heard anything in the house which gave evidence of a human being inhabiting it.

'Alas!' said Hensman, 'is the cup of promised happiness to be for ever thus dashed from my lips? Whenever I appear to be upon the point of making some discovery which will place Alice again in my arms, the bitterest disappointment succeeds, and, as if by magic, all my fondest hopes are blasted even in the bud.'

'By Heaven, Hensman!' said the Lord Warden, 'I know not what to say to console you. These circumstances are as inexplicable to me as they can possibly be to you.'

'Time will solve them all,' said Elkington, 'although at present they are so abundantly mysterious. I should advise, however, that a secret sentinel, not in the costume of the guard, but in plain apparel, should be placed upon this house, and that he be relieved every two hours, so as to be able to come to the castle with a full report of anything that may have occurred during the time that he has kept his watch.'

'That shall be done,' said the Warden, 'as well as anything which can be suggested as likely in any manner whatever to solve these most mysterious circumstances.'

'And I,' said Hensman, 'I am once again completely baffled, and standing in the wide world. I know not even which way to turn in search of her who has been torn from my protection, and concealed from me by such diabolical and devilish arts. Oh! Alice, Alice, this uncertainty is dreadful, and in time will poison my very spring of existence.'

'Come Hensman, come,' said the Warden, 'these lamentations do not sit well upon you, believe me. A mind like yours should not give way to them; and although perhaps you do not put abundant faith in the prediction, I never in my life felt so strong a presentiment that all would in the end be well, as I do regarding this, I hope, very temporary obscuration of your felicity.'

'Oh, forgive me,' said Hensman, 'if sometimes, my Lord, the impatience of my grief gets the better of my judgment. I will hope for better times, and in the mean time with heart and hand let me still consider myself your servant ever.'

'My friend, Hensman, rather call yourself, for have I not been indebted to you for my very life. Come on to the castle, and we shall yet be able to concert some measures which, with truth and honesty to back us, will enable us to get the better of these inveterate Jesuits.'

CHAPTER XXVII.

What befel Alice in her new Prison.

WE left Alice in a position so extremely precarious, that it behoves us to take back the reader to a condition of her fortunes, for we are by no means pleased to leave her in such a desperate strait as that in which the villany of Sir Rupert Brent had placed her.

For some time she lay perfectly quiet in the chest, after Sir Rupert Brent had been so hurriedly called away by a message from the abbess touching the great danger the convent was in, a danger which we know not to be exaggerated, inasmuch as we are already aware of what circumstances ensued immediately after the first demonstration of hostility at the convent gates.

She now really considered herself as completely lost, and abandoned by all hope, and she gave herself up to a kind of despair which had in it more of apathy than usually characterised her despair.

Had she preserved her ordinary courage better under these circumstances, she would sooner have discovered that she was comparatively free, but it was some time before, in making an effort to remove from the uneasy posture in which she lay, she found that the lid of the chest was open, and that she could, without difficulty, throw it back.

Oh, what a moment of joy was that, to feel that at all

events, she was comparatively free! and although the place was in complete darkness around her, she felt as though one of the greatest boons of earth had been conferred upon her, by the mere fact that she was enabled to walk a few short spaces, and to be free from the really frightful confinement to which she had been subjected.

She began now to think that her confinement in the chest had had a double object, first, probably, to completely blind her to the route that was pursued when she was taken from the sepulchre cell, and, secondly, in order that yet another experiment might be tried by the crafty Jesuit upon her fears.

She could have no possible notion of where she was, for the darkness was complete, but as she moved along, feeling the walls of her prison, which she found were of wood, she stumbled upon a pitcher containing water, and by its side she found a loaf of bread, both of which convinced her that it was intended she should remain there a prisoner, and that, whatever terrors she had been subjected to, her death had by no means been determined upon.

A feeling of hopelessness came over her which showed itself in tears, and she felt her heart greatly relieved as she wept freely and abundantly. The indomitable spirit of resistance, likewise, which usually characterized her, returned, and she was better able to bend all her energies to the one great object of her reflections, viz. the making an escape than she had before been able to do.

She felt confident from the panelling of the walls that the room she was now confined in was the mere ordinary apartment of a house, and not by any means intended originally as a prison.

It might be a portion of the convent, or it might not, for she had her doubts as to whether or not she had been carried any distance through the open air during the time she had been compelled to take up her abode in the chest.

But she soon satisfied herself that her situation was vastly improved from what it had been, for the air she breathed now was pure and clear although cold, and by listening intently she could hear the sound of wind among trees, which was a most grateful one to her, and one which she listened to for many minutes with undivided attention.

Then, by a careful examination of the walls, she discovered what she made certain was a window, although it was closed fast by shutters, which did not permit the least ray of light to penetrate them.

These shutters were on the inside, so at all events there was a hope of discovering their fastenings, and so being perhaps enabled to release herself; and she was the more eager to set about this great object, because she could not but suspect her present place of confinement would be but a temporary one, and that she was only placed in it upon some sudden emergency which would soon pass away, and that then, perhaps, the sepulchre cell would receive her.

'Chance circumstances,' she said, 'have given me this opportunity, which, if properly embraced, will lead to my escape, and that it may so lead no exertions shall be wanting on my part.'

She drank as much water as her thirst impelled her to do from the pitcher, and then, without overturning it, she managed to stand upon it, and so reach higher up to the window to discover how the shutter was fastened.

Her hand fell upon the head of a screw, which, to her great joy, she found she could turn with ease, and when she had done so a very slight amount of force indeed sufficed to draw the shutter down into a recess which was made for its reception, and in comparison to the previous darkness of the room a perfect blaze of daylight beamed within it.

It was almost with a shriek of joy that Alice Hensman welcomed the soft and beautiful light. It seemed something, indeed, like the near approach of liberty to see the sun shine, although it was declining in the west, and its abundant glories were rapidly fading into twilight.

'Now,' she cried, 'now I have hope; my children, I shall see you once again; I shall look upon your face, too, Ranulph, which I thought would not greet my eyes in this world. This is joy, indeed, and already I feel something of the sensations of actual liberty; yes, I shall be free, I shall be free!'

The window readily yielded to her hands, and she looked out into a garden which she saw was immediately beyond, and from whence had come the pleasant sound of the wind among the trees. With a most anxious glance Alice measured the distance with her eye from the window to the green sward beneath it. It was a fearful leap, but what will not any one dare for that sweetest of all earthly possessions—liberty, and especially liberty from such a persecution and such a species of dreadful oppression as that which Alice was suffering from?

What a noble object, too, had she not to achieve along with freedom! She had all the world to gain, and nothing to lose. Her husband and her children—those dear possessions which made the sum of all the joy existence could offer to her—seemed to beckon to her to take the leap.

She climbed the window sill—she breathed one short prayer to Heaven—and then sprang into the garden below.

Really unhurt, but feeling a great shock in consequence of the height, she lay for a few moments ere she recovered her energies, and then the dread that some one might be in the house and yet defeat her object probably inspired her with more strength than under ordinary circumstances she could at all have hoped for, and, rising to her feet, she looked eagerly around her for some means of leaving the garden.

The evening was coming on with great rapidity, for the sun, when it reached within a short distance of the horizon, had suddenly sunk behind a bank of heavy clouds, producing by that means a sudden obscuration of light, such as in this climate by no means ordinarily ensues. Then as Alice observed a door in the garden-wall at some distance from where she was, and had already moved some paces towards it, she saw it suddenly open from the outside, and a man made his appearance.

He took a key from the outside of the lock, and placed it in the inside; he then turned it in the lock, and no doubt, as he thought, for better safety, left it there, and walking across the garden carelessly, while Alice shrank from observation behind one of the trees, he entered the house.

Here was an opportunity not to be lost, and, caring little where the door in the garden might lead to, so that it led away from that detested mansion, she flew towards it, unlocked it, and passed out.

She found herself in an open space, which she immediately recognised as being some short distance from Winchester.

'I am free!' she shrieked, 'I am free!' and she flew rather than ran towards the city.

The chance passengers she met were amazed, and some of them terrified, to see a woman rushing along with such a frantic speed, her hair dishevelled, and presenting every appearance of having gone through something fearful in the way of adventure, which was not yet entirely over. But heeding nothing, and attending to no one, Alice Hensman proceeded towards her own home, her thoughts being wholly and solely intent upon her children, whom she hoped soon to have the joy of embracing again, after the short but severe career of peril and of suffering that had separated her from them.

The distance was considerable, but she achieved it in a wonderfully short space of time, and finally stood panting upon the threshold of her own house, where she paused a moment to recover breath before she entered it.

Then she knocked loudly for admission, and waited in a perfect agony of impatience for some one to answer her demand.

All was still; she heard no sound within the mansion, and again and again she knocked, while each time her heart seemed to sink within her at the thought of some evil she could not define, but which began to beset her mind with all the horrors of uncertainty.

She glanced up at the house; that glance was sufficient to show her that the windows were closed, and it had a deserted appearance.

'Gracious Heavens!' she exclaimed, 'what has happened? has death been busy in my house, or has he, who persecuted me and made me a prisoner, adopted the fearful plan of taking the children as hostages, in case I should myself escape. Oh, horror, horror, if it should be so!'

'Why, Mrs. Hensman,' said a voice behind her, 'can this be you?'

'Ah! who speaks?' she cried, turning quickly; 'who is it that knows the wretched Alice Hensman?'

'Why, Mrs. Hensman,' said the man, 'don't you know me? I am a neighbour, and live nearly opposite to you.'

'Yes, yes, I think I recollect you; now I know I do. Speak to me, I charge you, speak of my children. Tell me, oh, tell me, whither they are gone; quick! if you have any human compassion speak to me of my children.'

'Well, all I know is, that Hensman took them away, but where he took them to I can't tell you, but surely he can, and you will find him at the Lord Warden's.'

'Yes, yes, at the Lord Warden's; I shall find him there, as you say, at the Lord Warden's.'

'Well, but, Mrs. Hensman,' 'what has happened, and what has kept you away from home?'

'I cannot, dare not, pause to tell you now—some other time; I must seek my husband and my children now at once.'

Turning now from the door, she, without a moment's hesitation, took her route towards the castle, hoping that there at once she should see her husband, or, at all events, obtain some immediate tidings of him; and as she went, she tortured herself with all sorts of surmises concerning the disposition of the children, until by the time she reached the postern gate, she was almost exhausted with anxiety, fatigue, and apprehension.

She spoke to the sentinel, and, upon announcing that she came to speak to the Lord Warden or to Ranulph Hensman, and that she was the wife of the latter, he allowed her to pass his post, saying—

'If you think proper, you can wait, but neither the Lord Warden, Master Secretary Hensman, nor, in fact, any one in actual authority, is within. There is some expedition on foot which has taken them all from the castle; what it is I know not, but you can wait.'

'Yes,' she said, 'I will wait, I will wait!'

'Go and sit down in the guard-room, madam, no one will molest you, and there you will find a fire; I mean the officers' guard-room, which is the second door on your right.'

Alice Hensman thanked him, and passed in, gratified, at all events, to hear that nothing had happened to Hensman; for the fact of his being out on an expedition with the Lord Warden signified that he was alive and well. She obeyed the directions of the sentinel, and found the way to the officers' guard-room, where there was a cheering fire, by the side of which she sunk, feeling that, at all events, she was in perfect safety now that she had got within the precincts of the castle.

There was but one deep anxiety remaining, and that was concerning her children; but now that her first great excitement was over and she was able to reason more calmly upon the circumstances, she by no means felt such uneasiness, because the assurance came across her that Hensman must have removed them to some place of safety, for, if they had been taken possession of by the Jesuit, he would not have forgotten to make use of such an argument to prey upon her fears.

'I will believe,' she said, 'that all is safe, and that, having thus fortunately escaped from Sir Rupert Brent, I shall now in serenity and peace be able to rejoin my husband and my children. All will be well again, and I have but to take care that Ranulph does not run into too much danger in seeking of the Jesuit an atonement for the evil he has done.'

Overpowered then by the fatigue she had passed through and feeling the cheering influence of the pleasant fire-side by which she sat, it is not to be wondered at that Alice should yield to the sleep that came over her, and in a few moments, letting her head sink upon the table by which she sat, she lapsed completely into sound repose.

CHAPTER XXVIII.

The happy Meeting, and the generous Offer of the Lord Warden.

NOTWITHSTANDING the cheering expressions which had been used towards Ranulph Hensman by the Lord Warden and John Elkington, the bereaved secretary came but with a heavy heart towards the castle.

His friends saw that it was an effort to him to converse, so after a time they confined their conversation to each other, with the exception of an occasional remark, and left Ranulph to pursue the train of his own sad reflections.

And sad, indeed, they were! for now all clue seemed to have been lost by which he hoped to trace the place of Alice's concealment.

Every attempt that failed he considered, and considered truly enough placed his enemies upon their guard, and delayed exertions which might have been employed in some contrary direction, which was much to be regretted. Little did he imagine the delightful and joyful surprise that was awaiting him when he should reach the castle, towards which he was returning with so much reluctance. Oh! what wings it would have added to his speed could he but have suspected the real truth! But no! there was no friendly spirit to whisper to him the least cheering intelligence.

On the contrary, he seemed to feel a sort of mental reproach, as he moved onward, because he was not at that precise time engaged in endeavouring to discover Alice's prison, and, but for the express wishes of the Warden, he would not even then have crossed the threshold of the castle, but would again have proceeded in succession to the convent and the Well-house, with the hope of obtaining information upon the subject so dear to him.

In the ordinary course of things the sentinel at the gate had been changed before the Warden's arrival, so that the soldier who now kept guard there knew nothing of the arrival of Alice Hensman, and consequently the secretary entered the castle without the slightest suspicion that he was again under the roof of her whom he loved so well, and whose enforced departure from him for a time had been a source of such unmitigated regret.

Captain Angerstein addressed a few words to Hensman, and they both walked onwards towards the officers' guard-room, which was then only lighted by the fire, which cast a bright red glow over every object.

'I must go forth again,' said Hensman, 'for I cannot rest.'

'Nay,' said Captain Angerstein, 'you ought to give yourself some repose. If you do not, you will find yourself in a short time thoroughly exhausted.'

'I cannot hope for repose,' replied Hensman, 'until that period of exhaustion actually comes. When it does I must perforce give way to it; so now, my friend, good night again; I will just see the Warden for a few moments, and then go off once more upon my weary pilgrimage.'

'Nay,' said the captain, 'step in for a moment and take one glass of Canary, to recruit your energies. I pray you do not refuse me.'

Ever kindly disposed as Hensman was to all who addressed a gentle word to him, he allowed the captain to lead him into the guard-room, when the first object that met their eyes was some person sleeping by the fire-side.

'We have a visitor here already,' said the captain, 'a female too; who can it be?'

Hensman cast his eyes upon the sleeping figure. His heart at once told him who it was, and, with a cry of joy which awakened Alice, he sprang towards her.

Words were too weak to give utterance to the full tide of delightful feelings that swelled within their hearts; each could only utter the name of each, and in another instant Alice sank fainting in her husband's arms.

More than five minutes elapsed before either could speak, and then only she gathered strength to say—

'Ranulph, Ranulph!—Our dear children, speak to me of them?'

'Safe—quite safe, Alice.'

'And well?'

'Yes, completely so. But now tell me by what happy chance have we thus met again?'

Amid sobs, and tears, and smiles, such as the heart over-flowing with joy can only know, Alice related to her husband all that had passed, and then, Captain Angerstein having given notice to the Lord Warden of the singular and happy chance that had occurred, he came himself with John Elkington to the guard-room, anxious to hear under what train of singular circumstances Alice had been existing, and how it was that, unaided, she could have made her escape from the power of such a man as Sir Rupert Brent; and when he heard the tale he was astonished at the amount of suffering she had gone through, at the same time expressing the bitterest indignation at the atrocities committed by the Jesuit.

'This man,' he said, 'is now stained with so many public and private offences that, for the benefit of society, it becomes absolutely necessary he should, at any cost of time and trouble, be captured.'

'Yes, my lord,' said Alice, 'but let me hope that even you will join with me in dissuading my husband to pause before he chances even the sacrifice of a life so valuable as his, in pursuit of such a man as Brent; better far that the Jesuit should escape the well-merited consequences of his numerous crimes, than that one valuable existence should be lost in the attempt to punish him.'

'I agree with you in principle,' said the Warden, 'but still it will not do to let great criminals escape because there may be danger in punishing them. Believe me, Mistress Hensman, that with as few unnecessary risks as possible, this Sir Rupert Brent shall be made to answer for his crimes.'

'I am not one,' she said, 'who would let a woman's fears stay the arm of justice.'

'Of that I am well assured,' said the Warden; 'and now, until this man shall have been apprehended, and have paid the penalty of his offences, as surely he shall, for I will hang him if I catch him, you, and your wife and children, Hensman, must reside in the castle; your duties necessarily bring you much here, as well as taking you about from place to place. I am quite certain that you will feel your mind more at ease when you know that those who are so justly dear to you are safe within these walls.'

'I cannot deny,' said Hensman, 'but such would be the case, and that the proposition is one which gives me the greatest pleasure and calls forth my utmost gratitude.'

'And I,' said Alice, 'how can I thank you sufficiently?'

'By accepting my offer,' said the Warden, 'as frankly as it is said: it is but a poor favour to offer to you, in this large edifice, a few spare chambers.'

'And Ranulph,' said Alice, 'when am I to see those little ones, who, you tell me, are safe and well, so far certainly quieting my fears, but not satisfying the longings of a mother's heart?'

'At once, Alice,—at once.'

'I intended,' said the Warden, 'to have entered upon the examination of the prisoner we brought from the Well-house, but do you go at once, Ranulph Hensman, and fetch your children. Your mind, as well as your wife's, will then be at ease, and I am certain I shall profit more by your advice and assistance. During your absence, I will order some apartments to be prepared for you.'

'Yes,' said Ranulph, rising, 'I will go at once; the distance is but short, and I shall soon return.'

'But you will not go alone,' said Alice; 'you know not what dangers you may incur, or what enemies may be lying in wait for you.'

'Oh, fear nothing on that score; do not seek to make me so sensitive of danger that I am not to go into the streets alone—do not do that, I pray you. Let it suffice, Alice, that when I go upon any enterprise calculated to bring me into collision with those whom I know would gladly take my life, I will adopt every precaution that even your fears could suggest.'

'And you will return, then, as quickly as you can?' said Alice, with a sigh and an expression of sadness.

'In truth, I will, be assured; besides, you will remember I am going to no lonely place, but through the open streets of Winchester, and the quietest thoroughfare I shall traverse will be one in which, in all probability, at every dozen paces I shall meet some one who will be more a friend to me than a foe.'

Somewhat reassured by these expressions, Alice looked upon the departure of her husband with less reluctant eyes, and probably the hope of so soon beholding her children tended in a great measure to banish her fears. She looked wistfully after him as he left the guard-room, and a tear for a moment quivered in her eye, but in the animated conversation of John Elkington, who remained with her while the Warden went to order some apartments to be prepared for her reception, she was compelled to forget a portion of her fears.

There could be no doubt, from the similarity of the description which Alice gave of the garden of the house from which she had escaped with that of the Well-house, that they were the same.

'They must be identical,' said Elkington, after drawing her attention to the fact, 'although by what means you were brought there from the convent I cannot imagine.'

'And yet it must have been so; and probably one of the objects for placing me in a box was that they might be enabled to carry me along some portion of the open roadway without exciting a suspicion that any nefarious transaction was in progress.'

'It may be so; but certainly the audacity of that Jesuit almost transcends belief, and I do hope that the time will soon arrive when we shall be able amply to repay him, not only for what he has done, but likewise for what he has attempted to do.

In a short time the Lord Warden returned to say that he had some apartments ready, which, he hoped would meet with the approval of Alice Hensman; and this kind way of putting a matter, which was really a great favour on his part to the Hensmans, excited her warmest admiration and gratitude, which, when she expressed, he stopped her by saying—

'Mistress Hensman, you must always now bear in mind, as regards these transactions, that you and your husband have become so associated with public affairs, in consequence of being so persecuted at this juncture by the Jesuits, that in serving you I serve that cause which the king has most nearly at heart, and consequently I feel myself justified, quite independent of any private feelings in the matter, in offering to you all the accommodation which this fortress can afford.'

He then led her to a corridor, from which branched a number of apartments, and conducting her into one, on the ample hearth of which a blazing log fire had been lighted, he said—

'Here, madam, you may rest in perfect safety, and moreover, now that we are alone, let me assure you that it shall be my especial care not to employ your husband in those matters which will bring him into immediate collision with the Jesuit party.'

With tears in her eyes, Alice thanked him for this proof of kindly consideration, and then bowing with as much grace and respect as he would have done to a queen, the Lord Warden of Winchester, who was, perhaps, the man, of all others, standing most high with the monarch, and immediately connected with the court then in England, left the room.

Alice found that this apartment was replete with all the comforts the age could afford, and she felt convinced that some of the furniture must have been hastily removed from the private apartments of the Warden himself. Among others,

was an escritoire full of books and papers, and likewise a writing table, on which lay a mass of literary matter, which, as it seemed to have been laid there for her amusement, she scrupled not to examine.

Believing then that Ranulph Hensman might yet be some time before he arrived with the children at the castle, she dipped into a short anecdotal sketch, called the 'Haunted Horn,' which was strikingly illustrative of feelings and habits even then beginning to be upon the wane among the better informed classes, and those who were making war upon the Romish supremacy.

She read as follows:—

'There was a broad glare of light shot from the huge pile of logs that had been heaped up on the fire of the guard-room, and it shed a genial warmth over the whole place, and many men were there seated on the settees with their partisans arranged in one end of the room, ready to be seized at a moment's warning.

'The steel helmets reflected the ruddy glow of the fire and their faces shone as the faces of men embrowned by exposure to many a winter's storm and many a summer's sun. There were few among them who had not seen active service in the field, and now they reposed in the quiet and security of a castle guard-room, where they performed the duty of mounting the guards at various points where they were required.

'Here they passed the hours in telling tales of their former exploits and in relating the many adventures both of themselves and those they had heard of in the various countries in which they had served, and of the different fabled events in which they heard their heroes had been engaged in.

'They, however, now sat still and silent; all gazed intently on the fire, as if they were intently busied with thought, reflecting probably upon something they had heard, and dwelling upon the merits of the case, but lost in deep thought.

' There was a strange appearance in men thus occupied, with arms in their hands and clad in steel, that reflected the ruddy glow of the fire at a hundred different angles; their silence, and the different motionless attitudes in which they sat, gave them all an almost unearthly appearance.

' Then suddenly there came upon the stillness of the night, which was only broken by the crackling of the logs, and the sudden roar of some fresh jet of flame, a sudden and spirit-stirring blast from a trumpet, which rang through the castle wards and rooms with a piercing effect.

' The men started and looked at each other, and he who had the command of the men called out in a loud voice, which was almost as sudden and clear as a trumpet, —

' "Fall in, fall in!"

' In another moment the men had started up to obey the order, and the room that had been so quiet and silent but a minute or so before, was now a scene of animated bustle. The heavy heels of the iron-shod boots resounded through the apartment, and the clank of arms sounded from one end to the other, but it lasted but a few seconds, and then all was as silent and motionless as before.

' Again on the night air rang the trumpet call, louder and more imperiously than before. For a moment the men seemed paralysed, and then the word was given to move.

' Out they went, and traversed a passage or two until they came to a postern door, which was opened, and then they entered upon the castle walls.

' The night air was chill, and the moon shone brightly, but it was every now and then obscured by the heavy clouds that were ever and anon driven across its disc. Some moments the earth was wrapped in darkness, and at others the moonlight showed every object, capable of casting a shadow, for miles.

' There was a wood to the right as you stood at the drawbridge, and there was a moat that surrounded the castle, over which the drawbridge was thrown. Now, however, this was up, and the communication by this means between the castle and the plain beyond it was closed.

' The men made the circuit of the walls, stopping every now and then to examine every object they could see, to ascertain the cause of the singular trumpet call.

' Soon they made the circuit of the walls, and questioned the various sentinels as to the fact of their having seen anything moving about on the space beyond the moat where any object that had moved would be seen.

' The answer, however, of each was, that nothing had been seen, save the shadows of the clouds as they passed beneath the moon, urged on by a fresh wind.

' At length, after coming to the drawbridge, having made the circuit of the walls, they met the warder.

' "Warder, ho!" exclaimed the leader of the guard.

' "Who goes there?" said the warder.

' "The guard. Have you seen aught to-night?'

' "Nothing," was the reply. "There has been nothing but air and shadows that I have seen or heard this night."

' "Have you not heard the trumpet call?"

' "I have. It was loud and clear enough to have awaken the dead from their sleep, had they been within its reach. I heard it, but saw nought."

' At that moment the same trumpet call sounded again, and seemed to fill the air by its sound and volume. The hills and dales behind seemed to echo and re-echo with the sound.

' "Down with the drawbridge!" exclaimed the captain of the guard, " and I will penetrate this mystery."

' The drawbridge was lowered, and the captain left a certain number of men to guard the drawbridge, with instructions to summon the reserve of the guard in the rooms below, and to post them on the bridge—one half to parade about in the direction which he was then about to take while the others guarded the drawbridge against any sudden surprise.

' "And now," said the captain, " follow me; but do not let the two bodies separate so far as to be beyond shout or out of sight."

' Giving this advice, he spoke to the second in command, and then he turned to his men and commenced a rapid march across the drawbridge, and then to the right, which led them through the wood we have before noticed.

' For some time they continued in sight, occasionally they were obscured in the darkness which enveloped the earth when the clouds hid the moonlight from their sight.

' Onward they pressed, and were in a few minutes traversing the woody glade, while in the meantime the defenders of the castle were in a state of commotion, assembling at all parts, strengthening such points as were deemed most advisable while the remainder were in readiness to start to any point which they might be called upon to defend.

' A party of five-and-twenty men marched away as far as they could hear or see those on the drawbridge, and be seen or heard by them.'

' They then halted, and, being near the wood, they remained stationary, listening with much attention to any sound that might proceed from their comrades who had gone into the woods.

' "I wonder," said the warder, " what all this can mean? I have kept good watch out upon the country, and yet I cannot detect anything. I have seen nothing."

' "But who could have rung out so clear a blast as that which we more than once have heard of late?"

' "Indeed, it must have been some one."

' "Ay! some one, and that one must have been within sight to have produced sounds so clear and startling, and to fill the air to an echo. Whoever they were, they have mortal lungs of good capacity."

' "I believe you; there's not a man in the castle that could have winded such a call."

' "When will Sir Hubert return?" muttered one of the men at-arms. "When shall we see him again?"

' "I know not; but I tell you what, comrades; to my poor mind there's but a poor chance of our ever seeing him any more in this life.'

' "Indeed, Stanton; and why?"

' "That horn was never winded by mortal lips."

' "Ay!"

' "Ay, Stanton, ay!"

' No, comrades, no. To my poor mind there are other beings as can wind a horn besides men."

' "Indeed, Stanton! tell us all about it."

' "Ay! thereon hangs a tale," said Stanton. "You see, I have served more masters than one; but I will tell you all when we get into the guard-room."

' "And why not here?"

' "Because we shall be interrupted, and moreover the guard-room is the best place for tales of one's early life."

' "So it is, so it is."

' "Here comes a stranger," said the warder.

' "A stranger! Where?"

' "Yonder. The moon's gone in now, and you will not be able to see him until the clouds have passed away. What he can want, or who he may be, I am at a loss to think," said the second in command.

' "He may be a traveller, and want rest and lodging till daylight returns," said another.

' "I hope it may be nothing worse than a traveller with such wants," said the lieutenant; " but hark! I can hear his footsteps; he is close at hand."

' As he spoke the cloud cleared off, and within some fifty or sixty yards a man, clad in armour, came up, walking slowly, and apparently much fatigued.

' "Who goes there?" demanded the guard.

' "A friend," was the reply. "One who has lost his way, and is now unable to recover it, or even to find a lodging, unless you will receive me."

' "I think I can promise you so much," said the lieutenant; the captain of the guard will be back presently.

' "Here they come," said the warder, " here they come. Well, they have gone round in quick time. See yonder they come with a gallant step."

' They looked round, and saw at no great distance the guard coming along at a good pace, while those who had posted themselves not far from the wood, catching sight of their companions, instantly turned about, and were in full march towards the drawbridge, which they reached pretty near about the same time as the main body.

' "Well," said the lieutenant, " what have you seen? It is a fine open country yonder, is it not?"

' "There is nobody about, there is plenty of moonlight, but nothing else much that I know of; but who on have we here? A stranger! you have done more than we have. Well, Sir Stranger, was it you that summoned us so cleverly by winding a horn? I must give you credit for what you did, though it cost us a march."

' "Indeed! but I am a stranger here. I came because

1 knew not where 1 was, and partly because 1 heard a horn wind, which promised me company, and perhaps hospitality."

'"Neither shall be wanting, Sir Stranger, if you can partake of them in the guard-room and a soldier's fare. We have no company in the castle, and we can do no better for you."

'"That will do, my good friend, and be a luxury, too. 1 have often supped upon a crust, a drink of water, and slept upon the bare earth, so that now 1 can consider such a promise a happy luxury."

'"Well, follow us, Sir Stranger."

'"The whole party now entered the guard-room, the watch having been set, and the drawbridge raised, the guard then turned in, and then before the fire some refreshments were set before the stranger, who at in silence, while Stanton replied to the earnest entreaties of his comrades to relate what he knew of any similar occurrence to that of the born.

'When 1 was in Burgundy,' began Stanton, '1 was sentinel over the drawbridge, and there 1 heard many strange tales, and saw many strange occurrences.

'One night 1 was walking backwards and forwards on my part of the ramparts, when we were all startled by the sound of a horn, blown so strong and clear, that every one in the castle heard it.

'1 had heard something of a talk about it, and everybody said that it portended a death in the family who owned the castle, but it was treated very lightly, as the owners were young and in good health.

'The next night there was a good watch set, to ascertain if the same sound would be heard again, and a guard was placed in readiness to rush out and examine the surrounding parts, so that no human being should be left there to trouble the castle with such sounds.

'The next night again we heard the horn sound clear and shrill. No sound could be more distinct, no one could mistake it, and out rushed the guard before the last note had left the lips of the blower; and every spot was searched which could possibly have concealed a child, but no born blower was found there, and the party returned to the castle.

'The next day there was to be holden, and then a 1 was gaiety and bustle, and the lord of the castle was gay and confident. He rode his best horse, mounted his best attire, and forth the whole party rode.

'There were many gentles and nobles who rode out on the occasion. There was laughter and joy that rang through the whole party, till the hunt began, and then the lordly stag became the object of every one's gaze and attention. Horse and hound were now laid on, and nothing more was thought of.

'Presently the scene changed. The stag fell; it had broken its own neck by throwing itself against an enormous branch of a tree, and the lord of the castle, who followed, first of the field, before he could rein up the horse, he, too met with a similar fate to Absolom, with this difference—he was caught by the neck, and not by the hair.

'He was borne home a corpse.

'That night, when all were buried in slumber, and the tears of grief, again came the sound of the horn—loud, shrill, and clear. 1t, however, ended with a deep, wailing note, that seemed to dwell upon the hills.

'"And that one did to-night," remarked the captain of the guard. "1 heard it myself.'

'"Have you seen the Lady Bertha?"

'"No, no. 1 have not seen her this day or two, and then she was very poorly; her maid seemed to say she had no hopes of her."

'At that moment the guard-room door was opened, and the personal attendant of the Lady Bertha entered in tears.

'"Well," said the captain of the guard, "what have we in the shape of news—is your lady well?"

'"I hope so in the world to come."

'"Is she dead, then?'

'"Yes, she died about half an hour since. She died, indeed, as the horn ceased to sound. 1 was so taken between grief and surprise that 1 could not come and tell you."

'"Well, well," said the captain of the guard; "place be with her, though she was no friend to the soldier or to our patron Sir Hubert Montalbert; but peace to her remains."

'"Then my enemy is dead," said the stranger, suddenly starting to his feet, "my enemy is dead, and 1 can now claim my own, and live without fear in my own name and person. Soldiers, 1 am Sir Hubert Montalbert."

'As he spoke he removed his steel helmet, and his open handsome features at once told the soldiers who he was, for he was well known to them.

'"Huzza!" shouted the men; "hurrah! Sir Hubert for ever!"

'The sounds were echoed from every heart in the castle, and Sir Hubert lived happily and respected by his retainers; and no more, while he lived, did the haunted horn sound at the castle.'

Alice laid down the MS. as the sound of hasty footsteps came upon her ears in the corridor.

CHAPTER XXIX.

The Execution of Leoni.—The Riot in London.

TRIALS in former days used to be very different kinds of things to what they are now. Our bluff old Harry never used to trouble himself or his crown lawyers about such supid people as jurymen. He named a commission, who understood the affair beforehand, and who either dozed while the matter was being laid before them, or paid no heed to it, having their minds made up as to what was to be done before they sat down.

They met to try and to convict the prisoner Leoni of an attempt upon the king's life; and they accordingly met, tried, and convicted the prisoner, which in this case he most righteously deserved, and when Leoni heard his doom, that he was to be executed on Tower-hill, he appeared to take the matter with more coolness than had been expected.

The secret of this, however, appeared when he formally denied the secular power to try him; that he was an ecclesiastic, and demanded that he be handed over to those of his order, to be dealt with according to ecclesiastical canon.

This, however, produced no impression upon his judges, who too well knew the king's mind upon such matters, and came well prepared with an answer, and who reproved him for an act which denied the king's supremacy in all matters, and which was in itself a crime, and that he (Leoni) had better not trust in such a demand, for it was, if possible, an aggravation of the offence of which he had been found guilty.

Leoni was hurried away, strongly guarded, by the officials, and he was to be carried from the scene of trial to the Tower by water, and thus avoid the route through the city, and to prevent any disturbance among its turbulent inhabitants, as well as any attempt which the Jesuits might get up to rescue the prisoner from the secular arm.

This day was dull, and little was seen on the water. The scene that the river now presents was very different then—where houses and streets now stand the wild duck and widgeon built their nests—wharfs were then only represented by tall sedges and bulrushes, and willows—different, indeed, is the scene upon the face of the river.

There was but little interruption in their progress; the barge being manned by several men-at-arms, besides j ilors and the oarsmen, who formed an effective guard against any attempt that might be made under ordinary circumstances.

The city was passed, and the difficult passage of London bridge was made. It was a difficulty at that time, certainly, for the number of the arches, and the narrowness of the spaces through which the water flowed, made it a most dangerous passage when the tide was going down.

Then, indeed, from the causes just mentioned, the water on one side was much higher than on the other, and the descent at such times from one side of the bridge to the other was really dangerous and fatal.

It was not often attempted at such times, but it was occasionally so, and the tide was much longer in getting down the river than now.

The barge had safely made to this spot and passed it, and then it breasted the Custom-house and fish market, after which it came in sight of the Tower.

'We shall soon be home,' said the head jailor, who was with the prisoner.

'Home!' involuntarily echoed the Jesuit.

'Yes, Sir Jesuit,' said the jailor, 'yes, we are as much at home in the dungeons of yonder fortress as you are in the cells of your monastery—aye, a great deal more so, for we can quaff and sing, and have our feasts right merrily.'

The Jesuit lifted up his hands as if he deprecated such doings and conversation.

'Aye, you of the Church, too, I am told can eat and drink

like other men, for all your white eyes and lifted hands. I tell you, Sir Jesuit, I have heard of jolly fat monks—men who could perform all the usual duties of a well filled board, and could sing a jolly song over wench or strong ale, aye, as well as ere a trooper in the fortress.'

'Friend, hold thy ribald tongue, thou knowest not what thou sayest.'

'Don't I, by Saint George! I tell you what, sir monk, I do know, and that is, you would all of you deny men the full and free use of their tastes.'

'When they are evil, we would.'

'But they are by no means evil—they are good—they are pleasant, and the enjoyment produced is great, and what would you desire more?'

'Cease, man, cease; I have other matters to think of just now. I have but a short time to live.'

'By Saint George, that is true. But here we are at Traitor's-gate; you will soon be in the quiet of your dungeon, and then you can meditate upon the future until you find yourself in it.'

They now pulled the barge up under the arched way, through the water gate, which was opened for their admission by those on duty, and who had seen them coming, having been on the look-out for them.

'Well, friend Staples,' said the sentinel at the gate; 'well how goes the matter!'

'It will be a shortening match.'

'A head off, I suppose!'

'That is the thing, neighbour, the worthy monk's cowl won't save his head on this occasion, that is very certain.'

'I thought so; there's but little chance against the king.'

'Hardly, and those who come in at Traitors'-gate after a trial have but a poor prospect of life.'

'Life to come.'

'Aye, aye, then indeed they will soon be at home; come, Master Leoni, out with you, stand upon the step, will you?'

Leoni now stepped out of the boat, and went up the steps, and followed his jailors to his cell, which was in one of the gloomiest and most solitary parts of the castle.

Here he lay without any prospect of help or aid, and yet the monk's spirit quailed not. He had great faith in the power of his order, but he also well knew the obstinate character of the king, and his power, which was by no means lessened by the subserviency of his ministers, and his people's submission to whatever he chose to dictate.

And yet there were among the people many who did not like to give up their ancient thoughts and ways and take to the new ways of the king; there were, besides, many in London who could not brook supineness and quiet, but who gloried in all the noise and mischief of a riot.

Among such were many who cared not for the cause of quarrel as long as there was a riot—that was the main thing —right or wrong, it mattered not.'

'Clubs,' cried one.

'Bows and bills,' cries another.

And then go the civic guards and the mob together with right good will—more broken heads and deep gashes than are reckoned to increase personal beauty.

Among the citizens of London—that is, what is usually called the citizens, being chiefly the rabble as a mass, with some of the more substantial men among them—among these the Jesuits worked, and sent emissaries to stir them up to riot and rescue, in case they should fail in their attempts to rescue their fellows from the hands of justice by the power of the Church, which had not as yet lost all its principles— save when opposed to the King's will.

Thus they exerted themselves with the utmost power and good will, until they were convinced they had nothing to hope for from the King.

Then, indeed, they began to work with the multitude, and to stir up their passions, and to urge them to rescue the prisoner from the guards on the morning of the execution. They were afraid that there was a strong force to aid them in disguise—that when they set the example they would be well supported—and those, who were only citizens in appearance, were really men-at-arms. Indeed, many of the Jesuits themselves would mix among the combatants, and aid them.

Thus prepared, the rabble was ready for a riot; as ready and willing as men could be. There were many desperate characters among them, who were paid to urge on others, and to take their part in the fray, which was about to happen.

While matters were thus going on, the time for the execution was fast drawing nigh, and various attempts were made to see the prisoner alone, by those of his order, but all in vain, they were refused admission, and informed that in whatever guise they came to the fortress, they would find it more easy to get in than out.

Of course such a hint as that was enough, and they were troubled with but few applications for admission after that, for the interior of the Tower was very different from the interior of a monastery, and the governor held a different sway to that held by a chapter of monks, be they of what order they might—save the Templars or the Knights of the Hospitalers —those orders being done away with long since.

Leoni himself was visited the night before the execution by the governor of the Tower, who sought to tell him that on the morrow he would expiate his crime on Tower-hill.

'I am not in your hands,' said the monk, 'but in the hands of Him who made me, and if it be His will that I suffer, then, I shall be resigned.'

'Be you in whose hands you may affect to believe, still you will find yourself in the hands of the executioner, whose axe will convince you of the practical certainty of your person being in his hands.'

'The curse of Heaven be upon you.'

'But the king wills it.'

'The King of Heaven!'

—'The King of England, whom the King of Heaven preserve peace be with you. Have you aught to say or confess?'

'Nothing.'

'Your odious and wicked crime was too apparent to be of any use in denying. You are a cloaked assassin, and will die in your wickedness.'

'I have power to confess and absolve myself.'

'Then, you are your own confessor. That is one reason why you are so bad. Your thoughts are not uttered to another, thus it is you have conceived so wicked a crime as that which you have attempted.'

'It was done for the glory of God, and of his Church.'

'Worse than infidel,' said the governor, 'can you persuade yourself that such deeds are at all acceptable to any power! You must, indeed, be a dangerous man. And yet I have heard of a nation of fanatical and professed assassins, but I never thought in a Christian country, and that, above all, an ecclesiastic should become one of them. Shame on you, man—shame on you!'

As the rough old soldier spoke he turned his heel upon the culprit, and left the cell, having locked and double locked the door with such energy as plainly bespoke the anger he felt with the monk.

Leoni heard all this and preserved his calmness until the governor had gone away, and then he became agitated by the fearful position in which he was placed, and from which there was, now, no escape.

'To morrow, eh! 'Tis fearful to die—to have the day and hour appointed—to know, to feel, that upon one certain minute we must cease to live. And yet we all must die, some sooner and some later; my course is run, and why should I hesitate about the moment, does it so much matter? my mortal career might be terminated a day or two after the time appointed for my execution. Why then should I fear the loss of one day? it can make no difference—but then there is the uncertainty of the difference being so small.

'I will not, however, despair until I can no longer hope. They will leave nothing undone for me; perhaps on the scaffold I may be rescued, anything may happen—of this I am sure, they will not desert me until every prospect of life has been lost.

'Then, indeed, the terrible reality will be but too practical, as the governor said to me; but they shall not see me blench. I will meet death, since meet it I must, with what firmness human frailty will permit.'

*   *   *   *   *   *

The hours passed away, and when the morning sun rose upon the Tower and its environs, there was a large concourse of people collected there; the scaffold was erected, and a strong body of men-at-arms was posted around it, while the gate through which the procession would pass was also guarded by a strong body of men-at-arms, as well as a patrol pacing the distance between the gate and the scaffold as if keeping the communication open.

The spectators stood still; little was heard save the low murmur of many suppressed voices.

The concourse of people appeared to increase slowly; but the mass bore angry faces, as though they had more in their minds than would admit of ordinary expression. A deep, suppressed murmur ran through the crowd, and the spectators looked on the men-at-arms with eyes which appeared to speak the thoughts that animated the minds of the men, and seemed considering if it would not be easy to overcome such an one, and they cared not how soon the fray began.

There was now a movement among the soldiery, and the crowd pressed more closely along the barriers to look towards the gate to ascertain the precise moment Leoni should issue forth from the gates.

'Neighbour,' said one man, 'if they behead this harmless priest, they all deserve to be hung themselves to the tallest trees betwixt here and York.'

'They do, they do!'

'Then why let them do such an act?'

'And who is to say nay to the king's commission?' said another; 'I fancy that there will be but little help when backed by the king's guards. Who shall say nay?'

'Why, we, to be sure.'

'We—the citizens of London?'

'Aye, to be sure; we have only to say it, and it shall not be done,' said the first speaker.

'I would it were as plain to me, neighbour, as it appears to you; I cannot perceive it.'

'Look you here, neighbour, if the good and merciful citizens choose to rise up and say this thing shall not be, and draw the sword to prevent it—'

'Draw the sword, neighbour?'

'Aye, neighbour, aye, I will do so.'

'You!'

'Aye, truly will I, for I cannot abide to see blood shed in such a case as this. Consider. Have you no conscience? Can you stand and see the good man murdered before your eyes? I cannot, and will not, that is the truth, neighbour. There will be many do as I do to-day, neighbour.'

'Well, if the good city wills it, I am one of them, and will do as they do.'

'Then give me your hand, neighbour; I will stand at thy side, and we will aid one another if there should be any need of our doing so.'

'Give me leave to say,' said the other, 'that I do hold this a most iniquitous proceeding; the man, for all we can tell, never lifted hand against the king.'

'No, I believe he would not.'

'And moreover he had no trial, such as he ought to have had, with our laws.'

'Laws, quotha! we have the king's will.'

'Le rot le veut is all that one hears now; it was not so in days gone by.'

'That is true, too true to bode us any good, if—if things go on thus.'

'Aye, moreover, if we succeed in letting this man loose, what can they do?'

'Nothing.'

'Surely nothing, because their object will be lost, and ours gained, the man will escape and he will not be taken again; so all that can be done, is to try and find out where he is, and who helped him.'

'And none could tell them, unless he admitted a participation in the act.'

'That makes it all safe; besides that, what citizen would betray another?'

'None who are citizens.'

'Here he comes—here he comes.'

This cry was uttered when the mob first caught sight of the cavalcade when it left the Tower, and the outer gates were opened to permit them to enter the Tower Hamlets.

'Aye, aye, there he comes, sure enough.'

There was a deep sound came from the mob and much confusion seemed about to take place, and the guards repressed them as they pushed forward to the front, and the cavalcade proceeded towards the scaffold.

'Stand back, make way—make way.'

There seemed a great many men who pushed forward to the front who had not been seen before; many of them were armed, and stout fellows enough.

Just as the cavalcade had reached midway between the scaffold and the Tower gate, the monk looked around, and thought he could gather comfort from the appearance of the mob; suddenly there was shout raised—

'To the rescue.'

The shout was raised in several quarters at once, and three separate attacks were made, one upon the scaffold, and one upon the postern gate, where the two great bodies of troops were posted.

The third attack was made upon the cavalcade, in which the prisoner was placed. This was the most determined attack. The others were false, but were sharp enough to prevent either place from sending aid to the cavalcade, which was broken in by the first rush of men upon the London guard, who endeavoured to make a stand, but were all thrown down and severely injured.

Then another shout arose as the prisoner was loosened from his bonds, and the attack ceased at all points, and then the mob began to retreat towards Thames-street, down by the water-side, to enable the Jesuit to escape, and seek the protection of the sanctuaries and other places for themselves.

However well the whole affair had been managed to this point, there was one thing they had forgotten—that was, they were sure to be seen from the walls, and some old heavy pieces of ordnance had been hastily brought to bear upon the thoroughfare.

Suddenly a loud explosion was heard, and at the same moment a dreadful sound came past them. A cannon-ball had been fired upon them, which had narrowly passed by many of them, killing only one man, and then burying itself in somebody's cellar, leaving a round hole in it.

There came another bang, and a cannon-shot came in among them, knocking over some of the foremost; this was quite unexpected. There was no fighting at long shots; they could not combat against such odds—they had not bargained for that.

They hesitated, and paused.

This gave time for a body of arquebusiers to file out of the Tower, while the cannon was pointed towards the thoroughfare, and prevented all attempts to pass—the dead bodies already occupied the ground.

Leoni was in the midst of the pass; there he was wedged, and kick and fight as he would, he could not escape. He was fixed. He had got so far, but could go no further, and he must share the fate of the mob.

Suddenly the word was given to fire, and the arquebusiers fired, and many of the mob were seen to fall.

'Charge' was the next word of command, and then the rapid steps and rattling of arms, the shouts of the soldiery, and the groans and defiances of the mob presented a scene of terrific confusion.

There was not more than half a minute occupied before the soldiers came in contact with the mob, and a scene of carnage ensued that baffles description.

The mob stood well, but they were taken at a disadvantage. They were surprised, and had to give way before the determined charge of men accustomed to discipline, and now there were but a few yards between them and Leoni, who struggled hard to get away; but so jammed was he, he could not even raise a hand to defend himself from those who were about to recapture him.

There was a fierce conflict raging around him; but the trained bands of the city coming up at the same time, the rioters were taken in the rear, and they fled in all directions, Leoni himself being thrown down; he endeavoured to escape by crawling towards the river, but he was seized and secured by the arquebusiers, who bound him securely on a horse, and thus carried him back to the scaffold.

The governor of the Tower was present: he was covered with dust, and hot from exertion, but he smiled grimly as he looked upon the culprit.

'Ha, Sir Monk! did you imagine that we were to be so easily flung as that?'

'The Lord's will be done,' said the monk.

'The king wills it,' said the grim old soldier; 'come, Sir Headsman, see to your work.'

There was a solid mass of soldiers around the scaffold and more were arriving, so there was no possibility of escape being effected, but yet the mob had gathered round the scene of execution, and many angry shouts and groans were uttered at the soldiery by them.

However, they took little or no heed of that, and the execution proceeded in dumb show. The monk laid his head on the block, and every voice was hushed—then, with one blow of the axe, the head of the culprit was severed from the trunk.

There was but little to do now, but no sooner did the crowd look upon the bloody trunk and the ghastly head than they gave a groan of execration.

Then after a time they began slowly to glide off and disperse, no more being seen of them.

The soldiery were collected together and the usual ceremonies were gone through, and when all was complete they were in due order marched off the ground and then filed through the postern door into the Tower.

Thus ended a fearful riot in which several lives were lost, but which ended without the object being gained for which it was originated.

In a more advanced age, it would have been quite impossible for so formidable a collision to have taken place between a government and a people, without being productive of much more important consequences than those which arose from the riot that accompanied the death of Leoni.

But we must recollect that, after all, the people in the time of Henry VIII. had scarcely begun to consider themselves a distinct and important portion of the body politic, whose interests required to be seen to, as much as any other state of the realm.

If a mob then arose and threatened violence, it was either from some very small grievance, which involved no general principle, or because they were incited foolishly to take part with some contending faction, in whose success they could have no interest.

Now, the case is indeed widely different, when a great and intelligent people have found out that they are the real source of all power, and the real strength of a state, and will no longer be cajoled out of those liberties, which they have a right to demand.

In this case, between Henry VIII. and the people, for a wonder, the king happened to be in the right; but then, we must bear in mind, that the populace had yet not quite succeeded in thinking they might possibly exist without a licentious, idle, debauched, and scheming priesthood.

When that discovery really was made, there were no more such scenes as the one we have described enacted, and the time, we believe, and most fervently hope, is not far distant, when the increasing intelligence of the people of England will be sufficient to convince them, that they can do without even the comparatively small amount of priestcraft which at present finds favour with the multitude, who have not yet got to a right state of mind upon that subject.

Sooner or later, however, it must and will come to pass in this country, that the doctrine of every man being his own parson will be well and perfectly understood, and the trade of religion will no longer be as it is, a good one for the younger sons of noble families, or aspiring but stupid youths of the middle classes, who think with their mammas, that an idle life in some country place is preferable to being, what by-the-by they know their incapacity to be, namely, an useful member of society.

CHAPTER XXX.

The Assassination of Ranulph Hensman.

RANULPH HENSMAN, when he left the Lord Warden's in pursuance of his promise to Alice to bring the children to the castle, felt all that degree of elation and mental exhilaration, which under the circumstances he may be fairly excused for feeling, and which was the natural reaction of his mind from the state of depression in which it had been.

The beauty of the night, for it was really one of the most charming and delightful description, would have been almost sufficient, under circumstances of the greatest depression, to have raised the mind from the greatest abyss of sorrow, and make it look forward with something like renovated hope to a happier future.

Although the season was advanced, and the latter part of September was close at hand, nothing could be more truly delightful than the soft breeze that played so gently through the streets of that ancient city.

The moon was young, but yet it had sufficient power to chase away much of the darkness of the night, and its mild beams shed a luxuriant lustre upon the towers and windows of the ancient cathedral, which reared itself massive and grand into the night air.

There were but few passengers abroad, for the hour was a late one, and probably there was not a great number of individuals even in that densely populated city endowed with sufficient poetic feeling to ramble forth, merely to enjoy the beauty of the night.

And now it seemed to Ranulph Hensman, as he gazed around him, that a new existence was dawning upon him.

'Surely,' he said, 'the clouded and stormy period of my life has now passed away—away for ever—leaving me the calm serenity and sweet joy, arising from a contemplation of present happiness when contrasted with pain and uneasiness which has passed away.'

The unexpected restoration of Alice to his arms gave him such exquisite delight that he scarcely believed it now in the power of malignant fate to do him harm.

'Surely,' he cried, 'evil Fortune has already expended against me the worst arrows in her quiver, and I ought, and may now consider, that I am free from any more of her rude assaults. I shall henceforward pass a life of serenity and happiness, and in the society of those dear children, and that companion of my earliest affections whom I love so well, I shall feel like one isolated from the world and all its storms, and, tasting of the purest felicity unalloyed by even apprehension of evil. I ought to and shall be very happy.'

These were, indeed, blissful anticipations—anticipations which we hope and trust to see realized by Ranulph Hensman, because we feel a sincere and deep interest in his fortunes; but which, alas! we can scarcely dare to hope for in the perilous times in which he lived.

But, still, it was something to anticipate so much happiness, it was something like a foretaste of the pleasure that he panted to be able to think he might possibly be blessed with.

Full of these pleasant reflections he hurried onward at a rapid pace towards the house in which he had left his children, and, in doing so, he had to pass the gates of the cathedral—that building which had been reared for such pretended holy purposes, but which, in reality, had become desecrated by the worst persons of those who called themselves the ministers of religion.

This part of his route was enveloped in deep gloom, for opposite to the cathedral, at that time, although now they have long since disappeared, was a row of stately trees, which cast a deep shadow far and wide, making a real night of that somewhat lovely spot.

And there was something about the grandeur of the cathedral, overtopping as it did surrounding objects, that made it look like the very genius of Solitude.

The sighing of the wind likewise among these trees had an impressive and a solemn effect, which was much increased by a low strain of ecclesiastical music that came from the body of the cathedral.

The priests were, or pretended to be, at their evening devotions, and as Ranulph paused and glanced towards the open doors of the building, he could not but consider how glorious a sign and symbol of extended civilization a Christian temple might be, if in better hands than those which now in England possessed them.

Scarcely had such a thought crossed his mind when he heard a footstep among the trees behind him, and, taught caution by previous danger, and the unsettled nature of the times, he placed his hand upon his sword, and as he did so, turning at the same time to the trees, from whence the sound seemed to have come, a voice, on the other side of him, spoke, saying,—

'Well met, Ranulph Hensman. You're late a'oot.'

Glancing at the man who uttered these sounds, Ranulph Hensman saw that he wore a dark habit, fitting closely, and that a sword was by his side, the scabbard of which he grasped in a manner which showed that in an instant he could have placed his right hand to the hilt and drawn it.

He regarded Ranulph Hensman with a strange and meaning glance as he again spoke, saying:—

'It seems surprising to me that you should venture out alone at such an hour as this, knowing as you must do that you have enemies in Winchester.'

'Sir,' said Ranulph, 'I do not pretend to know you—nor do I wish to do so. Pass on your way and let me to pass on mine.'

'Nay, now,' said the stranger, 'you're grown wonderfully calm and cool. I am a Jesuit. You and I met in the vaulted chamber, in that ancient part of the cathedral where by trickery you intruded yourself.'

'I thank you for the declaration, and in the king's name I arrest you.'

'Take that for your insolence,' said the man, and, drawing

darted on one side and avoided the thrust, wh ch certainly else must have taken his life. As it was, the man rushed forward with such vehemence and force that the point of his sword struck against a tree that was immediately behind Hensman, and the weapon snapped in two with a ringing sound.

'Vile assassin!' cried Ranulph, as he immediately drew the trusty blade he knew so well how to wield—' vile assassin, take the reward of such treachery!' and then, unquestionably, the life of the Jesuit would have paid the penalty of his ill success had he not flung himself to the earth, and so escaped the pass which Hensman made at him.

At the moment, then, two men came out from beneath the shadow of the trees, and, with drawn swords, immediately attacked Ranulph.

Seeing, now, that he was nearly encompassed by assassins, and feeling quite convinced that he had fallen into an ambuscade laid for the express purpose of taking his life, he summoned all his energies to his aid, and slowly retreated, warding off with most admirable skill the attacks of both his enemies.

The clash of swords was furious and incessant, while he who had broken his weapon against the tree did all in his power, by voice and gesture, to animate his companions to complete the work they had begun.

'Kill him. kill him,' he cried; 'and so shall we do the best service to our cause that has been done for many a day.'

Ranulph uttered not a word, but, as coolly as if he had been practising a mere assault of arms in a fencing school, he warded off the murderous and furious attack which was made upon him, and which now had lasted several minutes without inflicting the slightest injury.

Engaged as he was with two persons, it would have been highly indiscreet of Ranulph to have assumed the offensive, for the consequence of his overpowering one of his opponents would have been sufficient to engage his attention for a few seconds of time, during which the other might have achieved his death.

But a most tempting opportunity occurred by one pressing forward closer than his companion, and, slightly stumbling as he did so, Ranulph Hensman could not resist the impulse of the moment, but inflicted upon him a severe wound.

He resumed his guard very quickly, but not so quickly as to prevent him from receiving a hurt from his other foe, who, however, finding that he was now alone opposed to such a practised swordsman as the secretary. (for his wounded companion had sunk to his knees, with his sword trembling in his grasp,) began to give way, and to fight with far less energy than before.

At this moment, from beneath the porch of the cathedral, there came a man with a drawn sword, who rushed furiously towards the combatants.

It seemed doubtful at first which side he intended taking, but, as he neared the spot, he called aloud,—

'Turn, Ranulph Hensman, and meet your proper foe. I am Sir Rupert Brent. Now, once and for all, let our swords decide our long-pending cause of quarrel.'

At the sound of that hateful voice Ranulph Hensman at once turned, and as his and the Jesuit's swords crossed, the man with whom he had been contending rushed forward, no doubt with the full intention of taking Hensman's life, which he would have done but for the hurry he was in, which caused him only to inflict a wound in the sword arm of the secretary, instead of running him completely through, which was his intention.

But, alas! poor Ranulph Hensman's hour soon came. The wound he had received was a sufficiently severe one to disable him, and the point of the sword dropped, leaving him at the mercy of one to whom such a heavenly quality was quite unknown.

It was with a positive shout of triumph that the villanous Sir Rupert Brent rushed forward, and plunged his sword into the body of the unhappy secretary.

'Die!' he cried, 'die, at last!' as he drew forth his reeking blade: 'die! and with the consciousness, too, that it is from my hand you receive your death-wound; and well I know, if aught can render death more bitter to you, that is a consideration which will do it.'

The secretary made a few unavailing efforts with his sword; he reeled forward like a drunken man, and then, with a gasping woo, after a vain effort to speak he sank upon one knee, for weakness prevented him from maintaining his feet.

'Ah! ah!' laughed Sir Rupert Brent, 'this is well; this is indeed sweet revenge; I have longed for this minute to come, and behold, it has come at last! Ranulph Hensman, Alice shall yet be mine, and let your dying thought be, that when I clasp the peerless beauty in my arms she will cry in vain for you to save her.'

With a deep groan Hensman fell backwards.

'Shall I finish him?' said the other men, levelling the point of his sword at Hensman's throat.

'No,' said Sir Rupert Brent, 'it is enough; I would have none other sword but mine drink his life's blood; it is enough I have done it, and there let him lie.'

'Be wary, some one comes. I hear a rush of footsteps; the townspeople are getting alarmed. Hark! do you not hear that shout?'

'What means it?'

'Some terrified and unarmed citizens saw the commencement of the conflict; they fled, and, having procured assistance, they come now, doubtless, to revenge the death of one who was a popular favourite.'

'Can it be so?' But I care not, for sanctuary is near at hand; but yet I can scarce believe it; it seems too incredible to me to think that such is the case. What have the populace to do with these matters?'

'They will make something to do with them, although having nothing in reality. See, they come, they come!'

Turning the corner of a street, there now appeared a disorderly and motley assemblage of persons, variously armed, and they approached the spot with loud cries of 'Down with the murderers! down with the murderers! Death to the assassins!'

'It is time,' said Sir Rupert Brent, 'it is time, indeed now, look for sanctuary.'

He stooped, and wiped his blood-stained sword on part of the apparel of Ranulph Hensman, and then, placing it hastily in its scabbard, he turned and made towards the church with as much expedition as he could, closely followed by his companions.

This manoeuvre was not, however, executed with so much quickness, but that it was discovered by the multitude, who with cries and shouts rushed forward to intercept the progress of the murderers. Their intention of seeking sanctuary in the cathedral was perfectly evident to all, and such a mode of proceeding was too common, unfortunately, to excite much surprise.

Having, however, the start of the people to a considerable extent, Sir Rupert Brent and his companion had no difficulty in reaching the cathedral. They rushed up the steps, and were met at the top of them by a monk, with whom they exchanged a few brief words, and then they plunged at once into the recesses of the sacred building, while the ecclesiastic stepped slowly forward to the verge of the threshold, and, taking from a secret receptacle in his breast, a small crucifix of burnished silver, he stood awaiting the coming of the crowd.

With shouts and cries of 'Death to the assassins!' 'No sanctuary for murder!' 'Down with them, down with them!' 'Justice for the warden's secretary!' and many other such exciting cries, they reached the church-doors, when that one priest stood firm, in the power of monkish superstition, to overcome all the excited passions of the multitude.

At that hour it was not very many persons who could be hastily collected together, and when they reached the cathedral door, instead of rushing in at once, which would have destroyed the charm which the monk intended to exercise over them, they paused from long habit, and at the sight of that emblem of their religion, which the priest with outstretched hand held out to them, many took off their hats and caps, and the angry passions which before had animated them seemed in some measure to subside.

The priest did not speak; he evidently hoped that the mere sight of his sacred habit, and the cross, would be sufficient to deter the multitude; and so, perhaps, it would have been, but for one man, who, pressing forward closer than the others, cried aloud,—

'No sanctuary for murder!'

The voice was so clear and distinct, and so emphatic, that it at once led the people to a similarity of thought with the speaker, and there was scarcely one in the whole assemblage who did not echo the cry, and loudly exclaim,—

'No sanctuary for murder!'

This was the first time that the people in anything like a body, had began to question the supremacy of the Church, or to hint at setting any limits to its vast assumed authority.

The ecclesiastic either was or affected to be perfectly astounded at this enormous extent of audacity, and before any movement could be made by the mob, he flung himself upon his knees before the church door, and holding up the crucifix in his hand, he cried, in a high and excited voice—

'Holy saints, who minister at the footstool of heaven's Master, intercede for these sinful people. Let not the curse fall upon them. Do not blast them as they stand with terrific consequences. They speak under the excitement of a moment, and will yet repent!'

It was not so much these words, as the manner in which they were uttered, which made them tremendously effective upon all but a very small minority of the persons assembled. In fact, with the exception of the bold man who had taken the lead in calling out, 'No sanctuary for murder!' there were but two persons who did not shrink back from the church doors with a shuddering sort of horror. And then the priest, seeing this state of things, at once added, 'Must I then pronounce the awful doom? Must I utter that curse which there shall be no escaping upon those who would disturb the sanctity of Heaven's temple?' the wavering people turned and fled, leaving but three persons who had courage sufficient to stand up for right against superstition.

These confronted the monk, and he who was foremost again spoke, saying,—

'I do not impute to you, Sir Priest, other than pure motives or sincere opinions; but I tell you that a most foul and cowardly murder has been committed, and is it proper, I ask you, that this temple of heaven should be desecrated by being converted into a place of safety for those who have done the deed.'

'Sanctuary,' said the priest, 'is one of the privileges of the Church of Rome.'

'Then,' said the stranger, 'one of the customs, if not one of the privileges of the people, has always been to convey any dead body found in the streets to the nearest church.'

'It is so,' said the priest, 'and you can bring hither the mortal remains of the man whom you say has been slain. The body shall be placed upon a bier close to the high altar, and masses shall be said for the repose of his soul. We can do no more; but the privileges of the church must be preserved inviolate.'

The stranger turned from the door, and, after addressing a few words to those who seemed inclined to support him, they all three walked towards the body of Ranulph Hensman, which they picked up and at once conveyed to the church.

It was met by the monk, who chanted a prayer as he preceded it to the steps of the altar, upon which he directed it should be laid.

'My son,' he said, in a soothing manner, to the man who had spoken such words of bold defiance to ecclesiastical authority; 'my son, you should be more wary of speech, and remember always that these proceedings of the Church, which seemed to affect you, are for wise purposes and the general good. You say that the murderer of this man has sought sanctuary here—I do not question the fact, although I know it not of my own knowledge; but, if such be the case, let us hope that, while here, he will seek by repentance to make his peace with offended Heaven and save his soul.'

'His wickedness,' said the man boldly, 'which induces assassination, should be punished by mortal means, and I cannot approve of the hypocrisy of a pretended repentance, and a making peace with Heaven after the commission of so serious an offence. It is a perfect mockery.'

'Dare you utter such words, and to me, beneath this roof? On your knees, obdurate sinner—on your knees, I say—and ask for pardon for such a deep offence.'

'Never, never, to thee. To Heaven above will I kneel and pray, but not to a mortal like myself.'

'Then,' said the priest, trembling with anger, 'I perceive that you are one of that damned sect of heretics, and who wage war against all the holiest observances of the Catholic faith.'

'I am a Protestant.'

'Hence,' cried the priest, stamping with rage; 'hence I say, and leave this place at once. No longer breathe the holy air which fills this temple. Away, sinner, away, and do not compel me to launch against your head such curses of the Church as must ultimately bring down upon you some exemplary judgment.'

'Curse away,' said the man, 'as you please. It matters little to me whether I have your blessing or your malediction. The one I consider as valuable and as effective as the other. I am about to leave here of my own free will, and not in consequence of any threats which you have uttered; but I tell you, priest, that the murderer shall not escape on this pretence of sanctuary, and, as trivial circumstances are sometimes amply sufficient to settle long-disputed points, it shall not be my fault if this question of sanctuary does not undergo such an alteration, from the proceedings of this night, that you will not know it in its new shape.'

The priest glared upon the man with eyes of the most intense hatred. He was evidently about to make some angry reply, but the stranger, who had thus within the very precincts of the church uttered such free and dangerous opinions, for they were then most dangerous, turned and hastened from the building.

'That man,' said the monk, 'must die, he must be picked out from among his fellows as a man by far too dangerous to the supremacy of the Church to be allowed to live. We do not want people who think so boldly for themselves. Thanks to Heaven, which in its handy-work makes so many wrong heads instead of right ones, the number of those who do think, and think boldly for themselves, is but few, indeed, and there ought to be but little difficulty in getting rid of them.'

He turned and looked at the body of Ranulph Hensman, which lay so calm and still upon the altar steps.

'There lies one of them,' he added, 'the Lord Warden's secretary, a man as troublesome to the Church of Rome and its interests, as ever lived—a man capable of revolutionizing a kingdom, and one whom it has been with us a great object to be rid of. There will be a great cavil about his death, and there may be a struggle between the Church and the people, but the Church shall triumph; and, now, that no provocation may be given beyond what is absolutely necessary, this body shall be properly attended to. It shall have holy tapers placed at its head and at its feet, and those whom curiosity shall bring into the church to mourn will look with awe upon the imposing spectacle of death, and if they come to brawl it shall go hard with us, but we will make them stay to pray.'

Muttering, then, unintelligible sounds to himself, and with a mixed expression, partly of rage and partly of exultation, upon his countenance, the priest passed out of the cathedral by a small door-way into the more private portion of the sacred building.

Within the next half hour, a wooden bier was brought into the church by some of the official persons connected with it, and the body of Ranulph Hensman was disposed upon it with all due form and solemnity.

Tapers were lit both at the head and at the feet of the corpse, and pieces of silver coin were placed upon the eyes. The priest laid a cross upon the breast, and then, with a sickly smile, he said,—

'We have him in death, although in life he was our bitterest enemy. We can well afford to pay him these attentive observances now, for he is innocuous to us dead, although a scourge while living.'

CHAPTER XXXI.

The Communication to the Castle.

THE man who had so boldly and in so dangerous a locality as Winchester Cathedral, avowed himself to be a Protestant, did not happen to know the secretary of the Lord Warden by sight, and consequently he was at a loss to gain information of the death that had occurred.

One of those, however, who had remained and sided with him, although they had not been quite so bold as he, recalled to his remembrance that some one in the mob had shouted out the fact that the murdered man was the secretary of the Lord Warden of Winchester.

Acting, then, upon the possibility that such might be the case, he made up his mind to hasten to the castle to relate what he had seen and heard.

And he was the more inclined to do this because of the known feeling in favour of Protestantism in the breast of the

Lord Warden, who it was quite notorious through the whole of Winchester, favoured that rapidly growing cause, and was ever ready to defeat, if possible, priestly cunning or oppression.

The recent remarkable attack, too, upon the convent of Benedictine nuns by order of the Lord Warden, had produced a remarkable effect in the public mind, and it was by no means straining at a conclusion, to think that this assassination had something to do with the preceding events.

Full of these thoughts, the man made his way to the castle, at which he arrived, just as a cavalier was issuing from its postern gate.

This cavalier was none other than John Elkington, who seeing a stranger stopped by the sentinel, turned back a pace or two, to ask him what was his business at the castle.

'I wish to see the Lord Warden,' said the man. 'There has been a fou' ... ... said that the party killed was the Lord Warden's secretary.'

'Gracious Heaven!' exclaimed John Elkington, 'it must be so. It was he I was going out to seek. Murdered say you? assassinated in the street? come with me and tell me all. Oh why did I let him go alone? my heart misgave me as I saw him leave the castle gates. Come in, come in, this is a dreadful tale for me to hear.'

'It's a dreadful one to tell, sir,' said the man, 'a very dreadful one to tell. I partly saw the deed myself along with many others, but we were too late to save the victim.'

'One man did it not?'

'No, sir, there were two upon him when I saw them.'

'And what became of them? You took their lives; you and your friends executed a retributive justice, or at least you have them prisoners somewhere securely?'

'Alas! no sir, they fled to sanctuary in the cathedral.'

'Sir Rupert Brent has done this deed, but were he hidden in the very bowels of the earth, I would drag him out to justice. No sanctuary can hold him—none shall hold him—and

although this will be a heart-breaking affliction to one, it shall do great good to many, for, through it, such a blow shall be struck at priestcraft as shall make Rome tremble.'

'Thank Heaven, sir,' said the man, 'that I hear such words spoken. Do I then speak to one John Elkington, who has succeeded in casting from him the trammels of priestly superstition?'

'It is my greatest pride,' said Elkington, 'to think that I belong to the new faith—that faith which will assuredly triumph—and to which I suspect strongly the secretary of the Lord Warden owes his death.'

During this brief animated dialogue, John Elkington conducted the stranger into the castle, and leaving him in a room for awhile, he went in search of the Lord Warden, to whom he related the painfully interesting intelligence that Ranulph Hensman had at last fallen a victim to his enemies, and was no more.

The Lord Warden was inexpressibly shocked at the news.

'Alas, alas!' he said, 'I blame myself—I blame myself much for this. I most certainly ought not to have permitted Hensman to go alone from the castle. It is a very sad thing to think that such a man as he, so noble and so full of abundance of virtues, should have fallen a victim to one like Sir Rupert Brent, who was his contrast in all essential particulars—I dread the effect of this upon Alice.'

'And I; but yet she ought to know it, and must know it at once, for she is not one who can bear suspense.'

'John Elkington, will you be the informant? I must own that as regards myself I certainly have not courage for the task; it is too fearful a one for me to undertake. I think I see her now, waiting with that patient look of quiet beauty on her brow, the return of him, alas! who will return no more.'

'Do not speak thus,' said John Elkington, 'or you will unman me for the task you yourself so much dread. She must be told, and Heaven grant me strength to tell her, and her fortitude to hear the news. But I told the man who brought the sad intelligence that I would bring you to him. Let me now do so, so that you may hear from his own lips the particulars of that most frightful event, of which he was an eye-witness, and concerning which, I assure you, he feels deeply.'

The Lord Warden accompanied John Elkington at once to the apartment where the man was waiting, and who then, with such full particulars as he was acquainted with related all that had occurred in relation to the death of Ranulph Hensman.

The man concluded by saying—

'And now, my Lord Warden, will it not be most monstrous that this foul murder should not be avenged upon its perpetrators, because they have availed themselves of the sanctuary? Is not this a creditable and most undeniable opportunity for putting an end to such an exercise of priestly power?'

'It shall be put an end to,' said the Warden; 'and the murderer shall not escape. May I hope, John Elkington, that you will take the conduct of this business?'

'I will; but it strikes me, my Lord Warden, that in the present juncture of affairs, this is just one of those circumstances in which the people ought to be called upon themselves to act.'

'How mean you?'

'I mean that I would not have you interfere with the arm of authority; but that I would have you leave this to me, with the full expectation which I have that I shall be able to make such a popular movement grow out of it as shall shake the power of the Jesuits to its foundation, and free England from it for ever. Will you, sir, who have made yourself already doubly active in this cause, bring by earliest morning to the cathedral as many persons as you can, upon whose perseverance and better judgment you can depend?'

'I will,' said the stranger; 'most certainly there are very many in the city known to me who are favourable to a change, and who justly consider such a thing as this sanctuary to be a most monstrous power wielded by the Church to screen offenders.'

'It is a monstrous power.'

'All those whom I know have such views I will pledge myself to bring with me, and the old cathedral shall ring again with sounds that have not been heard within its walls since one stone of them was placed upon another.'

'You are a hearty and a true friend to the cause; if there be many such in Winchester, it will be here that the first blow against Catholic supremacy is struck in England.'

'It is in vain,' said John Elkington, 'that I shrink from the task I have to perform. Alice must know, and I must tell her—I will go at once.'

He turned and left the apartment with a heavy heart, and marching along the corridor he sought those apartments which, by the kindly consideration of the Lord Warden, had been devoted to the use and service of the Hensman family.

Alice was standing at the door of the apartment with deep anxiety depicted upon every feature of her countenance.

'Has he come, has he come?' she cried, as she rushed forward to meet Elkington. 'Oh! why is he so long? why comes he not? Speak to me, good Master Elkington, and supply my mind with some reason why he comes not to me.'

Elkington paused and looked her fixedly in the face. She saw in a moment the mournful expression of his countenance. A half suppressed shriek came from her lips, and she clung wildly to his arm.

'No, no,' she cried, 'it cannot be; nothing has happened to him—nothing could have happened to him!'

'Alice Hensman,' said Elkington, in sad and mournful tones; 'Alice Hensman, we are all the victims of chance, and we know not from hour to hour what fate may destine for us.'

'Those words,' she exclaimed, 'those fearful words, what do they prognosticate? For what would you prepare me?'

'Alice you have shown that you possess resolution—you have shown that, in circumstances of difficulty and danger, you have been fully equal to any difficulties that may arise. You have shown a spirit above that of woman in your own defence, and that you possess a soul capable of high resolves. If ever there was a time, when you are called upon more than at another to exercise those qualities, it is now.'

Alice heard him with blanched cheeks and lips, from which even every particle of colour had fled. She seemed like one newly awakened from a dream or like one still under the influence of some agony of spirit almost too great for mortal endurance.

Then she clasped her hands despairingly, and looked in the face of John Elkington.

She spoke; and it was in a low, anxious whisper that she did so, saying—

'This is a vision, this is a vision! it is no reality—it cannot be—I must be sleeping.'

'Nay, Alice; let me conduct you to your room, and some of the domestics of the castle will wait upon you; but let it better come from my lips than from any other less friendly and sympathising with you. that you must wait until you meet him in a happier and better world than this before you look again on Ranulph Hensman.'

She did not scream. No cry of anguish, such as might have been expected, proclaimed the heart stricken agony with which she listened to those words; but for a moment or two she looked such unutterable grief, that Elkington involuntarily exclaimed,—

'Heaven help her now!'

She then moved her arms, like one feeling their way in the dark, and then a shudder came across her frame, and, but for the saving arm of Elkington, she would have fallen insensible upon the floor of the corridor.

Deeply affected, he carried her into the apartment from whence she had come, and laying her gently upon a couch, he went to summon some of the female domestics of the castle to attend upon her, and then, repairing at once to the Lord Warden, he told him of the sad condition to which the dreadful news had reduced her.

'I will go at once,' he said, 'and see what is to be done in stirring up the people to avenge the death of Ranulph Hensman, for far better now is it that the murderer should be dragged from his place of refuge by the populace themselves, than that it should be done by an exercise of armed authority.'

'I have given the subject,' said the Warden, 'as anxious consideration as I could do in so short a space of time, and I am completely of your opinion. At the same time, should that fail through a want of resolution, or from any other cause on the part of the people, I am willing at once to make use of all the power I have, and of all the authority I possess, to get justice done upon Hensman's murderer. Go, John Elkington, and then, in due time, report to me all that has been accomplished.'

'I will, and in the mean time let me beg of you, as regards Alice, to send at once for her children; and when she recovers from this death-like trance into which she has fallen, let her at once see them, and the remembrance then that she has still some duties to perform, will nerve her more than all the arguments we could bring forward to assuage her griefs.'

'It is a good thought, and it shall be immediately acted upon. Hensman informed me of the place where his children were being taken care of, and I will make it my business to send for them at once.'

These events had dipped so far into the night that when John Elkington left the castle it wanted not above an hour or two to the earliest dawn of day, and he hurried towards the most populous part of the city, in order that he might, with as much expedition as possible, carry out the proceeding he projected.

How far he was successful, and what ensued on the following morning at the cathedral church, our readers are already acquainted with from a perusal of the first few chapters of this work; and as regards those proceedings, we have but to account for the presence of Alice Hensman and her children on the occasion, and then to rapidly proceed to the denouement of our tale.

When Alice recovered, she found her children about her, and all the effect that could be expected from their appearance was at once produced; so much so, indeed, that she was left alone with them, it being considered by the Warden that if anything would tend to tranquillise her, it would be an unobserved association with those little ones whom she loved so well.

But he was far from expecting the result to ensue that actually did, for, unknown to any one, she left the castle, taking her children by the hand, and proceeded to the cathedral church, to take her last look of Ranulph Hensman, even in death, and to call aloud for justice on his murderer.

CHAPTER XXXII.

The approaching Conflict.

THE Lord Warden, John Elkington, and a third person of the name of Master George Hatton, sat together in a small apartment of the castle in earnest conversation the day succeeding that on which such strange occurrences had taken place in the cathedral.

George Hatton was an old man, with thin, grizzled locks, and a sharp expression of countenance that betrayed much speculation and observation. There was a perpetual twinkle of the eye too, which seemed to say that he enjoyed considerably all that he found out concerning human nature; and when we add that he was the most celebrated leech or doctor of his time, we give abundant reason for supposing that he was perfectly well acquainted with human nature in all its varieties.

This learned individual had a watch, which was in those times rather a rare and wonderful possession, and every now and then he consulted it, as if he were impatient for some event that was to take place at a given time.

'You have no doubts, learned sir,' said the Lord Warden, 'I presume, with regard to your intelligence?'

'None in the least,' said the doctor, and again he looked at his watch; 'none in the least, although I consider the time has come, and rather wonder he is not here.'

'I am glad to hear it,' remarked John Elkington; 'and I make no sort of question now but that the next few days will be indeed productive of the most important results, and that we shall be fully enabled to originate such a movement at Winchester as will be felt throughout the length and breadth of England.'

'Most assuredly,' said the Warden. 'How glad the priests of the cathedral seemed to be to get rid of Ranulph Hensman; they seemed quite willing that all their holy candles should be upset, as well as the vase of consecrated water, provided Hensman was removed.'

'Precisely,' said the learned doctor; 'and never more surprised was I than when, upon suddenly arriving, I found such a commotion in progress; I could scarce believe my eyes that things had gone so far already; but of course it's all the more p'easant for you to know. I will be with you again, gentlemen, very shortly, but when a doctor of reputation has a great case in hand he dare not tamper with it.'

'Think you really now,' said the Lord Warden to John Elkington, when they were alone, 'think you really that Sir Rupert Brent will keep his word?'

'Undoubtedly, he must do so; he has made his election to stay at the cathedral until the combat takes place. It is well guarded, and were he to attempt to leave sanctuary to proceed anywhere but to the lists, he would be torn to pieces by the people.'

'I like the plan of having the combat so close to the castle as its outer court, for there cannot be a doubt we shall collect as spectators the whole of the Jesuit faction in Winchester; of course, they consider that by the death of Ranulph Hensman they are free from the probability of recognition, as only he saw their faces in that vaulted chamber which was their place of meeting.'

'Unquestionably; and when the combat is over, let the drawbridge be raised and the outer gate closed, so that all are made prisoners at once. Nothing will be easier than for the town's-people and really harmless visitors to prove who and what they are, while among the remainder we shall find those men whom we seek as companions of Sir Rupert Brent.'

'Hark! what is that? Is it the sound of horse's feet in the court-yard?'

'It is; and so, perchance, the doctor is more exact than we thought he was in the time he mentioned.'

They waited anxiously for several minutes, and then a page came into the chamber to say—

'Please you, my lord, there is a gentleman, who calls himself Sir Richard Lee, of York, craves admittance.'

''Tis he!' exclaimed both the Lord Warden and Elkington in a breath, and then the Warden added, 'You will show Sir Richard Lee into the small painted chamber.'

'Yes, my lord.'

In a few moments the Warden and John Elkington rose and walked to the apartment that had just been mentioned, which was a small one, and yet one of the handsomest in the building. It was called the painted chamber in consequence of the panels of the walls each containing some work of art

as a representation of some portion of English history, while the ceiling was profusely adorned with rich carving.

The Lord Warden and John Elkington spoke to each other earnestly as they approached this chamber, and when they reached the door of it, they opened it cautiously, entered, and then closed it with great care behind them.

A conference between them and Sir Richard Lee, which lasted nearly an hour ensued, and then the learned doctor was sent for, who joined the counsel, which continued for as long again, and when that was over, the Warden and Elkington left the apartment, and conversed together in the same quiet and mysterious manner which had before characterised them as they approached it.

. . . . . .

The evening of the day arrived which had been fixed upon for the conflict in which Sir Rupert Brent was to be engaged with his accuser, and he had, as yet, made no attempt to leave the cathedral.

It was a remnant of the chivalric usages of an age gone by, as well as a hope of entrapping the whole of the Jesuit party, by getting them to be spectators of the approaching combat, that induced the Lord Warden to permit the trial by combat in the present case; because, as we know, putting out of sight entirely the criminality of Sir Rupert Brent, as regarded Ranulph Hensman, there was ample ground for his prosecution on other charges which, if not of quite so serious an import, would still have been quite sufficient to ensure his condemnation.

But the higher objects of a political character that were involved in his defeat prevailed, and, having not the shadow of a doubt that victory would declare for John Elkington, or for the champion he had pledged himself to procure, the Warden let the matter take its course.

On this evening, however, preceding the conflict, there was ample evidence to show that Sir Rupert Brent began to shrink from it, and he made a powerful attempt to leave the cathedral—an attempt which, singular to relate, was frustrated by those whom he considered his own friends; and if we, in our capacity of being enabled, in consequence of gathering authentic details, long after the events occurred, conduct our readers to a singular meeting, which took place about two miles from Winchester, they will better understand why it was that the Jesuits themselves would not allow Sir Rupert Brent to avoid the combat.

At that distance from the city, in a westerly direction, there was a farm-house, which had been the scene of a cold-blooded and deliberate murder, and so unenviable, in those superstitious days, was the reputation which the place obtained in consequence, that, after two or three persons had attempted to reside in it, and till the fields, it was completely given up, and suffered to go to decay and ruin.

On the evening, however, on which we speak, and about an hour after sunset, just as a small, drizzling rain, had set in, along with a partial fog, which certainly presented the smallest possible inducements to any one to be abroad, several men might have been seen wending their way along the hedge-rows, and across the fields, towards that solitary and deserted house.

These people, when they reached it, concealed themselves in some portion of its outbuildings, and soon others came, until at last there were twenty-one persons present.

Then, one stepped out in front of the door-way, and clapped his hands together, upon which those who were hidden made their appearance, and the whole party adjourned into a large barn, or out-house, capable of containing a great number of persons, the roof of which was in many places open to the air, and which, altogether, presented a melancholy spectacle of decay.

Then noiselessly did these men collect, and stood in a throng with such anxious and stern countenances, that no one could have supposed it other than some matter of the first importance which had brought them together.

After a few moments one stepped forward as spokesman, and addressed the others in the following strain :—

'My friends, the trifling events which first commenced in this city, and made the existence of our body known to the authorities, we are now all well assured arose from the passions of an individual.'

There was a general murmur of assent, and the speaker continued,—

'That we have nearly all fallen victims to the obtrusive and undisguised libertinism of Sir Rupert Brent there cannot be a doubt, and although we were slow for a time to believe that these personal projects and private revenge of his interfered much with our public duties, we are now convinced that such is the case.'

' Quite convinced,' muttered several.

' There are but twenty-one of us here,' continued the speaker, ' there were twenty-six, but the remainder have entirely and completely fallen victims to these private affairs of Sir Rupert Brent. What was it that induced first of all that pest to us, Ranulph Hensman, to make prisoner of Sir Rupert? Nothing but the mad perseverance of the latter in his passion for the secretary's wife. What induced this very Hensman to risk his life, by coming to the vaulted chamber, but personal feelings of revenge which ought never to have been awakened?'

' 'Tis true,' cried another, ' and upon that occasion we must not forget that a trusty servant of the Church met his death.'

' Yes,' said the first speaker, ' that is one death, and then by the mob, on the occasion of the attack on the convent, another of our body became so mal-treated that he has since died; a third fell by the sword of Ranulph Hensman on the night of his own assassination; a fourth lingers in the dungeon of the castle, as well as the faithful door-keeper of the Well-house, who, no doubt, was severely injured at his post, and after owing all these evils to Sir Rupert Brent's personal passions, he would feign leave.'

' Aye,' cried another, ' and we owe much more than the loss of a few lives. We have brought down upon us the attention of the King and all his creatures, and our actual number is known, and the whole attention of those inimical to our interests, centred at Winchester.'

' I cannot but agree, said a tall, dark man, ' with all that I have heard. There are self-evident truths so clear and distinct that no one can dissent from them, but we shall find that, out of all these evils, there springs at least some great good. We shall find that, by concentrating this attention upon Winchester and our proceedings, we have an opportunity, as our private advices from the Court of London tell us, of striking a great blow.'

' Yes,' remarked the first speaker in an animated manner, ' yes, if we be not now foiled at once by the fears of the very individual who has caused us so much trouble and uneasiness. It is only by Sir Rupert Brent meeting his enemy fairly to-morrow in the field that we can at all hope to accomplish our greatest object, since Leoni has so frightfully failed.'

' He has frightfully failed, indeed; but Brent must now appear in the lists to-morrow, and were he not at the present moment well-guarded by persons at the convent, upon whom we know we can depend, there cannot be a doubt but he would escape, and, getting off to the continent, defy us, and at once sacrifice to his own slavish fears the greatest cause we ever were engaged in.'

' It must not be, it must not be!' cried several excitedly. ' He shall fight, he shall fight!'

' Unless he do fight,' continued the speaker, ' unless we produce him and show that he is ready for the combat, there will be no lists, and consequently we should lose the opportunity of singling out the person against whom all our force is to be directed.'

' He shall! he shall!'

' My friends, I rejoice to hear that you are fully aware of, and animated with, the importance of this affair. It matters little to us now whether Brent live or die, but he shall and must answer our purpose to-morrow. His patent of knighthood from the Court of Rome gives him power to require the trial by combat, and he shall have it. If it interfered not with our objects, he might play the dastard to his heart's content, but it does interfere, and interferes immensely too, and he shall not recede.'

' We swear it,' cried the others, ' we swear it.'

' 'Tis well,' said the speaker, who uttered all he said with animation and fluency, ' 'tis well, and we understand each other; let us now to town, and relieve those who are keeping watch and guard over Brent. We will have him with ourselves, and we will not leave him again, until we have placed him face to face with his antagonist.'

This was unanimously agreed to; indeed, we might almost say, with acclamations did they respond to the sentiment, and with mutual asseverations they swore that, rather than allow Sir Rupert Brent to escape and leave them to reap

the consequences of their own folly, they would themselves take his life, so that if any excuse at all had to be made for his non-appearance, it should be the excuse of death, since nothing short of that should possibly excuse him.

They then, with anxious countenances and excited gestures, proceeded to deliberate and descant upon some deed which they had made up their minds to commit, and which was evidently of the greatest importance, both as regards its results and the danger attending its commission, of any that had ever fallen under their observation.

' If done at all,' cried one, with excited gestures, ' it must and shall be done with that degree of boldness that shall make it respectable even in failure, for, after the attempt which has failed in London, the eyes of all Europe will be directed upon the perpetrators of a new attempt of a similar character. England's King must die!'

' He shall die,' cried several excited voices.

' The causes of failure,' continued the orator, who most attracted the attention of his companions, in consequence of his specious delivery and admirable address, ' the causes of failure in the former instance are about to be summed up in the one explanation, that there ought to have been more than a single arm to inflict the blow. My advice is, now, that we all and each consider ourselves as bent upon the enterprise. Here are twenty-one of us, and surely we shall all find, or the majority of us, some opportunity of attempting, if not accomplishing the purpose, and it will be bad indeed if one man succeed in escaping the vengeance of such a host.'

' All, all!' cried the others, ' we will all do the deed.'

' This is well—this is the fair road to success; and so, after all, we shall make, as it is our special business to do, and as we always pride ourselves upon doing, misfortune an element of success, and, from the small vices of Sir Rupert Brent—those vices which threatened at one time, by interfering with business of higher motive, to be our destruction, shall become useful, and full of the elements of that ample and complete success, which, from the first, we have promised ourselves, as well as promised others, and which, if we fail in achieving, aims a death-blow at the reputation of our society —such a death-blow as we shall never recover.'

' There is abundant argument,' said another, ' in what you say. Is it not universally believed and admitted to be one of the fundamental rules and principles of our association, that any individual of us can be required to commit any act whatever, however desperate, and that he will do it, even at the certainty that the next moment must be the last of his existence?'

They drew their swords, and as the dim light, which burnt from an oil lamp that was placed upon the floor, for there was nowhere else to put it, shone upon their excited countenances and glittering weapons, any strange eye that could have looked in upon them would have gathered materials for shuddering reflection, as to what fierce and unholy purposes leagued those men together.

' We need not swear fidelity to each other!' said one.

' No,' cried another, ' the suggestion of such a thing is needless. The general oath that binds us together as a fraternity, amply suffices.'

' Then let us at once to town, except such of us as choose to make this place a lodging for the night.'

' Hush! Who comes?'

' Our scout, Andrews. I know his tread; and hark! do you not hear his whistle?'

' T's he!'

A mere lad now glided into the place, apartment it could not be called.

' Be warned,' he said; ' be warned. I saw a man even now cross the fields towards the house. He seems, by the imperfect glance I caught of him, to be a harmless country person.'

' He must die,' said one; ' it is a fatal curiosity that brings him hither; he must and shall die!'

' Aye, shall he,' cried the fierce speaker, who took such pains to inflame already such angry passions—' aye, must he, were his life the second best in England. Go out again, Andrew, and bring us further information of his movements.'

The lad left the place, but presently returned and said, ' I have discovered that he is a shepherd—a lamb has strayed from his fold, and he comes to seek it in the ruins of this old house.'

' Did you utter anything to him?'

'No; I gathered that much from his own muttered discourse to himself.'

'I propose,' said one, 'that if he comes not in here, he be allowed to go in peace; but we cannot trust an idle tongue with the secret of our meeting; and if he enter this place, he must die.'

'Be it so, be it so!'

There was a death-like stillness amongst the conspirators, and there was the appearance, but far, very far from the reality, of every angry passion being hushed and still. Scarce a word was spoken, save in the lowest whisper, and, unconsciously to themselves, they fell into groups of picturesque aspect, the mysterious effect of the whole being much heightened by the position in which the rays of light proceeded, and which, going upwards, cast strange shadows upon the countenances and the apparel of the men, making some of them look hideous, and perhaps a little improving some countenances that, under ordinary lights, had more of the ferocity, while they had all the cunning of the fox.

And so they waited, minute after minute, until the evil stars of that poor doomed man brought him to the place. There was no fastening to a door that swung idly upon one hinge; he pushed it open, and was face to face with those furious men, who now wore all that appearance of calmness and composure which portends a coming storm of no mean amount of fury.

He started back, but the quiet of the assemblage seemed to restore to him some confidence.

'My masters,' he said, 'I fear I intrude upon you, but a lamb having strayed from my flock, I thought to find it here?'

'Perhaps it's got among the wolves,' said one.

'Wolves, my masters! there are few wolves in Britain now, though they do say one was run down by the cross-roads at Winchester Hollow. But may I be so bold as to ask what brings you here?'

'Most certainly you may. You must understand that a most mysterious circumstance—'

'Yes, yes,' said the countryman, and he listened intently to this speaker.

Two of the Jesuits from behind plunged their swords up to their hilts in his back.

The shriek that burst from the unhappy man was of the most heartrending and frightful character, and then he stood for a few moments after the weapons were withdrawn, writhing and clasping his hands, before he pitched with a headlong gesture, as if he were diving in some pit on to the floor, and there he lay, with his ghastly face upturned, and the eyes becoming each moment dim and glazed in death, gazing frightfully upon the countenances of those around him.

'A necessary act incurs no blame,' said one; 'this place was sacred to our meeting. I would not number on my list of friends he who would needlessly take a life, but be who intrudes upon our councils must surely die.'

It was strange that in after ages a would-be poet paraphrased the Jesuit's words, and found a paltry excuse for a vapid sentimentality in sentences similar to those uttered by the lips of one of the most vicious of men.

'Let us go,' said one, as he sheathed his blood-stained sword, 'let us go, and we will leave here the bleeding witness of a deed which will only do something more to add to the unenviable reputation of this frightful place.'

'Yes,' said another, 'a deed which in its consequences will enable us to meet here with greater security than ever, if it should become necessary that we hold council together after that deed which I fully hope and expect we shall ere long reckon among the things that are done.'

The fog was still dense, and the rain fell in the same cold drizzling sort of mist which had before characterised it, as those bold, bad men made their way back again to the ancient cathedral town.

CHAPTER XXXIII.

The Trial by Battle.—Sir Rupert and his Friends.

FROM what we have already related, in connexion with those affairs that were about to come to so important a climax, the reader will perceive that, like all men who are capable of staining their souls with great crimes, Sir Rupert Brent wanted that true courage which would have enabled him to outface the circumstances of difficulty and of danger in which he was placed.

It was quite clear and evident that he fully expected to find the sanctuary he sought in the old cathedral, and his disappointment in that particular having forced upon him the only other real alternative that, under the circumstances, he could be said to have, he now would have done anything to escape from the consequences of that situation.

There are many thousands of men—and Sir Rupert Brent, the Jesuit, was one of them—who are strong and powerful in proportion as those whom they wish to oppress are weak and irresolute, but who, if they be opposed firmly and consistently, shrink into their original nothingness, and become almost incapable of action.

If the Jesuit could but for one moment have seen all that was to occur contingent upon the death of Hensman, he would have adopted some widely different mode of doing that deed. He would have let Hensman, on that occasion when he did meet his death, escape altogether, than have so far mixed himself up personally in a transaction as to be forced to bear all its consequences.

Therefore was it, that observing such a shrinking spirit in him at the last moment, those who called themselves his friends, but who now, probably, he considered to be his bitterest foes, resolved upon making a personal sacrifice of him rather than forego their great object of a public nature.

It was, indeed, a most terrific feeling for such a man as Sir Rupert Brent to know that he was thus trapped and hemmed in, as it were, upon all sides, and that his enemies were intent upon his destruction, while his friends were equally intent upon giving them the opportunity of achieving it.

Allusion has been made already to an abortive attempt of his to leave the cathedral, and when he found that that did not succeed, then, and not till then, did he become fully aware of the manner in which he was hemmed in and surrounded by difficulty.

It was not a course calculated to improve his health or strength either; and no wonder that both somewhat failed. Let us take a glance at the murderer in his place of concealment.

There he was, caged up like some wild animal—some existence dangerous to be let loose, and which it was necessary, for the well-being of society, to surround with massive walls, lest he should do yet more mischief.

He felt like some wild animal, caged and prepared for slaughter; and although the area of the cathedral was extensive, and he had the full liberty of walking where he pleased beneath its roof, yet he chafed and fretted at his confinement as much as if it had been within the narrowest space.

It is night, and about the same hour when those bold bad men are assembled at the farm-house we have mentioned, where they committed such a deed of blood as ought to have hurried them to perdition.

The damp mist which was without had likewise found its way into the sacred building, and the consecrated candles that burnt upon the high altar and at the shrines of the different saints, shone themselves with a pale and sickly lustre.

It was just one of those early autumnal evenings which put us in mind of gaunt, cold, sterile Winter, and which, in our fickle climate, will sometimes occur so suddenly that it shall seem as if we stepped at once from the bright and beautiful summer-time to such a cold and comfortless season.

And Sir Rupert Brent could guess well the desolate and the dreary appearance of things without, but not so desolate and dreary were they as his own heart.

The cathedral door was open, but yet he dared not pass out by it; he had tried that, and two men had sprung, as if by magic, to the threshold, and stopped him.

Then he knew that he was guarded, and that it was not intended that he should be permitted to leave his prison.

He had the key of the secret door about him; and although it was scarcely with a chance or hope of success, he did make an attempt, by means of that, to leave the place.

If he could at once have passed out of the sacred building, it was his intention at once to have betaken himself towards London, where he knew he could find opportunities of concealment, such as a country place would not afford him.

The moment, however, that he unclosed the door, and put his foot across the threshold, he was met by an armed man, who opposed his progress.

'What means this?' said Sir Rupert. 'Why do you stay my progress?'

'I am ordered so to do,' said the man, 'by those whom I dare not disobey.'

'And who are they?'

'My masters.'

'But if I resist that order, and insist upon my right to incur whatever danger there may be in my leaving here, what will be the consequence?'

'My orders are to give an alarm, and get the assistance that is within call; but if you persist, I am to kill you.'

Sir Rupert Brent glanced at the man, and he saw that there was a calm, steady determination about him, which it would be quite useless to attempt to resist. He turned away from the door, and the sentinel himself closed it.

'Lost, lost!' he exclaimed. 'They have resolved upon my destruction, and I have no hope left. The time gets on apace. What am I to do? Whither am I to betake myself? Am I to be caged here until it shall seem pleasant for those who intend my destruction to achieve it? Am I now, after all that I have suffered, to be hunted to death, whether I will or no? But I see it all. I now perceive the position in which I am placed. Some object is to be achieved by forcing me to this conflict, and those who force me care not if I be sacrificed, so that it be fully carried out. And shall I submit to this?'

He glared around him with eyes of fury, but despair was at his heart, and well he writhed under the feelings which he could not smother; he at the same time felt how vain it was, if his Jesuitical associates really meant to surround him, and leave him no chance of escape, to battle with them.

What could he do against a score of men, each as well versed in deceit, and bred up in the same school of abundant cunning as himself?

He felt that it was hopeless, and that it was a kind of desperation that lent him courage to exclaim—

'If it be really true that, like a bear, they have chained me to a stake, and I must fight, it shall be done; and if it be done, even in desperation, I will yet strike a blow for life and liberty. My bitterest curses light upon them all! and if there be a malediction more intense than another, and more full of bitter consequences, that malediction I launch against the world, which I despise and hate. And yet I hope—ay! even yet I hope—to be enabled to achieve something that shall make my name a terror to those who have oppressed me, and which shall, to some extent, satisfy the bitter feelings of my heart.'

And so, full of these gloomy reflections, at one moment breathing defiance and hatred, and at another letting his heart sink within him, at the frightful thought that death must be near at hand, Sir Rupert Brent passed that miserable night.

And now the morning began to dawn, the thick mist continued—seeming, indeed, to be rather more dense than before, but it assumed a whiter aspect, as the light of the coming day struggled through it. The candles upon the altar burnt with a more sickly glare, looking like the very spectres of lights, and adding much to the superstitious terrors that began to creep over the soul of the Jesuit.

Oh, it is a strange phenomenon of human nature, that only among the most ignorant and the best informed do we find the highest amount of superstition.

The ignorant believe in the supernatural, because they are so ignorant, and the highly-wrought intellect and richly cultivated imagination, often gives way to the strangest and wildest fancies, while, for a short period, the judgment appears to slumber, instead of correcting those strange vagaries of the mind.

And now, as the dim and uncertain light of early dawn began to make itself felt, crowds of teeming fancies took possession of Sir Rupert Brent.

He trembled and turned pale at his own shadow; his countenance was ghastly, and more than once he turned abruptly on his heel with a sudden start, as though he expected to find behind him something strange and hideous.

His steps became faltering and unequal, and more than once he said, in low, deep tones,

'Oh, that the day were come!—Oh, that the day were come!'

He sat down in one of the confessionals to rest himself, for he was sadly wearied with his long night vigils, and there, with his head sunk upon his breast, and his arms folded, he gave way to the presence of dark and gloomy thoughts.

Perhaps, at that terrible moment, the many particulars of a dark and gloomy career came across his memory—perhaps he pictured to himself the many foul deeds that he had done, the actual murders he had committed, and, like the phantasma of a dream, there floated before his eyes frightful visions of the past.

But, at length, an uneasy slumber came across him. His thoughts became confused and disjointed. The past and the present mingled themselves inextricably together, and it was not until some one touched him suddenly upon the arm, that he sprung upon his feet with with an exclamation of alarm.

Immediately before him stood two of his jesuitical associates—two of those men who were determined, let his terrors be what they might, that he should fight, and that nothing should save him from the approaching conflict.

'It is morning, Sir Rupert,' said one, 'and it is time after the, no doubt, refreshing night's repose you have had, you should prepare yourself for the approaching battle.'

'Refreshing night's repose!' said Sir Rupert. 'Is it well to mock me thus?'

'We know not why you call it a mockery; you have been undisturbed, and surely might have had as refreshing a night's repose as you could wish.'

''Tis well; say what you please, I know your motives—I am to be a sacrifice.'

'A sacrifice? what a strange conclusion!'

'Yes; I say a sacrifice.'

'It may be so,' said one of the Jesuits, coldly, 'but why it should be I know not. You yourself commit a crime, which, at such a time, had far better have been left undone. You are accused of it, and you claim the now rarely and forced right of trial by battle. The time has come for the conflict, and you seem to shrink.'

'Many men seem honest and full of friendly feelings,' said Sir Rupert Brent, 'and yet 'tis only seeming, for they really are not so.'

'A most just remark; we have taken care to provide you with a horse and arms; you will want for nothing to give eclat to the combat, and your patent of nobility from the Court of Rome must and will secure to you a worthy opponent. As a Knight of the Holy Roman Empire, you are a match for any one, and should no individual of sufficient rank step forward as a champion to meet you, why then you are free, and the accusation against you falls aimless to the ground.'

'That is a poor chance indeed,' said Sir Rupert; 'but I am ready. I now know who are my friends, they may be summed up in a small compass, and I know who are my foes—they are sufficiently numerous; but I do not shrink, I will fight, although a hundred devils were tugging at my heart.'

''Tis bravely said; this way, this way!'

Smothering his resentment, and controlling the bitterness of his anger as best he might, Sir Rupert Brent followed his associates through a private door of the cathedral to prepare for that coming conflict, which, if he met it at all, was to be met by desperation, and not by that true courage which is the character of a noble heart.

.   .   .   .

And now we will look towards the castle, and see there what preparation was being made for the event of the day.

By the very earliest dawn the Lord Warden rose, and collecting together the men-at-arms who were not occupied in holding the various posts about the fortress, he busied them all in the construction of the lists in which the combat was to take place.

This he had determined should be in the large outer courtyard of the castle, which comprehended a space amply sufficient for such a proceeding.

Posts were stuck up at intervals, and to them strong rope was fastened, over which was hung a quantity of crimson cloth, so that lists of about 150 feet in length were duly prepared for the combatants.

The whole area was strewn with sand and gravel, and various raised seats were placed for those who were to be judges of the field as well as for those who were more immediately interested from personal feeling in the issue of the combat.

The precision with which the Lord Warden gave his orders, and the promptitude with which the disciplined men whom he had to deal with executed them, enabled him in the short space of about two hours to see that everything was perfect, and then it wanted but one hour to the period which had been named for the conflict to take place.

Leaving competent persons to take charge of the lists, and

giving orders that all comers should be admitted freely to view the proceedings, he repaired to a chamber in which a rich and costly morning repast was laid, and it seemed somewhat strange that upon that occasion a quantity of plate was displayed, which the Lord Warden, who was most specially plain in his own habits and modes of life, never dreamt of incumbering his breakfast-board with.

Sir Richard Lee was there as well as John Elkington and the learned doctor, and they all partook of the really rare and beautiful repast which was laid before them, and which in itself must have cost a considerable sum of money, inasmuch as everything was at it which the most profuse prodigality could procure.

When the breakfast was over a brief consultation ensued, and then the whole party repaired to the armoury of the castle, which was an extensive vaulted room, containing suits of mail in abundance and every description of offensive and defensive armour, from the earliest ages down to the present time. Then, with the exception of the doctor, who looked with an eye of great indifference upon such warlike appurtenances, they commenced arming.

The Lord Warden put on a demi-suit of mail, while John Elkington, with the assistance of the armourer, arrayed himself in complete steel from top to toe.

Sir Richard Lee put on a suit of costly chain mail, many of the links of which were of solid gold, and a helmet, the vizor of which, when down, did not admit of the smallest particle of the face being seen, inasmuch as there were only a close collection of small holes opposite the place for the eyes, and a row of little apertures, through which the wearer could draw breath.

It took some time to complete this arming, and just as they had nearly finished and Sir Richard Lee was belting on one of those double-edged Norman swords with the plain cross hilt, which the knights of the middle ages knew how to use so effectually, a loud blast of trumpets from the court-yard announced that the time approached for the conflict.

CHAPTER XXXIV.

The Combat.

THE report of the intended wager by battle at Winchester had spread far and near, and the various circumstances attendant upon the affair had been exaggerated in every possible way by the active tongue of rumour.

But that the affair was one of serious import and contained more matter for reflection than actually met the eye, there could be no doubt, and while a few kept away for fear that some circumstances might arise productive of danger to all who were present, a great many more came, urged by curiosity, to be present at the scene.

These kind of meetings were each day beginning to be more rare, and Winchester had not been the scene of such a proceeding for many a long day.

The general knowledge, too, that the accused party, who was thus about to make so desperate an attempt of justification, was one of those knights of Rome, combining in himself a lay dignity with an ecclesiastical authority, added greater to the general interest with which the affair was viewed. And if we join to this the popular feeling, that there was some connexion between the present proceedings and the singular and unprecedented attack upon the Benedictine convent, we have done enough fully to account for the deep public interest which the affair excited.

When it was found that the sentinels at the castle gate had orders to permit free ingress to all who wished to view the judicial combat, an immense number of persons immediately availed themselves of the permission, and among them came several of the ecclesiastics, who, with habitual respect, were made way for by the mob, and secured, as they always did upon occasions of interest and ceremony, the very best places.

At that time the taste for variety and beauty of costume had not, as it has now, departed from the land, and, consequently, the throng of persons there assembled presented, indeed, a widely different character to the black, sombre hue which characterises a modern assemblage. The distinction of ranks, too, as regards dress, was strongly kept up, and the people engaged in various business transactions in the town no more thought of apeing the appearance and costume of a higher class, than they would of flying.

As a consequence of this state of things the gay and brilliant costumes of the more aristocratic portion of the community came out in bold relief, when contrasted with the sober suits of the citizens, and the dark flowing garments of the monks, of whom there appeared a larger sprinkling than those, who were acquainted with the city of Winchester, would at all have expected upon such an occasion. At every instant there were fresh arrivals of some kind or another, on horseback and on foot, until, at length, the court-yard was densely crowded in every part, except that which had been railed off for the lists, and a space towards another entrance than the one at which the public had been admitted.

This entrance was kept exclusively for Sir Rupert Brent when he should arrive, and the men-at-arms likewise preserved a clear passage from one of the entrances of the castle towards the lists, by which the Lord Warden could at any time enter.

This was the state of things when the heralds, as it was their duty to do, at a quarter of an hour before the appointed time for the combatants to be ready, blew a long and loud blast upon their trumpets, which awakened every echo about the castle.

Now there was an anxious pause of some minutes' duration, and many tried to better their position for seeing the conflict, while a confused clamour at the outer gate testified to the anxiety and disappointment of fresh arrivals, who could not procure admittance to the already crowded arena.

Then there was a cry of 'Way for the Lord Warden!' and the multitude shrank back a little from pressing so closely on the men-at-arms, while a side-door of the castle opened, and the three armed figures of the Lord Warden and his two friends advanced.

The doctor, in his black gown and curious, conical-shaped hat, brought up the rear, and when this party had reached the centre of the lists, and the Lord Warden had sat down for a minute on the seat destined for his reception, he rose again, and made a sign to our old friend, the wine-bibbing herald, who was standing close by in his emblazoned coat, dangling his silver trumpet in his hands.

At that sign he advanced, and raising his trumpet to his lips he blew a flourish so loud and long, that the throng of persons stared in wonder at its continuance, and could hardly believe it over, even when its last echoes had died away among the ancient towers of the castle.

Then, unfolding a scroll of paper which had been rolled round a portion of his trumpet, he read as follows.—

'Whereas a foul murder having been committed upon the person of Ranulph Hensman, a learned Clerk in Winchester, by one Sir Rupert Brent, a Knight of the most Holy Roman Empire, I, Robert de Warren, of Westmoreland, Lord Warden of Winchester, and of the King's Council, now declare—

'By virtue of authority from Henry, by the grace of God King, I appoint that the judicial combat claimed by the before-mentioned Sir Rupert Brent, in justification of his asserted innocence, and such a person of equal rank who shall come forward as the champion of the accusation, shall now take place. God save the King!'

The herald again placed his trumpet to his lips, and this time he was joined in the blast he blew by the two special heralds who had been appointed to attend in the lists.

Then the Lord Warden rose, and waiting for a moment until silence was restored, he said,—

'I now call upon Sir Rupert Brent to appear!'

There was a sudden movement among the multitude of persons, and a general glance in the direction of the private entrance of the castle, from which the Lord Warden and his friends had emerged, and coming slowly along was seen a female, over whose head was cast a veil of black crape, and who advanced with slow and measured steps, leading by the hand two children, while a third clung to the sombre robes which she wore.

Those who knew the circumstances of the case recognised in this mournful figure Alice Hensman, and in the children those little ones who had been rendered fatherless by the atrocious wickedness of Sir Rupert Brent.

A murmur of sympathy ran through the crowd; a way was made for her to the seats, on one of which the Lord Warden had for such a fleeting moment placed himself.

It was Sir Richard Lee who now advanced, and taking Alice by the hand led her to a seat, while the children grouped themselves at her knee, looking on with wonder and awe at the proceedings which were taking place.

The presence of Alice was absolutely necessary as the accuser of Sir Rupert Bent, and hence, at that moment, when the Lord Warden called upon him to appear, she had emerged from the castle to proffer her complaint.

When she was seated, and Sir Richard Lee had in a low tone said a few words to her, the Lord Warden again spoke, saying, in a loud tone which was heard by every one present,

'I here call upon Sir Rupert Brent, a Knight of the Roman Empire, and accused of the foul murder of Ranulph Hensman, to appear!'

The herald blew a shrill note upon his trumpet, but no answer was made to it, and all eyes were bent in vain upon that entrance to the court-yard, which it was known was set apart for the entrance of the accused, and where one of the heralds had stationed himself ready to give immediate notice of the arrival of Sir Rupert Brent.

Again a sonorous blast from the herald's trumpet rang through the place : then all became still, and there was no response.

The crowd began to get almost frenzied with impatience, and a cloud of care came over the countenance of the Warden, who began himself to suspect that after all Sir Rupert Brent might find some means of evading the coming conflict, notwithstanding all the exertion that had been made to bind him to his word, and to prevent him from having the smallest opportunity of escaping from its fulfilment.

What the friends of the Lord Warden thought, who were clad in such complete armour, no one had an opportunity of even surmising, for the vizors of helmets were closely down, and not the smallest portion of their countenances was visible.

Indeed, there could be but few people present able now to recognise in the mail-clad figure by the side of the Lord Warden John Elkington, who had always professed to be but a humble follower of one of the nobles of the court.

The Warden whispered something to Sir Richard Lee, who nodded assent, and then, by a sign from the Warden, the herald again, and for the third time, blew the loud note of summons to the conflict.

Scarcely had the last echoes of the sonorous sound died away, when the other herald, who had been placed to give notice of the coming of Sir Rupert Brent, was near trampled upon by a horseman, who dashed at full gallop through the entrance, and appeared in the lists.

This horseman was attired in a complete suit of brass armour. The horse he rode was white, and a waving plume of white feathers adorned his helmet.

The armour of itself seemed perfectly new and to be of a costly character, inasmuch as it was most richly embossed, and those who were acquainted with the value of such matters saw at a glance that it was one of the most complete suits of mail which the age could produce, and must have cost an extremely large sum.

The caparisons of the horse were of a similar character, corresponding in amount to the suit of mail which was upon the man, and a most superb charger it was—such a one indeed as could scarcely have been matched, and certainly not surpassed in England.

There came behind him, mounted upon a smaller horse, a lad attired in the costume of a squire, bearing the lance and shield of the knight who preceded him.

The terrified herald, who had so nearly been ridden over by the advancing stranger, as soon as he recovered himself, put his trumpet to his lips and blew a loud and shrill note, upon which the armed man, who so suddenly and with such defiance had made his appearance, raised the vizor which covered his face, and exhibited the countenance of Sir Rupert Brent.

And never, perhaps, had that countenance worn such an aspect as it then did.

The face looked like that of a corpse, from which the eyes were glaring with a horrible lustre, while the lips, which were of an ashy paleness, contributed to give a spectre-like appearance to the countenance.

All eyes were bent upon him, and for a moment he seemed to recoil il beneath the universal gaze. Then, by a great effort —an effort which was observable by his clenched teeth and his knitted brows—he contrived to summon resolution enough to commence the part he had to act.

He brought his charger so abruptly to a stand-still that the noble animal was almost thrown upon its haunches, but Sir Rupert Brent sat unshaken in his seat, and by his easy carriage in the saddle showed, at least, that whatever might be his other qualifications, he was no mean proficient in horsemanship.

He saluted the Lord Warden, who, upon his appearance, had taken the highest seat as master of the lists, coldly and haughtily, and then, wheeling round his charger, he addressed a few words to the squire who accompanied him, and who then communicated something to the herald.

'I see before me,' said the Lord Warden, 'Sir Rupert Brent, who is accused of the murder of Ranulph Hensman.'

'Where is my accuser?' said Sir Rupert, in a deep hollow tone.

'Here,' cried Alice, springing to her feet, 'I accuse you, Sir Rupert Brent, of the murder of my husband; I accuse you of that foul deed which has made me a widow, and these children fatherless; I accuse you of assassination, and I dare you to disprove the accusation, villain that you are. You know you did the deed, and, even now, your eyes dare not look on mine. Conscious guilt is upon every lineament of your countenance. Murderer! assassin! I and these hapless children are your accusers.'

She pointed with both hands in his face. Her attitude was expressive, and full of passion mingled with grief, and as the children, who clung to her, raised a wailing cry, it seemed as if they, too, were joining in the accusation against their father's murderer.

'What say you, Sir Rupert Brent,' asked the Lord Warden, 'to this accusation of so foul a character?'

'I say that I am innocent, and that innocence I am prepared to defend, and assert face to face and arm to arm, against any one of rank equal to myself, who shall produce my gage, which I cast down in the cathedral.'

'It is here,' said John Elkington, stepping forward, and holding up the glove which Sir Rupert Brent had cast at his feet, on the occasion of the Ordeal by Touch, in the old cathedral, so short a time before.

'I may not fight,' said Sir Rupert, 'with any one of lesser rank than myself, while, as a knight of the holy empire, I am of rank sufficient to meet the highest.'

'You shall be satisfied,' said the Lord Warden. 'Let the herald proclaim your own rank, and the challenge you give; you shall be found a fit competitor.'

The herald, to whom the squire of Sir Rupert Brent had made a communication, now advanced, and after a preliminary flourish of his trumpet, he cried,—

'Now, know ye all men that Sir Rupert Brent, a Knight of the Roman empire, and Chevalier of the Holy Order of Ignatius, declares his innocence of the crime imputed to him, and is willing to meet any one in single combat, who can claim to be his peer in defence of his innocence, and he prays that Heaven may preserve the right.'

There was a pause of not above a second's duration, when the other herald of the lists sounded his trumpet long and loud, and then spoke, saying,—

'The challenge of the accused Sir Rupert Brent, Knight of Rome and Chevalier of the Noble and Holy Order of Saint Ignatius, is accepted, and he will be met in arms by the Most Noble and Honourable John Talbot, Earl of Surrey, high marshal of England, companion of the garter, knight of the golden fleece, and privy counsellor to the king.'

'The Earl of Surrey,' gasped Sir Rupert Brent, while the multitude who were then present looked astounded at hearing thus proclaimed the name of one of the most renowned noblemen and accomplished warriors of the age. 'No, no,' cried Sir Rupert Brent; the Earl of Surrey—no, no, he is not here.'

'He is here,' said John Elkington, stepping forward and unclasping the vizor of his helmet. 'He is here, and in the John Elkington who in the cathedral church promised to find you one who would meet you face to face in support of the innocent and oppressed, the widow and the fatherless, you behold the Earl of Surrey.'

The loud and enthusiastic shouts that arose from the people at mention of this name, which was then one of the most popular to the public ear that could be uttered, made the old castle ring again, and it was many minutes before anything like order or silence could be restored among the people.

Then Sir Rupert Brent, who was actually seen by many to tremble as he sat upon his horse, spoke, saying—

'I deny the fact; I will not take the word of any adventurer who chooses to proclaim himself the Earl of Surrey.'

'As master of the lists,' said the Warden, 'and consequently referee with regard to any disputed point that may arise, I declare upon my honour that this knight is the Earl of Surrey. I trust that such a declaration from me will be considered amply sufficient to set at rest any scruple that may arise upon this occasion.'

At these words, freely and boldly spoken as they were, there arose another loud and enthusiastic shout from the people, and when it had subsided, Sir Rupert Brent spoke in so loud, harsh, and so strange a voice that it was evident he was struggling with all the evil passions of his soul.

'Be it so,' he cried; 'I accept the proof, and am ready for the combat.'

'My lord,' whispered a page to the Warden, 'there are some persons pressing forward to leave the court-yard.'

'Bid the sentinels,' replied the Warden in the same low tone, 'close the gates, and let no one pass out.'

The page bowed, and went to fulfil his errand.

Then a most magnificent war horse, fully and completely caparisoned for the lists, was brought out of the castle stables by a couple of pages, who led the noble animal to and fro before the eyes of the admiring multitude, until the Earl of Surrey should be ready to mount him.

Now that John Elkington had turned out to be so illustrious a personage, it was curious to see with what eyes of interest his slightest movement was followed by the people and how completely Sir Rupert Brent was cast into the shade by the superior interest attached to that illustrious earl who was certainly, at the period, one of England's proudest nobles.

The Earl of Surrey was a man who had made his name illustrious by the liberality of his views, his distinguished

talents, and the great personal courage that had characterised him upon many occasions of great merit, that he deservedly stood extremely high in the opinion of all classes of persons.

We are certain, in bestowing this high eulogium upon that nobleman, nothing has transpired, in the progress of the events detailed in this narrative, which can at all retract from him, and we have had pleasure in presenting him to the reader, as finding sufficient time from his high public duties to become the champion of the oppressed.

No doubt, at the very mention of his name, Sir Rupert Brent felt that he was a doomed man, for the idea of him contending against such a practised knight as the Earl of Surrey he felt it was almost preposterous.

Probably, too, the movement that was made towards the castle gates was made by the Jesuits with a full conviction that something seriously uncomfortable to them and to their party was likely to ensue.

Probably they thought that the presence of the Earl of Surrey betokened something more important still, and that some plot was on the tapis which might fairly and in their destruction.

The page was far more rapid in his movements than they, and had given the Warden's order to the sentinels before those who attempted and wished to leave the court-yard could accomplish such a purpose.

When they found themselves so hemmed in, the suspicion that something was wrong became almost a certainty, but still they were too cunning to make a tumult, when a tumult would have been absolute destruction to them, and they reserved themselves ready to act upon the offensive or defensive as the occasion might require.

Sir Rupert Brent, with moody look, cantered his horse to the further end of the lists, and there waited until the pre parations should be complete, which he now felt were certain, in any case, to lead to his destruction.

That he would be conquered by the earl, if he were not killed by him, he felt certain, and in the former case his death was inevitable, because he knew that he would be handed over to the not very tender mercies of the Warden, who, however kind and benevolent a man he might be upon ordinary occasions, was not at all likely to call those qualities into a state of requisition on behalf of such a man as Sir Rupert Brent.

Possibly the agony of these thoughts, and the absolute certainty now that his doom was fixed, gave the Jesuit that courage which is the result of hopelessness and despair. It was sure either to do that or to depress him so completely and entirely that he should not be able to move a finger in his own defence.

It did, however, both to the gratification of the Earl of Surrey and of the Lord Warden, produce the contrary effect, and when they next turned their eyes upon the Jesuit's face they saw one of the most remarkable changes that could be imagined had taken place in it. In lieu of the look of ashy paleness, which it had before worn, it had a crimson hue; and the eyes, which had before looked ghastly, and wore almost the aspect of death, now flashed as if of fire, presenting an appearance which at once proclaimed what fierce and angry passions ran riot in his brain.

He sat erect upon his saddle, and every limb of him seemed rigidly set, and was expressive of the determination of his soul to conquer or die. He moved not, he spoke not, but more resembled a sculptured warrior on a sculptured steed than a living man and horse.

Now the charger of the Earl of Surrey, at a signal from him to the squire who led it, was brought close to him, and he accomplished that feat, which very few, even in that age when athletic exercises were considered of vast importance, could accomplish. He placed one hand upon the pummel of the saddle, and without any further assistance at once vaulted on the charger's back.

This, for a man clad in complete armour to do, was no easy task, and the assembled crowd, to whom anything like physical prowess is always admirable, greeted the achievement by a cheer. But when the lance—a long, heavy, and cumbrous weapon—was handed to the earl, and he, after poising it for a moment in his hand, flung it quivering up into the air like a dart, and then dextrously caught it as it fell, there was such a clapping of hands, and such loud shouts of ' Long live the Earl of Surrey !' that the hearts of the Jesuits must have died within them.

Then the Earl took his place in the lists, and intimated, by a salute to the Lord Warden, that he was ready.

A priest stepped forward to utter a prayer, but Sir Richard Lee made an impatient gesture, and then the Lord Warden cried, ' This is an affair among men, we want no interference of priests.'

' The curse of the Church be upon you !' cried the monk.

' Clear the lists,' said the Warden, ' of the impious man who arrogates to himself the right of cursing any of God's creatures.'

The priest retired without another word, and, as he did so, he drew the cowl of his habit completely over his face. Let us suppose it was with a creditable idea of hiding from general observation the fact that a minister of Heaven could get quite as angry as any other man, under the most ordinary circumstances calculated to create or to inflame passion.

Now there was no obstruction to the commencement of the combat; each knight held his lance in its rest, and the heralds stood ready, with their trumpets nearly at their mouths, and their eyes bent upon the Lord Warden, to catch the moment when he should give the signal for them to blow the spirit-stirring strain that should call upon the antagonists to commence the fight.

The Warden waved his hand; a loud blast from the trumpets immediately succeeded, and the horses of each of the combatants started at the sound and dashed forward at a furious gallop.

There was scarce an instant of time ere they met. The lance of Sir Rupert Brent was aimed at the breast of his antagonist, but, by a dexterous movement of his body, the Earl of Surrey escaped the weapon, which glanced off him harmlessly, while he struck his own lance with so true an aim, exactly at the head of his opponent, that the fastenings of the helmet were shattered to pieces by the shock, and the casque and its vizor was torn from the head of the Jesuit, at the same moment that the point of the lance, which had entered the bars of his vizor, carried away a portion of his skull, and left him streaming with blood. He swung out and fro in the saddle for a moment —he uttered one cry of pain and rage, and then he fell from his horse, with a heavy crash, upon the ground below.

' God preserve the right !' said the Earl of Surrey, as he flung his lance to the squires that rushed forward to attend upon him.

Dismounting then in a moment from his charger, he drew his sword, and stepping up to the prostrate form of Sir Rupert Brent, he turned it face upwards with his foot, and pointing his sword towards his throat, he said,—

' Villain, do you now confess your crime ?'

' He is killed,' said the Lord Warden, rushing forward, ' and if not, I pray you leave him now to a less noble death than the Earl of Surrey can inflict.'

Sir Rupert Brent opened his ghastly-looking eyes, and with one arm that was at liberty, for the other was doubled up under him as he lay, and broken by his fall, he strove to clear away the blood from before his vision that streamed from his gaping wound.

' May the curse of the dying——' he said, and then his utterance failed him, and he could say no more.

A priest dashed forward from among the people, and kneeling down by his side, held up a crucifix before his glazing eyes, and this seemed to restore him for a moment, and, gathering all the energy that remained to him, he shrieked to him rather than said,—

' Away—away with this mummery—begone—begone !'

' Do you reject,' said the priest, ' the holiest consolation of religion ?'

' The consolation of delusion !' said the dying man. ' What is religion to me ? Heaven is a cheat, and there can be no hell like that in my own breast !'

' This is dreadful,' said the monk.

' My lord, my lord !' cried a page, ' Sir Richard Lee is betrayed—he will be murdered—he will be murdered !'

The Earl of Surrey and the Lord Warden turned with the quickness of thought, and there they saw that, taking advantage of their temporary absence, a crowd of armed men had attacked Sir Richard Lee, who was defending himself as best he might against such fearful odds, and using the Lord Warden's chair as a barrier between him and his foes.

The danger of Sir Richard Lee was but of momentary duration, for the attack of the Earl of Surrey and the Lord Warden upon his foes, was of so fierce and terrific a nature, that at each stroke of either of their swords one fell, and the astounded men-at-arms having now recovered from their sudden panic, rushed likewise to their rescue, so that, in the course of a few short moments, eight men, with drawn swords in their hands, were seized, while no less than eleven lay dead or wounded on the ground.

' Are you hurt—are you hurt ?' cried the Lord Warden to Sir Richard Lee.

' No, no—a mere scratch on my left hand; but the villains did their best. My Lord Warden, the time is come when an end may be put to some mysteries that now surround us; but who comes here ?'

From the private entrance to the castle there came a tall figure, wrapped up in a cloak, and leaning upon the arm of the doctor. They went directly up to where Sir Rupert Brent was lying, and the doctor, stooping to the wounded man, said,—

' Do you not repent of your evil deeds ?'

' Raise me a little,' said Sir Rupert.

Two of the men-at-arms did so, and then, clenching his fist, he shook his arm above his head, and with difficulty spoke,—

' May my bitterest curse light upon you all ! May you all live lives of misery and distrust, and die despairing as I do. No, no, I do not quite despair, for I have had one victim, in— Ranulph Hensman.'

' If that be your consolation,' said the doctor, ' I tell you to despair, for as he lay on the altar steps of the old cathedral, I saw that he was but in a trance of death, and, guessing the nature of his wound, I said nothing, but had him removed at once to the castle. You know that not six hours elapsed from the infliction of what you thought his death wound to his removal carefully on a litter from the cathedral.'

'No, no, he is no more. The blood flowed from his wound, when I touched him in the church.'

'Yes, because the warmth and the weight of your hand, he being alive, favoured the superstition. He lives, and will be restored to his wife and children.'

'A lie—a cheat—a fabrication! to make me despair.'

'Behold him here!' said the doctor, 'a living witness to the truth.'

He stepped aside, and pointed to the tall figure in the cloak, that had come with him from the castle, and this figure, dropping the mantle from before his face, exhibited the pale, but well-known features of Ranulph Hensman.

The Jesuit cast but one glance upon him, uttered a wild shriek, and fell back a corpse.

. . . . . .

The intense surprise of the multitude at these events, all of which occurred with marvellous rapidity, was depicted upon every countenance, and many looked forward to a scene as likely to occur between the singularly restored Ranulph Hensman and Alice, who had so mourned his death; but, when they saw him merely press her hand and smile gently upon his children, they became aware that she, likewise, was in the plot, and had before had the happiness of knowing that the Jesuit's sword had not proved fatal to her husband.

A thousand voices at least uttered cries of exultation and congratulation; but what was the surprise of all then assembled when they saw Sir Richard Lee sit down in the seat which the Lord Warden had vacated, and then John Elkington, taking Ranulph Hensman by the hand, led him up to Sir Richard's feet, when, to the surprise of all present, he knelt humbly.

Then Sir Richard, drawing his sword, laid it lightly upon Ranulph Hensman's shoulder, saying,—

'Rise, Sir Ranulph Hensman; and we are certain that we have not a braver knight in our dominions than yourself.'

'It is the King!' burst from every throat.

'Yes,' said the Lord Warden—'Long live King Henry, who has honoured his good and loyal city of Winchester with this visit, and has confounded the traitors that would step between him and his people.'

————

CHAPTER XXXV.
The Conclusion.

BUT little more remains to be told in order to bring our narrative to a perfect close. On that day Henry the Eighth promulgated the first of his decrees against the convents and monastic institutions, and formally banished the Jesuits from England; abolishing likewise sanctuary, which, after these events, never again became popular among the people at large.

One of the Jesuits, who was taken prisoner upon the failure of the infamous and cowardly attempt upon the life of the King, confessed the whole particulars of the plot, and cleared up the mystery of the Well House.

It appeared that there were two circles of brickwork in the well; the inner only contained water, and the outer a spiral staircase, which communicated through subterranean passages with the vaults of the Benedictine convent.

Such, therefore, were not only the means by which Alice Hensman had been removed from the convent, but by such a contrivance it was that the conspirators in the Well House had so mysteriously escaped the great vigilance of the Lord Warden on the occasion of the adventurous attack which had been made upon the Well House.

The circumstances made a great noise throughout Europe, and struck a severe blow, even in continental countries, at the supremacy of the Jesuits. Ranulph Hensman lived long and happily with Alice, and went to the tomb full of honours, being the founder of an illustrious line that at present stands high in the state, and some of the members of which, perchance, scarcely know that they may date the origin of their wealth and their honours to the superstition of the ORDEAL BY TOUCH

THE END.

LONDON: Published by E. LLOYD, 12, Salisbury-square, Fleet-street.

www.ingramcontent.com/pod-product-compliance
Lightning Source LLC
Chambersburg PA
CBHW081212170626
46811CB00010B/3259